# DANGEROUS GROUND

LEAH NASH MYSTERIES BOOK 6

## SUSAN HUNTER

Severn River
PUBLISHING

DANGEROUS GROUND

Copyright © 2019 by Susan Hunter.

Severn River Publishing
www.SevernRiverBooks.com

This is a work of fiction. Names, characters, businesses, places, events and incidents are either the products of the author's imagination or used in a fictitious manner. Any resemblance to actual persons, living or dead, or actual events is purely coincidental.

ISBN: 978-1-951249-63-2 (Paperback)

## ALSO BY SUSAN HUNTER

**Leah Nash Mysteries**

Dangerous Habits

Dangerous Mistakes

Dangerous Places

Dangerous Secrets

Dangerous Flaws

Dangerous Ground

Dangerous Pursuits

Dangerous Waters

Dangerous Deception

Dangerous Choices

To find out more about Susan Hunter and her books, visit

severnriverbooks.com/authors/susan-hunter

*For my husband, Gary Rayburn,*
*who does more kind things in a day*
*than most people do in a month.*

# 1

I parked my bike just inside the cemetery gates. It took only a few steps down the tree-lined path for the heat and humidity of a mid-summer Wisconsin day to slide away into the cool dark shade. Overhead, the soft murmur of thousands of leaves stirring in the light breeze accompanied me as I walked slowly toward my sister's grave. Both of my sisters are buried in the cemetery just a few miles outside of Himmel, Wisconsin. My father is as well. But today it was Annie I'd come to visit.

My heart beat a little faster as I neared the gravesite. I'm not afraid of the dead. It's the memories they leave behind that haunt me. Quiet Annie with her soft voice and big blue eyes, too shy to join the other laughing, shouting kindergarteners at recess—but the first to run over to comfort a little boy struggling not to cry on the first day. Imaginative Annie, commandeering our wide front porch as a sailing ship for her and her cat, Mr. Peoples, to travel around the world. Kind-hearted Annie, sharing her Halloween candy with me when I'm forced to surrender my own treats as penalty for talking back. Sweet, brave, compassionate, eight-year-old Annie, who ran into a burning house to save Mr. Peoples twenty-two years ago, and never came back.

Over all the years since, people—my mother, my aunt, my therapist (yes, I went that route once), my best friend—have reassured me that her death wasn't my fault, that I was just a child. But, I was older. I should have been watching over her. I should have seen her slipping back to the house after we'd all escaped. In my deep heart's core, I can't ever forget that.

Now and then, and always on her birthday, I go to the cemetery to see her. I know that she isn't really there. But her grave is an anchoring spot for me. I catch her up on the good, the bad, and the ugly happenings in my life. She knows what hurts me, and she knows what frightens me—secrets I don't share with anyone else. I tell her what our mother is up to, and how others she knew in life are doing. I say all the things to her that I would if she were still here. I try to make up for the fact that I'm alive, and she isn't. But, of course, I never can.

When I'm talking to her at the cemetery, it feels as though she can really hear me. And I know that she answers. Not right there, at the grave, but later, in unexpected ways. Sometimes, I hear Annie speak to me through a chance remark a stranger makes, or a phrase that leaps out at me from a book, or a sudden flash of insight on a problem I'm wrestling with. I don't share that belief with very many people. If I did, I might be forced to resign my membership in the Doubting Thomas Society, to which all good journalists should belong. But I can't accept that those occurrences are just coincidental. I really can't.

So, on the anniversary of her birth, once again I sat down on the bench in front of her grave and told her how sorry I was that she had died. That I hadn't saved her. That I still missed her. And then I told her what was really going on in the seemingly successful life of Leah Nash, former small-town reporter, current true crime author, and soon-to-be business failure.

When I say I talk to Annie, I mean that literally. I have a one-sided, out-loud conversation with her, though only when I'm sure I'm alone. Some people already think I'm crazy. No need to give them additional proof. On this particular day, I had a serious problem weighing on my mind.

Not long before, I had made what seemed, at the time, like a brilliant decision. The *Himmel Times Weekly*, the paper where I'd started out in journalism, and where I'd found a home again after a self-inflicted career injury, was closing. I decided to buy it. I asked a wealthy, community-minded, local attorney, Miller Caldwell, to invest with me. And then I asked a lot of other people—reporters, an editor, stringers, office and sales staff—to work very hard, for very little money, in the hope that together we could keep the *Himmel Times* alive.

It was exhilarating at first. But it had become an increasing source of anxiety for me. Just as we were getting off the ground, *Grantland County Online*, a digital-only news site (and I use the term "news" loosely), had gotten a major infusion of capital and a new publisher. Now *GO News*, as it's more commonly known, was kicking our butt.

"The scariest thing, Annie," I said, "is that we're barely keeping our heads above water, while *GO News* keeps getting bigger. They don't have the expenses we do—no print edition, no delivery costs, and they don't spend a lot of staff time fact-checking. Plus, they started *Tea to GO*. Did you know that the cool kids say, 'spill the tea,' when they mean 'what's the gossip?'

"*Tea to GO* is full of '*What married school official was seen in Milwaukee with a very attractive staff member last Thursday night? Did we say late, last Thursday night?*' That kind of garbage. It's almost all blind items—the better to avoid lawsuits, my dear. But people are eating it up. Every time you go into the Elite

Café, someone is trying to figure out who the latest gossip is about."

I paused for a bit of a wallow in self-pity. It wasn't as if I hadn't tried to shake things up at the *Times*, to get us moving ahead, but so far nothing I'd done had made much difference.

"We have a good team. Miguel is much happier since he gave up the managing editor job. He really didn't like bossing people. And Maggie McConnell is doing great in that spot. She's got the instincts, the skills, and forty-five years in the news business behind her. If she could only spin gold out of straw, she'd be perfect. But since she can't, we're making do with a budget so lean it might as well be made out of turkey burger.

"I gave Allie Ross—you remember, I told you about her. She's the high school kid we've been using as a stringer. Anyway, I gave her a part-time job for the summer in the office. She's doing the routine stuff, obits and inside pages copy—weddings, anniversaries, club news. She's got promise, but she's only fifteen. Troy, the other reporter besides Miguel, is a little bit of a suck-up—and his news judgment isn't quite there yet. Still, he's a hard worker. The stringers are a pretty mixed bag.

"Now, here's a twist I bet you didn't see coming. I hired Mom to take April Nelson's place as office manager. I know, I know, it's a dicey move. But she's smart, and efficient, and she gets the job done. Plus, she comes cheap. It's been a little challenging, I admit. Remember when I used to get mad at her and say, 'You're not the boss of me!' and she'd send me to my room?

"Well, now *I'm* the boss of *her*, only I don't get to send her to her room. Yes, OK, I'm not supposed to be doing the day-to-day. That's Maggie's job. I understand that. But I can't just hide away in my office and write my next book if the paper is falling apart two floors below me, can I?

"Everybody took a leap of faith when we reopened the *Times*, and everyone is putting everything they have into it. I can't let them down. I have to find a way to keep us afloat. I just didn't know it would be so hard, Annie."

I paused for a breath before I wrapped things up.

"And then there's Gabe. I don't know. I like him as well—no, probably better than—anyone I've gone out with in a long time. He makes me laugh, and he's really smart. And he likes strong women who speak their minds. In my experience, a lot of men don't. So what's the problem, right? Well, it's not exactly a problem. It's more that I'm afraid a problem might be coming. Lately, it feels like he's pushing me a little, like for a commitment or something. Can't we just enjoy each other? Can't we just *be* without getting all serious, and defining things, and making plans? I don't want to change things. That's when things go bad, when you try to change them."

I slumped back against the bench with a sigh. Usually, when I lay everything out to Annie, it makes the issues seem a little more manageable. This time it all still felt overwhelming.

Then, a voice spoke.

———

Fortunately for my mental health, it wasn't Annie's. I turned and looked behind me.

"Coop! How long have you been standing there?" I asked, trying to remember exactly what I'd said out loud. It's not that Coop and I have major secrets. He's my best friend, after all. Still, I don't tell him *everything* I tell Annie.

"Long enough," he said with a grin that didn't offer me much comfort. I tried to move the conversation away from my chat with Annie, particularly the Gabe part.

"What are you doing here?"

"Your mom said you were here. I called your cell, but it didn't go through."

"Yeah. It's a dead zone—pun totally intended—in the cemetery, except for the hill. What did you want?"

"Nothing. I brought something for Annie."

I looked down at his right hand and saw that he carried a
small pot of pink flowers. Pink was Annie's favorite color. Tears
sprang to my eyes. I quickly blinked them away.

"That's so nice. Why?"

He shrugged. "I know what today is."

I'm all about keeping my tough outer shell polished, but I
was so touched, I couldn't keep up the facade. "You're a pretty
great friend, you know that?"

He smiled, but he looked embarrassed, and tried to cover it
by moving to put the flowers next to Annie's headstone.

"Did you really come just to put flowers on Annie's grave?"

"No, not just for Annie. I took some to Rebecca, too." He was
kneeling, positioning the flowers, with his back to me. I couldn't
see his expression.

"Oh."

Rebecca had been Coop's wife and my nemesis until she was
killed last year. I wasn't happy that Coop had lost someone he
loved, but I couldn't pretend I was sorry she was gone. She'd
done everything she could to break up our twenty-year friendship and came close to succeeding. I couldn't think of anything
nice to say about her. So, I employed the Thumper rule, and
didn't say anything.

Coop apparently didn't want to get into the subject of
Rebecca either, because as he stood and turned to me, he said,
"I'll walk out with you. I've got my truck. We can throw your
bike in the back and you can ride home with me."

"Yes, please. I didn't realize it was so hot. I just about sweated
to death pedaling out here."

"Yeah, I can see that," he said, taking in my damp, bedraggled hair, slipping from its hair clip, and the beads of moisture

coalescing into a river of sweat running down the side of my forehead. "You kind of look like you just took a shower." He sniffed the air, "Except you don't have that shower-fresh scent."

"Shut up," I said. "I'm a head-sweater from way back. Deal with it." I smiled though, because there's something very nice and very easy being with a person who really doesn't care how you look—or in the present situation—smell.

We walked together in companionable silence, until I'd decided he hadn't heard any of my one-sided conversation with Annie. That dream died in the next minute.

"So, what's going on with you and Gabe? He's a nice guy, Leah. You're not getting ready to toss him overboard, too, are you?"

"No. Why would you say that? And what do you mean by 'too'?"

"You really want to go there?" He cocked an eyebrow. It's a not very funny running joke between Coop and my mother that I always find a reason to cut my romances short.

"No, I don't. I thought you didn't believe in illegal surveillance, and what do you call lurking around cemeteries where people are having a private conversation? It's nothing. Really."

He looked at me for a second, but all he said was, "OK."

Our conversation was cut off as a tall woman in her fifties, her hair pulled back and hanging in a long, gray braid down her back, appeared and abruptly crossed the path in front of us.

"Hello, Marcy," I said.

She looked up as though surprised we were there.

"Leah. Coop." She nodded but didn't stop to talk. We knew where she was going. To the top of the hill on which sat a small granite building that resembled an ancient Greek temple. The family mausoleum held Marcy's grandparents, her own mother, and Marcy's baby daughter, Robin. One day, it would hold Marcy, too.

We watched in silence as she reached the building, pulled a key out of her pocket, unlocked the door, and slipped inside, like a ghost gliding through a wall. It had been sixteen years since Marcy White's baby had died, and she still came every week. People said she brought a different book each time and read it to Robin. They said it like it was something weird, or even crazy. Not me, though. I understood why she did it.

"You know what, Coop?" I asked, as we continued on down the path.

"What?"

"I'm calling bullshit on death."

---

## 2

"Hey, I haven't seen you for almost a week," I said, as I tugged at the seatbelt in Coop's truck. "What's been keeping you so busy? If you're heading up some big new investigation, give me a hint. We need to get the jump on *GO News* somehow."

"Sorry, you're not the only one with some work issues. I'm not heading an investigation right now. I'm heading up a 'Community Task Force.' "

He put air quotes around the phrase Community Task Force and a clear note of sarcasm in his voice.

"Why do you sound so disgusted? You didn't mind being on the burglary task force a few months ago."

"Because that was a real job. It was working with other police agencies in the county to put some bad guys away. This task force is pretty much paperwork and public relations, as far as I can see."

"Yeah? What are you tasking about?"

"After *GO News* did the story last month on James Shaw sending that email to one of his students, it got a lot of parents riled up. Then that middle school sexting thing happened up in Sawyer County, and somebody had the bright idea that what we need to protect kids in Grantland County—because the police aren't doing it—is a vigilante group of parents. You know, go on social media sites, trap sexual predators, that kind of thing."

"Really? Who's behind it?"

"Not sure exactly. An administrator at the high school got wind of it and called the chief. That's how the task force idea came up—to head off the crazy. Chief Riley's theory is that you get stakeholders with different viewpoints—like law enforcement, school personnel, parents, counselors, and they'll come up with ideas and recommendations everyone can get behind. The parent vigilante thing will die a natural death. He hopes. The first meeting is next week."

"Boy, I don't know. As long as kids have phones, hormones, and a limited grasp of long-term consequences, I don't think 'recommendations' from parental units and cops will have much impact."

"Yeah, I know. But the chief is most concerned about giving the parents something to do, so they don't get in the way of real investigations or get into dangerous situations themselves. I get why they're so worried, though," he said, putting the truck in gear and starting toward town. "It's a tough time to be a parent. You always found plenty of ways for us to get in trouble when we were kids. Now, with social media it's ten times worse."

"Oh, yeah, like I was always the one."

His silence said it all.

"All right, so I was always the one. But you didn't have to go along with me. But, back to why you're so pissed off about the task force. You just said that parents have it tough. Couldn't this be a way to share information, support each other, figure out what's worth worrying about, and what isn't?"

"Could be, I guess, but organizing, coordinating, liaising, and basically riding a desk for the next couple of months is not what I want to do. The main reason that I didn't go for the captain's job when it was open is I like a mix of supervising and investigating—not full-on paperwork. Erin Harper would be better for this kind of thing."

"Why, because she's a girl?"

He shook his head. "Don't even try that. You know I don't care what gender she is. But Erin's got ambitions, she likes to organize, she's smart, she's political, and she likes being in the public eye. I talked to Rob about it, but it was a no go."

"What did he say?"

"Not much, just that we all have to do things we don't like sometimes. The task force is something Chief Riley wants to see happen. I need to be a team player. You know, I never had a problem with Rob when he and I were both lieutenants. Now that he's captain, he's not acting like the same guy anymore."

"Power corrupts? Or maybe ..."

"Maybe what?"

"Could Rob be jealous because you got all that publicity for closing out Rebecca's case?"

"I don't think so. He was never a glory hound. Just a good, steady, reliable cop."

"That's not exactly how I see him. He's always happy to be a source, because he can't wait to talk about his awesome investigating—but only if we're reporting things the way he likes. Ever since *GO News* opened up shop, he feeds them information we can't get hold of, because they trade journalism for access. And if we print something Rob thinks is critical, he freezes us out for weeks. Plus, he has that stupid cocky attitude that comes with the job—sometimes," I amended. "Present company excluded. Can't you talk to Riley? Tell him you're being benched?" I knew that the Himmel police chief, Mick Riley, valued Coop.

"No, I want to stick to chain of command. I'm not going over Rob's head. I'm just gonna have to deal with it, see if things get better. If they don't, well, I take action."

"Action? Like leave?"

"Not too many other options. Besides, maybe it's time for a change."

I didn't like the sound of that. Himmel without Coop would feel pretty empty. But I didn't need to go there yet. I went back to something he'd said at the beginning of the conversation.

"What's going on with James?"

James Shaw was the JV football coach and a biology teacher at Himmel High School. Coop and I had graduated with him. Just before school got out for the summer, he'd been accused of sending a sexually explicit email to a tenth-grade girl in one of his classes. Now, he was on suspension and under criminal investigation.

"You'd have to ask Erin, it's her case. But I think you know how much you'll get from her. Off the record, it doesn't look good." I'd had a couple of run-ins with Lieutenant Erin Harper over the last year. She's a hard one to figure. Just when I think I've broken through and she trusts me, she throws me in the deep freeze.

"But do you really think James would do something that totally gross and stupid?"

"It doesn't seem like him, no. But one thing I've learned in this job is that people can surprise you in good ways—and bad. He's been drinking too much ever since his divorce. I have no idea what's been going on in his head. I hope it isn't true, but there was enough evidence to charge him, so ..."

"Even so, I don't see it. It doesn't fit."

We had pulled up in front of the *Times* building. As I unbuckled my seatbelt and reached for the door, I said, "I'll see you tonight, right? At the reunion reception at the Elks?"

"Planning on it. Did you hear Ryan Malloy will be there?"

"I heard."

"Lots of people will be excited to see him, Himmel's own Hollywood actor. Don't you want to hear what he's been up to?"

"Not really." I put as much casual unconcern as I could muster into my voice, "Can you help me get my bike out of the back? I want to catch the staff before everyone leaves for the day."

"Sure," was all he said, but I didn't appreciate the amused look in his gray eyes.

———

I unlocked the door next to the *Himmel Times* street entrance, wheeled my bike in and tucked it under the stairs that lead to my third-floor apartment. Then I turned the knob on the other door in the stairwell and stepped into the *Times* offices, which occupy the ground floor of the renovated downtown building where I live.

My mother was at the reception desk, talking to our summer hire, Allie Ross. Courtnee Fensterman, our receptionist, should have been there but she rarely is.

"So, what are you up to, Allie, besides doing Courtnee's job?"

"Go ahead, Allie," my mother prompted. "Tell Leah what you're thinking about."

"Well," she said, hesitating a little. "Like I was telling your mom, I mean, I'm really happy to be at the paper for real, not just as a stringer. I don't mind working on the reception desk, or taking classified ad calls, or proofing stuff. I like helping lay out the pages. And it's really fun to sit in on the story budget meeting. But—"

She paused to twist a strand of dark, curly hair around her index finger, then let it go and said in a rush, "I have an idea for a story of my own, with my own byline. A real story, not just who won the drawing at the Lions Club barbecue. But I know that's important, too."

She added the last bit quickly, as though to forestall a rerun of the talk I'd overheard Maggie give her the week before, when she had chafed a little at typing up Mrs. Hooper's recipe column. Shades of me at that age.

"What's your idea? Have you pitched it to Maggie yet?"

As though conjured up by the sound of her name, Maggie McConnell, the *Times* managing editor, came barreling around the corner as I finished speaking.

"Has who pitched what to me?" Maggie's voice is rough-edged, the legacy of a now-vanquished smoking habit, and it can be a little intimidating.

Allie looked at me. I nodded encouragement.

"Me, Maggie. I want to pitch a story idea to you. It's got a local angle, like you always say we need. It's timely, and it's got news people can use." She stopped, screwing up her courage.

"Well, go on. Don't leave me hanging."

"OK, well, you know that three kids from my class got the measles when they went to New York for the choir trip in May. So that's the local angle. And also there's been a bunch of outbreaks in other states, so that's the timely part. And Wisconsin has one of the higher rates of unvaccinated kids, and that's the news people need part. I want to do a story about vaccines and how things could get really bad if more people don't vaccinate their kids."

"How do you know Wisconsin has a high rate of unvaccinated kids?" Maggie demanded.

"I looked it up online, on the state health department site."

I was impressed, but all Maggie said was, "All right, go on, go on."

"I was thinking I could interview the kids who got measles, and I could ask the county health department what they would do if we get an outbreak in Himmel like there was in Minnesota. And I could interview somebody who knows about epidemiology at UW?" She finished her sentence on an uptick, her voice faltering a little as she tried to read Maggie's face for signs of approval.

My mother and I held our breaths for Allie. She's not the most self-confident kid, and Maggie, while not unkind, is always blunt. This time, she was silent. She retrieved her tortoise shell glasses from the top of her head and was pressing one bow against the corner of her mouth, as she often does when thinking. After a minute, she shoved her glasses on her nose, stared at Allie and said, "I like the idea. I like that you showed initiative. But you aren't ready for a story like this. It's a controversial subject. There's going to be pushback. We have to be absolutely sure the facts are correct and our reporter has a thick skin. It's not a story for a beginner."

At Maggie's first words, a smile had begun spreading across Allie's face, but as Maggie finished, the smile vanished. She bent her head to hide her disappointment, and I felt a pang of sympathy.

"Come on now, it's nothing against you, kiddo. You just need more experience," Maggie said, recognizing Allie's disappointment. She can be a steamroller, but she reads people pretty well.

"Yeah, sure. It's OK, I understand," Allie said, but her eyes were downcast and her voice barely above a low whisper as she struggled not to embarrass herself with tears.

"Maggie, I know you're busy, and Troy and Miguel are doing double-time this month trying to get out the special edition with all those beautiful advertising dollars, plus the regular paper. How about if you let Allie work on the story, but I work with her? I'll mentor her through the whole thing. It's not breaking news, so it's not like it has a short deadline. There's plenty of time for us to back and forth on it."

"Really, Leah? Would you do that?" Allie was looking at me like I'd just tapped her with my magic wand.

"If Maggie doesn't mind, sure I would. What do you say, Maggie?"

As Maggie slowly put her glasses back on top of her sensible gray bob, the look she shot me pretty clearly said, "Stay out of my newsroom decisions, please." Except without the please and with a few choice adjectives. However, what she said out loud was, "You're the boss."

I knew she wasn't happy, and I knew why. I shouldn't have second-guessed her. She was right that a vaccination story would be a tough one to do. Himmel has a very vocal anti-vax parents' group. Hence, the three kids who got the measles. Some sources could give Allie a bad time. She'd have to be extra vigilant about fact-checking and sourcing. And she'd have to be careful not to let balanced coverage slide into "he said, she said." I'd jumped in too quickly—a besetting sin of mine. But I couldn't back out on Allie now. I'd just have to make sure she turned in one heck of a story.

"OK, great then, Maggie. Allie let's get together Monday. Say nine o'clock. We can strategize your story."

"Monday? But I could do it tonight, or tomorrow," she said.

"I like your enthusiasm, but I can't this weekend because—"

"Because, *chica,* you're going to make Ryan Malloy so sad that he broke your heart."

We all turned as Miguel Santos walked into the reception area. Now, if you want to talk heartbreakers, he's one. Tall, slender, beautiful dark brown eyes with lashes that look like extensions, warm light brown skin, a killer smile. Plus funny, smart, and kind. He's the whole package. Some of the heart-breaker part comes from straight women realizing that he's gay.

"Who's Ryan Malloy?" Allie asked, her eyes alight with interest.

"Just some guy I went to school with," I said, shooting a death stare at my mother. She's the only way Miguel could have heard about him. "So, Allie, let's nail down a time on Monday and we can talk."

"He's Leah's first," my mother said, blithely ignoring my attempt to change the conversation.

"You never forget your first," Maggie said, jumping in quickly—maybe to get a little of her own back by keeping a topic alive that I so obviously wanted to kill. "What was it, Leah? First romance? First sex? First broken heart?"

"It was nothing. It was junior year in high school. We went out for a while, then his family moved to Seattle. End of story."

"He was a good-looking kid, nice manners, but he was a conniver. Plus, he was in love with himself. He wasn't a good choice for Leah, but you couldn't tell her anything, then. Or now, come to think of it. She was crazy about him. She moped around the house for weeks after he dumped her."

"OK, Mom. This is super fun, but can we end this episode of *Carol's Revised History* podcast? I didn't mope for weeks after Ryan left. For the record," I said, looking around the room, "whatever I felt then, however Ryan or I behaved, it was **sixteen** years ago. I'll be as happy to see him this weekend as I will anyone else I haven't thought about in years. Besides, he always attracted a crowd, and that will be even truer now that he's an actor—even if he's not a very famous one. I probably won't even get a passing nod when he walks through the horde of admiring fans."

"All the more reason to let me style you for tonight, *chica*. Come on," he said, taking in my sweaty hair, makeup-less face, baggy T-shirt and dirty tennis shoes. "We have a lot of work to do."

"Miguel, chill. You know it's not a fancy party, just a drinks reception at the Elks for the start of the reunion weekend. The big do is the dinner/dance tomorrow night, and I already have an outfit for that. I'm going casual tonight. I've already got my clothes laid out on the bed. Get out of the closet."

He half-turned from sliding hangers draped with my "good" clothes along the closet rod and flashed me a grin.

"I was never in the closet, *chica*. You know that. But, seriously, we are so going shopping for you. Soon. Show me what you have for tomorrow night."

"Mom got it for me last week when she went to some boutique in Madison. She doesn't think I know how to dress myself either," I said, as I walked into the office next to my bedroom and retrieved the garment bag hanging on a hook next to the door.

"Oh, *Moonflower Magic*! I love that store. Carol has such good taste," he said, pulling off the protective plastic and holding up a dark green, crossover-front dress with a deep sort of drapey V-neck in a soft, silky material.

"Perfect! This will bring out the green in your eyes. And you need some shimmery green eyeshadow. You still have those strappy sandals?"

"Yes. But they hurt my feet."

"For one night, you can do it. Don't you want sweet revenge on Ryan Malloy? You will look so hot! No one puts Leah in the corner," he said, looking so incensed on my behalf that I had to laugh.

"All right, all right. I'll wear the dress, the sandals, and I'll even take a stab at some shimmery eyes. But not because I want sweet revenge. Because it will make you happy."

"You have the sparkly hazel eyes, the great smile, the thick, beautiful hair. Why do you fight me when I tell you to flaunt it?"

"I guess I'm not a flaunting kind of gal. Besides, you see me through eyes of love, my friend. In reality, I'm an OK-looking Midwestern chick who cleans up nice. I'm pretty fond of my nose, though—one thing at least that I can thank my father for. And Mom contributed some nice eyelashes to the gene pool." He shook his head in mock despair.

"I give up," he said.

"That isn't true, I know. Look, you can style me up like your favorite Barbie doll, but I'm still not going to be making any former boyfriends drop at my sandal-clad feet. Especially not Ryan. Mom's right. He could give Narcissus a run for his money."

I reached over and tousled his carefully coifed hair. "I'll see you later. You're going to the drinks reception at the Elks, right?"

"I want to, but Maggie needs me to shoot some photos in Omico. It's the Little Miss Firecracker pageant tonight."

"Lucky you. Well, don't worry about missing the reception. I don't think all that many people will be there. It's just a low-key get together to start the weekend off. Lots of people won't even be in town yet. The fun, fun, fun starts tomorrow. Now, I've got to go take my shower. Gabe and I have a hot date for dinner at McClain's tonight. There's a special on Davey Burgers."

---

When I finished blow-drying my hair and putting on some mascara and lipstick, my phone rang. Gabe.

"Hey, you. I'm almost ready. I'm getting hungry and the Davey Burgers are calling."

"That's why I'm calling, Leah. I'm sorry, but I can't make dinner. Something came up."

"Oh," I said, trying to keep the disappointment from my voice. "Got an issue with a case—or a client?" Gabe is a criminal defense attorney, and his hours can be long and erratic at times.

"Both. I can't make dinner, but how about I meet you at the Elks? I'll get there as soon as I can."

"Sure, no worries. I'll see you there."

"Great. I shouldn't be late. From what Carol tells me, I'd better not be, or you might fall under the spell of your movie star ex-boyfriend."

Geez Louise, who hadn't my mother told about my high school romance?

"No doubt you're taking a chance, but I'll be true to you as long as I can. Just remember, I considered Ryan Malloy pretty charming once upon a time."

"Yes, but I'm your fairy tale prince now, right?"

"Absolutely. Get your work done. I'll see you in a while."

I stared at my phone for a few seconds after I clicked off the call. I understood that Gabe had several cases going, and he probably had to meet with a client, or do some other lawyer stuff. Lord knows, I'd cancelled out on him enough times when I was under a deadline. Still. I'd really been looking forward to dinner with him—not to mention the Davey burgers. I sighed and walked into the bedroom to get my clothes for the reception off the bed. And then I started to laugh.

Laying on my bed was a sundress patterned in cream, coral and pale-yellow colors. A pair of yellow flats was lined up neatly on the floor directly below the dress. Miguel must have dug deep to unearth that ensemble from the depths of my closet. I couldn't remember the last time I'd worn it. The black crop pants and yellow T-shirt that I'd picked out as my outfit for the evening were nowhere to be seen.

**3**

---

"Leah, this is my friend Kristin Norcross," Coop said.

I had just inhaled two Figgy Blue Bites from my plate of *h'ors d'oeuvres* when Coop showed up at my elbow. The fresh fig halves, topped with Wisconsin blue cheese, candied walnuts, and a drizzle of honey are sticky, but worth it. I rubbed my fingers off on a napkin and put out my hand.

"Hi, Kristin. Nice to meet you. Have you tried the *hors d'oeuvres*? Marcy White is catering, and they're unbelievable."

She was my height, about five six, with shoulder-length auburn hair and wide-set green eyes. The hand she offered me was slim, and her fingernails were painted an orangey red that matched her lipstick. She had a nice handshake. Not a death grip, but firm enough to give you something to hold on to.

"Nice to meet you, too. We just got here, but I'll definitely make a visit to the snacks table."

"You'd better do it fast. There won't be much left if Leah hits it up again," Coop said.

I crossed my eyes at him as Kristin said, "I don't believe that. Leah couldn't stay so fit and trim if that were true."

"Why, thank you, Kristin. But on the issue of Figgy Blue

Bites, and anything else Marcy makes, I'm afraid Coop's right. I can't resist, and I can't deny it. She may not be the friendliest person in the world, but Marcy sure knows how to show a canapé some love. I've gone to many a wedding and a few funerals that I would've passed up, just because I knew Marcy was doing the food."

Kristin laughed.

Coop said, "You think she's kidding, but she's not."

"Coop said you've been friends for a long time. It's easy to see that."

"Oh, we go way back. The things I could tell you about Coop. Like the time in seventh grade when he had a mad crush on Bethany Miller, so we—"

"All right, all right, Kristin doesn't want to hear all that. Where's Gabe?"

"Not a very subtle way to change the subject, but OK. Your seventh-grade secrets are safe with me—for now. Gabe is running late. He'll meet me here after he finishes up some work thing. Gabe's a lawyer," I said to Kristin. "He used to be a prosecuting attorney like you, but he's in private practice now. And he's not a native Himmelite either. Coop told me you're from Hailwell, is that right?"

She nodded. "We lived there until I was fifteen, then my mother got a job offer in Nebraska and we moved. But I love Wisconsin, and we still have a lot of family here. I was really glad to get the job in the district attorney's office and move back to the area."

"How do you like working for Cliff Timmins?"

"It's interesting," she said, and grinned.

I definitely liked this girl. I glanced at Coop, and it was obvious he did, too. I noticed then that he must have gone to the barbershop after he dropped me off, because his dark hair was styled as opposed to just brushed. It was short but just long enough for the top to sort of side sweep over and give it a little zip. He was freshly shaved and smelled of some nice citrusy scent. The light blue shirt and khaki pants ensemble he wore wouldn't set Miguel's heart singing, but it worked for Coop. He seemed more relaxed and happy than he'd been in the afternoon.

"I hear you're working on another book. I really enjoyed the last one," Kristin said.

"Thanks, that's nice to hear. I wish everyone felt that way. *Family Secrets* hasn't done quite as well as *Unholy Alliances*."

Quite as well? Who was I kidding? It hadn't made half the sales of my first book.

"That's hard to believe. The story about your family, and the cold case with the cheerleader—it read like a suspense thriller, not a true crime book. And there was so much heart in it. You did an amazing job."

"Kristin, from your lips to the ears of readers everywhere." I saluted her with my glass.

"I thought you two would hit it off. I'm going to take Kristin around and introduce her to some more people," Coop said. "We'll catch up with you and Gabe later."

---

"Leah, can I buy you a drink?"

I didn't need to look up to see who it was. The voice was exactly the same one that I remembered: deep, intimate, sexy.

He was holding out a glass of red wine, which I generally avoid because the color is very dangerous for someone with my propensity for spilling things.

"Sure, Ryan."

He'd had a Hollywood smile in high school, and his time in actual Hollywood seemed to have increased its wattage. His impossibly blue eyes were as clear and bright as they had been back then, and I knew the color was real, not enhanced by colored contacts. However, his teeth were so astonishingly white they had to be veneers. Golden hair messily tousled made him look younger than his early thirties, no doubt an advantage for an actor. His best feature, ironically, was the only imperfect thing about him—a strong nose with a slight bump on the bridge. It saved his face from being pretty instead of handsome.

"To old friends," he said, handing me the glass and then gently clinking it with his own before he took a drink.

I nodded and took a small swallow.

"You look great. And I hear you're doing great, too. Your books, I mean."

"Thanks," I said, my tone cool.

He was going to have to work for it, if he wanted me to make nice. Ryan hadn't broken my heart, but he sure as heck had bruised it. If he had just dumped me when his family moved, like a normal, self-centered teenage boy, it would have been much easier. Instead, he'd talked about how we'd work at our long-distance relationship. We could email, we could call— texting wasn't much of a thing back then. And he'd be home for the summer. He could stay with his older stepbrother, Steven, who lived in Himmel. He didn't want to end the good thing we had together. And I, in the depths of my first love, fell for it.

Maybe he'd been afraid that I'd stop helping him "revise" his English papers—which was really more like rewriting them —if he said we should break up when he told me he was moving. Maybe he thought I'd cry and get hysterical. And maybe I would have. I'll admit it. I did have a pretty serious crush on him. But so what? Deal with it, man! But he didn't. He just left town with his family, and I never heard from him again.

And yes, I was sad, and I was upset—though I still maintain I did not "mope." But then I got hopping mad, because by not calling and not answering my email, Ryan cut me off from the catharsis of telling him what a jerk he was. I didn't have the chance to take him up one side and down the other—a specialty of mine that has given me solace during many a break-up—romantic *and* professional. But now, it seemed, I had my opportunity. I waited to hear what he said next, like a cat waiting for just the right moment to pounce.

"You're not still mad at me, are you, Leah?" He flashed a rueful smile. "I'm sorry. I didn't mean to lose touch. You were always special to me. But you know how it is—you move away, things get hectic in the new place, you mean to call, you don't get around to it, and then, well, it's too late. Too much time has gone by."

"You didn't exactly 'lose' touch, Ryan. Lose implies you misplaced something you want to find. You didn't 'lose' our relationship. You tossed it in the trash like a crumpled fast-food bag on your way out of town. If you'd wanted to find it, you could have answered my emails or called me, yeah? Just an honest, direct, parting of the ways."

Irritation flashed in his eyes for a second, but he suppressed it quickly.

"I guess I didn't behave very well. You're right. I was your average, self-absorbed high school kid. It wasn't about you. It was just where I was in my life then. I didn't stay in touch with anyone from Himmel, not even James. I feel bad about that, I really do. I hear things aren't going so well for him these days."

If he was trying to steer the conversation off the dangerous emotional ground of our teenage breakup, he'd just taken a wrong turn. Because the way he had treated James Shaw was, in my view, much worse than the way he'd treated me.

"You could say that. It looks like he's going to lose his job and maybe go to prison. He's had a pretty hard-knock life since the accident."

In late April of our sophomore year, Ryan and James had spent the night at Ryan's family cottage on Gray Lake. It was still too cold for most people to be on the water. But they decided to take the speedboat out, even though Ryan wasn't supposed to use it without his stepfather there. They were screwing around, going too fast, daring each other to do ever more stupid things. When James stood up, Ryan gunned the motor and took off as a joke. James fell overboard. Ryan circled back to pick him up, but he didn't cut the motor soon enough. James was caught in the propeller. His right leg had to be amputated below the knee.

"Yeah, the accident was a really rough thing. I feel for James. You might not think so, but it was tough on me, too. I was pretty broken up about the whole thing. But, you know, you've got to take life as it comes. Accidents happen. You have to move on.

"From what my mother tells me, James has been making bad decisions for years, and blaming all his bad calls on that one day on the lake. James was always kind of a 'poor me' guy, but he didn't used to be stupid. I mean, come on, what was he thinking, trying to hook up with a high school girl? Especially with all this 'Me Too' stuff going on. He can't blame the fact that his life is a mess on one piece of bad luck from years ago."

"I'd call losing your leg more than a piece of bad luck. Especially for James. It crushed his dreams. He was a great football player, Ryan, you know that. Coop says he was the best high school quarterback in the state. It had to really hurt watching you play his position. He wouldn't be human if he didn't think about how he would've been recruited by a Big Ten school. That he might've been drafted by the pros. Instead—"

"Instead, he's a second-rater. Yeah, I know, I know. I hear what you're saying. Look, I feel bad for the guy. It was awful, what happened with the boat. But James just wouldn't get over it. When I got 'his' quarterback position on the team—" He paused to make air quotes around the word his.

"He was so pissed off and jealous. It really messed with his head. And that's on him. You think my life's been so easy?"

"Yes, actually, I do. A mother who thinks you walk on water, a rich stepfather, good looks, a decent amount of brains, and enough charm to get what you want. You're like the guy who was born on third base, and thinks he hit a triple."

It was quite satisfying to have my say, and I stood ready to have Ryan react angrily. Instead, he shook his head and took a drink of his wine.

"All right, maybe I had a few breaks to start with. And maybe I knew how to use them. But my life hasn't been so perfect either. I've been beating my head against the Hollywood sign for eight years. I get a second lead on a sitcom, and it's cancelled in six weeks. I get a part in a decent film, and all my scenes get cut. I do voice-overs for local bank commercials, and scramble to pay my SAG dues. I'm good looking and I'm a good actor. I'm not bragging, it's just the truth. But there's a thousand other guys just like me out there. You need an edge, something extra to break into the club. And even if you do, you've still got to suck up to the casting directors—and they're mostly all women—or you don't get anywhere."

"If they're mostly women, I can't imagine that's a problem for you."

"Imagine again. I had a thing with one of them that turned out to be *Fatal Attraction* times ten. She's got a real nasty streak and a lot of influence. I've been practically blackballed for the last year. I can't even get a voice actor gig on a cartoon. That's why I'm going indie."

"Going indie?"

"Setting up a production company. Commissioning a script myself. Playing the lead, and maybe directing, too. I've got a partner lined up already. We're just working on the financing. If Ben Affleck can be a triple threat, so can I."

"That sounds expensive. Financing a film, I mean."

I realized as I spoke that he had completely turned the conversation away from the way he'd treated me in high school and onto his current issues. Just like the old days, it was all about Ryan. But whether he had heard me or not, I'd said what I wanted to say. It was quite freeing. With it came the knowledge that Ryan was just the same, but I wasn't. High school Leah would have continued the take down, bent on proving that she was justified in her anger, determined to not only wrest a sincere apology from him, but to leave him begging for mercy under the lash of her tongue. Now, don't get me wrong, that still held a certain appeal. But the pull wasn't overwhelming.

"It is expensive. Very. But I've already got some backing lined up. I'm thinking about doing some filming here. Maybe using some local talent from the community theater. It would cut down on my costs and who knows? Maybe the next Jennifer Lawrence is right here in Himmel. Which reminds me, I wanted to talk to you about—"

"About financing? Sorry. This one-book wonder has her own money problems."

"No, not financing. I have something else in mind. That is, if you forgive me for being a jerk in high school?" He tilted his head slightly to the right as he looked down at me and placed his free hand lightly on my arm.

Oh, what the hell. It *was* sixteen years ago.

"OK, fine. I forgive you."

"That's a relief. Now for my proposition. I—"

"Wait a second. If there's any propositioning going on with Leah, I think I should be the one doing it."

# 4

Gabe had materialized beside us. He smiled and put his arm around me as Ryan stuck out his hand.

"Hi. I'm Ryan Malloy. Leah's old high school boyfriend."

"Gabe Hoffman. Leah's new grown-up boyfriend."

Gabe isn't overly tall, about five nine. He wears his dark brown hair a little long, parted on the side, but no amount of hair product can keep it from flopping down on his forehead at some point. Sometimes he has a dark stubble beard, which looks good, but tonight he was clean-shaven. He has great eyebrows, thick, straight, and very expressive. But his eyes are my favorite thing about him. They're so dark, it's hard to see the pupil, and so intense that when he looks at you, you know you've got his full attention.

"Hey, you. I was beginning to think you weren't going to make it," I said.

"What? And miss the chance to find out your darkest secrets from all the people who knew you when?"

"I think my mother has already spilled those."

"So, Gabe, what is it you do?" Ryan asked.

"I'm a lawyer. How about you?"

Ryan looked taken aback, as though someone had asked a policeman in uniform what he did for a living.

"I'm an actor. I played the oldest son, Owen, on the cable series *Streetwise.*"

"Sorry. I don't watch a lot of TV."

"Did you see the movie *Sweet Revenge* last year? I had a great part, but the lead had it in for me, so most of my scenes got cut. There's a lot of backstabbing in Hollywood. It's a tough business."

"Ever thought of giving up, trying something else?"

"No, not yet, anyway. I was just telling Leah that—"

"That you have a proposition for her? Yeah, that's where I came in."

Ryan smiled. "A business proposition. I'm putting together a production company, to do my own independent films. I'll be producing, directing, acting. I've already got the script for the first one. But I think Leah's book, *Family Secrets*, would make a great second film. With changes, of course, you know, to punch up the storyline."

"Wait a second, Ryan. *Family Secrets* is true. If you "punch up" the story, it wouldn't be."

"You don't film a book, Leah, you film a story. Look, we'll get together and talk about it."

"How long are you staying?" Gabe asked.

"I'm not sure. Kind of depends on how things come together for my production company. And there's my mother, of course. I'm here because she's not doing well."

"I heard that, Ryan. I'm sorry," I said.

"Yeah, her cancer came back. She did chemo, for a while, but now she doesn't want any more treatment. The doctors said it could be weeks or months, they can't really say. I can't stay forever, of course. If I can get the meetings I need set up, I'll have to go. But Steven will be here, so it's not like she'll be alone."

"Steven?" Gabe asked.

"My stepbrother, Steven Burke. The 'car king.' You must have seen his really bad commercials on local TV. He's got three dealerships and makes tons of money—so he's always telling me."

"That must make you feel better, knowing your stepbrother is here when you can't be," Gabe said.

"Oh, sure. He's good to Mom. Of course, he'd better be."

You might think that last remark meant that his stepbrother, Steven, would have to answer to Ryan, if he treated Ryan's mother badly. But it probably referred to the fact that Ryan's stepfather, Jonas Burke, had left everything to Ryan's mother when he died. The intent was that when Joanna passed away, the estate would be divided evenly between Ryan and Steven. But it actually meant that if Joanna wasn't happy with her stepson, she could cut him off with nothing.

"Your mom must be happy to have you staying with her again," I said.

"Oh, I'm not staying at the house. I'm out at Gray Lake at the family cottage. I think it's easier for mom that way, less commotion. She's got home health care people in and out, and the housekeeper is there. I think it would be too much for her if I was at the house all the time."

As much as Joanna doted on Ryan, I doubted that. It was more likely that Ryan didn't do well with the role of dutiful son for more than a few hours at a time. What exactly was it that had made me crush so hard on him all those years ago? It had to be the looks. It couldn't be the character.

I took Gabe's hand as I said to Ryan, "It was good seeing you again. But there are a couple of people I want Gabe to meet, and I'm sure you've got other old friends that you want to catch up with."

"Yeah, I do. But I want to talk to you again about your book. Here, put your number in my phone and I'll get in touch next week."

As he started to hand it to me, a wave of perfume heavy with musk wafted toward me. I stifled a sneeze. Ryan must have caught the scent too, because instead of passing me the phone, he turned and looked behind him.

The woman who approached put her hand on his arm. She was petite and looked even more so next to Ryan's six feet. Her light brown hair was long and wavy. She was still beautiful, with large dark eyes, a short, straight nose, and full lips that she licked nervously with a delicate pink tongue. I recognized her right away, but I was shocked to see her, and at the change in her. Her eyes, under their smoky makeup, were puffy. The whites were etched with tiny red veins, as though she'd been crying. It was possible that she had been drinking, not crying. Or maybe she'd been doing both.

"Ryan, I can't believe it's you. I wasn't going to come, but I had to."

---

Ryan had a perfunctory smile on his face, the kind you give when you're madly trying to remember who this person, who seems to know you, could possibly be. Gina Cox had been in our grade, but she was really quiet, really shy. Until we were seniors. Then she became the class wild child. I didn't know her well in either of her incarnations—churchy Gina or crazy Gina.

She realized that he didn't know who she was at about the same time I did.

"Ryan! Don't you recognize me? It's me, Gina." Her voice grew louder. She released the hold she had on his arm, while at the same time releasing the aroma of Jack Daniels as she swayed slightly on her stiletto heels.

"Gina! Oh, yeah, sure," he said.

" 'Gina, oh yeah, sure,' " she repeated, mocking him. "I thought you'd be glad to see me. I thought—no, that's not true. I *wanted* you to be glad. Like I wanted you to call me. Or answer my emails. But you never did. And you wish I wasn't here now, don't you?"

Wait. What? Why would Ryan call Gina? He was *my* boyfriend before he left. Gabe looked at me, and I shrugged. This was news. I was curious to see how it played out. Apparently, so were others, because the buzz of conversation had stopped and clusters of people were watching the unexpected drama. Though he'd always enjoyed being center stage, this time Ryan looked very anxious to exit.

"No, no. It's great to see you, Gina. But, uh, the thing is I have to make a call. You know how it is, my agent, he's always after me. I'll catch up with you later. You're looking good!" Ryan had pivoted, ready to walk away, but Gina clamped her hand back on his arm.

"Am I, Ryan?" She gave a sad little smile. "What a liar you are. You haven't changed. But I have. Look at me. I'm thirty-three years old, and I look like I'm forty-three. You know why, Ryan? You know why? Because my life's been shit, that's why." Her words had begun to slur.

Ryan tried again to walk away.

Gina raised her voice. "You don' get to walk out on me again. Look at me!" A little spit shot out of her mouth as she shouted. The drops landed on the lapel of the sport coat Ryan wore over his pristine white T-shirt and jeans.

"I know I look like hell. Why wouldn't I? I've been living in hell. You know that, Ryan? You should know that." Ryan attempted to lead her away.

"No! You listen to me. You—everybody, you should hear this. You wanna hear this, right?" She spread her arms wide and addressed the crowd. "Well, you're gonna. He's gonna, too!" She looked at Ryan, and he put a hand back on her arm, trying to move her away from the audience, which was surely as rapt with attention as any he'd ever had for any scripted drama he'd ever been in.

"Shh. Easy there, Gina, we can talk. We can catch up. Let's go—"

"No!" She pulled her arm out of his grasp, stumbling a little, then regaining her balance. She turned back to the onlookers and spoke again, like an actor breaking the fourth wall on a television show.

"Hey, you know what? I got an idea. A great idea. How about a movie about a real small-town sleaze? It's a trage-a, a trage-a com. A tragicomedy. Part funny, really, really, funny. And part sad. See this guy. This guy, see, he ruins his best friend, and he gets away with it. Nobody blames him. Nobody ever blames him for anything. And then this guy—he's not very nice—" She turned to look over her shoulder at Ryan. "You're perfect for the part, Ryan."

For the third time, he tried to walk away, but she grabbed him by the arm again. Short of throwing her down on the floor or walking out dragging her behind like an anchor, he didn't have much choice but to stand and take it. And Gina had more to say.

"So, yeah. This, this, movie. It's about a high school kid, and he hurts his best friend real bad. He, he maims him. He destroys him. Wait, I said that, didn't I?" She shook her head as if to clear it and again swayed, but she was tethered to Ryan and maintained her balance.

Gabe whispered in my ear, "Leah, we have to stop this."

"No, wait, just a second. I want to hear what else she's going to say."

"So this guy, he cheats on his one girlfriend, with this dumb, stupid, other girl. He says *she's* the one he really loves. And she can't believe it. He's like a prince, and he picked *her*. She is so happy, so, so happy. She doesn't even care about lying to her parents, or the people in her church. Did I say she's a good girl? She is. She was, that is. She really was." A small sob escaped, and tears began to roll down her cheeks, leaving trails of black mascara behind. "But she lied to everybody—her parents, her church family, her friends. But you know who she really lied to? To herself."

"You're drunk. And you don't know what you're saying. Please, stop embarrassing yourself."

"I'm not embarrassed, Ryan. Are you embarrassed? It's just a story, isn't it? Just a dumb story about a dumb girl who ruins her life. That's why it's funny. Because she's so dumb. Don't you get it, Ryan? Don't you? I loved you. I made my parents ashamed, because of what I did. I made *myself* ashamed. I don't love you now, Ryan. I hate you! I wish you were dead! I wish I was dead!" She began pounding his chest with small clenched fists. "I hate you! I hate you!" He grabbed her hands and pushed her away as she began sobbing.

None of us could look away, nor, it seemed, could we move, although her abject pain and humiliation was terrible to witness.

Then Marcy White appeared, like a guardian angel in a white chef's outfit, a white headscarf covering her hair. She gently pulled Gina away. As they moved toward the door, the much taller and sturdier Marcy bent her head down so it touched the top of Gina's as the younger woman sheltered in the curve of her arm. Gina's loud sobs had subsided, but she was crying softly. She clung to Marcy as the older woman comforted her like a mother reassuring a child after a nightmare. It was one of the most surprisingly tender moments I'd ever witnessed.

**5**

———

"Well, that was pretty intense," Gabe said.

"Pretty awful, too," Kristin added.

The four of us, Gabe, me, Kristin, and Coop had moved to a table at the far side of the room and were rehashing Gina's meltdown. Also, cleaning up on a plate of Marcy's *hors d'oeuvres.*

"Obviously, this Ryan was the boyfriend from hell, but she must have really loved him to be that upset this many years later. It was excruciating to watch. But who's the other girl she was talking about? The one Ryan was cheating on? Someone in your grade? I hope she wasn't in the crowd, that could be a little humiliating."

"Yes. Couldn't it?" I said dryly.

A flush crept up Kristin's face as she made the connection. "Oh, gosh. It was you, wasn't it, Leah?"

"Yep. It sure was."

She covered her eyes with her hand as she shook her head. "I'm mortified."

"Don't be. If I'd found out sixteen years ago when it happened, I would have felt bad. Now I'm just surprised at how clueless I was. I had no idea Ryan was seeing anyone else. And if I *had* suspected it, I never would have picked Gina as the girl."

"Why not?" she asked.

"She was super-religious. Her family belonged to the Church of the Covenant of Jesus. It's seriously strict. Her dad is a warden or an elder or whatever they call them. You know, one of the guys who run things. They had their own school through the eighth grade. When Gina came to high school in the ninth, she really just hung out with the other kids from her church school. The only person not from her church that I ever saw her with was James. And I think she only knew him because he worked at her dad's hardware store, and so did she."

"Not my James," Gabe said.

"Yes, your client, James Shaw," I said.

"Is he the one who sent a sexually explicit email to a student? Are you representing him?" Kristin asked.

"Allegedly sent the email. Yes, I am," Gabe said.

"Is that your case?" Kristin asked, turning to Coop.

"No. It's Erin Harper's. The captain saved me for the big assignment. The Community Task Force on Sexting and Social Media."

"No," I said. "Don't get started on that. It will just make you mad all over again."

"Let's go back to the love triangle of Ryan Malloy, Leah, and sad little Gina," Gabe said. "I'd like to know more about that."

"And I'd like to know if there are any Figgy Blue Bites left. And I could use another glass of Pinot," I said, standing up. I wasn't upset about Ryan's long-ago infidelity, but you can only dwell on the guy—and the girl he cheated on you with—for so long. "You guys talk amongst yourselves. And when I get back, I'll take the floor and answer any questions Kristin might have about the life and times of Lieutenant David Cooper. And I just want to say, Kristin, how happy it makes me that you don't call him David."

She looked puzzled, and Coop looked disinclined to explain, but I just let it lie there. That would be for another conversation one day. I pushed back my chair, but as I stood to go, an unwelcome sight greeted me.

"Uh-oh, incoming. Coop, engage the enemy while I make my escape."

But it was too late.

---

"Hello, Leah. I just had to stop and let you know you're a featured player in the lead item for *Tea to GO*."

"Don't even think about tagging me in that rancid, blind-item gossip column, Spencer."

Spencer Karr is the new owner/publisher of *GO News*. To make things even more fun, his parents are Paul Karr, the man who wants to marry my mother, and Marilyn Karr, the ex-wife who wants to kill her. And she wouldn't mind taking me down with my mother as well.

"Jealous, much? *Tea to GO* is one of the reasons *GO News* is kicking your ass. Don't get all hormonal at me, because you didn't think of it. And don't worry, it's not a blind item. I was an eyewitness to everything, and it all played out in public. It's a little too late to be discreet, don't you think?"

"I think you're mixed up, Spence." He hates being called Spence. "You're not kicking our ass. You *are* an ass. Just like you were in high school. Come on, even you can't seriously be thinking about running an item about what went down just now with Gina and Ryan. You can see what a wreck she is."

"No, I'm not thinking about it. I've already posted it. You surprise me, Leah. We don't censor coverage at *GO News*. It's all the local happenings, all the time. What makes me think that you're more concerned about yourself than you are about Gina? Maybe your reputation as an investigative journalist is overblown? You missed a story that was right under your nose."

I shook my head in disgust, "That was sixteen years ago, you moron. Maybe you're still reliving what you wish were your glory days, but I'm not." He continued as though I hadn't said anything.

"I was stunned to learn about the love triangle. From the look on your face while Gina was ranting, you were, too. Who knew Himmel High School was such a hotbed of sexual intrigue? Here, what do you think? The layout looks good, doesn't it?"

He thrust his phone under my nose and showed me the *Tea to GO* item accompanied by an extremely unflattering photo of me staring at Gina and Ryan. My mouth was half-open and I had a dazed expression on my face. The only thing missing to make me look like a total idiot was a thought balloon reading "Huh?" over my head.

"Spencer, you didn't really need to do that," Coop said. He had risen from the table and come over to where we were standing.

"That's where you're wrong, Coop. It's got everything readers like: an actor who's a handsome bad boy, Ryan; a beautiful, heartbroken woman, Gina, and a spurned, less attractive girl-friend, Leah. Oh. I definitely had to do this."

Spencer's not a very big guy. I was wearing flats, and we were eye level. Next to Coop, he looked even shorter. But he makes up for his small size with his large ego.

"You're still riding to Leah's rescue, I see."

"Leah doesn't need anyone to rescue her, Spencer. I'm just going to suggest that you think about what you're doing. Ryan's here because his mother has terminal cancer. Gina's obviously got some emotional problems. What's the point of highlighting that on your news site? Couldn't you take it down?"

"No. I couldn't. How can people trust *GO News* if we don't report news as it happens? The public loves celebrity news. Of course, when we run it and the *Himmel Times* doesn't, well, that doesn't look so good for the paper. I understand that. But then, it hasn't been looking good for a long time, has it?"

"I think you're stretching it to call Ryan a celebrity, except in his own mind," I said. "And Gina definitely isn't. Just like you're stretching it to call your online gossip sheet a news publication."

"You're really getting worried, aren't you, Leah? You should be. The latest circulation numbers for the *Times* don't look so good. Ours are climbing. Well, nice chatting. I think I'll order a bourbon at the bar to sip while I check our site stats. I'll bet the clicks are climbing, even as we speak."

# 6

I'd invited Gabe back to my place, but I wasn't that disappointed when he said that he had an early meeting with a client, and he had some work still to do for it. I needed to do some thinking about the evening, and a few other things.

It was a warm night and my third-floor loft was stuffy when I walked through the door. I know life isn't about the things we own, and that money doesn't buy happiness. Still, the proceeds from my first book that had allowed me to claim this space as mine had definitely given me a down payment on contentment. The loft is open and airy, full of sunlight that spills through the tall arched windows on nice days. The brick walls of the old department store it was once part of are a nice reminder of the history of the building. The gleaming countertops and stainless-steel appliances, the open layout from kitchen to living room, and the highly polished wooden floor give it a nice modern feel. A bathroom, bedroom, and small office complete my happy little home. But my two favorite things in the whole place are the gas fireplace that warms up cold nights, and the window seat where I can sit and look down on the street and the traffic below.

In fact, within five minutes of entering, I was on that very window seat, clad in my summer pajamas—an oversized UW T-shirt—with a Diet Coke in my hand. A light breeze entered through one of the open windows but didn't do much to dispel the heat that had built up all day. I rubbed the icy cold can across my forehead, giving myself a pleasant shiver. I had two things on my mind—Ryan and Gina, and the paper. I took them in order as I watched the mostly empty street below.

It hadn't made sense, at first, that Ryan had been seeing Gina on the side while he and I were dating. But the more I thought about it, the more I realized that the odd couple had been me and Ryan, not Gina and Ryan. I remembered how surprised I'd been when he'd started chatting me up in the cafeteria. And, OK, I'll confess, how flattered.

Ryan was without doubt the most popular kid in our class. Even the teachers liked him. He usually went for girls who were prettier, flirtier, more waif-like, and, shall we say, less outspoken than me. Gina was three out of four—definitely not a flirt—but so much prettier than any other girl in school, and so unlikely to express herself, that she was definitely Ryan material. If I'd been more objective at the time and less infatuated, I would have seen that Ryan had been enamored of my mad skills with a research paper, not with me as a person. He had been seriously in danger of being put on academic suspension and losing his spot on the basketball team when he first showed interest in me. But he was good at masking his motives, and I was very ready to fall for his attention and charm. Soon after, it didn't seem unreasonable for him to ask for my help with his English homework. After all, we were a couple.

My mother knew what I was doing, told me it was unethical to do Ryan's homework for him, and ordered me to stop. Of course, I did not. Coop had also told me I was being stupid, which I had vehemently denied. I rationalized that Ryan had done the basic work, and I was just guiding his writing and "finessing" parts of it. Which I was, if by finessing you mean writing whole paragraphs and taking the time to make sure the sentences sounded like something he would write, not something I would turn in.

In retrospect, Ryan and I hadn't spent all that much time together. While I was busy being the power behind the basketball, the hand that rocks the free-throw, or whatever cliché you care to toss out about a female who subordinates herself so a male can reach his goals, he was with Gina. Obviously—at least on Gina's side of it—things had gotten a lot more serious between the two of them than they had between us.

Ryan had pressured me for sex, but so had most boys I'd gone out with. I wasn't ready. I told him I didn't want to be pushed, and he backed off with reasonably good grace, which I had counted as a mark in his favor. But his chivalrous sensitivity was no doubt because he was already involved with Gina, and he had just made a pro forma try with me.

Of course, he'd left town with nary a backward glance for me. I'd given him what he needed, and he was off. But he'd done the same to Gina, who had given him much more. And now I thought I finally understood the sad and seemingly inexplicable transformation Gina had undergone between our junior and senior years.

Ryan had left in January of our junior year. In April, Gina's grandmother, who lived in North Carolina, fell and broke her leg in two places. Neither of her parents could travel south to help out. Her mother had to take over the hardware store while her father did the spring planting on the small farm they owned. So, Gina, the dutiful daughter, was dispatched to assist her grandmother. She finished the school year down there, came back sometime over the summer, and returned to Himmel

High School for the start of our senior year. But it was a whole different Gina who showed up in September.

She didn't hang out with her church friends anymore. She put blue streaks in her light brown hair and got her nose pierced. Yes, those are fairly typical things for your average teen trying to establish her own identity. But she also started spending her time at school with the stoner kids. She got put on probation for skipping school. Then, she really crossed over to the dark side when she started going out with one of the Grangers.

That sort of sounds like she took up with the son of a ranching family who lived next door to the Cartwrights. Trust me, that wasn't the case. The Grangers are a sprawling extended family who live in and around Himmel, many of whom have spent at least a few stays in jail, and virtually all of whom have had some kind of run-in with the police. Mackie Granger, a low-level drug dealer of mostly weed and some pills, was Gina's chosen beau. He should've been in our class, but he dropped out in our junior year. Mackie lived with his grandfather, who was in an alcoholic haze most of the time. He had no idea where Mackie was at any given moment, and no interest in finding out.

We were all stunned by the change in Gina. Her church friends may have reached out to her, I don't know. But the rest of us didn't. We stood by and watched the train wreck happen, more in amazement than concern, because we didn't really know her, and we were self-involved teens with problems of our own. It was a source of idle speculation—maybe she got into drugs while she was in North Carolina, maybe she was just fed up with the strict rules of her parents and her church, maybe she'd always been wild and just finally let it out. None of us connected her metamorphosis with heartbreak and definitely not with Ryan.

Eventually, she and her parents had a massive blow-up, and rumor had it that her dad threw her out in the spring of our senior year. She wound up leaving town with Mackie. I hadn't heard, or thought, of her since. Funny, although not really, that both her life and that of James Shaw had taken a nosedive after close association with Ryan. I suppose I should count my blessings that mine hadn't.

Then, as if on cue, came the phone call I'd been expecting.

---

"Hi, Mom."

"Leah, what on earth happened at the reception tonight?"

I wasn't shocked that my mother had already heard, she's very plugged in to the Himmel grapevine, which operates at warp speed. If it ever achieves comparable accuracy, there will be no need for news outlets of any kind, print or digital. The only thing that surprised me a little was the timing of her call. It was eleven-thirty, not all that late, but my mother is usually in bed reading by then.

"What did you hear?"

"Paul has a news alert on his phone for *GO News*—I know, don't say anything. Spencer is his son, after all, and he wants to support him."

"Yeah, I hear Hannibal Lecter's dad felt the same way."

"Leah."

The rivalry between *GO News* and the *Himmel Times* was beginning to cause some awkwardness between my mother and Spencer's father, Paul, which I felt a little bad about. Paul's a good guy. But his son isn't. Still, I backed off at the warning note in her voice.

"OK, so you saw the story online then?"

"No, Paul told me about it. I know how *GO News* sensationalizes things. Was it really that bad?"

"Yes. It was."

"I feel terrible for Gina. Paul was upset, too. Gina's parents, Peggy and Warren, have been his patients since he first opened his dental practice, and he always liked Gina. She was such a shy, pretty, little thing, until, well all that business with Mackie Granger. I told you Ryan wasn't worth your time."

"Yes, yes, you did. Score another one on the *Mother Knows Best* board. One of these days I'll have to start taking you seriously."

"I wait in eager anticipation."

"Do you know why Gina is here? I can't imagine she came just for the reunion," I said.

"It's her mother's seventieth birthday next week. Peggy's been in touch with Gina over the years, but Warren said she couldn't come home. Peggy finally stood up to him and told him that she wanted to celebrate her birthday with Gina. When Peggy had that heart attack last year, it scared both her and Warren. I think that's why he finally relented, but he won't let Gina stay at the house. She's at the Himmel Motel. I hope this thing at the reception doesn't rip the scab off that family wound again."

"You know Paul's son is a jerk, right?"

"I prefer to think of him as Marilyn's son."

"Really? You mean there's a chance Marilyn had a liaison with the devil, and Spencer is his spawn? Paul could walk away clean then."

"Leah, that's not funny."

"Yes, it is. A little bit. And it's not like I said it to Paul. Does the story online say anything about Marcy White?" I asked.

"Marcy? No, why? How is she involved?"

"She wasn't involved exactly. She did the catering—which as per usual was the best ever. I don't care that much about seeing all the old Himmel High grads tomorrow, but I am totally stoked for Marcy's grilled Mediterranean chicken kebabs."

"Honestly, you'd think I never fed you."

"Mom, no offense, but putting Marcy's cooking next to yours, it's really not fair. You're the queen of comfort food. But Marcy, she's the Leonardo da Vinci of all things edible."

"Point taken. Marcy's an artist in the kitchen. But you didn't answer me, what did she have to do with Gina and Ryan?"

"She rescued Gina. We were all staring with our mouths open, watching Gina pounding Ryan's chest and crying her head off. Then, Marcy just walked up, put her arm around Gina, in this very gentle way, and led her off. I've never thought of Marcy as a comforting sort of person. She's pretty abrupt and socially awkward. Even her food isn't comfort food. She's about the last person I'd expect to be so tender-hearted."

"Well, Marcy was always very fond of Gina. In fact, Gina was the only babysitter she trusted with Robin. Don't judge her so harshly. Losing a child is the most devastating thing that can happen to a mother. And she didn't just lose her daughter. She and her husband Doug divorced as well. Grief doesn't always bring people together. Sometimes it tears them apart. After Doug left her, Marcy just pulled inside a shell. For years. I think, though, she's trying to come out of it a little, now. I hope so."

I was quiet for a minute.

"You've still got it, Mom. Nobody can make me feel like a callous jerk better than you."

"Thank you. I'm here to help."

"What makes you think Marcy's trying to reach out more?"

"Well, besides what you just said, she joined the St. Stephen's Care Committee last month. The other day she went with me to visit Ryan's mother. Those visits to the terminally ill are hard to make, even if you like the person. And Marcy was never overly fond of Joanna. I was a little nervous about what Marcy might say, but it was Joanna who made things awkward."

"How's that?"

"Years ago, they were on opposite sides of the vaccine issue. Marcy was almost militant about it, even before Robin was born. But Joanna and her first husband Ed were just as adamant on the anti-vax side. It made for some heated discussions. I think Joanna appreciated that Marcy had put old arguments aside to come and see her. So, she tried to offer an olive branch herself. But she chose an unfortunate way to do it. She told a story—wait, I hope this doesn't open old wounds for you. It's about Ryan moving."

"You know, you can drop that anytime. What was the story?"

"That when she and Ryan and her second husband Jonas started the drive to their new home in Seattle, they were only on the road one day before she and Ryan got so sick with the flu, they had to stay over in Fargo for a week. Jonas had been vaccinated and he was fine. But Joanna and Ryan were miserable. Joanna told Marcy that she was a convert from then on. She never missed a vaccination again. Well, you know, and I know, that Marcy's baby died because she was too young to be vaccinated, and she caught the flu. But Joanna didn't know that, because Robin died after they moved. I held my breath, expecting Marcy to lash out, but she just gave a sort of tight little smile. Then I started jabbering about the weather, and we all got through it. So, yes, I think Marcy's really trying to come back from a dark place she's been in for a long time."

"Well, good, I guess. But now that I've had a lesson in non-judgmentalism, let's go back to Spencer and *GO News*. How bad do you think Paul would feel if I killed his only son? I mean, would it be a deal-breaker for your relationship? Because I'm starting to think taking him out is the only way I'm ever going to get the *Times* on solid financial ground."

I was joking, of course. Sort of. But my mother heard the undertone of anxiety in my voice and zeroed in on it.

"I know the numbers aren't great, but I thought you and Miller had a plan to keep the paper afloat for three years of rebuilding. It hasn't even been six months."

"We did. We do. But we didn't—I didn't—factor in *GO News*. It was barely a gleam in Spencer's squinty little eyes when Miller and I bought the paper. I had no idea it would take off like it has. But he doesn't have the overhead we do, and he doesn't really care if he breaks a story first. It's his *Tea to GO* column that's driving a lot of the visits and the clicks on his site, and advertisers are noticing. When he wants real news, he just steals it from the *Himmel Times* online site. He might have his staff reorganize and reword it a bit, maybe make a couple of calls for quotes, but then he puts up a story based on our legwork."

"I'm sorry, hon. I know how much keeping the paper alive means to you."

"It's not just that I think community journalism matters, Mom. It's all the people who believed in me. They signed on to work at the *Times* instead of looking for other jobs, because they thought I could make it happen. Maggie, and Miguel, and Troy, and the stringers, the sales staff, everybody. Not to mention Miller, who's already sunk a ton of money into this. I don't want to let them down."

"I know you don't, sweetheart. And you won't. You'll find a way. And Spencer will get his comeuppance—short of homicide, on your part, I hope. And you know Miguel is in your corner. He thinks you make the sun rise and set. He'll do anything he can to support you."

While I'd been moaning to her about the paper and she'd

been trying to cheer me up, unbeknownst to me, my erratic but occasionally inspired subconscious had been hard at work. As she said the word Miguel, an idea burst into my brain.

"Mom, Mom, stop talking, please! You're a genius, I love you. I have to go. Call you later. Bye."

## 7

Early Saturday morning is usually not that busy at the Elite Café and Bakery, where Clara Schimelman, the owner, is to baked goods and sandwiches as Marcy White is to canapés and main courses. But this morning, possibly because of the influx of former Himmelites come to frolic at the All Class Reunion, there was a line-up at the bakery case before eight a.m.

Fortunately, Clara spotted me coming in. I nodded and claimed a table in the back. When she had a minute, I knew she'd be over with my standard order, chai latte and whatever kind of cookie or muffin she thought I should have. In the meantime, I scanned the crowd and saw Charlie Ross at a table with his daughter, Allie. Ross was talking. Allie was staring at the floor with her arms crossed. I quickly quashed my impulse to go over and say hello. I had no desire to walk into the middle of whatever parent/child clash was happening.

The bell over the door jangled, and Miguel bounced in. I waved, then watched as he stopped by the serve-yourself coffee urn, tossed some money into the honesty box—a way to circumvent the long line at the counter—and poured himself a large cup. His progress to my table was slow, because he had to stop and chat with people who called his name as he made his way to me.

"You're like Norm coming into *Cheers,*" I said. "Do you know every single person in this town?"

"I'm a friendly boy."

Miguel is from Milwaukee, but he moved to Himmel to live with his aunt Lydia, his mother's sister, and his uncle Craig when he was in high school.

"I've lived here almost two-thirds of my life. But I can go into Walmart and not see a single person I recognize. Right now, here in the Elite, I don't know half the people, not even by sight."

"But you and your *mamá*, if a name comes up, you always go, 'Oh, that's Roger's cousin. He's married to Angela's sister, the one who used to be a nun.' " He spoke in a very creditable imitation of my mother going through her oral ancestry.com version of who's who in town. But I didn't like the implication that I was following in her footsteps on that front.

"OK, my mother does that, yes. And my Aunt Nancy, but I definitely don't."

He smiled, but he didn't say anything.

"Besides, knowing *about* someone isn't the same as knowing them. And you know everyone."

"I try. I like people, *chica*. You're more ... selective," he said, after possibly searching for a word to stand in for judgmental.

"Well, the reason I wanted to see you this morning is tied into your hyper-active friendly gene. I have an idea that I think will help our circulation, and that you'll have fun doing. And there's no one but you who could pull it off."

"I love it!"

I couldn't help laughing. "You don't even know what it is."

"I mean I love that you want me to help," he said, in earnest.

"*Chica*, I felt so bad when I told you I didn't want to be the editor anymore. I felt like I abandoned you, I—"

"Hey, stop it. You weren't happy, and I'm really glad you were honest with me. You did a great job. But being in the office so much, bossing people, running the budget—well, that just wasn't you. Maggie's a much better fit as managing editor. She's doing well. Everyone is, really, all of you guys are working your hearts out. But still, we're struggling more than I thought we would, thanks to that asshat Spencer Karr and *GO News*."

"Leah, here. I give you raspberry Kringle, very good today." Mrs. Schimelman had magically appeared at our table. She set a cup of chai and a plate of pastry in front of me. "You, I didn't see come in," she said to Miguel.

"Just coffee is good for me. I love your hair, Mrs. Schimelman. Very sassy!"

Her face broke out in a big smile, and she flicked Miguel's arm playfully with the white kitchen towel that is always slung over her shoulder. "Such a *schmeichler* you are! Your Aunt Lydia cut it for me."

"No, no. I'm not a flatterer. I told you Making Waves is the best salon in town. Aunt Lydia does magic on your beautiful hair."

She laughed with pleasure, causing her ample body to shake, then turned to me. "Leah, what we gonna do with this boy?"

"Oh, I have something in mind. And you just confirmed my hunch that it's exactly the right thing to do. Read all about it Thursday in the *Himmel Times.*"

"Oh," she leaned in confidentially, "I read the *GO News* today, and—"

"*Et tu*, Mrs. Schimelman?" I said.

"No, I already eat. But that poor little Gina. Why did Spencer Karr put that in his news? Such a mean little boy he was. Like his mother. He wasn't so nice to you neither. You gonna do clap back at him in your paper?" Mrs. Schimelman prides herself on her millennial slang.

"Indirectly," I said. "I'm playing a long game. That's why I'm meeting with Miguel."

"Oh, a meeting. OK. I go, you talk. You," she said, looking at Miguel, "come back when you hungry. I make you something special."

"You're special enough for me," Miguel said with a wink. He really is one of the few people I know who can carry off a wink.

Mrs. Schimelman sashayed away, her hips rolling and her shoulders shaking with laughter.

"OK, charm boy, time to get serious. My idea is you, being you. I want you to write a daily online column that's a cross between *Queer Eye* and *Dear Abby*. We'll call it *Ask Miguel*, or *Ask Me Anything*, or I don't care, whatever you like. People can ask you about their hair—like Mrs. Schimelman did, or what to wear to prom, or how to break up with their boyfriend, whatever. And you will just be you. Funny, friendly, smart and every once in a while we'll run a prize. *A Shopping Day with Miguel*, or *Dinner and a Movie with Miguel*, or *A Makeover with Miguel*. We'll run an expanded version on Thursdays when the print edition comes out."

To my surprise, instead of falling in with my brainstorm, he was shaking his head.

"What? What's the matter? You don't like it?"

"No, no, it's fine. I can do that, no problem. But I don't see how that will help the paper?"

"Easy. Half the reason people read *GO News* is the *Tea to GO* section. We don't want to sink *that* low to pander to the public, but hey, that doesn't mean we won't do any pandering at all. But ours will be classy. Not mean-spirited gossip and nasty innuendo. You said it yourself, you like people. And the thing is, they like you back. I really think a daily piece from you will bring new eyes to the paper and keep the readers we already have. Are you in?"

"For you, always."

"I know it's extra work, and as soon as we turn more—well —any profit, I know Miller will support a raise." I didn't truly know, because I hadn't talked to my mostly silent partner yet, but he hadn't let me down so far.

"*Chica*, it's never about the money. I think it will be fun. And if you think it will help, then, let's do it."

---

Miguel and I roughed out some ideas to introduce the column using Twitter, Instagram, and other social media platforms, as well as our website and the print edition. He left for his aunt's salon to spread the word the old school way, through the stylists at Making Waves, who saw a sizable percentage of the Himmel population each week.

I called Miller, who said he had a few minutes to talk and suggested I drop by his law office, which isn't far from the Elite. As I stepped out the door of the café and started walking up the street, a voice called from behind, "Hey, Nash, you got a minute?"

I turned and saw Charlie Ross hurrying to catch up with me.

"Not much more than that, Ross. I'm walking over to Miller Caldwell's office for a meeting. What can I do for you?"

Detective Charlie Ross and I were once completely at odds, but he'd changed some—or maybe I had—and we got along pretty well now, most of the time. I liked the way he'd stepped up from weekend dad to full-time father when his ex-wife took off with a boyfriend and left Allie behind. Ross still gets pretty cranky, though, when he thinks I'm investigating things I shouldn't—which is a fair amount of the time.

"It's about Allie."

"Yeah, I saw you guys were having a pretty intense conversation."

"Somethin's botherin' her, Nash. She's bein' all moody and keepin' to herself. When I ask her what's going on, she says nothin', or she tells me not to be a helicopter parent. Which I didn't even know what that was 'til I looked it up. And I'm not," he added, though I suspected he might be, a little bit.

"She's an adolescent girl, Ross. It comes with the territory."

"I don't know. I read this article that said teen depression is gettin' to be a big thing. Allie had that crush on Gus Fraser last fall, and that didn't work out so great. She never talked about him since he went to live with his aunt, but I dunno, maybe she's hidin' how sad she is or somethin' like that. Or maybe she's missin' her mom. She says no. Which I'm glad, because last time I talked to my ex, she's got no interest in havin' Allie go visit her and the boyfriend in Texas. I'm kinda lost here, kinda over my head. I was wonderin' if you noticed anything when she's at work, or if she said anything to you?"

"No, I haven't noticed anything. She seems fine at the office. But I'm not really around her that much. Though I did promise to help her on a story she wants to do. Did she tell you about it?"

"Yeah, last night. It's about the only thing she's seemed excited about lately. So, do you think you could talk to her, maybe? Try to find out what's buggin' her? Maybe it's some kind of girl thing she doesn't feel right talkin' to me about."

"I don't know, Ross. I don't think it's a good idea for me to get into the middle of something between you and Allie." Besides which, I had enough on my plate without taking on a big sister role. And I hadn't been much of a success at that with my own teenage sister, Lacey.

"Come on. It's just a conversation. And who you kiddin' anyway? You love gettin' in the middle of places where you don't belong. And Allie looks up to you. She thinks you're all that. No matter how I tell her different."

I could see how much he wanted to help his daughter. I would have given a lot to have a dad who cared about me that much when I was Allie's age.

"OK, fine. I'll talk to her. But if she doesn't want to open up, I'm not going to pry or push her. Kids need some space."

"OK, OK. That's good. Thanks, Nash. I owe you one."

---

"I think it's a fine idea, Leah. But I also think you don't need to worry so much about the paper. It's only been a few months. You have to give a new business time." Miller Caldwell had leaned back slightly in his executive chair as I outlined my brainstorm for using Miguel.

"But, Miller, I feel like I dragged you into this, and I—"

"No. Stop right there," he said, bringing his chair upright as he straightened and held up a well-manicured hand. "You're a powerful personality, Leah, but neither you nor anyone else can 'drag' me into a business deal I don't want to make." He smiled.

Miller used to set female hearts aflutter with that smile. He looks every inch the politician he had once aspired to be: tall and fit, with well-cut brown hair going silver, tanned but mostly unlined skin, steady, clear blue eyes, and a row of even white teeth. Miller had struggled a long time over coming out as a gay man because of his family. When he finally did, it had meant unyielding bitterness from his now ex-wife, Georgia. She had channeled her hurt into vicious accusations that destroyed any hope he had of holding onto his position as president of the bank, or of having a political career. His children had been bewildered and for a time estranged, though things had improved there. His elderly father won't speak to him, still. But I've never heard him complain, or say anything against anyone in his family, not even Georgia. Instead, he's just turned his energy to his law practice and his money to re-energizing Himmel.

"I believe that community journalism is central to a growing, forward-looking town—the kind of town Himmel once was. The kind of town I think it can be again. And I believe in you, Leah. You and the *Himmel Times* are part of my master plan."

"Well, I hope you're as smart as you are good-looking, because with *GO News* in the picture things are turning out to be way harder than they looked when we started this partnership."

"I'm not worried about the survival of the paper. You and Maggie are more than capable of meeting any challenge Spencer Karr presents. You've already come up with a good countermove using Miguel. No, what does worry me is the blind items *GO News* uses, and the way people can jump to conclusions. Someone is bound to be hurt, whether that's what Spencer intends or not."

"My money is on he doesn't care. It's a game to him, and he'll do pretty much anything to win. But," I said standing to leave, "we'll just have to try and stay a step ahead of him. Thanks for the pep talk."

# 8

"How about some lunch?" Gabe asked when he called a little before one.

"You missed your chance. I just finished a delicious bowl of Honey Nut Cheerios."

"I'm sorry. Work took longer than I expected, and then I had to take Barnacle for a walk." Gabe had taken in Barnacle, a small, mixed-breed terrier, on a temporary basis after his elderly owner died. Just until a new owner could be found. Four months later, it looked like that would be Gabe.

"Are you sure you can't go? I was going to take you to McClain's for the Davey Burger we missed last night." He sounded genuinely disappointed.

"Don't worry about it. You can buy me multiple drinks tonight instead. No worries on the food, Marcy is putting on the spread, and it will put Davey Burgers to shame. That is, if you're still planning on going."

"I wouldn't miss it, especially after last night. Do you think another of Ryan's girlfriends will show up?"

"Anything's possible with that guy. Cocktail hour starts at

seven. It may take me from now until then to practice walking in the shoes I promised Miguel I'd wear. I'll see you later."

"Can't wait."

———

"You look amazing," Gabe said, as he stepped into my apartment and held out a vase filled with tulips.

"Thank you. Compliments *and* my favorite flowers? What's the occasion?"

"The occasion is," he said, as he put the vase on the counter and then pulled me into his arms, "that I'm spending the evening with a smart, beautiful, famous author, who also happens to be my favorite woman in the world."

He kissed me in a very satisfactory way. When we stepped apart, I said, "I thought Mrs. Schimelman was your favorite woman."

"It's close. Her *rugelach* puts her right up there, but you've still got the edge. Especially in that dress. Very sexy."

"It takes a village. My mother bought the dress, Miguel accessorized it, and gave me makeup tips. I just tried to follow instructions."

"I'll thank them at dinner. By the way, am I likely to have to fend off any more old boyfriends tonight?"

The teasing note in his voice was nice to hear and his dark eyes were warm with affection.

"You seem in an awfully good mood tonight. What's up?"

"You know me, I'm just a happy guy."

"Did something break in the case you're working on?"

"Not really. It's the James Shaw case. He swears he didn't send the email, but the evidence is really strong. It came from his computer. It went out at three a.m., so it's not like a student could have sneaked into his classroom and used it. I'm not sure where to go with it."

"You're a litigation genius, didn't you tell me that? You'll find a way."

"I said that when I was trying to impress you. Hey, wait a minute. Are you trying to distract me from your romantic past?"

I laughed. "Nope, nothing to see here."

As we walked out to the car, I slipped my arm through his and he gave my hand a squeeze.

"I think this is going to be a really fun night," I said.

---

The multi-purpose building at the fairgrounds just outside of Himmel was the site for the Himmel All Class Reunion. Cars jammed the lot and music flowed through the open doors and spilled out into the warm evening air. The play lists had been my mother's contribution to the evening. Her taste in music is eclectic and spans multiple decades. At the moment a Frankie Valli song was playing. The next one could be anything from The Doors to Lizzo. A portable dance floor had been set up outside next to the building. Fairy lights were strung from poles to provide romantic lighting. Tiki torches and citronella candles were in evidence to keep the mosquitoes at bay while alumni danced the night away.

"We've never danced together before. I can't wait to get you out on the floor tonight," Gabe said.

"Um, yeah. There's a reason for that. To say I'm not a great dancer is a gross understatement."

"Lucky you, I am. I can show you the way."

"You can try, but I've brought many a dance partner to tears. I'm just warning you."

"I'm not afraid."

"Leah, I told you that dress was made for you. Don't you agree, Gabe?" My mother, looking extremely pretty, and way younger than someone who is approaching sixty at a pretty fast clip, was wearing a sleeveless, sparkly, midnight blue dress. It deepened the color of her eyes, and the high silver heels on her feet showed her legs off to advantage.

"I do, Carol. You look great, too. I can see where Leah gets her looks from."

"You don't have to suck up to her, Gabe. She already likes you."

"You stay out of it. Let him suck up if he wants to. I never turn away a compliment," my mother said.

"Who's complimenting my best girl?" Paul asked, as he came up carrying two glasses of wine and handed one to my mother.

"Gabe is," I said. "He's trying to curry favor."

"You're a man with a discerning eye, Gabe," Paul said, putting an arm around my mother's shoulders and smiling down at her. He always looks at her like he can't quite believe his luck, which is one of the reasons I like him.

"I hope you save a dance for me, Carol," Gabe said.

"You're going to need a break with a good dancer, after you go a few rounds with me on the dance floor," I said.

"Come on, you can't be that bad. Right, Carol?"

"Believe it, Gabe. Not only does my beautiful daughter march to a different drummer, she dances to the beat like Elaine on *Seinfeld,* bless her heart."

"Yes. You'd better start fortifying yourself with alcohol as a preventative measure to take the pain away—literal and emotional. In fact, we both should. I'll have a Jameson on the rocks, please," I said.

My mother spotted someone across the room that she'd been trying to lure into serving as producer for the next community theater production, and she had dashed away when Gabe went to fetch the drinks. He was stuck in a crush of people at the bar. So, Paul and I were on our own. As he sipped his wine, I gave him one of those closed-mouth smiles you use when you're trying to convey noncommittal friendliness. The slightly uncomfortable silence wasn't because we don't like each other. We've always gotten along well—except for that unfortunate short period when I thought he might have committed murder. But ever since his son Spencer had returned to town to take over *GO News*, things had been a little strained. We took great pains to walk around the subject of Spencer and the havoc his new venture was wreaking on the *Times'* bottom line. It was hard for both of us, and sometimes it made our one-on-one conversations feel more like verbal bumper cars than pleasant chats.

At the moment, from the look on Paul's round, open face, and the sheen of perspiration faintly visible at his receding hairline, I deduced that he had something he needed to say. I was pretty sure what it would be. Before starting, he brought his hand to his face. With his thumb and index finger, he made the drawing down gesture you use on either side of your lips when you think you might have leftover lunch crumbs lodged in the corners of your mouth. Then he swallowed hard and started talking.

"I'm sorry, Leah, about that story on Spencer's news site this morning. I don't understand him sometimes—or most of the time, I guess. He's always been closer to Marilyn. I was glad when he came and asked me for the money to invest in *GO News*, instead of going to her. I thought it meant he wanted to build more of a father-son relationship with me. I didn't realize that *GO News* was going to turn out like it has, but I didn't put any strings on the money I gave him. I never meant for Spencer's new business to cause you problems."

"Paul, it's OK. Spencer and I have issues, it's true. But that doesn't need to involve you. He's your son. I get it."

"No, let me finish. Your mother, you, me, we've all been walking around what he's been doing. But he really crossed the line today with that article about you, and Ryan Malloy, and Gina. I know her mother, Peggy, has to be beside herself. She's been trying to get Gina and her father to forgive and forget, and this is going to make things that much harder. I've been going over and over in my mind what I could have done differently when Spencer was growing up. Maybe I spent too much time building up my practice and not enough time with him. I think I failed my son, for him to turn out the way he has. I feel ashamed of him. And I feel ashamed of myself. I'm sorry, Leah."

I hoped that I would never be the cause of a look on my mother's face like the one Paul had on his. Beneath his furrowed forehead, his sandy-colored eyebrows were drawn together in a frown of pain, and his brown eyes were so sad it hurt to look at them. I glanced around, hoping to see my mother heading our way, but she was still across the room, talking. I'd have to wade in.

"Paul." I touched his arm lightly. "You're a good person, and no one is a perfect parent. Just like no one is a perfect child. When Spencer does something really good, you don't take credit for it, do you?"

I couldn't actually think of anything good that Spencer had ever done, but there must have been something in thirty-three years.

"So, when he does something pretty bad, you don't have to apologize for it, right? And you definitely don't have to take the blame. Think about it. He only got half his genes from you. We both know that Marilyn's contribution to the DNA had to be a lot to overcome."

He gave a half-smile at that. Encouraged, I pushed on.

"It's not all on you, this parent/child thing. You did your best. Now, Spencer has to decide the kind of person he's going to be. It's out of your hands."

"I love my son, Leah. But I don't like him. It's a hard thing to realize."

I was pretty much out of comforting phrases, and pretty soon I was going to find myself saying, "You're right. Your son is a creep. Get rid of him." Which I knew would not be helpful. Out of the corner of my eye, I saw my mother wending her way toward us through the crowd. If I could just keep nodding supportively and patting his arm, she'd be here to take over before I said something I'd regret.

"I want the kind of relationship with Spencer that your mother has with you," Paul was saying. "Open and easy. You like each other, you like spending time with each other. But it's never been that way between Spencer and me, and it's been worse since Marilyn and I divorced."

"Well, I—"

I wasn't saved by the bell, but by a loud shout and a scream from outside.

"Somebody help, please! He's going to kill him!"

## 9

———

Paul and I joined the horde of people who rushed out of the open doors to the side of the building, next to where the dance floor was set up. Two men were pounding each other so hard, you could hear the *thwack*! of closed fists against muscle and bone. One of the men was Ryan Malloy. The other was James Shaw.

As I watched, James landed a punch to the solar plexus that knocked the wind out of Ryan, causing him to double over and sink to his knees. James had put so much into the hit that he lost his balance. His leg with the artificial limb shot out from under him and he fell. Coop rushed to where both Ryan and James, bloodied and breathing hard, were on the ground.

"I shoulda done that seventeen years ago," James shouted, shaking off Coop's arm as he reached down to help him up. "I can do it," he said, his words slurring.

Coop turned his attention to Ryan, who was now sitting up and looked somewhat better than James.

"What happened? What's going on with you two?" Coop asked Ryan.

"I don't know. I was just standing over there." He pointed to a spot a few yards away as he gasped out the words, "talking to Steven, and out of nowhere, James is at my elbow, shouting some crazy shit. The next thing I know, he's punching me." Ryan was on his feet by then, dabbing at a small streak of blood on his cheek with a tissue someone handed him.

"Two different nights, two different people want to take a swing at you? You're not a very popular guy, are you, Ryan?" Coop asked.

"Hey, I didn't start anything."

"It's true. I saw the whole thing," Steven Burke said. Steven, Ryan's stepbrother, was standing at the front of the growing crowd. He's putting up a good fight against encroaching middle age—workouts with a personal trainer, a haircut that minimizes his beginning baldness, trendy glasses, and his most important accessory, his much younger second wife, Lily. But he still looks pretty much like what he is, a past president of the Rotary Club, sliding inexorably into his late forties.

"James there is drunk as a skunk. He came over to where Ryan and I were talking, and just started yelling and swinging at him."

I'd been watching James's slow, painful, and humiliating efforts to get back on his feet. Just when I couldn't stand it anymore, Gabe pushed through the crowd and walked over to him.

"Hey, let me give you a hand."

This time James took the help that was offered. With Gabe's assistance, he staggered to his feet. His nose was bleeding, and he angrily wiped it on his sleeve.

"What are you doing, man?" Gabe asked.

"Gettin' satisfaction."

"James, come on, you've had too much to drink. Let's get you home."

"No!" James stood up to his full height, and the word came

out of him with a roar. The crowd, which had been focused on Ryan, turned and stared as he pointed his finger at Ryan, swaying enough that I worried he might go down again.

"Everybody loves Ryan. Every bubby, ev'ry all. Everyone. But I know you. You—I. It was you—" He paused and shook his head, as though he realized his words weren't coming out right.

He tried again, "It's all you. You're a nar-narcis—" He was struggling to get out the word narcissist. He regrouped. "You're a poser. You're a fake, you're a liar—"

Shouts from the onlookers began to drown him out.

"You're the liar, Shaw!"

"You're a pervert!"

"You should be in jail!"

"Pedophile!"

James stopped. He looked around at the crowd as though surprised they were there. He started to speak again. I saw Gabe say something to him in a low voice. James shook his head again. Then, for a second, he stared straight into the faces of friends, neighbors, students he'd taught, now adults themselves —people he'd known all his life. His expression, both baffled and hurt, seemed to say, *you know me. You know I would never do what they said.*

But without a word, he shook off Gabe's hand on his shoulder and hobbled away across the fields.

———

Once the show was over, we all began streaming back into the building. Whether by chance or intent, Marvin Gaye was crooning "What's Going On," but before I could ask Gabe the question, Spencer Karr materialized beside us.

"I'm going to start following you around, Leah. Twice now

I've picked up lead items for *Tea to GO* and you've been front and center both times."

"Please don't." The lenses of his hipster glasses caught the light, so I couldn't see his eyes, but I had no doubt they were alight with malice.

"But your boyfriend is the one I want to see right now." He leaned over me toward Gabe. "What can you tell me about your client James Shaw's assault on Ryan Malloy? Why did he attack the man who used to be his best friend? Is there any connection between Gina's attack last night and James's tonight?"

"Shouldn't you be asking Ryan Malloy those questions?" Gabe nodded in the direction of a table where Ryan sat surrounded by solicitous females—including Spencer's mother Marilyn—plying him with cool compresses and warm sympathy.

"Oh, I'll be talking to Ryan. But I want to get James's side of the story. At *GO News* we like to get all the facts," he said with a smirk that made me want to grab him by the neck of his untucked shirt and shake him.

"All the 'facts' that fit your narrative. Anything that doesn't, you delete," I said.

"Jealous much, Leah?"

I turned my back to him. "Let's go find our table, Gabe."

"So, I'll put that as no comment?"

"I'll tell you what you can put that as. You can—" Gabe's firm squeeze of my hand and the words he whispered in my ear kept me from traveling too far down the road of regrets.

"Don't feed the beast, Leah."

---

We made our way through the milling alumni, spouses, and significant others, and found our place cards at a table on the far side of the room. Coop and Kristin, and Jennifer Pilarski and her husband John, were already seated. I was surprised to see Steven Burke there, too—without his wife Lily.

As Gabe and I sat down, everyone was talking about the fight between James and Ryan.

"I don't understand why you didn't arrest James," Steven Burke said to Coop.

"Ryan's OK. I'd say James got the worst of it, and he's not in any shape to cause more damage. Ryan said he didn't want to press charges. Besides, I would've had to involve the sheriff's department, because we're in their jurisdiction. I didn't see any need to escalate things."

"Well, it still seems to me that he should face some kind of consequences. On top of everything else, he must have been drunk driving," Steven insisted.

"He didn't drive. He took a Ride EZ car. We saw him get out. Besides, Steven, don't you think he's facing plenty of 'consequences' already? Didn't you hear how vicious some of the crowd was? It kind of creeps me out that people I know can morph into a mob like that," Jennifer said, plucking the maraschino cherry out of her drink and biting into it. Jen and I have been friends since kindergarten, where we first bonded in the time-out corner. Now, she works as a secretary at the Grantland County Sheriff's department. She's a curvy woman with bouncy brown hair and a belly laugh that gets everyone around her laughing, even when the joke's not all that funny.

"It was hardly a mob, Jennifer. He's been charged with a serious offense," Steven replied.

"Charged but not convicted. He hasn't gone to trial, Steven," Gabe said.

Steven ignored Gabe and directed his response to Coop.

"Aren't we supposed to believe the victims? Isn't that what women want these days? To be believed? Don't you believe that young girl James was stalking? That's your job, isn't it, Coop?"

"When we take in a complaint from anyone, man or woman, our job is to listen, to respect, and to investigate. That's what my department did in James's case. Then, we turn the evidence over to the prosecutor's office. It's his call."

"And if the evidence is there, we prosecute," Kristin added. "Which is what my office is doing. But Gabe is right, James is accused, not convicted."

"Look, I'm a simple man. I call it like I see it. I didn't build my business on nuance. I understand the police and the prosecutor have to follow the rules. Though to my way of thinking, a lot of those rules are written to coddle criminals. But I've got a question for you, Gabe. Why would you defend a man like James?"

"What sort of man would that be, Steven?"

"A man who uses his position as a teacher to take advantage of young girls. The police have the email, for God's sake! James is a sexual predator. What he did is disgusting."

"It would be, if it were true. James says it isn't." Gabe's voice was steady and calm.

"He has to say that. But you don't have to be his lawyer, right? I'll just give you some free advice—I don't charge by the minute like you lawyers do. If I were trying to build up a law practice, I wouldn't take on James Shaw as a client."

"I'll take that under advisement." Gabe kept his tone light, but I knew he was irritated.

Steven, however, seemed to take Gabe's response as a victory, and his tone became less aggressive.

"Well, I think we can all agree that regardless of how we feel about his guilt or innocence, James shouldn't have been here tonight. Everyone just wants to have a good time with old friends. James didn't belong, and he got what he deserved."

It was on the tip of my tongue to say that maybe Ryan had gotten what he deserved, a long-deferred payback for the "accident" that had robbed James of so much. Jennifer saved me by jumping into the troubled conversational waters.

"Well, guilty or innocent, James is lucky the sheriff isn't here tonight. Art Lamey would have locked him up in a heartbeat. Just the kind of thing he likes—no danger and plenty of pats on the back for being tough on crime. Lord help us all if he gets elected in the fall." She took a large swig from her glass, finished off her Brandy Old Fashioned, and shuddered.

"There's not much chance he won't be, is there?" Kristin asked. "Just yesterday the county clerk told me that no one else has filed. I know I'm new here, but is Sheriff Lamey really that bad?"

"He's worse than that bad. He's dumb. OK, I can deal with that. He's full of himself. So what, right? Not that unusual in a boss. No, what I can't take is that he's a wimp who would throw his grandmother under the bus to save his own sorry self. Sheriff Dillingham, my boss before him, he had his quirks, but he was a stand-up guy," Jennifer said.

She turned to her husband then and with comic despair said plaintively, "John, honey, please, would you get me another Old Fashioned? Just talking about Lameass getting elected for four years is depressing me. I need something to perk me up."

John and Jennifer Pilarski embody the cliché that opposites attract. He's an unassuming man with thinning blond hair and wire-rimmed glasses—an introvert foil to Jennifer's exuberance. He reached over and took his wife's empty glass.

"Anyone else want one?" he asked.

"I do," said Steven, "but I'll come with you."

"You know what, I think I'll go grab another beer before they start serving dinner," Coop said.

"I'll come, too," Kristin said.

As they left the table, Jennifer said to me, "Steven doesn't seem too pleased with the assigned seating, does he? Maybe I shouldn't have changed the place cards."

"You did? Why?"

"We got here first. I didn't think you'd want to sit with Spencer Karr and his mother, so I switched them out. Was I wrong?"

"No, you were absolutely right. But where is Lily? This is prime trophy wife showtime for Steven."

"That's probably why he's in such a bad mood. He said she couldn't come because she had to take care of a sick girlfriend. My bet's on a healthy boyfriend."

"Jennifer, you have a very suspicious mind. It's why I like you so much. And, because I like you so much, I have to tell you. You'd better watch what you're saying about Art Lamey. You're one Old Fashioned away from getting yourself in the time out chair at work."

"What do you mean?"

"Jen, come on. You're breaking the cardinal rule of small-town life. You can't be calling Art Lamey 'lameass' and criticizing him in front of people you just met, or who, like Steven, might not share your opinion. What if it turned out that Kristin Norcross is related to Art's wife? She's from around here. Just watch what you're saying until you know who you're saying it to."

"I'm not worried. Anyone related to him already knows what a lameass he is. Besides, Kristin doesn't strike me as a gossip."

"No, me either, but the point is, neither of us know her well enough to know for sure. And don't forget, Spencer Karr is always lurking. He could start chatting her up. Then, before she knows it, she's spilled some tea that's going to make a big, ugly stain all over someone's life. I don't want it to be yours."

As I finished, I looked at Gabe for support and saw that he had an amused expression on his face.

"What?"

"What do you mean what?"

"Why are you smirking?"

"This is my bemused expression. I'm definitely not smirking. I've never seen you in the Hermione role before. You know, the intelligent, brave, sensible one. I've always thought you were more of a Tonks, the smart, brave, impulsive one." He grinned, and I thought what a nice smile he has. But I still gave him some serious side eye.

## 10

I had almost enough Jameson in me to make dancing seem like not such a bad idea by the time dinner and speeches were over at nine o'clock. Coop—who is a surprisingly good dancer—had already led Kristin outside to the dance floor under the stars. Gabe was chatting with Miguel, who had just introduced him to his new beau, Christopher. He seemed nice but was probably not destined to be around for long. Miguel's romances usually only last a couple of months. I went to the bar for one more Jameson to fortify me before I exposed Gabe to my dancing deficiencies.

"Marcy! What are you doing tending bar? Where's Derek? Isn't it enough that you created the most delicious, the most beautifully presented, the gold-standard-setting meal for reunion dinners? The chicken alone gave me a new reason to live."

I always try to get a smile out of Marcy, because it's such a challenge. I rarely succeed and tonight was no different. Still, she did nod and that might have been a fleeting ghost of a grin that briefly touched the corners of her mouth.

"Derek's on a break. Bar's been busy tonight."

"I'll make it easy on you. Just a Jameson on the rocks."

As she gave me what I noted was a generous pour, I ventured into the periphery of the personal with her.

"You did a really good deed last night, the way you took care of Gina Cox—calming her down, making sure she was all right—that was really kind of you."

She seemed surprised as she handed me the drink. "Gina's a nice girl. I didn't like to see her that way. I got her back to the motel. Sat with her a while. That's all."

"It was more than the rest of us did. I think we were all a little bit shell-shocked. I don't know if you know this, but I was the girl Gina was talking about—Ryan's supposedly exclusive girlfriend." As I spoke, I saw Ryan himself walking toward the bar, and I really didn't want to kill the pleasant, slightly fuzzy feeling my Jameson was beginning to give me.

"Well, thanks again for a wonderful meal. I hope you don't have to work too late."

"Don't worry about me. I'll be on my way soon."

Before Gabe and I stepped outside, I turned to see if Ryan had actually continued to the bar once he saw Marcy there. But of course he had. Nothing pierced his armor of self-esteem. He was standing at the bar, flashing his million-dollar smile at her as she handed him a drink.

---

"You looked beautiful tonight. And you danced pretty well, too."

I sat contentedly in the crook of Gabe's arm, my feet-killing sandals long-since kicked off, and my legs curved under me on his comfortable sofa. His dog Barnacle snored softly in his bed in the corner of the room.

"Thank you. It was the extra Jameson, I think. Freed up my inhibitions, let my inner Janet Jackson out."

He kissed the top of my head, and when I lifted it to look up at him, he said,

*"Then turn not pale, beloved snail, but come and join the dance.*

*Will you, won't you, will you, won't you, will you join the dance?"*

"Please tell me that you're not calling me a snail, because if you are, your romantic patter needs some work. Or are you just English majoring me again?"

"I am," he said, picking up a strand of my hair and twirling it around his finger. "It's Lewis Carroll."

"Mmm. Does it mean you want to start dancing again? I'm not sure I'm up for it."

"Not right now. I was thinking more about how hard it is to let go, and give ourselves over to something new, and trust that it will all work out. It's hard to leave the safety of the shore, isn't it?"

I sat up straighter. "Wait, are we having a philosophical discussion? Because I'm really not quite sober enough to fully participate."

"That, I know. I kind of like you this way."

"What, you don't like me unless I'm half-drunk? Are you trying to take advantage of me? My mother told me about boys like you."

"No," he said. "I like you just the way you are, all the ways you are. But when you're a bit tipsy, like now, your defenses come down a little. I get a glimpse behind that tough facade."

"It's not a facade," I said firmly.

"Yes, it is. We all have some defenses to keep ourselves safe. But it's nice to have people you feel safe enough with to let them in, even without a double Jameson, isn't it?"

"Maybe," I said, but I was thinking, *We're not there yet.*

I woke up before Gabe, not hungover, exactly, but a little thick-headed. It was about nine-thirty Sunday morning, long past my usual getting up time. I slid out of bed, went to his dresser, pulled open the bottom drawer and pulled out a T-shirt, a pair of shorts, and some clean underwear that I'd started keeping there. My running shoes were stashed under the bed.

Barnacle started bouncing around my heels as soon as I opened the bedroom door. I closed it quickly behind me.

"Shh! Gabe's sleeping," I whispered. "Let me brush my teeth and get a quick shower, and then I'll take you out. Don't wake him up," I added sternly. He gave me a reproachful look but trotted dutifully back to the living room.

One of my favorite things to do is stand under a hot shower, which I know is not very responsible, environmentally speaking, but it feels so nice, it's hard for me to resist. I try to make up for it by always recycling, and never using those little plastic pod things to make coffee. I know, it's not good enough, but baby steps, right?

This time, however, with Barnacle waiting and my fear that the water pipes might wake Gabe up with the odd banshee wail they sometimes emit, I moved fast. I towel-dried my hair, yanked it into a ponytail, pulled on my clothes, and was in the living room in under fifteen minutes.

That was still at least five minutes too late.

Contrary to his apparent compliance with my orders, Barnacle had not gone back to his bed. He had gone rogue.

The living room looked like a mini tornado had come through. Trash from the wastebasket was spilled across the floor, the remains of one of my sandals, its strap well-chewed, peeked out from under a chair. A stack of mail had fallen off an end table, and paper from a torn book was strewn around the room.

"Barnacle!" I said in a loud, stern whisper. "Look what you did! What got into you?"

He lowered his head and retreated to his basket, his head on his crossed paws in front of me. I sighed.

"Look, I know Gabe wasn't here most of last night, and he didn't get up early to take you for a walk. And maybe you don't like it that I'm here cutting in on your time, but come on, this is not acceptable."

He stared at me.

"OK, fine. Don't offer to help."

As I gathered up the chewed paper that littered the room, I spotted the remains of a half-destroyed paperback under a chair and pulled it out. I turned to Barnacle.

"Seriously? Out of all the books here, you picked the one I wrote to tear up? This is starting to feel personal, buddy."

He had the grace to hide his face in his paws. I worked quickly, which was pretty easy given that I had to trash almost everything. I didn't get out the vacuum, because I didn't want to wake Gabe. When I finished, I grabbed a small sack to take care of what Barnacle left behind on our walk, and got his leash down, but he didn't do his usual going-for-a-walk-dance.

I knelt beside him. "Oh, come on," I said. "I forgive you."

Just as I was hooking up the leash, my phone rang. Miguel.

"Hey, you, what's going on?"

"Everything. Everything is going on, *chica*. Ryan Malloy. He's dead!"

"What?"

My voice was so loud, it startled Barnacle into barking, which in turn brought Gabe stumbling into the living room.

"How did he die, Miguel?"

"I don't know. I'm just getting here to his cottage. I'll call you."

"No, I'm coming out. See you shortly."

"What? What's going on?" Gabe asked, now fully awake.

"Ryan Malloy is dead. I've got to get out there and see what the story is. I'll talk to you later. Sorry, Barnacle," I called over my shoulder as I left.

## 11

As I turned down Lakeside Drive, the gravel road that circles Gray Lake, I saw that I was just behind Charlie Ross's SUV. We traveled about a quarter mile to the first curve in the road. The Burke cottage is just beyond the bend, but we couldn't go any farther because of all the Sheriff Department cars, an ambulance, a fire truck, and other vehicles clogging the road. I spotted Miguel's bright yellow Mini Cooper, looking cheerily out-of-place up ahead as well. A group of people, curious neighbors from around the lake, I guessed, were milling around on the road.

Ross pulled over and parked. I did the same and scurried to catch up with him as he started walking toward the family cottage where Ryan had been staying.

"Ross! Hey, wait up."

"No time, Nash. And no one is allowed to talk to the press—Acting Sheriff Lamey's orders. Check in with him if you want information."

"Ross, no, you don't understand."

"I understand Ryan Malloy is dead, and I need to get to the scene before Lameass screws it up."

"I'm not asking for information—at least not yet. I have something to tell *you*. I was with Ryan last night—we all were, me, Gabe, Coop, Kristin Norcross, Jennifer and John Pilarski. Steven Burke, too. A little after eleven, the reunion was winding down. Ryan seemed like he might have had one too many Jack and Cokes. So Coop took his keys and called Ride EZ to take him home."

"Wait a minute, are you sayin' to me—"

"Yes. Exactly. I'm telling you that Ride EZ should have a record of when Ryan was picked up, and when he was dropped off. So, you'll have a way to narrow the time of death window. Now will you quit being so crabby?"

"I'm 'crabby' because this is my case, but I'm gonna have Lamey with his foot on my neck the whole way. Once he realized who got killed, he shot over here like a bat outta hell. Figures he's gonna grab some headlines on this one, I'm guessin'. You know, the kind of stuff *GO News* goes for. *'Sheriff solves celebrity murder.'* I was way across the county, so he got a head start on me. Probably trampled all over my crime scene."

"I'm sorry, Ross. I mean it. I know Lamey's a pain. Who found Ryan?"

"Warren Cox."

"Warren Cox? Gina's dad? What was he doing out here?"

He shrugged.

"I hear his daughter got into it good with Malloy at the Elks Friday night. Maybe her dad wanted to have his own little talk with the guy. I would. I heard, too, that James Shaw started a fight with Malloy at your shindig last night. Seems like your boy wasn't too popular."

"*My* boy? Where did you hear that?" My mind went to Allie's surprised interest in the newsroom on Friday afternoon, while my mother offered her version of my adolescent romance with

Ryan. I saw then that Ross was grinning, and I rolled my eyes at him.

"Well, James might have started the fight, but he definitely wasn't the winner. He wound up flat on the ground. He couldn't even get up for a while. When he did, he went limping off by himself."

"Yeah? Well, could be James went home, sobered up, and got mad all over again. This time he decides to have the advantage over Malloy, and he brings a gun to a fist fight."

"So, Ryan was shot?"

"No, not gonna play that game. You wait until the sheriff releases that information. I sure as heck shouldn't be seen talkin' to the press about it. I got enough problems. Could you back off a little? I don't want anybody to see me walkin' up with you attached to my side."

"You're hurting my feelings, Ross. OK, I'll walk three steps behind, but you have to promise to keep the *Times* in the loop. I don't want us to be scooped on this by Spencer Karr."

"I don't gotta promise you anything," he said gruffly, but I was pretty sure he'd give me what he could.

---

"What have you got?" I asked Miguel, who had come running over when he saw me. Both of us were confined behind the crime scene tape, along with the usual contingent of onlookers. Years of reporting have taught me that nothing brings out people like someone else's misfortune. Oh, I know, I know, some people are there to offer support, but I feel pretty confident saying that most of them are there to watch the show.

"Not much. Sheriff Lamey didn't want to tell me anything. Until I told him I wouldn't be able to use the photo of him if I didn't have anything to report. That's when he told me that Ryan was shot, and that Warren Cox found him. I already sent it to Maggie, and there's nothing on *GO News*, yet."

"Wow. You're getting pretty good at tricking people into doing what you want them to do. The sheriff can't resist seeing himself online or in print."

"I learned from the master," he said, with a slight bow to me.

"I'm not sure I think that's a compliment. Any sign of Spencer Karr—or Andrea?"

I had hired Andrea Novak as the social media manager at the *Times*, but I'd also had to fire her—or rather, Miguel had to, at my insistence. Despite several warnings, she had continued to be sloppy with the facts and irresponsible in what she printed, and as a result caused a serious problem for the paper. But she'd found a safe haven at *GO News* as Spencer's assistant in the fact-free zone that is *Tea to GO*.

"No, but the sheriff is going to do a press conference later today. Andrea will be there, for sure. Sheriff Lamey has a crush on her." He did a fairly good impression of Andrea's well-practiced hair flip and sly smile, followed up by a facial expression that approximated Lamey's lecherous grin.

I suppressed a laugh. "Come on, stop it. We shouldn't be laughing at a murder scene."

"I'm not laughing. You are. I'm just telling you, Andrea, she has the inside track. And Sheriff Lamey, well the heart wants what it wants," he said.

"Eww. Enough. Lameass and Andrea is the stuff nightmares are made of. Have you tried to reach Ryan's stepbrother, Steven? I think we should leave his mother out of this, at least for now."

"*Chica*, I've got this. Don't you have some work to do on your pages for Clinton?"

Clinton is my agent, who would not let me rest on the laurels of my second book and pushed me to start on the third before the final edits were even done on the second one. Which actually turned out to be very prescient of him, because there weren't enough laurels from *Family Secrets* to provide a very comfy place to rest.

"Yes, I do. I was just—"

"You were just not trusting me, again," he said, looking down, with a note of reproach in his voice.

Instantly, I felt guilt stricken. Control—mostly of other people, not myself—is my middle name. I'm aware, but I relapse fairly often. Especially where the paper is concerned. Miguel deserved my confidence, not my hovering.

"No, Miguel. That's not it at all. I do trust you. You know that. Why—" I stopped as he looked up and I saw the teasing gleam in his dark brown eyes.

"I cannot believe you'd manipulate me like that."

"Just practicing my skills, *chica*."

———

The honk of a horn made me jump as I was opening my car door. I looked up and saw a red Prius pulling in just behind me. A woman with a glorious halo of curly red-gold hair unrolled her window and leaned out.

"Leah, hi! I thought that was you."

"Hey, Betty. How are you?" The black lab sitting in the front seat beside her looked expectantly at me, then gave a polite bark. "You, too, Allen. How are you doing?"

"We're fine. What's going on? Why are there so many cars here? And what's everybody doing milling around by the Burke's cottage?"

Betty Reynolds was the nurse in our family doctor's office for years. When her husband, Carl, retired, they moved to Texas, but they kept a cottage at Gray Lake, and they spend the summers there.

"You haven't heard?"

"Heard what?"

"Ryan Malloy is dead."

"Oh, my gosh! What happened? Poor Joanna, this will devastate her. And she's already gone through so much."

"That's what the police are trying to find out. Ryan was murdered. Shot last night at the family cottage."

She gave a sharp intake of breath. Allen reached over and put a heavy paw on her arm.

"What, Betty?"

"Last night I woke up, because I heard a loud popping noise. I figured it was the college kids who rented Dorsky's cottage. They've been setting off fireworks and poppers all week. I thought about calling it in to the Sheriff's Department, but instead I just closed the window and went back to sleep. What if it wasn't fireworks? What if it was a gun? What if I went right back to sleep, while Ryan was getting murdered?"

"What time was it?"

"I don't know. I didn't look at the clock. I went to bed about eleven—Carl was already sleeping. Nothing wakes him up. I read for maybe twenty minutes, then I fell asleep. It might have been midnight, one o'clock? I'm not sure."

"You should talk to Detective Ross. He's in charge of the investigation. He's at the Burke's cottage now."

———

Maggie's car was in the parking lot behind the *Times* when I pulled in. I resisted the urge to stop in the newsroom and check on how coverage of Ryan Malloy's death was going. Miguel already had what I'd learned, and I'd just be getting in the way. Resolutely, I went in through the back and took the three flights of stairs to my place. There's an elevator, but I rarely use it.

My phone rang as I stepped inside.

"Hi, Mom."

"Leah, is it true? Has Ryan Malloy been killed?"

"Yes. He was shot."

"I can't believe it. He was holding court at the reunion last night, looking like he didn't have a care. Then, a few hours later, he's dead. And so, so young. Who could have done it? Did someone break into the cottage?"

"I don't know, but I doubt it. Break-ins around here don't usually result in dead bodies. Warren Cox found him. Ross already knows about the fight James Shaw had with Ryan last night, so he's probably on the suspect list."

"Oh, no. I can't believe James would kill Ryan. He's such a gentle person. And they were best friends once."

"Well, they weren't looking so BFF-y last night. I don't know how far Ross will travel down that road. But I bet Art Lamey will push in that direction. From Lamey's perspective, zeroing in on James will show his department is fast and furiously moving to solve the murder of a beloved citizen—or at least a semi-famous one. Even if it turns out not to be James, it's all about making it look like things are happening. Lamey can use this case as evidence that he's the get-things-done sheriff the county needs."

"Ugh! He's such an awful man. I wish Charlie Ross would consider running against him."

"Ross? Mom, seriously, do you see him managing a department, keeping things cool with the other police agencies in the county, not to mention getting along with the County Board of Supervisors? It would be like putting me on Coop's Community Task Force. I don't have the patience, neither does Ross. He's not good at making nice."

"Getting along with people isn't 'making nice,' Leah. Most of us think of it as being respectful of others."

"Hey, I'm respectful—unless people are acting like idiots.

And that would be a lot of the people Ross would have to deal with as sheriff."

"Sometimes I wonder if I should have said no to that pack of wolves who were raising you. But they begged me so hard, I had to take you."

"Funny."

"It was, wasn't it? Go back to last night, though. How long did you stay after Paul and I left the reunion? Was Ryan still there when you left?"

"Things started winding down around eleven—not long after you guys took off. Gabe and I and the rest of our table stayed. We were all standing around talking, and Ryan came up to our group. He wasn't falling-down drunk or anything, but he seemed a little fuzzy. Steven left then, which didn't show much brotherly concern. Coop talked to Ryan and got him to give up his car keys. Then he called Ride EZ to take Ryan home. We waited around until the car got there. After Ryan left, we all did, too."

"Ride EZ? I'm surprised Tammy Granger's making a go of that business. Especially because she uses her family as drivers. A lot of people are a little leery of the Granger clan."

"With good reason. I didn't know it was a Granger family enterprise. I won't be hopping in the backseat of a Ride EZ car any time soon. Not unless I'm looking for a fast ride to the nearest drug dealer's house."

"That's probably wise." Her voice shifted tone. "We shouldn't be joking around. Think of what Joanna Burke is going through. Ryan was the world to her. And the worst is yet to come."

"What do you mean? I can't imagine she'll ever feel worse than she must right now."

"Oh, but she will. She's numb right now. But that will wear off. When it does, the despair that descends is unbearable."

"I'm sorry, Mom. I didn't think." Of course she knew how Joanna would be feeling, she'd felt it herself, twice.

"There's a pain in outliving your children that no one who hasn't experienced it can understand. It's a break in the natural order of things. You're thrown into a chasm of sadness so deep, you think you'll never climb out of it. But, eventually, you do. What makes me feel so terrible for Joanna is that she won't be able to. She doesn't have long to live, and every day that she does, she'll feel the ache of her loss. Drugs can ease the pain of her cancer, but nothing can take away the pain of losing her child."

She spoke with such profound understanding of Joanna Burke's suffering that I wished we were in the same room instead of on the phone. I wanted to wrap her in a hug. I fumbled for words and in the end I just said, "I love you, Mom."

"I love you, too, sweetheart. I'll talk to you soon. I think I'll go over to see Joanna now."

## 12

————

After talking to my mother, I poured a can of Diet Coke over lots of ice and took the glass to my window seat. A few people were walking down the sidewalk, but there's not much happening in downtown Himmel to draw a crowd on a Sunday afternoon. A new coffee house had opened across from the *Times* offices a few weeks earlier. I watched as a couple came out of the door holding hands. The woman looked a little like Gina Cox— petite, with long, light-brown, wavy hair. But when she smiled up at her boyfriend, I saw that she was much younger and much happier.

How would Gina feel, when she heard the news about Ryan? She'd been so desperate for him to answer her, to tell her why he hadn't loved her the way she had loved him. As though once she understood, her pain would end. I hadn't felt that way about Ryan, but I had once felt the same about my ex-husband, Nick. I hadn't ever allowed myself to feel that vulnerable again. Was that why Gabe scared me?

Wait, what? Where did that come from? Gabe didn't scare me. Nobody did.

*Yes, they do,* said a little voice inside my head. *Any man who wants to get close to you scares you. Look at Ron in Charlottesville. Dave in Miami. And then you run away.*

I hate when my little voice comes up with crazy ideas like that. I didn't run away from Ron, or Dave, or anybody else. They just turned out to be less than I thought they were. They disappointed me, and we called it quits. That's all.

*Really? Or do you set the bar so high, no one can ever reach it? That way you won't get hurt.*

Whoa. What the heck was in this Diet Coke? I got up from my window seat and dumped it in the sink. In minutes I was on my bike, riding to see the one man who has never disappointed me, or scared me, or let me down. I could use some sensible conversation that didn't involve weird ideas from my subconscious.

Father Gregory Lindstrom stood outside his apartment, holding three grocery bags and struggling to unlock his front door as I rode up on my bicycle. I parked it in the bike stand in front of the building.

"Father, hi!" I called. "Let me help."

He turned and smiled. "Leah, hello."

I smiled back, suddenly feeling much better about myself. He has that effect on me.

"Let me take one of those bags for you," I said, lifting it out of his arms.

"Thank you. I'm afraid I got a little carried away with the sale prices at Aldi's today," he said.

I followed him into his small kitchen and set the bag on the counter.

"Would you like some iced tea? I have some in the refrigerator. I'm going to prepare a late lunch. You're welcome to join me, if you like." He's a short man with a fluff of white hair and glasses with thick lenses that can obscure the kindness in his light blue eyes. At seventy-something, he's very fit and energetic, and still loves wading in icy trout streams in his favorite secret spots in northern Wisconsin and the Upper Peninsula of Michigan.

"Iced tea sounds great. Actually, lunch sounds pretty good, too. What are you making? Can I help?"

"A hot dish. Cheesy beef, rice, and cabbage. It's a little heavy for a summer day, but I've had a craving for it lately. I don't need any help, but I'll enjoy your company while I cook." He poured me a glass of tea and pointed to the round wooden table to indicate I should grab a seat.

"I didn't know you knew how to cook."

"Oh, yes. My mother taught me when I was young. She was an excellent cook, and this dish was one of her specialties. When Mrs. Malone retired as housekeeper at St. Stephens, and I moved here after the rectory burned, it seemed the right time to take the task on myself. I quite enjoy it, too."

As he spoke he moved around the kitchen, putting his groceries away, keeping out those things that were part of the recipe, and pulling various bowls and cooking implements out of drawers and cupboards. The gentle clatter made a homey backdrop to our conversation.

"Is this a casual visit, Leah? Or do you have something on your mind?" he asked, deftly chopping a green pepper with quick sure strokes of his knife.

"I haven't seen you much lately. Just wanted to catch up."

"Your mother tells me you're working on your next book. You didn't give yourself much time to relax after completing *Family Secrets*, did you? I just finished reading it. Very fine work."

"Thanks. I can't afford to take time off. I'm glad you like the second book, but not enough other people do. It isn't selling as well as the first, and my cash reserves are running low. Buying the paper did a pretty good job of depleting my finances. So, say a prayer that book three is the charm, and we can keep the *Times* afloat."

"Are things that bad? I've been enjoying the paper. I've heard other people who say the same."

"That's nice to know, but *GO News* is making it tough."

"Ah, yes. I know that's quite widely read as well." He fell silent as he used the back of his knife to slide the pepper pieces to the side of his cutting board before starting on the onion.

"You heard about Ryan Malloy?"

He nodded. "I went to give his mother Communion after Mass this morning. I was there when the police brought the news."

"I'm glad she wasn't on her own. It had to hit her hard."

"It was a terrible blow, as it would be to any parent. Still, she responded with what I can only describe as stoicism. Although that may have been due to the numbness of shock."

"Mom is going over to see her. She's probably there now."

He nodded as he moved the onion aside.

"I'm sure Carol will be a comfort to her." He began chopping a head of cabbage and waited for me to continue. When I didn't, he looked up, his eyes quizzical.

"Leah? Is there something else on your mind?"

"There is. But I don't know how to say it without sounding like a letter to *Ask Miguel*. Did you hear I'm having Miguel start an advice column? Maybe I should write to him about it. '*Dear Miguel, My boyfriend is a wonderful person—funny, smart, kind, and I like him a lot. How can I dump him? Signed, Confused in Himmel.*' "

The heated pan sizzled as he dumped in the meat and

vegetables and gave them a stir. He let the silence hang between us, until I went on.

"See, it's like this. You know Gabe Hoffman, right?"

"Yes. I've met him several times. With you, Leah."

"Yeah, I know. I'm just trying to work up to it."

"Maybe you shouldn't try, you should just say it."

I took a deep breath and exhaled before I let out my thoughts. "Well, Coop and my mother, they always tease me that I dump the men I go out with as soon as the newness wears off."

"Do you?"

"No! It's just that after a while, they usually do something I can't accept, and so we break up. It's no big drama. We just shake hands and say goodbye ... more or less," I added, thinking of a few occasions that hadn't gone quite that smoothly.

"So, now Gabe's done something that you can't accept?"

"No, Gabe's great. But I like how things are now. We laugh, we talk, we work together sometimes, we have fun."

"That sounds very nice," he said, as he sautéed the vegetables.

"It is nice. That's my point. Why does it have to change?"

"Is it changing?"

"I'm not sure. He's just showing some signs, you know, like he wants to be more serious."

"And you don't?"

"No. Well, maybe, I'm not sure. I know, this is really stupid, isn't it? I just start feeling really anxious when someone gets too close."

"Someone, or some man?"

I didn't answer for a few seconds, beginning to think I might have had better luck with my inner voice than with Father Lindstrom's perceptive probings.

"Well, to be honest, some man, I guess. My track record isn't that great. My unique talent seems to be getting involved with men who wind up disappointing me."

While I'd been talking, he'd added rice and water to the skillet, put the lid on, and turned the burner to low. Then he poured himself some iced tea and sat down across from me before speaking.

"Men who disappoint you, Leah? Or who abandon you?"

For some reason the word abandon hit me like a punch in the stomach.

"Nobody abandoned me. We just broke up, that's all. That's totally different."

"I see."

I went on as though he'd challenged me, instead of simply nodding and taking a sip of his tea.

"Well, it's obvious. If someone is abandoned, it means they're helpless. They can't take care of themselves. They need someone else to support them. That's not me. I don't need anyone to take care of me."

"I agree. Leah the adult is a very competent, capable person. But what about Leah, the child, whose father left, whose sister died, whose mother was wrapped in her own deep grief and had a baby to care for as well? Did that Leah feel abandoned?"

I squirmed uncomfortably on my chair. I'm all about psychoanalyzing other people, but it's not an exercise I enjoy when I'm the one on the analyst's couch.

"That doesn't really make sense. My mother didn't leave me, and my sister Annie *died*, for Pete's sake. She didn't have any choice about it."

He let the silence hang between us.

"All right. Maybe I did feel sort of cast adrift. Maybe I couldn't understand why my father would just take off. Maybe I did think it was my fault—that he couldn't forgive me for not watching over Annie. But that was a long time ago. Do you mean that I'm drawn to men who on some level remind me of my father, because I'm trying to see if this time I'll be worth staying around for? And I break up with them, so that this time I won't be—" I hesitated. Funny how hard it was to say that word. I forced it out. "Abandoned?"

Again he stayed quiet, his eyes gently inquiring. When I couldn't stand it any longer, I started talking again.

"I suppose you think that my relationships end badly because I don't let anyone in, not really. Because I know you can't really count on anyone. So, whether they leave or I leave, it doesn't matter, because I'm still whole. Because I didn't give any of myself away, I can't be 'abandoned.' That when someone tries to get too close, it scares me and I push them away. Is that what you're saying, Father?"

"I don't believe I've been saying anything, Leah."

I felt my face flush. Where had all that come from? I hadn't known that's what was hiding inside me. How had Father Lindstrom known? I felt embarrassed and exposed and eager to get onto safer ground.

"I'm sorry, Father. I didn't mean to go all *Dr. Phil* on you. I'm just trying to figure out what to do if Gabe wants more of a commitment than I do. I don't want to hurt him, but I don't want to be rushed into something I'm not sure of, either. Of course, on the other hand, maybe he's not thinking that at all, and I'm just finding problems where there aren't any. Or possibly, making excuses because I really *am* scared of getting too close and then getting hurt. But I'm not a scared kind of person. About most things."

"Leah, you would make an excellent addition to a law firm. You could play devil's advocate very effectively while a defense attorney is laying out his strategy. You argue both sides of the case very well."

"I thought I had a handle on this trust stuff after the last go-round with Nick. But I keep having the same doubts. I really like Gabe. I don't want to mess things up between us. But I don't want to fool myself either." I crossed my arms on the table and dropped my head onto them in an exaggerated gesture of despair. Then I popped back up and said, "What's wrong with me, Father?"

"Nothing. You find it hard to trust. That's understandable. You had your heart broken when you were very young, by the death of your sister, the abandonment by your father. And later in your life by other relationships that didn't last.

"But to love is to be broken at some time—by death, or betrayal, or abandonment. It's inevitable. It's life. But if we put a hard shell of fear over our broken heart to protect it, it has no room to grow. To live life fully is to have a heart that expands, not contracts, with each loss. To know true contentment in life, you must knit your broken heart together with a loose and giving stitch, so that it can grow large enough to hold compassion for other broken people in the world."

I sighed. "No offense, Father. But I was hoping for a more practical answer."

"Understanding that life is nuanced, not black and white, *is* practical. We lose a great deal if we see people only in one light. My mother used to say, 'Don't make the perfect the enemy of the good.' If you trust Gabe, if you let him in, he may disappoint you at times. He may not be all the things you want him to be. But if he's enough of the things that are important to you, perhaps that is sufficient."

He patted my hand, then got up to see to his hotdish, which by then was smelling really, really good. By the time we finished eating, I was in a more mellow mood. Music might soothe some savage breasts, but for me, a nice Wisconsin hotdish works just as well.

My phone buzzed in my pocket. I didn't recognize the number, but it was local.

"Sorry, Father. I should see who this is."

"Certainly," he said, standing up and gathering our plates.

"This is Leah Nash."

"Leah, this is Joanna Burke. It's very important that I see you as soon as possible."

## 13

Joanna Burke's house, a brick, two-story Colonial, was set back from the street by a long, curving driveway. The wide expanse of lawn was as precisely mowed as a golf course green. In contrast, the flower beds were a riot of exuberant plants and colors. Bees buzzed among the blossoms as I parked my bike and walked up the brick sidewalk to the front entrance. I recognized geraniums, day lilies and cone flowers, but my horticultural knowledge didn't stretch far enough to identify the many other varieties that bloomed in a joyful salute to summer.

A small woman with gray-hair and red-rimmed eyes opened the door when I rang the bell. She wore khaki pants, a navy-blue untucked blouse, and sensible shoes.

"Yes?" Her expression was that of someone about to close the door on a person selling political or religious salvation.

"Hi, I'm Leah Nash. I'm here to see Mrs. Burke."

"I'm sorry," she said, shaking her head and beginning to shut the door. "She's resting. There's been a death in the family." Before I could explain that Joanna had asked to see me, a voice called from inside the house.

"Wanda, who's there? Is it Leah? Bring her to me, please."

She turned her head and called back. "Yes, Mrs. Burke."

But I could see she was not happy about it.

I stepped across the threshold into a large, bright foyer with a highly polished dark wood floor. A staircase led up to the second floor, but Wanda led me down a hallway to the right. Our shoes made no sound on the plush runner beneath our feet. I followed her through the first open door.

"Here she is, Mrs. Burke."

Ryan's mother was seated on a cream-colored sofa staring at, but I doubted seeing, her beautiful front lawn. She turned to face me, and I tried to hide the shock I felt at the change in her. She had been a striking blonde with a wide smile exactly like Ryan's. Now, she looked like the last page in a four-part carbonless form—a faint copy of the woman she had been. The cancer treatment had left her hair thin and fine, sticking out in places like the down on a baby chick. Her pale skin was hatched with fine wrinkles across her cheeks, and her eyelashes and eyebrows were gone, leaving her face with a naked, vulnerable look. But she was beautifully dressed in a pale green, silky tunic and black pants, and her narrow feet were encased in black slippers with gold embroidery on the toes.

"Leah, thank you for coming. Please, sit here beside me," she patted a spot on the sofa next to her with a hand that seemed too frail to support the large diamond ring and wedding band that jiggled loosely on her thin fingers. I was surprised at how strong her voice still was. "Would you like something to drink? Tea or water?"

"No, thank you."

"All right, then. Wanda, you don't need to hover. Thank you."

Wanda looked like she would have preferred to stay to protect and serve, but she left with a nod, closing the door softly behind her on the way out.

"I'm sorry Wanda almost turned you away. She's a wonderful cook and housekeeper, but since my health took a bad turn, she's appointed herself my protector, too. She means well."

"No need to apologize. I'm very sorry about Ryan. I know this is a terrible time for you. I wish there was something I could do to help."

"There is. I want you to find his killer."

---

She had refused to say why she needed to see me during our brief phone conversation, but I had suspected something like this, and I was prepared with my response.

"Oh, Joanna, no. I'm so sorry. But I'm a journalist, not a detective. The sheriff's department is handling Ryan's case, and I know the lead investigator, Charlie Ross. He's very good. He'll get to the truth of things, I'm sure."

I wished that Ross—and Coop—were there at that moment. They both seem to think that I live to jump into the middle of their cases. The truth is, I've only ever dug into closed or cold cases that sometimes overlap with theirs. Well, maybe a live one or two, but only when I was asked, and there was a good reason to say yes. It's not like I search them out. And this was definitely one case I didn't have any desire to be a part of.

The hand she reached out and put over mine was as light as a sheet of tissue paper. But her voice was firm.

"Leah, it has to be you. My son is dead. My only comfort is that I'll be dead soon, too. But I have to know who killed him. I need to know that person will be punished. Ryan was my light, my life."

It was true, I knew. It wasn't that Joanna hadn't loved her husband Jonas, or presumably Ryan's father, but in Joanna's eyes there was Ryan, and then there was everyone else.

"I understand," I said. "But even if I thought I could be useful, I really couldn't get involved. I'm working against a deadline for my next book, Joanna."

She lifted her hand and made a dismissive gesture, as though writing a book were nothing in the face of her overwhelming loss. A fair point.

"It won't take you long—it can't. I won't be around that much longer. I don't know your Detective Ross. But Sheriff Lamey is who came to see me today. It was clear to me that he isn't very bright. He seemed to think that Ryan's death is a career opportunity for himself. I have to be sure that Ryan's killer is found. You've done it before for your own family. I need you to do it for mine. Please." Her tone was urgent, her words demanding, but it was her eyes that made me say yes, despite my reluctance. Two blue wells of pain so deep, I had to look away.

"Well, I guess I could try, Joanna. But it won't be easy. I don't have the resources the police do. I—"

"What you have is better. You knew Ryan. He mattered to you. And that matters to me."

It seemed beyond cruel to tell her that I didn't feel any of the emotion she was attributing to me. I was sad about Ryan's death in the same way I would be sad for anyone's loss of life, but he had long ago ceased to matter to me in any serious way. I tried to gently remind her that it had been many years since he and I were close.

"Ryan and I had a nice conversation at the reception on Friday night. Did you know that we hadn't seen or spoken to each other since the day before your family moved to Seattle?"

"Yes, he told me you two caught up. I remember what a crush you had on him. Who could blame you? He was a beautiful boy. A beautiful man. Ryan is—was—no, he *is*, so precious to me." She ended on a half-sob. But she quickly got herself under control.

"I'm not going to cry. I'm not going to allow myself to feel anything until you find his killer. When I know that whoever took him away from me will be punished, then I can let go." She dabbed at her eyes and cleared her throat before going on.

"Did you know Ryan was finally going to get his break-through as an actor? He decided to stop trying to get discovered, and to make his own luck. He was going to produce his own movie—direct it and star in it, too. He would have been wonderful."

"Yes, he mentioned that. He seemed very excited."

I wanted to ask her more about Ryan's movements over the weekend, who he had been seeing locally, whether she had any ideas about who might have killed her son. But I could see that first she needed to talk about him as her wonderful son, not as a murder victim.

"Did Ryan always want to be an actor? I don't remember that about him."

"No, not until he had the lead in a play his senior year in Seattle. He was so good! Everyone said so. He was a theater major in college. Jonas, Ryan's stepfather, worried about acting as a career, but I never did. I knew Ryan would succeed. When Ryan wanted something, he got it, no matter what."

I thought of Gina and didn't doubt it. I thought of James, too. And the accident that had taken away his hope of a football career—and had given Ryan James's spot on the team.

"Ryan was my miracle boy. I lost two babies before he was born. Miscarriages in the second trimester. The doctor said I'd never carry a baby to term. I had to spend the last four months in bed when I got pregnant with Ryan. I made a bargain with God. I promised that if He gave me a baby, he'd have the best life that I could give him, and I'd never let anything happen to him.

"Do you know, I boiled Ryan's pacifiers every day, and if one fell on the floor, I'd boil it again before I'd let him touch it? My mother used to laugh at me. I had wall-to-wall carpeting installed, so he wouldn't be hurt if he fell when he was learning to walk. I had a baby monitor in his room until he was three. When I read about how dangerous vaccinations were, I refused to allow Ryan to get any. I never even let him watch violent shows on television.

"But I don't think I was overprotective. Ryan was a marvelous athlete, and I let him play every sport he wanted to. And he excelled at all of them. I worried, yes, but what Ryan wanted, I wanted. I just made sure that he had the best padding, the best helmet, whatever it took to keep him safe. When we bought him his first car, of course he wanted a fast sports car. But I insisted he get one with the highest safety rating. I did everything I could to keep my promise to protect him. I truly did, but he died anyway, didn't he? My son died." Despite her determination not to break down, she couldn't help herself. Who could? She put her face in her hands and began to sob.

I reached out and put my hand on her shoulder, but I didn't say anything. After a few minutes, she gradually regained control, lifted her face, and pulled a tissue from the box sitting on the table next to the sofa. She wiped her eyes and blew her nose gently, then said, "I loved him so much, you see, and I can't bear to think I failed him. You have to find his murderer. You have to."

"Well, then, we have to think about who didn't love Ryan, Joanna. Clearly someone had it in for him."

"But that's what makes it so hard, don't you see? I can't think of a single person who didn't like Ryan. Everyone loved him, wanted to be his friend—or his girlfriend," she added with a wistful smile. "He was so handsome, wasn't he?"

"Yes, he was. But people can be jealous of someone who seems to have it all, like Ryan. Not everyone is happy for someone else's luck. Ryan had been back in town for a while. Who did he socialize with? Did he look up old friends, or make new ones?"

"I'm not sure. He didn't stay here at the house. He was out at the cottage, you know. He needed a place to work in peace and quiet. And except for the fact that I'm dying, I'm really doing quite well. Hospice people come in regularly, and there's a home health care aide who comes every day and helps me get up and dressed. She even helps me bathe. I never realized before, but the helplessness of illness is almost as awful as the illness itself. But I'm not complaining.

"Steven's been very helpful, too, taking care of all the bill-paying and banking and that kind of thing. And his wife, I mean, his first wife, Jill, has been good to me, as well. Anyway, there was no need for Ryan to stay here. I couldn't expect him to do all those things and still work on his movie. And he's always loved the cottage at the lake. I sent Wanda out to clean and take him a meal sometimes, even though he never wanted me to fuss. But that's a long way of saying I don't know if Ryan saw old friends or made new ones, isn't it? He could have, but he didn't mention it to me."

"He didn't ever just casually say that he'd run into so-and-so, or that he'd met a new neighbor at the lake, nothing like that?"

"Not that I can recall. We talked a lot about his script, and who he wanted to be in the film. It amazed me how someone as talented as Ryan was could have had such a hard time getting roles. But the competition is very fierce, he said, and the system is rigged in favor of people who already have an in—someone in the family who's already in the business. He worked so hard to succeed, and he was determined. That's why I knew he would." That sounded like Ryan. His mother was terminally ill, but the conversation was all about him.

"Well, what about family time? How did Ryan and Steven get along? Any friction there?"

"No, of course not. Steven loved him. I don't mean to say they were close—how could they be? Ryan was still in high school when Jonas and I married, and Steven was already married to Jill and getting his business going. But Jonas always insisted that we were a family, and both Steven and Ryan would be treated equally. So, if you're thinking there's some kind of money issues between them, there wasn't. Jonas left everything to me, and when I die, the estate will be split equally between the two of them, just as he wanted. Besides, Steven probably wouldn't mind if it wasn't. He's doing very well financially. You can't turn on the television without seeing an ad for one of his car dealerships."

I hadn't really been thinking about a money motive. I was heading more along the lines of sibling rivalry—an adult Steven who'd felt displaced in his father's affection or felt that Ryan had stumbled into a very easy life when his mother married Steven's father. Which, it appeared to me, he had. But the money motive is a classic.

"Joanna, not to be crass, but how much money are we talking here?"

She looked taken aback, as most people do when you get down to cash on hand. I've never thought of money as a measure of a person's worth. Maybe that's because for most of my life, if that were the yardstick, I would have definitely come up short. To me how much money you have is just a fact, neither good nor bad, like what color your eyes are, or if you take your coffee black. Or your Jameson straight.

I realize, however, that most people feel differently, and would find it easier to tell you the details of their sex life than their bank statement. So, I restrain myself from asking, usually, but I had to know in this case.

"Well, Jonas was very good with money, and he was fortunate, very fortunate, with his investments."

"OK, so are we talking fortunate like the two of them will divide a couple hundred thousand in assets—or a couple hundred million?"

"No, nothing anywhere near that. Jonas left an estate of four million, more or less."

"I see. I'm sorry if I sounded rude. I'm not saying that money is a motive in Ryan's death, but it sometimes is, in even the nicest families."

Despite Joanna's protests—or maybe because of them—I would definitely be following the money. She nodded and expounded on the happy family theme.

"All of us have had dinner together once a week, since Ryan's been back—Steven, and his wife, Lily, and Ryan and me. With Jonas gone, and my ... situation, I wanted to bring us together as more of a family. Ryan only had me. I hated the thought of him being alone, after I die. Ironic, isn't it? I've lived my life, but I'm still alive, and my son is the one who is dead." Her voice faltered, but she didn't break down.

"What about James Shaw?" I asked. "Did Ryan get together with him? They were good friends for a long time."

"No, he didn't. He was shocked when I told him that James had sent a pornographic email to one of his students! Given Ryan's career and his production company starting, he didn't think it would be a good idea to be associated with a sex criminal."

"You do know that James has only been charged, not convicted."

"Of course, you're right. I don't mean to be unkind. It's a shame about James. He always idolized Ryan. And even though Ryan was so much more popular than James, he always included him in everything. Ryan had such a good heart. Even after the accident, Ryan was never angry at him."

"Why would Ryan be angry at him?" I had trouble keeping the astonishment out of my voice. How could the guy who caused the accident be mad at the guy who lost his leg?

"Why, because, some people blamed Ryan. It really hurt him. It was so unfair. Especially because he and James never would have been on the boat if James hadn't insisted. Ryan told us James just wouldn't take no, and then he was so careless, jumping around and showing off until he fell into the water. Still, Ryan always insisted it was his fault as much as it was James's. That's the kind of person he was. Ryan tried to stay friendly with James, but finally he had to walk away. James was just so bitter. But I know Ryan forgave him."

Wow. Quite a different version of the story than any I'd heard before.

"Did anyone tell you that James and Ryan got into a fight at the dance last night? Quite a serious one. James started it, apparently."

She was nonplussed for a moment. "No, I didn't know that. The sheriff didn't tell me that. I don't want to be kept in the dark, Leah. I don't want to be humored. I want to know everything there is to know about my son's murder. You will tell me everything you find out, won't you? I don't want you to hold things back because you think I'll be upset." Her dry, papery hand clutched mine and her breath had quickened. I put my other hand over hers and pressed gently.

"Joanna, I promise that I'll find out what I can. And I'll tell you what that is. But, seriously, don't discount the police. I won't argue with your take on Sheriff Lamey, but Detective Ross is good at his job. Now, I'm going to let you get some rest. I'll send your housekeeper in on my way out to see if you need anything."

## 14

I didn't have to go hunting for the housekeeper, she was hovering in the hallway when I left.

"I'm sorry, Wanda, I didn't catch your last name."

"It's Stone. I'm Wanda Stone." She was a good four inches shorter than me, and she drew herself up like a mama bear facing down a threat to her young.

"Well, I just wanted to say that I'm leaving now. Joanna is pretty drained."

"I'm sure she is," she said, in a voice as tart as sauerkraut.

"I only came because she called and insisted she had to see me. I thought it would upset her more if I refused." This short, round woman with tight gray curls and snapping brown eyes had me feeling as guilty as my third-grade teacher, Mrs. Whitney, used to. And I hadn't done anything—at the moment, I mean, not in Mrs. Whitney's class.

"Look, I can see you care about her very much. I feel terrible about what's happened to her, and I'm going to try and make things a little easier for her. I—"

"Oh, I know. She wants you to find out who killed her son.

Don't look at me like that, I wasn't listening at the door. Mrs. Burke told me after she got off the phone with you. I told her then that I didn't think it was a good idea, and I don't think it's one now. She shouldn't be agitating herself, and you shouldn't be helping her do it. She has so little—" She broke off to wipe the tears that seemed to surprise her by spilling out of her eyes mid-scolding. "So little time left. But where Ryan is concerned, she's never had any common sense. Excuse me, please. I have to see to her."

---

As I rode my bike home, I started sorting out my priorities. I'd have to let Ross know what I was doing. He wouldn't like it, but he'd be even madder if he heard about it from someone else. And I doubted that Steven had been as fond of his stepbrother as Joanna believed. Why would he be? Ryan was an interloper who had come between Steven and his father's fortune. He might have to be pleasant to him for Joanna's sake, and the sake of the inheritance she had control of, but it seemed unlikely that he actually liked him.

I stopped thinking then and focused on pumping my bike up Prospect Hill, the steepest climb in town. But the reward is to rocket down the other side, the wind blowing in your face and the glorious feeling that this time, you just might lift off ET-style into the sky beyond.

Sadly, instead of floating into the clear blue, I just glided to the end of the street, and then pulled over because my phone was ringing. Gabe.

"Hey, you. I've had a pretty interesting afternoon, how about you?"

"Leah, I can't talk. James was taken in for questioning on

Ryan Malloy's murder. I'm heading over to the sheriff's department now."

"That was fast. Poor James. Come over when you're through. I'll make dinner."

"Sounds great, but I'm not sure when I'll be done."

"That's OK. I'll scale it back from the Beef Wellington I usually make on Sundays to something that won't get ruined if you're late. How about sandwiches? I've got a brand-new jar of peanut butter, so it will still be special."

He laughed and said, "That sounds perfect. But could you do me a favor? Barnacle's out of the food he likes and I was on my way to the store when James called. Could you—"

"Yes, I could pick some up and feed him. But you know, I seem to be spending more time with your dog than with you lately."

"I thank you, and Barnacle thanks you. And, I'll make it up to you."

"You bet you will. I'll see you later."

———

Back home after feeding Barnacle, I pulled together my three favorite things for a thinking session: a yellow legal pad, a pen, and a shot of Jameson over ice. It had been a long day, and it was, after all, after five o'clock. Then I sat on the window seat, with one leg tucked up under me and my pad of paper on my lap, to begin organizing my early thoughts about who might want Ryan dead.

With Ryan gone, Steven wouldn't have to share anything, and even if his business was booming and he didn't need it, there are a lot of people who always want more. And maybe he wasn't doing as well financially as Joanna believed. After all, he had just purchased his third car dealership, the one in Madison, which would have taken a chunk of change. What if it was turning out to be a bad investment?

Then there was his wife, Lily, twenty-years his junior and quite a big spender. She'd moved into the house he'd owned with his first wife, but word on the street was that she had done massive renovations to it, and now wanted to sell it and buy another, bigger one. Supposedly, she had her eye on the Dunn house, a huge home on a high bluff overlooking the Himmel River. The asking price was a million five. Oh, yes, there were lots of uses Steven could put an extra couple of million to, not least of which was keeping his young wife happy.

Now, what about James? And Gina. Both of them had reason to blame Ryan for some really bad stuff that had happened in their lives. Gina fought with Ryan the night before he died. James had come at him with no provocation—according to Steven—on the very night Ryan was killed. I didn't want to think that James was involved. But I knew from personal experience that too much alcohol can distort your judgment and make you do things you ordinarily wouldn't. Although to date, I hadn't killed anyone.

So, what about Gina? She was, as my Aunt Nancy would say, "no bigger than a minute." It was hard to imagine her facing down Ryan and killing him. On the other hand, she'd been furious at him. And how big did you have to be to take someone down if you had a gun? Lots of women in Wisconsin know their weapons and how to use them.

Finally, there was the man who found the body, Gina's father, Warren Cox. If he had been as clueless as me, and word had reached him about what had happened at the reception at the Elks on Friday—which in Himmel it was almost impossible that it hadn't—he might have reacted very violently toward Ryan. Although he had lost his daughter because of his intractable stubbornness and his unforgiving nature, he might not see it that way. He could blame Ryan as the cause of his family falling apart. And he might have decided Ryan should finally pay for it.

Once you let your mind roam free, it's surprising how many suspects you can come up with.

## 15

---

"You know, I think this is one of the finest meals you've ever made," Gabe said, after finishing the last bite of his sandwich and taking a swallow of Supper Club beer. Barnacle snored lightly on the couch.

"Thank you. Although seeing that I fed you a PB&J sandwich on slightly stale bread with a side of bottom-of-the-bag broken potato chips, I'm wondering if you're not being a touch sarcastic."

"Never. Well, hardly ever. And don't think I didn't notice you brought out the real plates for me, not the paper ones. I'm easy. What can I say?"

"Sometimes you are," I said, in a slightly passive-aggressive way.

He looked at me quizzically, but I backed away. I hadn't had time to process my talk with Father Lindstrom yet. I wasn't ready to get into it with Gabe.

"So, now are you satiated enough to tell me what happened with James this afternoon? How much trouble—or should I say how much more trouble—is he in?"

"A lot, I'm afraid. They didn't arrest him, but they were

leaning on him pretty heavy. And it definitely doesn't help that he's already been charged with sending that email to his student. If you want to know any more than that, you'll have to join the defense team."

I wasn't sure if he was kidding or not.

"I'm serious. I could use the help. But I can't tell you anything more specific unless you're part of the team. Which at this point, as usual, would be just you and me. I could use somebody else to help me bail water on this one. James's alibi story leaves a big hole in the bottom of our boat, and we're going to sink fast."

"Before you drown in your own metaphor, sure, I'd like to help James. But I already promised Joanna Burke that I'd try to find out who killed Ryan. She doesn't trust the sheriff's department."

"I'm with Joanna there. I don't mean Charlie Ross. I think he's a fair enough guy. It's Lamey who worries me. He's taking a very active part in this investigation. And James is his favorite suspect. Did you enter into a contract with her? Is she paying you to investigate a specific person? Did she say she believes James did it?"

"Of course I don't have a contract with her, and she's not paying me. It's not like I do this for a living. She doesn't care what I turn up, as long as she knows who killed her son. I only said that I'd help because she's devastated, desperate, and terminally ill. It doesn't get much worse than that."

"All right, then. No problem working with me to help James."

"But what if I find evidence that James is guilty?"

"I don't think you will. But if you do, then we deal with it."

We paused for a minute while Gabe got another beer out of the refrigerator. I poured a Jameson for myself and turned off the air-conditioning to let in the breeze that had started outside.

As we moved toward the sofa, Barnacle, not wanting to share the space with us, scooted to the other end. I put a Spotify playlist on shuffle to let it stream quietly and randomly in the background. Sometimes I think better to music. Then, we sat down to work.

"OK, the most obvious reason to suspect James is the fight he had with Ryan at the reunion. Let's talk about that," I said.

"Yeah, that's not a good thing. And I'm not sure James is telling me the whole truth about it, either. Which is also not a good thing."

"Why, what's he saying?" I asked.

"Wait a minute, are you definitely on board, or not?"

I never like Gabe more than when I see him digging in to work for a client. His eyes spark with determination, and you can hear the passion in his voice. Now, he held my gaze, waiting for the answer he had to know I would give.

"You're really into your nautical imagery today, aren't you? Yes, I'm on board."

He leaned over and kissed me. Then he handed me a dollar bill.

"This makes it official. The pay isn't great on the good ship Gabe Hoffman, but we really appreciate our crew."

"Noted. So, then, what did James say about the fight with Ryan?"

"He said that he'd been drinking on and off all afternoon. Mostly on. That he wasn't planning on going to the reunion for obvious reasons. But he was online looking at *GO News* to see if they'd put up anything new about his case. He can't seem to stop torturing himself. It's like rubbing your tongue over a sore tooth. It doesn't help any, and it just reminds you how much it hurts."

"How did he get from perusing *GO News* to beating up Ryan at the reunion?"

"There was an item online about Ryan setting up his own production company, maybe using some local talent in his first film. James says he got thinking about how close he and Ryan used to be. He drank a little more. Then he got the great idea to go to the reunion, just to say hello to the guy who used to be his best friend."

"That doesn't sound quite right, Gabe. We both saw him whaling on Ryan. And heard him say that stuff about Ryan being a poser and a fake."

"I know. I said the same to James. But James says he only got mad because Ryan ignored him, then tried to turn away like he wasn't even there."

"Well, that might be true. It's how Ryan acted when Gina approached him Friday night."

"According to James, Ryan's attitude made him lose it. He's been under a lot of pressure from the email accusation, and he's got a lot of anger with no place to go. Ryan's brush-off was the match that set it all on fire. Plus, he was drunk."

"Well, adding in the drunk part—which he definitely was— makes it sort of plausible, but it's still pretty weak."

"I agree, but I pressed James pretty hard and that's the story he's sticking to."

"What did he do after he left the fairgrounds? Does he have *any* alibi for last night?"

"Not really. He says he was so drunk that he got turned around going home. Wound up over by the north entrance to the fairgrounds. He walked down a gravel road for a while, but then he realized he'd gotten turned around somehow. He was heading in the wrong direction. His leg hurt so bad, he had to sit down and rest before he went on. But he must have passed out. Next thing he knew, someone was shaking him. He doesn't know what time it was, except that it was dark. The man got him up, got him into a car, and drove him home."

"Who?"

"That's where the story earns its fairy tale credentials. A random Good Samaritan, apparently. James can only remember bits and pieces. He remembers the guy helping him up the walk at his house, but he says he doesn't remember anything else until he woke up in his recliner in the morning."

"That's a terrible alibi. No wonder Lamey is pointing at him."

"Why do you think I said I need you to help bail the water out of our sinking boat? I'm sure that James is hiding something, but the cops couldn't budge him on his story. And I can't convince him that he needs to tell me the truth, the whole truth and nothing but, or he could wind up in prison for a very long time. Also, did I mention the missing gun?"

"What missing gun?"

"When they asked him about a gun, James said he had one that belonged to his dad. A Glock 19. He never used it, just kept it, because his dad gave it to him. He doesn't know where it is. After the divorce, he realized it was missing when he unpacked boxes at his new place and couldn't find it. He meant to call his ex-wife, see if she had it mixed up with her things, but it didn't seem that important. He never got around to it. He didn't report it missing to the cops, because Wisconsin doesn't require it."

"Hmm. That's not so good. But the police can't have the ballistics report yet. They can't know if the bullet—or bullets—are even the kind that would be used in James's missing gun. What about the motive? What does Ross think it is?"

"Actually, Lamey led the questioning. Charlie didn't say much."

"That must have been killing Ross. What was the focus?"

"Jealousy and revenge. James is a failure, his life is going to hell, he sees a story about his old friend Ryan's success, he gets drunk, enraged, and confronts Ryan at the reunion. He's humiliated in front of everyone, goes limping home to nurse his anger, then decides to make Ryan pay for everything he's done to him. He goes out to the cottage and kills him."

"A lot depends on time of death, don't you think? I talked to one of the neighbors. She heard what could have been gunshots not long after midnight. She thought it was fireworks and went back to sleep. But if it was the killer shooting Ryan between midnight and two a.m., then it's hard to pin it on James. There's no way, as drunk as he was, that he could have pulled it together enough to get home, get his car, drive ten miles to the cottage, shoot Ryan and then drive back home. He'd have had a hard time just getting the key into the ignition last night."

"Unless they argue that James was faking it. That he wasn't as drunk as he seemed. It's not as though anyone gave him a breathalyzer or a blood test."

"Yeah, but a whole lot of people saw James in action, and I think most of them would say that he was well and truly drunk. But, I see what you're saying. James has a strong motive, a possible opportunity, and if his gun turns up and matches the ballistics on the bullets, oh, boy."

"Exactly."

"We've got to get him to tell us what really happened after he left the reunion."

"I like the sound of we, Leah. Thanks for agreeing to help."

When he smiled at me and looked so happy, I wondered why I found it so hard to just let go and let him in.

"You're welcome. Now, what about Warren Cox, Gina's dad? Ross told me he was the one who called in the body, and usually that's someone the police are very interested in checking out. Do you have anything on Warren?" I asked.

"Just what you told me. Lamey and Ross certainly weren't giving me any information on alternate suspects. Any ideas?"

"Always. When I asked Ross what he thought Gina's dad was

doing at Ryan's, he tossed out the possibility that Warren had heard about Gina and Ryan's encounter Friday night, and had decided to confront Ryan about it. If Warren Cox was as clueless as I was about Ryan and Gina's extracurricular activities—and it only makes sense that he was—then he would have been shocked when he heard the story. He might have decided that Ryan was to blame for Gina leaving her church, going over to the dark side, disgracing her parents—basically for destroying the whole Cox family. And in that case, it was time for retribution. From what I understand, there's some serious eye-for-an-eye stuff in the Bible. And what if Warren didn't wait until ten a.m. this morning to pay him a visit?"

"You're thinking he drove out last night, confronted Ryan, things escalated, and he shot him?"

"It's possible," I said.

"But why would he go back this morning to 'discover' the body?"

"Maybe he does the deed last night, but he leaves something behind. He doesn't realize it until this morning. Say it's a shell casing. Warren knows there could be fingerprints on it. He has to get it. But there's a good chance his car will be seen. The lake's a busy place on Sunday mornings. So, he gets whatever he came for, calls in the body, and has a story ready to explain why he was there.

"Warren is an upright church-going man, never done a wrong thing in his life. Even without the autopsy, the medical examiner can tell Ryan's been dead for hours—much longer than the half-hour it took for Warren to find the body and wait for the cops to arrive. Right away that takes him out of the frame. Add in that everybody knows about the huge fight James and Ryan had at the reunion. Boom! All eyes are on James, and Warren skates."

"That's pretty good," Gabe said.

"Thank you. I've got more where that came from, just give me time."

I noticed that Gabe was smiling again. "What?"

"You really love this, don't you, untangling all the threads, weaving them together again into the story of whodunnit. If Art Lamey asked you to work with him on a case, you'd jump in just as fast, because you just can't resist the chase, right?"

He was a little bit right, but I would absolutely draw the line at Art Lamey.

"Don't even say that. Lamey is such an odious little toad. And he'd never ask for help from a woman—from anyone, really. He wants this chance to show off what a law enforcement badass he is. Closing the case in record time would be nice publicity leading up to the election this fall. Not that he has much to worry about, no one else has filed. Maybe I should run for sheriff."

"I think you're kidding. But in case you're not, the filing deadline is almost up."

"Yes, I'm kidding. Maybe. How is it that people like Lamey wind up in charge of anything?"

"Murphy's Law? I don't know, but let's get back to James."

"Right. He's my first stop tomorrow." I started to get up.

"Where are you going?"

"To get some paper and a pen and start making my list. I want to see James first thing, I have to talk to Ross, to—"

"Do you have to do that at this very moment?" He leaned in and took my face in his hands and lowered his head to kiss me.

After a few minutes I said, "Well, maybe it could wait until tomorrow."

For the rest of the night, we didn't talk about James or Ryan, or much of anything else. We just listened to music and looked out at the moon. After a while, Gabe pulled me to my feet. I had just enough Jameson to relax in his arms and dance passably with him to Etta James singing "At Last." You wouldn't think it, but Gabe can be quite romantic. Something that fits in nicely with my love of 1940s films and current Hallmark movies. I will happily own up to the first and deny to the death the second.

When we went to bed, murder was the farthest thing from my mind.

## 16

---

After Gabe—and Barnacle—left early Monday morning, I took a quick shower and mindful of the weather forecast for another hot and humid day, donned a pair of cargo shorts and a green tank top. Then, I sat down at my desk to make a list of people to talk to: James Shaw, Steven Burke, and Tammy Granger, owner of Ride EZ, the car service that picked Ryan up from the reunion dance. I was just getting ready to leave when a text came in.

*Are you still good to meet at 9?*

Shoot. I'd forgotten about meeting with Allie. I now wished I hadn't so blithely promised I had time to help her with her vaccination story. But I couldn't bail on her. Plus, I'd promised Ross I'd poke around a little and try to find out if something was bothering her.

*Absolutely. See you shortly.*

Instead of taking off, I treated myself to a delicious and nutritious Cheerios breakfast, plus a Pop Tart, for the extra energy. After that, I looked around at the beer bottle left by Gabe, the empty plates from our sandwich supper that I hadn't put in the dishwasher, and various other odds and ends that were cluttering up the kitchen. I tidied things up before Allie arrived. After all, if she admired me as much as Ross said she did, I really should set a better example.

By the time she tapped on the door, things looked quite presentable.

"Come in, and let's see what you've got so far," I said, leading her over to a seat on the sofa.

We spent over an hour strategizing the vaccination story. She'd come prepared with a list of who she needed to talk to and the questions she should ask. I suggested some sources to try, and some ways to fact-check the information she got, and reminded her to make sure she identified herself as a reporter before she set up any interviews.

"Feel ready to really dig in, now?" I asked.

"I do. I think it's going to be an awesome story. I want to show Maggie that I can do it. That I'm not just a stupid kid."

"She doesn't think you are, Allie. But people have strong opinions on both sides of the issue. Even if you write the fair and accurate story that I know you will, it doesn't mean people aren't going to come after you if it's something they don't like. That can mean some nasty phone calls and emails to the editor. I think Maggie was just trying to save you from that for your first big story."

"Maybe. But, thank you, for getting her to change her mind. You won't be sorry."

"I don't expect to be."

I was rewarded with a happy grin—which made me realize I hadn't seen many of those from Allie lately. Maybe there was something to Ross's concern.

"How's your new book coming?" she asked.

"Slow. But if my agent happens to call—and he's due to—don't be surprised to hear me say it's going great. He gets very nervous when I get behind schedule, which I am. So, I find it best to just reassure him and move on."

"He sounds like my dad."

OK, there was my opening to try some casual probing.

"Why do you say that?"

She sighed and leaned back against the sofa.

" 'How's school? How come that Aubrey kid doesn't come over anymore? Why don'tcha go to that new teen center, you could meet some kids there?' "

She did a fairly good imitation of Ross's voice and speech pattern. "I keep telling him I'm fine. The other day he asked me if I had boy troubles!" Her voice rose in amazement and horror at the idea of discussing romance with her father.

I took a step into the minefield of adolescent emotions.

"Well, do you?"

"No." She answered quickly and firmly, in a tone that said the subject was closed. Which made me suspect that I—and Ross—had hit pretty close to the mark.

"OK, well, that's good. Remember the other day, when my mother was going on and on about my crush on Ryan Malloy when we were in high school, and I said I wasn't that upset when he dumped me? Actually, I was. But I didn't want to talk about it to anyone back then. I just needed time to get over it in my own way, without my mother or anyone else trying to 'help.' Parents. What are you gonna do?" I cringed a little inwardly, knowing I sounded like one of those too jolly adults trying to "relate" to kids.

Allie was looking down, twisting a piece of hair. I didn't say anything else. After a few seconds, she raised her eyes and the look in them seemed both pained and embarrassed. All she said was, "Thanks for helping me with the story. I'd better get back downstairs. Courtnee's taking an early lunch, and I said I'd watch the desk."

"So, you finally decided to pick up the phone. It's not nice to ghost your agent, Leah."

"I wasn't ghosting you, Clinton. I've just been pretty busy, and I've missed a call or two."

"Am I wrong to hope that 'busy' means busy working on your book?"

"Well, some, yes, definitely. But—"

"Leah." He dropped the teasing tone he often uses when he's trying to gently nudge me into focusing on pages due. He sounded deadly serious. "I've got some bad news. Endres Press isn't going to exercise their option for your third book."

I felt an uncomfortable flutter in my chest and the urge to cover my ears and start humming to drown out Clinton's voice. I'd been counting on a rebound from the slow sales of my second book with a strong third entry into the true crime field.

"Is it because the sales haven't been great for *Family Secrets?* My first book is still selling all right. Maybe the second one is just sophomore slump. I can make this one better. I can—"

"*Family Secrets* is a good book. It just came out at a bad time. Everyone's into Hollywood crime stories at the moment. But I know now why Endres Press hasn't been returning my calls. They're in a massive reorganization. Your editor is gone, along with a whole lot of other people. They're in a very shaky financial situation. They want to put their focus on the star power of their best-selling authors."

"Of which I'm obviously not one."

"Hey, I didn't call to bring you down."

"Well, if you called to fire me up, I have to tell you, it's not working."

"No. Wrong attitude. I've already started shopping the rights to your new book. I'm taking your book proposal all over town.

But, sweetie, I'd love to be able to say it's in the final draft. Can I say that?"

I was only half-listening. What was I going to do? My first book was still selling, but for how long? I'd already used the advance I'd received for my second book to pay down the loan I'd taken out to buy the paper. I did a quick mental calculation to see how long I could last with what I had in the bank. Not long.

"Leah? Are you still there?"

"Yes, I'm still here. What did you say about a final draft?"

"How far are you?"

"Pretty far."

"Does that mean pretty far along to the finish line, or pretty far from starting?"

"I hate that you know me so well. But I haven't had as much time as I thought I'd have to get going. A lot of writers take a year, or two years between books. I've got a paper to look after, too. I—"

"OK, stop. I love your feisty little newspaper project, you know that. It's a great back story, sweetie. But it can't be the lead right now. I'm going to be selling my little heart out for your book, and you need to be writing your little heart out. Send me some pages. Soon!"

I went downstairs in search of comfort in the form of cookies or some other treat that I hoped my mother had brought in for the staff. She usually does on Monday mornings. I got to the break room just in time to see Miguel take the last bite of the chocolate chip cookie in his hand. The plate in front of him was empty.

"You realize that you've just consumed the only thing that was standing between me and complete desolation."

"Why, *chica*? What happened?"

"Oh, nothing. Everything. Endres Press isn't going to publish my next book. But hey, that works out great, because I've barely started writing it. But wait, no, it doesn't, because I need to get it written and about five hundred more books if I'm going to hold up my end of the Miller/Leah newspaper business."

"But why? You are the best reporter, the best writer! Why won't they publish your book?" The surprise in his loyal brown eyes provided some much-needed salve for my wounded self-esteem.

"Thank you, Miguel. You just earned a bonus. That is, you would if we had bonuses to give. They're having financial problems at Endres Press, and they're going to focus on their best performers. Which I am not at present. Clinton assures me he can sell the next book. The problem is, I have to write it. At the same time I'm supposed to be investigating Ryan Malloy's murder."

"What? You're investigating?"

I realized then that I hadn't talked to Miguel since I saw him at the crime scene. Prefacing it with the admonition that it was off the record and not for publication, I filled him in on my conversation with Joanna and my commitment to help Gabe.

"You can check with Gabe for comment—it's not a secret that James was brought in for questioning, but keep me out of it. Somehow, I'm going to have to figure out how I can write a book about a past crime and investigate a new one at the same time."

"No worries. I'll keep it low-key. But let me help."

"No. With all that you're doing at the paper, I can't have you do something extra for me—again. I just asked you to take on *Ask Miguel*, but at least that's for your real job. How's that going, by the way?"

I regretted having confided in Miguel, not because I couldn't trust him, but because I should have known he'd want to help, no matter how overloaded he was. If I could change the conversation, maybe he'd drop it. I got some unexpected help as Maggie, Troy, and Allie came through the door. I looked at the clock. Noon. Time for lunch.

"*Ask Miguel* is going to take over our website if we let it," Maggie said. "We've had more hits on that page than we have anything else, and it's barely started."

"That's great. Are we getting any emails coming in?"

"Are we!" Allie said enthusiastically.

I was glad to see that our earlier, strained conversation seemed to have passed from her mind.

"That's all I've been doing all morning. I've been screening them for Miguel into categories: romance, family relationships, job problems, personal issues minor, and personal issues major. Miguel wants to answer one from each on Thursday for both editions, print and online. The rest of the week, he'll just do a few each day."

I looked at Miguel. "You've really got this organized and under control, haven't you?"

He nodded with a but-of-course expression on his face. "I told you, I've got this."

"What kind of questions are coming in?"

"Oh, some are about bad boyfriends, or mean girls, or strict parents, or ungrateful kids, that kind of stuff so far. Nothing majorly serious, though some are kind of sad," Allie said. "It's kind of crazy what people will tell about themselves—although it's anonymous, so I guess that's why."

"Yes. It's been my experience that people will say things anonymously that they'd never say if they had to do it in public," Troy said. He'd been so quiet, I'd forgotten he was there —which is often the case with Troy. He's earnest, bright, and a bit clueless socially. With his carefully parted brown hair, his well pressed khakis and his always tucked-in shirts, he looks like the upright and somewhat uptight Eagle Scout his resume said that he had been. Still, I find his freckles and the way he pushes his wire-rimmed glasses up on his nose rather endearing.

"My advice, kids, is don't say anything you wouldn't want to see on the front page of the *New York Times*," Maggie said. "Because things have a way of coming out. And thank goodness for that, because finding the truth beneath the surface is our bread and butter." She walked over to the refrigerator, pulled out a brown paper bag, and sat down to eat the sandwich it contained.

Her move toward the food seemed to animate everyone else. Allie got a bag of chips from the snack machine and poured some coffee from the pot on the counter. Troy heated a container of what looked like green-tinged tofu and smelled strongly of broccoli and garlic in the microwave. Miguel, apparently satisfied by my mother's cookies, contented himself with a Coke from the machine. I got a Diet Coke myself, poured it over a glass of ice and joined them. Maggie often used lunchtime to get a rundown on where everyone was on their assignments. I had pledged anew to myself— after I had intervened in Allie's vaccination story—to stay out of day-to-day news operations. Still, I like to hear what's going on.

"Troy, how's your story on the Community Task Force coming?" Maggie asked.

"Fine," he said around a mouthful of his tofu concoction. "There's a kick-off meeting tomorrow I'll be at. This afternoon, I'm going to interview the assistant principal at the high school and Lieutenant Cooper for some background. I've already talked to a couple of parents."

"Good. What about talking to some kids from the high school? Find out what they think about it?"

"Yes. Sure. I didn't think of that." He turned to Allie who was seated across from him.

"Allie, where do you and your friends hang out in the summer? I'd like to find a group of kids together."

She seemed a little flustered as Troy focused on her. Did she have an unrequited crush on him? At least it better be unrequited. Troy wasn't that much older than Allie. He was just twenty-one, but at Allie's age, a six-year difference is a bridge too far.

"Umm, well, some of the kids like to ride the bike trail out to Founders Park, and then they hang out at the picnic tables near that little snack stand there. And nerds like me go to the Young Adult Book Club at the library on Thursday nights. And there's always some kids at the Teen Center the Methodist Church runs. It sounds basic, but it's pretty cool."

Troy had pulled out his notebook and was jotting things down as Allie talked. When she finished, he gave her a sweet smile, and I saw him through Allie's eyes. A smart, "older man" who was kind, and kind of cute.

"Thanks, that's a big help. But what about you? Want to be one of the voices of Himmel youth? What do you think? Is sexting really a big thing at school?"

When Allie blushed a lovely shade of pink at Troy's continued attention, I was pretty sure I was on the right track. The moodiness Ross was worried about could be caused by the fact that she had a thing for Troy and knew he didn't reciprocate it.

"I-I don't know really. None of my friends are into it, that I know of, anyway." She looked as though she'd like to conjure up someone, if it would help Troy out.

"Well, you could ask me, Troy. I think I know a lot more

about sexting than Allie." An aggrieved-looking Courtnee was standing in the doorway, proud to be a self-proclaimed expert in the sending of salacious messages and semi-clothed or nude photos of herself.

"And just because I had to trade lunch times with Allie, because I had to drive my mom to the podiatrist, that doesn't mean I'm supposed to take care of everything, all by myself, at lunchtime, does it? I already helped three people, and all you guys are doing is sitting around talking and laughing. I can hear you way out front. How do you think I can do it all alone? Isn't anybody going to help me?"

So many replies struggled to get out, but I held them back.

Allie sprang up immediately. "I'm sorry, Courtnee. Sure, I'll help."

That seemed to be the signal for everyone to start getting up and moving on. Having successfully broken up a gathering of which she was not a part, Courtnee flipped her long blonde hair and flounced back to her station. Troy headed out to do some interviews. Maggie went to her office. When Miguel started for the door, I put my hand on his arm to stop him.

"I meant it. You've got enough going on. I can't let you take on helping me, too. I've got this."

"Hey, did you forget? I'm *Ask Miguel*. I'm the one with all the answers. And my answer to you, *chica*, is 'Oh, I will be helping'. Count on it."

Actually, I was pleased that Miguel was insisting on helping me, despite his heavy workload. I didn't want to take advantage of him, but I was going to need some backup if I wanted to keep my promises to Joanna and Gabe—and Clinton.

## 17

My first interview had to be with James Shaw. He lived on a dusty, dirt and gravel country road outside of Himmel. Heat radiated off a cracked asphalt path that had a spongy feel under my feet as I followed it to the house. I knocked on the aluminum-framed screen door and took in my surroundings as I waited for James. His nondescript, faded-blue ranch-style house could use a power wash. The lawn was mostly dirt and crabgrass. A half-hearted bed of drooping flowers had given up the struggle against an invading force of aggressive weeds. The whole aspect of James's home seemed a sad reflection of where his life was at the moment.

He didn't answer my knock, but I knew from the parked pickup in the driveway that he was home. I pounded again, harder, and this time I called through the screen, "James! Hello? James! It's Leah Nash. I'm not leaving until I talk to you, so you might as well come to the door."

A few seconds later I stepped back as he appeared behind the screen. He pushed the door open and said, "Hi, Leah. Come in."

His hair was wet, as though he'd recently exited the shower, and he wore a red UW T-shirt over a pair of black shorts. He was unshaven, but not in a sexy stubble way, more in a bleary-eyed, life-sucks-so-why-bother way. As I followed him inside, my eyes were drawn to the prosthesis attached below his right knee. I'd only ever seen James wearing jeans or khakis after the accident. His strength and his natural grace as an athlete meant he walked smoothly, with an almost imperceptible limp. It was easy to forget he had an artificial limb. But today the metal and leather miracle that enabled him to walk, though not to play pro football, was on display.

Uncluttered is the kindest way to describe the living room he led me to. The laminate wood flooring in a light oak color was bare, no area rugs in sight. A brown recliner upholstered in corduroy sat in one corner, angled toward the television mounted on the opposite wall. Next to it was a tray table on which rested a sweaty glass containing half-melted ice cubes and an amber liquid.

A built-in bookshelf behind the chair held textbooks and a few novels, as well as a photo of an older couple I recognized as James's parents. No pictures on the walls, no other family photos, there was nothing else in the room but an old couch with plaid upholstery. Although it was bright and sunny outside, the living room was dimly lit. A dusty Venetian blind the same color as the beige walls covered the only window, its slats half-closed against the heat of the sun. The room looked like the living space of a guy who had given up.

James motioned me toward the couch as he lowered himself onto the recliner. The fabric on the cushions was scratchy against my bare legs.

"Sorry, do you want something to drink?"

"It's a little early in the day for me," I said, giving, I admit it, a slightly judgy look at his glass.

"It's iced tea, Leah. I'm off the hard stuff."

"Wise choice. You're in some pretty big trouble, James. Speaking as a veteran of big trouble myself, I can tell you alcohol just makes it worse."

James and I weren't close friends in school, but in a class of two hundred and fifty kids, you pretty much know who everyone is. And James was a big deal at school until our junior year. Tall, strong, quick-moving, he played varsity football as a freshman and was quarterbacking when he was a sophomore. The only thing that kept him from being as popular as Ryan was his shyness. He barely said two words in class discussions, and if he had a girlfriend, I never heard about it. I know some of the girls liked him—my friend Jennifer was one. She swore he looked like the kid who played Kevin on *The Wonder Years*. I didn't see it exactly, but he did have a head of thick dark hair and expressive dark brown eyes. But James was just too shy to pick up on the signals—and Jennifer's were loud enough to require some serious introvert avoidance to ignore them.

He still had the dark hair, but his eyes held a guarded expression, as though he was on the lookout for the next blow from Fate to fall. Given his experience, I couldn't really blame him. Instead of being a top pick for an athletic scholarship at a great school like the University of Wisconsin, he had lived at home and worked while going to a UW branch campus to earn his teaching degree. When he graduated, he landed a job teaching biology and coaching JV football at Himmel High School. Honorable work, yes, but a far cry from his dreams. He married, but his wife had an affair and divorced him. Then came the email accusation and now, hard on its heels, was a potential homicide charge.

"I talked to Gabe this morning. Thank you for agreeing to help me. I'm sorry I didn't answer the door. I thought it was someone from *GO News* again. Andrea Novak. She shows up everywhere I go."

"Ah, Andrea. I'm familiar with her work. We fired her at the *Times*, but she found a happy home at *GO News*," I said. "My best advice is don't talk to her, ever. Not even to say no comment. She's a shark, and if you toss her any chum, she's going to gobble it and you up."

"Yeah, I found that out the hard way."

"How's that?"

"Last March I joined a mentor program for kids who've had amputations. This Andrea, she called and said she was doing a feature on a ten-year-old kid from Omico that I was working with. She wanted some quotes about him. His mom said it was fine, so I gave them to her. Then Andrea asked me about my own experience. I said that was personal, and I didn't want to comment. She said she wouldn't use it in the story, but Austin—the kid I was mentoring—was too young to really explain what it's like. She said it was just for background, to give her a feel for how I coped. That she'd write a better story if she understood better, so, I said OK."

"And?"

"And nothing, right then. She did a nice story on Austin. I kind of forgot I'd even talked to her. But then all hell broke loose at the end of the school year over the email that got sent to Emily Farrell. That's when Andrea used all the stuff I told her in a big story about the predator schoolteacher. Didn't you read it?"

"I try not to read *GO News*. It's bad for my mental health. I know they ran a pretty harsh story, but I stuck with the *Times* reporting. I didn't read theirs."

"Harsh is one way to put it. Things weren't going that great the day I talked to her, and I'd had a beer ... or three, or four, when she called. I was pretty frank."

"Like how frank? About what?"

"Extremely frank, about everything. I said I hated being held up as a role model for how you can adjust to losing a limb. I said everything was harder, from getting up in the morning to having sex with your wife. I told her I'd been so depressed I considered suicide. That in the beginning I only made it through because of my parents, and what it would do to them if I killed myself. And even now, all this time later, some days are so hard I wish I was dead.

"I said that every time I strap on my prosthesis in the morning or take it off at night I'm reminded how much I've lost. That sometimes the anger and resentment I feel at every able-bodied man I see is overwhelming. She used all of that and then some. Made it sound like I was some crazed 'handicapped' pervert who couldn't relate to women his own age, so I took out my aggression sexually on young girls by trying to ruin their lives."

"Man, James," I said, "That story must have been brutal."

"It was. My mom cried when she read it. I called *GO News,* asked them what the hell? Spencer Karr asked if I said it. I said yeah. He asked did Andrea agree it was off the record. I told him not those specific words, but she knew what I meant. He said if she didn't promise off the record, then it was on me. They could use whatever I said. I was so mad I hung up before I made things worse."

"Good thinking."

"But since then, Andrea's texted me, and called me, and emailed me to say she's sorry I 'misunderstood' and she'd love to give me a chance to clear things up."

"Don't do it!"

"I won't. But like everything else in my life now, it doesn't matter. They've still got everything I said before, and that's going to make a real nice addition to the story they do when I get arrested for Ryan's murder."

"Hey, hey, let's not go there yet."

He looked steadily at me for a few seconds before shaking his head. "Don't, Leah. You know, and I know, it's coming. Gabe knows it, too. I didn't send a sexual email to Emily Farrell. The only thing I've ever sent her are what I send all the kids: reminders when papers are due, or study guides for a test, or something else to do with their class. Nothing personal of any kind, ever. And I didn't kill Ryan.

"But no matter how good a lawyer Gabe is, there's no way to prove either one. People have already made up their minds about the email, and they're gonna do the same thing about Ryan's murder. I'm finally getting the message—I may as well just stay down, because every time I try to stand, I get hit in the head with a two by four. Ever since the email accusation, no one talks to me. They whisper behind my back, or they post terrible things on the web. The 'brave' ones say something nasty to my face. Not one person has come up to me and said they believe I didn't do it. Not one."

I hated the resignation in his voice, but I understood why it was there.

"James, you hired Gabe, and Gabe hired me. You do what you need to do, feel how you have to feel. But Gabe is going to mount the best defense he can for you, and I'm going to give him as much information as I can to help him do it. Still, even putting the email stuff aside, you're in a hell of a mess."

"I don't need you to tell me that. But what am I supposed to do? What can I do? I can't prove I didn't send the email, and I can't prove I didn't kill Ryan."

"Not if we don't get to work, you can't. Let's talk about Ryan. Now, you told Gabe that you drank too much Saturday—I don't think anyone who saw you would dispute that. And because your judgment was so messed up, you decided to go to the dinner dance and catch up with Ryan. You hadn't talked to him since he moved away sixteen years ago, but you out of the blue felt the need to see him. Do I have that right?"

"Basically, yeah. You drink too much, you do dumb things, you know?"

"Oh, I know. But when you saw Ryan at the reunion, you went pretty quickly from saying hello to throwing punches. What did he say to you?"

"Nothing. That was what made me mad. He acted like I wasn't even worth looking at, like he didn't recognize me."

"That's what he did to Gina Cox the night before."

"I know. I mean, that's what I heard from some people."

A little bell went off in my brain.

"Which 'some people' would that be, James? You just told me everyone either gives you a wide berth, or they insult you. So, who was it you had a casual chat with about the reception Friday night?"

His face flushed, but he fixed me with a defiant stare. What was he hiding, and why?

"I'm on your side, James. So is Gabe. You do understand that, right?"

No answer, but he lowered his eyes and stared into his now empty iced tea glass.

"All right, let's break this down. Who might talk to you, when no one else will? Someone who knows what it's like to be shunned, right? It's Gina, isn't it? You saw Gina, and she told you what Ryan had done to her."

Still no answer.

"You used to work at her dad's hardware store. So did she. Did you know about her and Ryan at the time?"

"Oh, yeah. I knew." He looked up and I was surprised at the anger that flared in eyes that had been so dull with despair a moment before.

"I knew, because Ryan treated me as bad as he treated you

back then. I told him I really liked Gina, but that I was afraid she'd be turned off because of my leg. I thought any girl would be. But Ryan said he'd talk to her, tell her what a good guy I was, try to get her to go out with me. Afterward, he said he was really sorry. She thought I was nice, but she just didn't think she could handle the leg thing. I knew then that I was a freak, someone people felt sorry for, not a whole person anymore."

"James—"

He waved off my sympathy.

"The next day, I went into the stockroom at the hardware store. Gina was there. So was Ryan. They were all over each other. Gina was just another girl to Ryan, but she was special to me. He knew that. He could have any girl he wanted, and he chose the only one that I cared about."

"Ryan was an ass, James, but that was a long time ago."

"You don't get it. Ryan got every damn thing he ever wanted. He wanted Gina. Why not? She was the most beautiful girl in school. But when he got her, he treated her like crap. Gina was too naive to realize what he was like. He pulled a con on you, too, Leah, and you were the smartest girl in school."

"Yes, he did," I said, torn between a small thrill at being declared the smartest girl in school (though I would've preferred the smartest *person),* and a slight pang that I would never be described as the most beautiful.

An off-the-wall thought came into my mind. "James, are you covering for Gina? Do you know something? Admit it. You saw her on Saturday. That's how you knew she had a run-in with Ryan on Friday night. Did she tell you she was going to see Ryan again?"

"No. I didn't see Gina, and she didn't tell me anything. I got in a fight with Ryan because I was drunk, and he tried to blow me off and it made me mad. That's all there was to it."

"You don't have the luxury of being Gina's knight in shining armor. The email accusation is bad, but a murder charge is infinitely worse. You could lose everything."

He laughed but it was a short, sharp bark, nothing funny about it.

"I'm a one-legged, divorced, JV football coach for a school that hasn't made the playoffs in ten years. I haven't done anything, and I don't have anything, and all that I can see in my future is jail time. I'd say I've already lost everything."

"OK, let's leave the Gina piece for now. Tell me about the mysterious guardian angel who picked you up and drove you home Saturday night after your fight with Ryan."

"I'm not making it up."

"I didn't say you were, but, James, you have to see it doesn't help anything if you can't remember more than that. In fact, it makes things worse, because it looks like you *are* making it up. Can't you flesh it out a little?"

"I'm sorry, I can't. Don't you think if I knew more, I'd tell you more? I just don't."

## 18

_____

After leaving James, I called Gabe on my way to Steven Burke's car dealership in Himmel.

"I think you're right. James isn't telling the truth about why he went to the reunion. I think he met up with Gina somehow on Saturday, and Gina told him what happened at the reception on Friday. James told me he used to have a crush on Gina. It sounded like he still does. Ryan was supposed to help him get together with her back in high school, and instead he went after Gina—and got her—himself," I said.

"Killing Ryan would be a pretty extreme way to get back at him for stealing his girl—sixteen years ago."

"Yes, but that's not what I'm saying. Follow me for a minute. I want to take a different path."

"Point the way."

"What if James's motive for lying is that he's protecting Gina? We don't know what she said to him when they talked. What if she told him how angry she still was? How she blamed Ryan for the way her life has turned out? What if, when she sobered up, she still had all the anger and desire for revenge that everyone heard her yelling about Friday night, and James listened to it all. Would it be so weird for him to think that she killed Ryan?"

"So he's willing to take the blame, even after she chose Ryan over him? That's some serious unrequited love."

"I hear you. But you should have heard James today. I don't think he ever got over Gina. And he's pretty convinced there's no way for him to get off the down bound train that he's on. If he has to go to prison for the rest of his life, maybe he thinks it's worth it to save Gina from getting on that train instead. I'm not saying it's the right answer. I'm just saying it's a possible one."

He thought about that for a minute, then said, "OK. Who's next on your list, Gina?"

"Steven Burke. I want to see what else he can give me on his little brother—excuse me, little stepbrother. After that I'll go to see Joanna and let her know that I'm working with you. And I have to remember to tell Ross what I'm doing, too. Oh, and with all the fun my day's been so far, I forgot to tell you how it started."

I gave him the sad news about my lost book contract, and my need to work on getting my third book in shape for Clinton.

"Leah, I'm sorry. That has to hurt—both financially and emotionally. Are you feeling like you need to step away from working on James's case? I understand if you do."

"No way. You can't dangle a juicy murder in front of me and then yank it away. Don't worry about it. I'll just have to put in some extra time."

"Well, when all this is done, maybe we can both reprioritize our schedules."

"I hope so. How about practicing tonight?"

"Let's try it. I'll call you later to see what's happening."

"OK. Well, I'm at Burke's Auto World now, talk to you later."

I hurried inside, but it was a short visit.

"Mr. Burke isn't in. Death in the family," said the bored

middle-aged woman sitting behind a sliding glass panel in the reception area. She half-turned her chair toward her computer and raised her arm to slide the glass barricade back, but I interrupted her mid-swivel.

"Do you know if he's at home today?"

"Nope. Couldn't say. Thanks for stopping by Steven Burke Auto World. Have a nice day." The monotone in which she spoke belied the message on the name tag pinned to her generous bosom: *"Great service is our business! My name is Sondra."*

---

The Burke house on Lark Drive was large, with a stone and wood exterior and lots of windows, but nothing particularly distinctive about it. Steven had lived there with his first wife Jill before their divorce. Maybe that was part of the reason his wife Lily wanted to buy the Dunn home on the bluff.

A bright yellow van with a ladder on top and lettering on the side that read, "Zimmerman Brothers Painting," was parked in the driveway. When I rang the front doorbell, it was opened by a woman in her late twenties with shoulder-length, luxurious, wheat-gold hair. Lily. I'd only met her once, at the open house we'd had in February to celebrate the re-launch of the *Himmel Times.* But she was memorable. Her green, slightly slanted eyes were fringed by a row of lashes so thick and long they had to be extensions. Her complexion was a tanned and luminous pink and gold, and her full, well-formed lips were expertly lined and colored a deep rose. She was barefoot and wore pink leggings and a white and pink clingy top that emphasized her large breasts.

"Bijou, would you stop!" she said impatiently to the small

white dog prancing and yapping excitedly around her ankles. To me she said, almost equally impatiently, "Yes?"

"I'm Leah Nash. We met a few months ago at an open house for the *Himmel Times*." Her face registered annoyance, not recognition.

"Yes?" She repeated with slightly more impatience.

"I'm sorry to bother you, but I'm here at Joanna Burke's request to speak to Steven about Ryan. Is he in?" It was a bit of a stretch, but only a bit. Joanna *had* asked me to find out what had happened to Ryan, though she hadn't offered Steven up as a potential suspect.

"Joanna's request?" Her perfectly waxed eyebrows drew together in puzzlement.

"Yes, she asked me yesterday if I would—" I searched for the right word. "If I would supplement the work the police are doing. She's very anxious to find out who killed her son. I'd like to talk to Steven if he's available."

"Wait a minute. Are you the woman from *GO News*?"

"No, I—"

"Yes, you are. You were in the picture with Ryan and that drunk woman who made a scene Friday night. I saw it online. I don't understand why Joanna would ask you to investigate. And what can my husband tell you anyway?" She spoke with a peculiar sort of drawl, as though she were playing the mean girl role in a movie about spoiled rich kids. It was an odd affectation.

"I'm not from *GO News*. I have nothing to do with it. As I said, Joanna asked me to find out what I could about Ryan's murder, because I'm a journalist, and I've consulted with the police on a couple of murder cases. We help each other out." That was another slight variation on the truth. I doubted either Coop or Ross would consider our sometimes parallel investigations as "consulting," but that's how I like to think of it.

"I'm just trying to get some background on Ryan, other than his mother's perspective. I'd like to talk to you as well as Steven."

She looked at me for another few seconds then said, "Well, come in, I guess. Steven isn't here. I can't tell you much, though."

She must have seen my nose wrinkle as we walked through the door, because she said, "Sorry, the paint smell is strong in here. I'm having the living room and family room done today. We'll have to use Steven's office to talk. It's the only place except the bedrooms and the kitchen that isn't being painted, or taped off, or used as a holding place for furniture. It's total chaos right now, but we're in the last phase of renovating. We had to completely re-do the kitchen, all the bathrooms and the entire downstairs. Steven's first wife did all the decorating for the house herself. Hideous. I hired an interior designer from Chicago, and it's made all the difference. Still, it doesn't change the fact that the house is just too small for us."

"Yeah, I heard you were looking at the Dunn house. Now that's a big place," I said. I followed her down the thickly carpeted hall, and then up a set of stairs, Bijou still bouncing at her heels.

"That's the trouble with this town, everyone knows everything. Or they think they do."

Steven's office was a good-sized space on the second floor, with gray walls, white trim, and a bay window that let in lots of light. A sleek black desk and a leather executive chair faced the window. An area rug in a muted red, white, and gray pattern covered the center of the dark wood floor. If this room represented ex-wife Jill's "hideous" taste, I was on Team Jill. I liked it.

"Steven must have a clear conscience."

"Why do you say that?"

"Because he sits with his back to the door. He's got a nice view, but I like to see who's coming at me." I gave her a disarming smile, which she ignored. She gestured to two leather theater-style lounge chairs along one wall. They faced a large TV screen mounted on the opposite side of the room.

"We can sit here."

"That's a nice set-up for watching sports."

"Oh, we have a theater room in the basement for that. These are just the chairs that didn't fit when we remodeled. Steven uses them when I want to watch *House Hunters* on the big screen, and he wants to watch football or whatever."

That told me something about their relationship. Steven must still be in the grip of true love. Not many Wisconsin men would give up their big screen viewing of the Packers or the Badgers so their wives could watch HGTV.

Lily perched on the edge of one chair, half-turned toward me. The now-silent Bijou curled up at her feet. I twisted sort of half-way around so I could see her. The chair made several rude noises as my sweaty legs in their shorts stuck to the leather. I waited half a second before beginning, in the hope that an offer of cold water—which would have been welcome—would be forthcoming. It was not. In fact, she didn't even wait for my first question to begin talking.

"I didn't know Ryan well at all, but of course I'm devastated by his death. It's unbelievable. I just met him for the first time when he came to Himmel because of Joanna's health. He's an actor—rather, he was an actor, and I'm an actor, so we had a lot in common."

"I didn't realize you acted. Was that before you married Steven?"

"Yes, mostly. I did some community theater, and some modeling and commercials when I lived in Milwaukee. I did a few television ads for Steven's car dealerships before we got married. You've probably seen them."

"No, I don't think I have. Sorry. Is that how you met Steven?

Doing commercials for his business? I'd heard that you worked for him as an auto sales rep. Is that wrong?"

"I'm sure you've heard more than that. Probably from the witchy wives of Steven's friends. They think I 'stole' Steven from Jill. As though she owned him. I didn't go after him. I didn't need to. I took a job in sales in the Omico dealership—just temporary. That's where we met. Steven and I worked together quite closely on an advertising project, and one thing led to another." She lifted her shoulders to indicate that she couldn't help it if men found her irresistible.

"It sounds like some of Steven's friends haven't been very welcoming to you. Is that why you weren't at the reunion Saturday night?"

"No, they don't scare me, the insecure old cows. I just wasn't up for a night of listening to everyone talk about their boring, small-town lives—family weddings, their brilliant children, and the latest novel their book club read."

The scorn in her voice irritated me. It's true that the topics she mentioned form the bedrock of many a small-town conversation. Admittedly, they're not always stimulating, but they're the building blocks of friendship and a sense of community—no matter where you live.

"Luckily for me," she went on, "a friend of mine from Ennisville tore a tendon. She had surgery and asked me to stay with her on Saturday while her husband was out of town."

"Not so lucky for her, though. A torn tendon can be excruciating."

"Oh, Mandy was fine. She just likes being the center of attention. Always has."

"Did you grow up in Ennisville, then?"

"Yes, but I got out of there as fast as I could."

"But your friend didn't?"

"No, Mandy finally got Thomas Scanlon to marry her. He's

the biggest fish in the smallest, most stagnant pond you can imagine. She'll never leave."

"You and your friend aren't much alike, then."

"Thank God, no. Mandy is one of those people who keeps clinging. No matter how many times I try to shake her loose, she just doesn't take the hint. I'm going to have to get harsh, soon."

Himmel is almost a metropolis compared to Ennisville, a town of about two thousand people on the shores of Lake Michigan—except in the summer when the population swells with the arrival of tourists and cottage-owners. However, I wondered how long it would be before Lily would decide to "shake loose" our comparatively large town—and her much older husband. I wasn't liking Lily very much. And I was really thirsty.

"I hate to bother you, but do you think I could have a glass of water? It's just so hot out today, and my throat is really dry."

Her annoyed expression reappeared.

"I'll have to go downstairs to get you one."

I think she wanted me to say *Oh, never mind, then.* I didn't.

"Thank you, I really appreciate it."

When she left the room, I stood and wandered over to look out the window. It was a nice view—big expanse of fenced-in yard, lots of shade, beyond the fence a small wood, and off in the distance, I knew, lay a marshy area and then the Himmel River. As I stood there, I heard the rattling bugle call of a sandhill crane through the open window. I leaned over the desk, stretching and turning my neck trying to see if it was flying overhead. They look like dinosaur-time pterodactyls to me.

"What in the hell are you doing?"

# 19

_____

I turned so quickly that I knocked a stack of folders off the desk.

"Steven! I'm sorry." I bent down to gather up the scattered papers, which looked like invoices and business letters and other office-type stuff.

He took several strides and glowered at me as I straightened up with a fistful of them. "I'll take those," he said, all but grabbing the papers from my hand. "Those are confidential business files. And this is my office. Could you kindly tell me what you're doing here?" He wasn't shouting now, but he wasn't very happy, either.

"I heard a sandhill crane, so I was looking out the window to find it. That's all."

Lily entered the room then and handed me my water, but her eyes were on her husband.

"Don't be such a bear, Steven. Everything but the bedrooms and your office are a mess with all the painting. I brought Leah up here to talk," she said, putting her hand on his arm. Her words came out in a much more sultry tone than they had when she and I had been talking. It seemed to have the desired effect.

"I see. I'm sorry. It's just that with the painting crew, and the carpenters, and everyone else we've been having in and out the past few weeks ... as I said, those are confidential files. I'm sorry, I didn't mean to sound rude."

"Sure. I understand." I bit my tongue to keep from adding that he had done a pretty good impression of rudeness, for not even trying.

"What is it that you wanted to talk to Lily about?"

"Joanna asked her to help find information on Ryan's murder," Lily answered for me.

Steven's eyes narrowed and his eyebrows came together in a frown. "You're not writing a story for the paper, are you?"

"No, I'm not. I don't work as a reporter anymore, Steven. I own it, remember? But Joanna doesn't have a lot of confidence in the Sheriff's Department under Art Lamey. She's desperate to find out anything she can, as quickly as she can. I couldn't say no when she asked me to help."

"You should have. It can't be good for Joanna to brood over Ryan's death. The police are professionals. I talked to Art this morning. He assured me they're closing in on a suspect. Joanna, and you, should let them do their jobs. If she doesn't stop thinking about it, she'll make herself even more ill."

"How can she think of anything else?" I asked. "She won't have any kind of peace until she knows who killed her son, and why. If anything, it might be what keeps her alive a little longer. The hope that she'll get the answers she needs."

"And you're going to do that for her quicker than the police can?"

"I didn't say that. All I'm saying is she asked me to help, and I'll do what I can. That's why I'm here. To ask you, and Lily, about Ryan—what you know about what he's been doing since he arrived. Or if you have any ideas about who might have wanted him dead."

"I know who wanted him dead. James Shaw. Isn't that obvious? He attacked Ryan. We all saw it. And if David Cooper had arrested him Saturday night, Ryan might still be alive."

"I can see why you'd suspect James. He's a possibility, but there may be others as well. It's the truth you want, right? Not just a quick arrest. This won't take long; I only have a few questions."

He exchanged a glance with Lily, then said, "All right. For Joanna's sake, I'll answer your questions."

Before he could take the power seat, his executive chair, I grabbed it and rolled it over to where the theater chairs were, saying as I did so, "You don't mind, do you? It'll just be easier for us all to talk. I'll sit here in front of you guys, and you two can sit in the lounge chairs. Thanks so much."

I smiled brightly at them both. I had learned the trick of manipulating a situation by moving fast, adding a sweet *thanks so much* and a smile, from Sharron, a very smart, very Southern, and very competitive reporter at the *Charlotte Observer*. It didn't always work for me. I don't have the social skills of a Southern belle—but it worked often enough.

"So, Steven, Lily was telling me that she'd only just met Ryan a month or so ago. But you knew him for sixteen or seventeen years. What's your take on him?"

"I could waste your time and mine, Leah, by saying that Ryan was a wonderful person, not an enemy in the world. But I won't. He was a user. He used my father, he used his own mother, he used everyone he came in contact with. He had it easy all his life. All he had to do was crook his little finger and Joanna—and every other woman—came running. His acting career was a joke. If he was any good, he would have made a success of it years ago."

"Steven, the man is dead. And I've seen some of his film work. I think he had talent. It takes time for actors to make it."

"Lily, you sound like Joanna. Film work! You mean two lines

on a canceled sitcom, or a thirty-second commercial? Give me a break!" He made a dismissive gesture with his hand. "I didn't have anyone subsidizing me the way Joanna—and my father's money—underwrote Ryan. Yes, I had a small stake from my father to begin with, but I built my own career. By the time *I* was thirty-three, I owned my own dealership. What did Ryan have to show for himself?"

"You didn't have much use for your brother, I take it."

"He wasn't my brother. He was barely my stepbrother. He was the son of the woman my father married. I'm sorry for Joanna, but Ryan Malloy's death doesn't have any impact on me, personally. I'm not glad that he was murdered. But I'm not going to be a hypocrite and pretend he was a great guy, either. He was entitled, and spoiled, and he coasted through life on his looks, and what some people thought was charm."

"I have to say I'm kind of surprised, Steven. You were all in for Ryan after the fight he and James had Saturday night," I said.

"I wasn't 'all in' for Ryan. I was pointing out that Shaw should pay the consequences for starting a fight. Like I said before, if Shaw had been arrested and put in jail, Ryan would still be alive."

"Why are you so certain James killed him?"

"He had a grudge against Ryan, you could see that for yourself Saturday night. Ryan was driving the boat when he lost his leg. And Shaw didn't make much of his life after that. Now, he'll be going to prison as a sexual predator. Maybe he took his last chance to get even, and finally Ryan's luck ran out."

"How could Joanna be so far off on how you really feel about Ryan?"

He shrugged. "Well, I wasn't going to tell her, was I? What would be the point? Joanna assumed everyone loved Ryan the way she did. So, I let her. For most of their marriage, Joanna and my father lived across the country. How I felt about Ryan never became an issue. And I'm certainly not going to tell her now. I trust you won't, either."

And though Steven didn't mention it, Joanna held the strings of a very big purse. If Steven upset Joanna, she could do whatever she wanted with the money.

"Not unless it becomes relevant," I said. "What about you and Joanna? She said you've been very helpful to her during her illness. How would you describe your relationship?"

"Cordial. I do what I can for Joanna, because that's what my father would want. And because Ryan made himself scarce until it became clear that Joanna wasn't going to recover this time. He couldn't wait to get his hands on my father's money."

"Lily, you sounded pretty positive about Ryan when we talked earlier. Did I get that wrong?"

She looked up from examining her flawless manicure.

"No, but I told you, I didn't know Ryan very well. I only met him a few weeks ago. He was always pleasant to me."

"What about Ryan's social circle? Do either of you know if he picked up with any old friends—or new ones—since he's been back? Have any gatherings out at the cottage?"

"No," Steven said flatly. "If he was having people out there, we wouldn't know, and we certainly wouldn't be invited. Lily and I have our own social circle. Ryan was a lot younger than us—"

"A lot younger than *you*, Steven," Lily corrected sweetly. "Ryan was actually a few years older than me."

Steven went on as though he hadn't heard. "He took over the family cottage and what he did out there and with who is anyone's guess." He began to shift in his seat, and I thought he was getting ready to dismiss me.

I forestalled him by turning to Lily.

"So, it must have been a shock for you, Lily, when Steven called to tell you Ryan was dead."

"What? No, he didn't call. I was here when Joanna called Sunday morning."

"I thought you were staying with your friend Mandy."

"Only if she needed me, but by late evening I could see she was fine, so I came home. You have to set boundaries with a me-me-me person like Mandy, or she'll just take advantage of you."

"You should have come over to the reunion dinner dance then. Steven sat at our table, and none of us said a boring small-town word about weddings, book clubs, or grandchildren."

"I didn't get back soon enough, but I'm sure it was very nice," she said, her voice conveying clearly that she was sure it was anything but. "I got home at eleven-thirty, just a few minutes before Steven did. Way too late for the reunion."

I nodded. "Yes, pretty much everyone was gone or leaving by then. Steven probably told you that Ryan got a little buzzed. We ordered a car service to take him home." I turned to Steven. "You didn't happen to call Ryan later, to see if he was all right, did you?"

"No, I did not. I was happy to see my wife, because I hadn't expected her to be home. We had a cocktail together, and then we went to bed. Ryan, and whether he made it home safe and sound, was the farthest thing from my mind. He was perfectly capable of taking care of himself."

"Maybe not that capable. He is dead, after all."

"If you're trying to make me feel guilty, don't bother. It's got nothing to do with whether or not I checked up on him. I believe James Shaw killed him. He was angry enough at the reunion. The sooner Art makes an arrest the better," Steven said.

Lily chimed in. "We've already told the police all this. If you work with them like you said, Leah, I'm sure you can get any other information you need from them."

Steven and Lily had both stood up as she spoke. I'd stretched it out as long as I could, but this interview was over.

"Yes, sure. Thank you both. I'll be in touch if I think of anything else I need to ask."

"I suggest you check with Art if you need anything more. Lily and I have a great deal on our minds just now, as I'm sure you can understand," Steven said.

# 20

---

I turned the air conditioner on full blast as soon as I got in the car and drove out of the Burkes' driveway. I went just a short distance down the street before pulling into the driveway of an empty house with a for sale sign on the lawn. I wanted to write down a few key things while my memory was fresh.

Neither Lily nor Steven had been crazy about talking to me. Sure, that might be because—as they had repeatedly pointed out—they had busy lives, they knew nothing, they'd had a death in the family, and they really didn't have time for me. But it might be because one or both of them had something to hide. Why had Steven just about thrown a headlock on me, just for standing next to his desk? What was in those "highly confidential business papers" that just having me in their near vicinity made him nervous? How confidential could car dealership papers be, anyway?

My friend Jennifer had cast doubt on Lily's story about a sick friend, and after talking to Lily herself, I thought Jen might be right. Steven's wife didn't strike me as the type to give up swanning around at the reunion, looking fabulous and collecting admiring glances from the men, and envious glares from the women all night. Himmel might be boring, but she would have enjoyed being the show-stopping stunner of the evening a lot more than playing nurse to her sick friend. Unless, as Jen had suggested, the sick girlfriend was actually a healthy boyfriend. Lily's story warranted some checking out.

I put my notebook in my purse and started to back out, when I glanced in the rear-view mirror and saw a woman about to walk right behind my car. I braked, rolled down the window and stuck my head out.

"Hey! Cil, what are you doing here?"

She looked up at the sound of my voice and smiled. Cil Chapman had been a year behind me in school. She's tall, with auburn hair and an infectious smile. With her at the moment was a short-haired black and brown dog that looked like a cross between a German shepherd and a dachshund. His pointy ears stood up on top of his long-nosed little head, and his legs were so short he had to move them double-time to keep up with Cil. I got out of the car as they walked up the driveway to meet me.

"We bought the house just up the street about six months ago," she said, pointing to a craftsman style bungalow next door to Steven and Lily Burke's house.

"Nice! Who's this little guy?" Her dog was trying to hide behind Cil without much success. I started to bend down and offer my hand, but she stopped me.

"Better let him come to you. Little Bob is a rescue dog Jay and I are fostering. He's pretty skittish, but he's a sweetie."

"Sure," I said, straightening up. "Don't tell me, that's why I didn't see you at the reunion Saturday. You were dog sitting."

She grinned, "We sure were. We got Little Bob Friday, and we didn't want to leave him alone, or even with someone else so soon."

"You missed quite a night."

"I heard. Did James Shaw really attack Ryan Malloy? Or was that just *GO News* going over the top again?"

"No, it was for real."

"And Gina Cox went after him the night before at the reception, my mom said. That was a shocker! Who would've thought poor little Gina and Ryan? I saw her picture, she's still really pretty and Ryan is—was still really hot and—" She put her hand to her mouth then as she remembered that I was also a part of the Gina-Ryan story.

"Hey, I'm sorry, I—"

"Don't be. High school was a long time ago. Thank God."

"That's for sure. How's Ryan's mom doing?"

"About as bad as you'd expect."

She was quiet for a second, then changed the subject. "So, what are you doing here? House-hunting?" She pointed to the for sale sign.

"No, I'm poking around a little into Ryan's murder."

"Really? For a book?"

"No, I'm helping out Gabe Hoffman, the new attorney who's in with Miller Caldwell. He's representing James Shaw."

"James has been arrested? That was fast."

"No, no. He's just been called in as a witness so far. I'm doing a little background research, you know, who Ryan's friends were, what he'd been doing since he came here, that kind of thing."

"Don't PI's usually do that?"

"Yeah, usually, but I'm cheaper."

"Have you talked to Steven and Lily yet? If their stepbrother/brother-in-law hadn't just been murdered, I'd have a couple of things to say to my next-door neighbors myself."

If it weren't for my hair covering them, Cil could have seen my own ears prick up enough to rival Little Bob's. I played it cool.

"Oh, why's that?"

"I'm not crazy about the way they care for their dog. Lily has a little Highland Westie, Bijou. She leaves him alone in the backyard way too much. He barks to go in, and they just ignore it half the time. Digging under the fence and escaping is Bijou's favorite pastime. His second favorite is running over to our house and barking at the front door until I take him home to be let in. It happens two or three times a month. Sometimes, if it's late, I just let him stay with us. Last night just about put me over the edge."

"Why, what happened?"

"Little Bob's had a hard time settling in. It's kind of like having a new baby in the house. Finally, he tuckered himself out and fell asleep on the couch. Jay went upstairs to bed, but I didn't want Bob to wake up alone, so I fell asleep right next to him. I mean, I really crashed. Until Bijou started barking at our front door. I jumped up, because I didn't want Bob to wake up. Side note, I don't think he'll be much of a watch dog, he barely stirred. I zipped out, grabbed Bijou, and took him back home. All the lights were out, but I leaned on the doorbell, hard. I was pretty ticked. No answer. I pounded on the door. No answer. I was getting really mad by then. Why should they be sound asleep when I was outside in my pajamas in the middle of the night?"

"What did you do?"

"I took the spare key from under the fake rock next to the front entrance, opened the door, and let Bijou in. I'm sorry, but I wouldn't be sad to hear that he dug a hole in Lily's new carpet!" Her face was flushed with indignation at the memory.

"Cil, what time was that?"

"I'm not really sure. Little Bob fell asleep, and Jay went to bed about eleven. But I don't know what time it was when Bijou dropped by. I was only half-awake. By the time I got back, Bob was curled up in a little ball, shivering and crying. I comforted him for a while, then took him up to bed. If I had to guess, I'd say it was maybe twelve-thirty, one o'clock. Why?"

I gave her a noncommittal answer. But I was thinking hard and fast. According to Lily and Steven, they had both arrived home well before midnight, had a nightcap and toddled happily off to bed. It looked like that might be a big fat lie.

---

After I said goodbye to Cil, I drove over to Joanna Burke's house, calling Ross on the way.

"Nash, I'm kinda busy here."

"You're not the only one. Listen—but don't get mad and waste time yelling at me."

"I don't like the sound of that."

"I'm serious. I'm helping Gabe with James Shaw's case."

"I shoulda known you'd pop-up in the middle somehow. But you're early. Shaw's not arrested yet."

"But you had him in for questioning. And Steven Burke said Art Lamey told him an arrest was coming soon. It's James, right?"

"Your boy is in big trouble, I'll say that much."

"What if I have some information that might point to someone else?"

"What is it?"

"I talked to Steven and Lily Burke. And I talked to one of their neighbors. The Burkes have a dog who likes to tunnel under the fence and visit them. On Saturday night late, the dog showed up at the neighbor's house. The neighbor, Cil Chapman, took him back to the Burkes, but there was no answer when she rang the bell and knocked. So, Cil used the house key the Burkes keep hidden under a fake rock, and let the dog in. The thing is, Steven and Lily Burke told me they were both home from just after eleven thirty on. But Cil is pretty sure it was later than that when she went over. Maybe more like twelve or twelve thirty, and no one was there. Why would Steven and Lily lie?"

"People lie for a lotta reasons. Most of them don't involve murder."

"Maybe. But don't forget, with Ryan dead, Steven is the only heir to a lot of money. Four million dollars is a pretty good motive. The autopsy must be done by now. What's the time of death window?"

"Lameass is doin' a press conference in about an hour. Come and hear for yourself. You can wait in line with the other reporters to get the word."

"Come on, Ross. I'm not reporting on it. And you know he won't give out anything that matters. Just give me a heads-up, off the record. What was the time of death?"

"Sometime between midnight when Ryan got dropped off at his cottage and four a.m. That's as close as the M.E. is willin' to go. You know how those guys are. He was shot twice in the chest with a handgun at close range. I'm inclined to think those poppin' noises Betty Reynolds heard were gunshots. We found one other neighbor who heard the same thing, in the same time range, between twelve and twelve-thirty.

"I checked out the kids that were settin' off fireworks all week. Told 'em if they didn't come clean, I'd be talkin' to their parents, and they'd be lookin' at a fine of a thousand bucks a piece. That brought 'em right around. They were too scared to stop and think no way could I write a citation with no evidence. Anyway, they admitted usin' fireworks during the week—it was the fourth of July, after all. But they used the last ones up on Friday."

"So for sure it wasn't fireworks Betty heard. That means the real time of death was probably between midnight and one. If the Burkes weren't at home then, aren't you curious about where they were?"

"That's what one of their neighbors says. Maybe it's true, maybe it isn't. Just once, could you let me decide what I need to investigate and why?"

"I'm just being helpful. What about Warren Cox? What's his reason for being at Ryan's house on Sunday morning? Was it to punch him out for Gina's sake, like you thought?"

"I didn't think anything. I just said that could be the case. It still might be. It's early yet. According to Warren, he prayed all night over what to do about Ryan, for takin' his daughter away from God."

"What did God tell him to do, shoot Ryan?"

"Nope. God told him to try and lead Ryan and Gina to forgiveness through that church of his."

"I see. But when Warren got there, uh-oh, too late."

"Somethin' like that."

"Do you believe him?"

"Right now I'm withholdin' judgment."

"What kind of handgun was used?"

"Don't know. Nine-millimeter bullets, so maybe a Glock 19 or a Sig Sauer P320. They're pretty common home defense weapons."

It didn't make me feel very happy that James's missing gun was a Glock 19.

"Did you find any shell casings?"

"No, whoever did it knew enough to pick 'em up. I can't tell you anymore, and I don't want any of this in your newspaper, unless you get Lamey to spill it. We sent off blood samples to the state lab for toxicology tests, but I feel pretty sure sayin' the bullets are what killed him. Now, go bother somebody else. I told you before, I don't need more trouble for talkin' to you."

"All right. You go your way, I'll go mine. But there's one thing to keep in mind. Everybody assumes Steven Burke is rolling in money. What if he isn't? He's the sole heir to the family fortune now. There's no doubt Ryan's death has improved his life. Follow the money. Just think about it."

"Thanks, but I got plenty of my own thoughts without thinkin' yours, too."

"Fine, but don't complain that I didn't let you know what I was doing. OK, I have to go. I'm at Joanna Burke's now. Bye."

## 21

Wanda, Joanna's housekeeper, answered the door even before the bell finished ringing.

"I'm sorry, Mrs. Burke is sleeping right now. I don't want to wake her up. Could you come back later?" That was a considerable improvement over my last meeting with Wanda. Perhaps I was growing on her.

"Oh, sure. I don't want to disturb her."

With Joanna sleeping, and Wanda slightly less frosty toward me, it might be a good time to see if I could wrangle a chat with her. I had a feeling those sharp little brown eyes didn't miss much.

"I don't know what you're planning for dinner, but I'm pretty sure brownies are for dessert. What a heavenly smell," I said. "Nothing like a warm brownie and a glass of cold milk."

I'll never know if it was my winsome expression, or my growling stomach that won her over. I hadn't had anything to eat since breakfast.

"Oh, you might as well come in, why don't you? No one else is going to eat them. I can't get Mrs. Burke to take more than a bite of anything right now." She led the way to the kitchen with me following close behind. A slight breeze came in through the open window and wafted a rich, chocolatey smell my way. In under a minute a plate of warm brownies sat in front of me, and a tall glass of milk was placed at my right hand. I reached out for a brownie, took a bite and internally swore fealty to Wanda forever.

"Wanda, never have cocoa, sugar, butter, flour, and eggs come together for a greater purpose. This is the best brownie I've ever had." I wasn't lying either. And it got me my first smile ever from Wanda, who dimpled and instantly looked much younger.

"They're nothing special, but they're made from scratch. That's why they taste so good. I never use a box mix for anything. It's not how my mother taught me."

"She taught you well. Seriously, these are great."

"Have another," she said, pushing the plate closer to me.

"You don't have to ask me twice," I said, with the second brownie already halfway to my lips. "I can't believe anyone would skip out on these."

She shrugged and helped herself to one of her brownies as well.

"Mrs. Burke was never one for sweets much. It was Mr. Burke who really loved my brownies. Steven, too."

"Have you worked for Joanna for a long time?"

"I used to clean house for her before her and Mr. Burke got married. Then after that, they hired me as a full-time housekeeper until they moved to Seattle. I could've gone with them, but I didn't want to go so far away and ... there were other things. Then, after Mr. Burke died and Mrs. Burke came back here five years ago, she looked me up and asked would I want my old job back. I had to think about it. But when she told me Ryan was staying in California, well, that made the difference."

I remembered her comment the day before, about Joanna having no commonsense where Ryan was concerned.

"You didn't care for Ryan?"

"It's not my place to say," she said, primly.

"You really don't have to say anything. I used to know Ryan pretty well—or I thought I did. I dated him in high school. When the family moved away, he and I had big plans to keep our relationship going long-distance. It's not surprising it didn't happen, we were only juniors, after all. It's the way it happened that left me with not very fond feelings about him. Ryan turned out to be a pretty untruthful, not-very-nice boy. I haven't said that to Joanna, of course. But I think I get where you're coming from."

She nodded. "His mother worshipped him. He could get her to say yes to anything. Mr. Burke, he tried to step in a few times when Ryan was out of line, but Mrs. Burke, sweet as she is, was like a tiger if anyone criticized Ryan. I couldn't stand the way he pulled the wool over her eyes. I don't think Mr. Burke liked it either, but he sure did love Mrs. Burke. Happens that way sometimes, when a man so much older marries a younger wife. He just doted on her, so he let her make all the decisions about Ryan."

"Was Ryan the 'other things' part of why you didn't move with the family to Seattle?"

"It wasn't just him. I really didn't want to go that far away from my own family. I grew up on a dairy farm outside of Omico, and most everybody is still in the area. But Ryan was what you might call the deciding factor. And he didn't get any better with age."

"How's that?"

"I could count on one finger the number of times he came back to Himmel to visit his own mother after she moved here. She always had to go out to California to him."

"But when her cancer came back, he came back to be with her."

"To be with her money, more like. I love Mrs. Burke. She's been nothing but good to me, but she had a blind spot for Ryan. And I don't hold with giving money away from blood."

"You mean because the estate would have been divided equally between Ryan and Steven?"

She nodded. "Mr. Burke never could say no to her. Now, I could understand setting something aside for Ryan, but I don't believe he deserved to be treated the same as Mr. Burke's own son. And he sure never appreciated all that Mr. Burke did for him. I just don't think that's right."

"It's a moot point now. Steven will be the only heir. Well, Lily, too, by marriage I suppose."

"Hmph. She's just as bad as Ryan. Two peas in a pod, I say. Or worse," she hinted darkly as I reached for my third brownie. But they were small. No, really, they were.

"I saw her earlier today. She said that she and Ryan had a lot in common."

"Ha! So that's what they call it nowadays."

"What do you mean?"

She shook her head, her lips pursed together, before she said, "I'm not one to gossip. Let the Lord be the judge, not me. But it's right there in the Bible. Leviticus 20:21."

As I may have mentioned before, I'm not top of the class in Bible studies, but given where our conversation seemed headed, I hazarded a guess. "Are you saying Ryan and Lily were having an affair?"

Her body language couldn't have been more clear as she pressed her lips even tighter together, tilted her head to the side and lifted one eyebrow.

"Are you sure?"

"Sure as my eyes and ears. Ryan was supposed to have lunch

with his mother last week. He called and cancelled. Said he had too much to do for his movie project. She was so disappointed, she almost cried. Instead, she sent me to take him the pie she had me make special for him. She felt so bad he was working so hard. He was working all right." She didn't have to use her fingers to make air quotes around the word working. Her voice did the trick nicely.

"You saw Lily and Ryan together?"

"Heard them is more like it. His car was in the driveway when I got there. That's strange, I thought, when he's got a perfectly good garage. I had my suspicions about them already. So, I peeked in the garage window, and there was her fancy car with the special license plate. SEXY-L."

"But maybe Steven was driving Lily's car for some reason, and he was the one visiting Ryan. Or, if it really was Lily, maybe they were talking about the movie he wanted to produce. Lily could have been asking him to cast her in a part." I didn't believe it, but I thought Wanda might provide more detail if she was defending her position.

"Ha! I'm not so old I don't know what a man and woman having sex sounds like. When I knocked on the door, the windows were open, and they weren't too quiet. But I stayed there," she said, with what I can only describe as grim satis-faction.

"Finally, Ryan came to the door with just a pair of shorts on. He smiles at me like the cat that's got the canary. 'Sorry, Wanda, I'd invite you in, but I've got a friend here,' he says. As if I'd want to come in. I just gave him the pie and left, but as I'm going, I hear her calling for him to come back. And I know that voice. It was Miss Snooty herself."

"Wasn't Ryan worried that you'd tell someone? Like his mother?"

"He knew I wouldn't. She wouldn't believe it, for one thing, probably not even if she saw them together with her own eyes. Or if she did, she'd make some excuse for him. There was no point in upsetting her. And don't you tell her either, especially now."

I nodded. I wouldn't tell Joanna, but I was definitely going to pursue this lead and see where I landed. If it came to nothing, she'd never know. If it came to something, there was no way she could be kept in the dark, but it would be the police, not me, who told her.

"Do you think Steven knows?"

"No. If he did, he wouldn't be giving that Lily every little thing—and every big thing—that takes her fancy. He bought her one of those condos in Colorado or Utah, or one of those places where everybody skis, for a wedding present. What's wrong with going over to La Crosse, I say? You can get a real nice deal there. Ski any time you like, and you don't have to pay almost half a million dollars for it. And now she's got him tearing up that nice house Steven and his first wife Jill lived in."

"Yeah, they were doing a lot of painting today when I was there."

"That's not all. *She* had to have a whole new room built, for her clothes! My brother Bernie did the work—she changed her mind and he had to pull the built-in shelves out three times! A whole room for a closet! I've never heard of such a thing. And Bernie still hasn't got paid for it."

I continued to stoke Wanda's animosity to see what additional flames might shoot up.

"I heard they're looking at buying the Dunn house. It's listed at over a million."

"He's going to be sorry he ever took up with her, if you ask me. Steven won't be the first man led to the poor house by a woman no better than she should be."

"Well, he must be willing," I said.

"That's what she's counting on. But she'll run through his money and leave him flat. I've seen it before."

I nodded to show my support for her position. She continued.

"And that's too bad, it really is. Mr. Burke, senior that is, he worked hard all his life to make that money. And Steven, he's a hard worker, too, I'll give him that, even though he did run out on that nice wife of his for this one. To be fair, though, he's been a help to Mrs. Burke, making sure she gets to her doctor appointments and taking care of her mail and paperwork and such for her. You'd think that wife of his that doesn't work could come by and visit or lend a hand one of these times, but I suppose she's too busy gettin' her hair done or her bikini wax or whatever fool thing they do these days."

I had eaten all that my stomach desired—though my eyes were still lingering on the brownie plate—and Wanda had given me plenty to chew over mentally, when the sound of a handbell rang through the downstairs.

---

"I'm sorry Wanda didn't wake me up when you got here, Leah."

I had waited in the kitchen while Wanda helped Joanna get herself around after her nap on the sofa, and now she was sitting in a wingback chair with her feet resting on a small stool. Although it was warm in the house, she had a soft pink shawl wrapped around her shoulders.

"No, that's fine. I didn't want her to. I'm glad you were able to get a little rest. I just stopped by to let you know that I'm going to be working with a friend of mine, Gabe Hoffman, who's representing James Shaw."

My announcement evoked a far stronger reaction than I had

expected. She leaned forward, her hands uplifted, palms facing each other in a gesture of frustration and incomprehension.

"But how can you do that? How can you work to protect a man who might have killed my son? Steven told me that he's the major suspect."

"Joanna, I'm not trying to protect James. I'm trying to do what you asked, make sure that whoever killed Ryan is found. If it's James, he'll have to face what he's done. But there may be other people who had a motive and opportunity, too."

"Who? Do you know someone else who could want to kill my son?"

I didn't think it was the right time to trot out Steven and Lily as potential suspects, and it wasn't really fair to them either, because I hadn't done enough digging to know if I was on the right track or not.

"I'm not sure, Joanna. Yes, James is a suspect, but there are still a lot of questions to ask. You don't want the wrong person arrested for Ryan's murder."

"Steven said that he was worried that involving you would make it harder for the police. He said I should remember that you're a reporter and that what you care about is a story for your newspaper, or a new book. I told him he was wrong. But now you tell me you're working with James Shaw's defense lawyer? I asked you for help, and now you're working against me." Steven must have been on the phone to her as soon as I left his house.

She was breathing harder and her face was flushed.

"No, Joanna, that's not true. I'm not doing that. I—"

"I'd like it if you left now. Please, don't come back."

## 22

I understood Joanna's reaction. But I felt bad about it. She'd been counting on me, clinging to the hope that I would find Ryan's killer. Then Steven had called and had stoked her up to believe that James was the one. So, when I told her I was helping Gabe, she felt like I had betrayed her. She was hurting so much, she couldn't hear what I said—or couldn't believe it, thanks to Steven.

As I drove into the parking lot behind the *Times* building, I noticed that it was just after five o'clock. I hadn't heard back from Gabe, so I called him.

"Hey, are you up for pizza at Bonucci's? We could make it later, say around seven? I'm not too hungry at the moment."

"It sounds good, but I have to pass. Just too much going on at the moment."

"Yeah? Well, I had quite an afternoon myself. Got a minute for a quick rundown?"

"Sure, what did you find out?"

I gave him the highlights of my visit with Steven and Lily; my friend Cil's help in discovering they were not where they said they were when Ryan was killed; Wanda's very interesting belief that Ryan and Lily were having an affair, and my unhappy last conversation with Joanna.

"So, in addition to feeling bad, I'm a little sad that Wanda will probably cut me off from any more brownie afternoons."

"You still have Clara Schimelman and the Elite Café."

"True, but Wanda would have made a great back-up. Are you sure I can't tempt you with Bonucci's pizza?"

"You can always tempt me, no pizza necessary. But, no, I can't make it tonight. And I've got court in the morning. How about a quick lunch tomorrow?"

"Sorry, tomorrow is going to be pretty unpredictable. People to see, things to do. I'm a busy girl. I'm investigating a murder, remember? Also, supposedly, writing a book."

"All right. How about dinner at seven? You can be un-busy with a little advance notice, right? And I'll make sure I am. I'll make you spaghetti bolognaise."

"Sure. See you at seven tomorrow. I'll report on my progress."

"That might take all night. Good thing you have a tooth-brush at my place."

---

I was disappointed that Gabe couldn't do pizza, but actually I wasn't all that hungry after my brownie extravaganza with Wanda. Besides that, I had some work to be doing. When I got to my place, I poured a giant glass of iced tea with tons of ice. Then I got my reporter's notebook, where I'd scribbled hastily written notes after each interview, out of my purse. I went through them with a highlighter, picking out the things that seemed most important. I transferred the key points to my trusty yellow legal pad and was just getting down to some serious bullet-pointing when my phone rang.

"Hey, Miguel."

"Hey! I'm right downstairs. I have to write up the press conference and post some photos online. Want me to come up when I'm done?"

"I'd love it, but I have to get some stuff done myself. I'm drowning in details—nothing fit for print though. Mostly inferences, oddities, and possibilities, with a bit of judgmental snarkiness thrown in."

"Tell me!"

"I will. How about breakfast tomorrow? I'll meet you at the Elite. So, what happened at the presser with the sheriff this afternoon?"

"Not too much. Sheriff Lamey said Ryan was shot by a handgun at close range. He wouldn't say what kind of handgun. He wouldn't give time of death, just in the early hours of Sunday morning. I talked to my friend in the medical examiner's office. She said between midnight and four a.m."

"Yeah, Ross told me that, grudgingly, but don't use it, OK? I don't want the sheriff to think Ross leaked it, and it's not critical to the story."

"OK. Sheriff Lamey also confirmed Warren Cox found the body. I think because Andrea asked him. Also, we all knew that already. I asked him if they had any suspects. But he would only say that 'all lines of inquiry are open.' But he probably means James Shaw, I think."

"I'm losing it," I said.

"I don't believe it. Why?"

"Warren Cox. Gina's dad. I forgot all about him. I should have gone to see him before I even talked to James today."

"There, it's proof. You need my help."

"No, Miguel. You've got plenty to do—which is why you're still at work at six o'clock. I'll get organized here. I've already started making a list. Wanda, Joanna's housekeeper, thinks that something was going on between Lily and Ryan. I want to see if I can get independent corroboration on that. I have to add Warren Cox. And I'm going to check on Steven's finances, and who the Ride EZ driver was who gave Ryan a ride home, and—" He stopped me before I went further.

"I'll take Lily."

"No, you won't. You don't have time."

"Too late. I already wrote it down. It won't take time. I'll just go to my Aunt Lydia's salon and chat. If there's something to know about Lily, someone there will know it. Unless you don't want me to go, because you don't trust me to get the information."

"Oh no, I know your ways now. Even if I can't see you looking at me with big, sad eyes. Of course I trust you. But it's like that thing on the coffee cup—*Lack of planning on your part does not constitute an emergency on mine.* I screwed up. You don't need to clean up after me. I told you this morning, you've got too much on your plate already."

"And like I told you, *chica.* Oh yes, I will be helping. This is easy, 1-2-3. No more talking now. I have to write and you have to organize. Change breakfast to lunch. I'll stop by the salon in the morning. See you at the Elite around noon."

And he was gone. And I was grateful.

———

After I hung up, I moved over to the window seat with my legal pad and pen. On the first page I wrote *Odd Things to Think About.* Then I started listing them.

- Warren Cox's alibi for Saturday night was God— impressive, but hard to prove

- Why had he really gone to see Ryan on Sunday morning?
- One possibility: to pick up spent shell casings from the gun he shot Ryan with
- Why had Steven and Lily both lied about being home when neither was?
- They were together, doing something nefarious
- They were each alone, doing something they didn't want known
- Were Lily and Ryan really having an affair, or was Wanda's dislike of them causing her to assume things that weren't true?
- See what Miguel digs up
- What if James wasn't making up a story about the kind stranger giving him a ride? How could we find him?
- James's lost gun was a Glock 19, which used 9 mm bullets
- Did Warren Cox have a handgun that used 9 mm bullets?
- Did Steven or Lily have a gun that used 9 mm bullets?

Then I went to a new page and made a list of things to do.

- Talk to Gina
- Follow up with Marcy White, see if Gina confided any useful information to her
- Ask Coop which Ride EZ driver picked up Ryan after the reunion
- Dig into Steven's finances
- Tell Ross about Ryan and Lily

- Talk to Warren Cox
- Spend at least a few hours writing on the next book
- Check-in with Allie on her vaccination story

Well, I could knock at least one of those things off right then. I punched in Ross's number.

"Yeah, Nash?"

"Hey, I had a chat with Wanda Strong, Joanna Burke's housekeeper. She thinks Ryan and Lily, Steven Burke's wife, were having an affair."

"Yeah? Why does she think that?"

I explained what Wanda had told me.

"So, if it's true, then either Steven, for jealousy reasons, or Lily, for lover's quarrel reasons, could have killed Ryan. And that could be why they're lying about their alibi. Because one of them killed Ryan."

"Maybe."

"You'll check it out?"

"What makes you think I haven't?"

"You already knew?" I couldn't help feeling a little deflated that my scoop was apparently old news to him.

"One of these times, you're gonna realize I don't sit around waitin' on tips from you. I gotta go. Bye."

I wasn't a hundred percent certain that he did already know, but I was a thousand percent certain that he'd be looking into it, if he hadn't already.

---

I made another call after hanging up with Ross, this time to Coop.

"Hey, what are you doing?"

"Getting ready to grill some hamburgers, why?"

"Is Kristin there?"

"No," he said, sounding surprised. "Why?"

"Because I need some help thinking, but I don't want to bother you if you've got company."

"No worries. Come on over."

When I pulled into Coop's driveway, the smell of ground beef grilling hit me as soon as I opened the car door. I followed the aroma to his back patio, where he sat in shorts and a T-shirt at the red cedar picnic table he'd made the year before. A Leinenkugel beer was in his hand, and a can of Diet Coke beside a tall glass filled with ice sat across from him.

"How do you want your burger?"

"I don't, thanks. At least not right now. I had a talk and eat interview with Joanna Burke's housekeeper not very long ago, and I'm still pretty full. But this Diet Coke will hit the spot, thanks."

As I slid onto the seat across from him I asked, "How's the Sexting Commission going?"

"It's the Citizen's Task Force. OK, I guess. We have the first meeting tomorrow."

"How many people are on it?"

"Fourteen members. Four parents from the local school districts, four administrators from the schools, four reps from the police departments in the county. A social worker from the teen drop-in center the Methodist church runs, and me."

"That's a pretty big group to work with."

"Yeah, well, the captain thinks I should add a few more. It's good politics, apparently."

"You're hating it, aren't you?"

He shrugged. "It's great, if you like spending all day on phone calls and paperwork."

"Well, once you get the first meeting underway, maybe it

won't be so bad. Some of the other members can take on a few things."

"Yeah, we'll see how it goes. Let's skip my day. Tell me what you've been doing, and why you need help thinking."

"Did you hear James Shaw was brought in for questioning on Ryan's murder?"

He nodded as he got up to take his burger off the grill.

"Gabe is representing him, and I'm doing some investigating, trying to find who else might have wanted Ryan dead."

"If I was Gabe, I might start wondering which you like best, me—or my cases."

"Good thing you aren't Gabe, then. And at least he trusts me when I get involved in his work."

"I trust you. I just can't control you."

"Is that a bad thing?"

"In a criminal investigation, it sure can be."

"Well, Gabe doesn't think so. Besides, Joanna asked me to look into it before Gabe did. She doesn't trust Lamey, and she doesn't know Ross. But that didn't last very long. She doesn't think I'll be objective because I'm working with Gabe, and Steven is pushing hard on James as the killer."

"I wonder why that is."

"I've been wondering the same myself." I proceeded to take him through my interviews for the day, including Wanda's belief that Lily and Ryan were an item, and the discovery that Steven and Lily were lying—well, probably lying—about their alibi.

He was quiet for a minute, then he said, "That's a lot of possibilities to run down."

"Tell me something I don't know."

"*Is* there anything you don't know?"

"Come on, Coop, don't tease me. I could use some help. I've got more suspects and motives at this point than I know what to do with."

"All right. You sure you don't want a burger?" he asked as he started on his second one.

"I'm sure. Just give me one bite of yours." It was delicious—crispy, caramelized texture on the outside, juicy on the inside. I gave it back, then said, "Wait a sec. Just one more bite."

He shook his head, pushed his plate over to me and got up to grill another for himself.

"What do you know about Steven's financial situation?" he asked.

"Not much, but I need to find out about it. Have you heard anything?"

"My dad said something about it a couple of months ago."

"Your dad? He doesn't even live here." Coop's father is a retired carpenter who moved to northern Wisconsin to be closer to his daughter, but mostly to his grandkids.

"No, but you know Dad. He likes to stay in touch. Probably one of his old coffee shop buddies passed it on."

Coop and his dad look quite a bit alike, but personality-wise they're polar opposites. Dan Cooper is a talkative, gregarious, happy-go-lucky kind of guy.

"Passed on what? Are you going to make me drag it out of you?"

"Dad said he heard Steven was overextended. That opening that third dealership put him in a financial bind. He wondered if it was true, that's all. He built the cottage at Gray Lake for Steven's dad, and did a lot of work there over the years, so he knew Steven as a kid. And with Dad, if he knows you, he's interested. No, let me rephrase that. Dad's interested whether he knows you or not."

"True. That's why he and I get along so well. We're both curious about people."

"Curious people, maybe. I'm not sure you need to stick 'about' in there."

"You love us, and you know it. And you make a great burger, too," I said, finishing the last bite of the one Coop had ceded to me, then smiling my appreciation.

He didn't smile back though. Instead, he got up abruptly and started putting condiments on a tray to take back in the house. "Things all settled down with you and Gabe?"

For a second I wondered how he could possibly be privy to my angst-ridden relationship conversation with Father Lindstrom. Then I realized that he couldn't be. Thank goodness. "What do you mean?"

"I guess it must be, if you can't even remember it. You know, at the cemetery, you were talking to Annie and it sounded like you were thinking about breaking things off with him."

"No, I told you it was nothing. Just a slight misunderstanding. But I want to go back to Steven's finances. If your dad has heard rumblings all the way up north, don't you think there could be something to it?"

"Possibly."

"Miller probably knows. He's wired into all the banking/financing stuff in the county."

"If he's Steven's attorney, he can't tell you anything. And even if he isn't, he's not one to name names."

"True. But I think he'd at least tell me if he's heard anything like your dad has. And he might give me an idea where else to look. Hey, as long as we're talking about things on my to-do list, did you happen to see who the driver was for the Ride EZ car that took Ryan home Saturday night?"

"No, I started to walk out with him, but he didn't want me to. I was just glad he gave up his keys without arguing. I didn't want to embarrass him as long he was was getting a ride."

"Yeah, you did good getting them from him. Maybe he wasn't drunk, but he was definitely buzzed. That reminds me, when I talked to Steven today, he revealed a major case of stepbrother envy. Even if money isn't the motive, he sounded like he could have taken Ryan out just because he found him so annoying."

"Do you think he might know about Ryan and his wife? I'd find my wife sleeping with my stepbrother fairly annoying."

"Maybe, which would be another tick in the motive column for Steven." I blew out a sigh so deep it made my lips vibrate.

"I've got so much running through my head that I may not get to sleep tonight. Which could be a good thing. A little insomnia might be what I need to get me going on my real job, which is writing books, as Clinton likes to remind me. I promised him I'd push hard to get a draft of the next one out to him soon. Endres Press dropped the option on my third book, so he's going to have to hustle to find a new publisher to take it."

"Why would they do a crazy thing like that?"

"You pass the best friend test. Your automatic assumption that Endres Press is crazy and not that I'm a terrible writer is very comforting. But, it's just good business sense for them. They're in almost as bad financial straits as the *Himmel Times* is. I'm not a big-name author, my second book has had 'disappointing' sales, and they need to focus on the writers who can bring them the most revenue. So, they cut me loose. But, Clinton's scrambling to find another publisher, and thank goodness he still has faith in me. I'll admit it, though, I did feel a little slippage of the ground under my feet when he told me this morning."

Coop's hand moved toward me, and he slapped my upper arm.

"Ouch! I'm not hysterical about it, you know. Besides, aren't you supposed to smack me on the face for that?"

"Mosquito. I think I got him before he bit."

Along with the departure of the sun on a humid Wisconsin night comes the arrival of the persistent little vampires of the insect world. I heard the familiar high-pitched whine near my ear, then felt a sting on the back of my neck.

"Maybe, but I think you invited an army in to avenge him."

Suddenly, we were both swatting at various parts of our bodies as the invading horde of tiny flying creatures proved that size doesn't matter.

"This is my cue to take off. Thanks for the burger, and for the thinking help. I'll talk to you later. And get some Citronella before our next grill out, please."

## 23

---

As I had predicted, I couldn't fall asleep once I got into bed. Ideas and questions kept racing through my mind. If Steven was the killer, what was his motive—money, sexual jealousy, or both? If Lily knew Steven had killed Ryan, would she really have given him an alibi for murdering her lover? I got out of bed and added it to my things to think about list.

I crawled back in, but still couldn't fall asleep, because then I started thinking about Gina and Warren and their motives. And then there was James, my main concern, with his super-flimsy story about a guardian angel who had not only watched over him, but had driven him home and put him to bed.

Finally, I got up for good. I sat down at my laptop on the theory that if I stopped thinking so hard about the murder, some answers would come. I focused instead on making real progress on my book. By the time the dark was beginning to give way to the dawn, I had written some solid chapters. Unfortunately, as I stood up and stretched, I did not also receive a flash of insight that brought sudden clarity to my confused ideas about Ryan's death.

I flopped down on my bed again, but this time it offered me

blessed relief, not tortured thinking. When I woke up a few hours later, I felt reasonably rested. A shower and some coffee revved me up for the day, and I pulled out my list and put things in order.

---

My mother had texted and asked me to stop in and see her before I went out and about for the day. When I walked through the newsroom on my way to her office, Allie was staring at a computer screen, a frown of concentration on her face.

"Hey, Allie. How's the vax story going?"

"Good. I made a lot of calls yesterday and got more information for it. I'm just trying to organize what I've got so far. Do you think you could take a look at it? Not now," she added hastily. "It's not ready yet, and I know you're busy."

"Of course I'll take a look at it. Let me know when." I smiled and turned to go, but she called me back.

"Leah, I heard that you're working with Gabe to help Mr. Shaw."

"Yes, that's right, why?"

"It's just, that is, I wondered ... do you think Mr. Shaw sent that email to Emily Farrell?"

"That's not what I'm working on. I'm helping Gabe because James is a person of interest in Ryan Malloy's murder."

"But Mr. Shaw wouldn't kill anyone!"

"I don't think he would either. But the police think he's a possible suspect."

"You mean my dad?"

"Sorry, Allie, that's all I can say about it. Your dad wouldn't like it very much if he thought we were discussing his case."

She nodded, but I could see she had something else she wanted to ask.

"What's going to happen to Mr. Shaw? Not about the murder, I mean about the email. It's really bad for a teacher to be charged with trying to hook up with a student, isn't it?"

"Extremely bad. If James is found guilty, he'll lose his job. He won't be able to get another one teaching, and he'll go to prison, maybe for a long time. Allie, do you know anything about this?"

"No!"

I looked at her for a minute. She gave me a clear-eyed gaze straight back—the same look I would give my mother when I told her that I was spending the night at Jennifer's. When in fact, Jennifer and I were both going to sneak down the back stairs at her house to attend a parentless party.

"Are you friends with the girl who got the email? Could she have set James up somehow?"

She looked shocked. "No! Emily would never do that."

"All right, I believe you. I believe James, too, but there aren't many people who do, and things don't look very good for him. I won't kid you on that."

She nodded but didn't say anything.

There was a good chance that Allie knew more than she was saying. But I couldn't pursue it right then.

---

"Hey, Mom. What are you working on?" My mother was at her desk, looking at a spreadsheet with the same frown of concentration I had seen on Allie's face.

"Oh, Leah! I'm just trying to make sense of these reports Courtnee ran for me."

"Good luck with that. What did you need from me?"

"Could you do me a favor and drop this box off at Mary

Beth's house?" She pointed to a carton in the corner of her office that was overflowing with naked baby dolls.

"OK, but why would Mary Beth want a box of dolls?"

"She's going to sew some outfits for them, and we're going to give them away to kids at Christmas. They're from Vesta's house. Some of the women from the Interfaith Council have been sorting through her things. She specified in her will—"

"Wait, Vesta had a will?" Vesta Brenneman had been an exceedingly eccentric old woman who had lived alone with her dog Barnacle—yes, Gabe's Barnacle—in a falling down house within which, for no reason she ever confided, was a large collection of unclothed baby dolls, among other oddities.

"Yes. She left the house to a cousin in South Dakota, and the contents to the Interfaith Women's Council, to be disposed of as it sees fit."

"That's surprising. She was always so cranky when anyone took food and clothes and things to her house to help her out."

"Just because she never liked you, it doesn't mean she was cranky to everyone. She just preferred to be left alone. This is her way of saying thank you. Now, I'll help you carry the box to your car."

As we walked out, I held the base of the box and she kept the excess dolls from falling out.

"I'm going to run over to Joanna's on my lunch hour today. Have you been by to see her since she asked you to investigate Ryan's death? I'm sure she'll ask me about it."

"Yeah, about that." I explained that Gabe was representing James and I was helping him, and Joanna didn't like it.

"Oh, no. Not that I'd want you to do anything else. I can't believe James would harm anyone. I feel for Joanna, though. She doesn't need all this emotional turmoil."

"I think Steven is the one stirring her up. He's got her convinced that James killed Ryan. Mom, have you heard anything about Steven's business not being as solvent as it should be?"

"No. He and his wife certainly spend money like they've got no worries."

"Maybe they don't. I'm just a little curious. Do you know Steven's ex-wife Jill?"

"A little, she's on the board of the community theater."

"Does she get along with her ex-husband?"

"I have no idea. Why?"

"I want to talk to her about Steven. I just wondered if she's likely to be protective, or vindictive."

"I'd put my money on vindictive. Steven wasn't very discreet when he left her for Lily, but I don't know Jill that well, so I can't say for sure."

"I'd prefer vindictive." We were at my car and my arms were getting tired. Also, sweat was starting to run down between my shoulder blades. Another sweltering day was well on its way.

"Mom, can you get the back door on the passenger side? I think there's room on the floor for the box."

She opened the door for me, and stepped aside, but not without comment as I wrangled the box into place.

"Honestly, Leah. Don't you ever clean out your car? I can't believe all this stuff on your back seat."

"It's my car emergency supplies. A blanket, a flashlight, jumper cables, a tool kit, an ice scraper, a bag of cat litter. A box of Pop Tarts."

"Most people keep their emergency supplies in the trunk."

"I did have all that in the trunk until I had to move it out, so I could put the nightstand you bought at Maggie's garage sale in it last week. Who needs Two Men and a Truck, when you've got One Daughter and a Car, right?"

Before dropping the box of dolls off, I drove to the offices of Ride EZ, located in the defunct Jorgenson's Tire Service. The sign for Jorgenson's had been taken down and replaced with one for Ride EZ, but it didn't look like much else had changed since the tire store had closed. The flaking paint on the pea-green cinderblock structure still created the impression that the building was molting. Inside, smells of rubber, oil, and gas seeped from the garage into the reception area.

The front door was unlocked. A glass jar of wrapped peppermint candies sat on a dented Formica counter, along with a stack of flyers promoting Ride EZ, and a plastic container filled with pens bearing the Ride EZ logo and phone number. Behind the counter was a wooden chair and a desk with an old computer sitting on it.

"Hello? Hi?" I set my purse down and leaned across the counter. "Is anyone here?"

A chair scraped across a floor somewhere beyond the reception area. A man in his late twenties appeared in the doorway. He had a thin-lipped mouth that he worked back and forth as he sucked noisily on what smelled like one of the peppermint candies, though it would have looked more natural with a cigarette dangling from it. His brown hair was slicked back, and he strolled into the room wearing a cocky expression on his narrow face. A dragon tattoo started just above one wrist and ended somewhere underneath the sleeve of his black T-shirt. Cole Granger.

"Well, well, well. To what do I owe the honor of Himmel's most famous writer comin' to my humble establishment?" Cole's family had come from eastern Kentucky, and despite living in Wisconsin since he was an adolescent, he still spoke with an Appalachian accent. I suspected he worked to preserve it.

"I thought this was your mother's business. Is she here?"

"You wound me, Leah. But then, you always hurt the one you love, ain't that right? I'm not workin' over to Timber's anymore. I'm what you might call the general manager at Ride EZ. Mama's stepped out for a little. Now, how may I help you?" He leaned on the counter stretching a little toward me. Instinctively I stepped back. He laughed, revealing surprisingly white teeth.

"Hey now, that's a dragon on my arm not the big bad wolf. You're safe with me darlin'. Unless you don't want to be. I was just gonna offer you a little piece of candy. I'm hooked now that I quit smokin'. You musta noticed my new pearly whites, all the ladies do."

"Knock it off, Cole. I came to find out which Ride EZ driver picked up Ryan Malloy Saturday night from the reception and drove him home."

"Well, now, why would you want to know that? Are you detectin' again, Leah? Gonna write another book, are you? We have already extended our cooperation to the po-lice."

He always exaggerated the word police, dragging it out into two long syllables, with the accent on the first syllable. "But I don't believe I can help you. Seein' as you're not a member of law enforcement. We assure our customers complete discretion. I can't be givin' out information about the who, what, where of things."

"Your customer is dead. I don't think he cares. Come on, you must have the driver's name recorded somewhere. Just tell me who it was."

He paused as though considering my request, then gave me a wolfish grin. "Why that would be me, darlin'. Now, seein' as it's you, and we got a special friendship, let me look on the computer here, and I can tell you exactly the time." He turned to the computer, clicked the mouse a few times, scrolled through the pages that appeared, then turned back to me.

"I picked Mr. Movie Star up at the reunion at eleven thirty-four. And I dropped him off at eleven forty-nine. All right here on the logs."

"How did he seem?"

"A little on the wobbly side, but he wasn't fallin' down drunk, if that's what you mean. Pretty quiet. Slept most of the way home."

"Were there any lights on in the cottage when you got there? A car in the driveway?"

"Like I told the cops, no, and no. No lights, no car. He got out and I left, end of story."

"You didn't wait to make sure he got in all right? You said he was a little wobbly."

"We're a ride service, not a babysittin' service. My work was over."

"Which way did you go out? Did you drive around the lake and come out on Washington? Or did you just go back to Marshall Road?"

"I went down Marshall, but I don't see as that's any business of yours."

The way he said it, I was pretty sure that he'd gone on to do something he shouldn't after he dropped Ryan off. "I just want to know if you saw any other cars heading in the direction of Ryan's cottage. I don't care what you were doing."

"I didn't see nothin,' just me and the dark. I went right home and read my Bible verses like mama taught me, and then I went to bed."

"Somehow, I don't think that's true."

"Now darlin', I'm truly offended that you would say that, after all we been to each other."

"We've been nothing to each other, Cole, and that's just how I like it."

"I know you're just playin' hard to get, but you'll come round one of these days. But you ever need a ride, you just give me a call, now," he said, taking a grubby business card from his pocket and slipping it into the front pocket of my purse.

A door slammed from somewhere in the back and a loud voice shouted, accompanied by heavy footsteps pounding down a hallway.

"Cole! Cole Rufus Granger, where is your lazy ass? You was supposed to pick up Austin and take him to his special camp today! You know Jimmy can't take him no more, and I told you specific last night that you had to get him. I had to leave my pedicure to drive him, 'cause you didn't show. I swear, boy, you ain't too big for me to knock you upside a your head!"

As the tirade finished, a fifty-ish woman burst through the doorway. She had a short shock of greenish-blonde hair and was wearing a bright red cotton dress. Her face was round, with close-set small eyes, and a tiny button nose. With her red-clad, round body, and wildly pumping little arms, she looked like an animated tomato.

"I'm sorry, Mama. It slipped my mind. Won't happen again." Cole bent down to give her a kiss on the cheek, but she swatted him away.

"You know this is my beauty day, Cole! Why I cain't have two hours to myself in this family, I don't know. Well, what are you starin' at?"

She had just noticed me.

"That there, Mama, is my good friend, the famous writer, Leah Nash. Leah, this is my mama, Tammy Granger."

"Are you the reason I had to leave with only half my toes done?" She pointed at the plump sandaled foot she thrust toward me.

"No, I just got here."

"Well, this isn't a social club. Cole has work to do, little as he seems to know it. Now, if you don't want a ride, you best be on your way. We got a business to run. Cole, I'm outa co-cola in my icebox, run down to the convenience store and get me some. Well, go on, now!"

Entertaining as it was to see the would-be gangster Cole reduced to his mother's go-boy, it was time for me to leave, too.

"If you think of anything else about the night Ryan died, let me know, will you?"

"You don't have to make up excuses, Leah. You want to call me, you just go right ahead. That's my personal cell phone number on the back of my card I give you."

"In your dreams." As I turned to leave, Mrs. Granger turned her wrath on me.

"Like my boy in't good enough for the likes of you? He's a hard worker and any girl would be blessed to have him, and he don't need nothin' to do with your skinny be-hind."

It amused me that Cole's mother had gone from berating to beatifying her son. And I enjoyed the part about being called "skinny," which I probably was in comparison to Mrs. Granger, though not in the world at large.

"Yes, ma'am. I have to agree. It's best if Cole and I have nothing to do with each other. I'm sure we'll both be happier that way. Nice meeting you."

## 24

Gina was the next person I wanted to see, and the Himmel Motel was right on my way back into town. The T-shaped brick building has twelve rooms for rent that are each still accessed by a heavy metal key, not a swipe card. A small apartment for the owners is located off the front desk area. The motel is just inside the city limits, in an area that was originally single-family homes, but gradually surrendered to commercial zoning. A few houses dot the street, but they're all rentals now. An alley runs next to the motel on one side, and there's a liquor store on the other. All the rooms open directly to the parking lot in the back. Two standing terra-cotta ashtrays occupy the edge of the lot as a concession to guests who aren't allowed to light up in the smoke-free rooms.

Inside the motel the rooms are nondescript and far from luxurious. Quilted polyester bedspreads in dark greens and blues, walls hung with generic prints, floors covered with thin, dark, geometrically patterned carpets. People book a room at the Himmel Motel because it's clean, it's reasonable, and the owners are accommodating. Not for the ambiance.

I stopped at the front desk to get Gina's room number. Gail

Ozick and her partner, Mary Ann Gilroy, own the motel. Gail, a chubby woman in her late sixties, was crawling around under the desk when I walked in.

"What are you doing down there? Did you drop something?"

She looked up at the sound of my voice and smiled. Then she hauled herself back up to a standing position, blowing a wayward lock of gray hair out of her face before she answered.

"No, this darn computer is on the blink again, and before I call to get it fixed, I want to be sure everything is plugged in. It's the first question they ask. Like I'm some kind of idiot. I know the darn thing has to be plugged in! Sometimes it feels like those young kids think nobody knew anything until they were born to explain it to us. But anyhow, what can I do for you, Leah?"

"I heard that Gina Cox is staying here. I just wanted her room number."

"Yes. Poor Gina. That wasn't a very nice article on *GO News*, was it? And then Ryan Malloy dying the very next night! You aren't writing a book about that, are you?"

"No, Gail. I just want to talk to Gina. How long has she been staying here?"

"Came in on Thursday. Planned to leave on Monday, but she extended her booking. Her mom is having some tests. You know she had that heart attack a while back. Gina said she's staying until the results come in."

"Have you seen much of her—Gina, I mean?"

"No, hardly at all. Some of the guests like to get a game of cards going evenings, or watch a baseball game on the big screen in the lobby. Mary Ann makes some popcorn and we all sit around and kibbitz, but Gina hasn't ever come. She pretty much keeps to her room. Her car's gone some in the daytime. I expect she's visiting her mother. She's nice, but not real friendly, if you know what I mean. I've tried to chat with her a few times, but she wasn't really interested."

"She was pretty quiet in school. She didn't even go to the reunion on Saturday."

"She didn't? Her car was gone, I noticed, when I did a last look around about nine-thirty.

"You didn't happen to notice what time she came back, did you?"

"No, Mary Ann and I were in our apartment. We're binge-watching *Downton Abbey*. I couldn't get her interested at first, and now I can't get her to stop watching. She has a crush on Lady Mary, but I think she's pretty snotty. We're on season two. I just love Anna and Bates, but his wife, can you believe her?"

"I haven't gotten around to seeing it yet, but I know Mom and Paul really liked it."

"Oh, you have to, you'll love it."

"I'll definitely check it out, but you were telling me what Gina's room number is?"

"Oh, right. She's in twelve, right at the end, just past the soda machine. I saw her car when I emptied the trash, but I don't know if she's still here."

"I'll check it out, thanks, Gail."

———

There was no answer at first when I tapped on the door. I waited a minute, then out of the corner of my eye saw the window curtains move. I knocked again, louder.

"Gina, it's Leah Nash. I know you're in there. I need to talk to you."

I heard the chain slide and the deadbolt lock click. The door opened. Although I'm not unusually tall, I felt like an Amazon as I loomed over the petite Gina. She stood with one hand on the doorknob, the other resting on the door itself, as if she were readying for me to attempt a forced entry.

"What do you want, Leah?" She looked up at me from under thick lashes that had no trace of mascara. In fact, she wore no makeup at all. Her light brown hair was caught up in a loose bun on top of her head. She wore a T-shirt and cutoffs, and her feet were bare. She looked a lot better than she had Saturday night.

"I need to talk to you," I repeated.

"What about?" She asked, her hand still poised to close the door in my face.

"About James Shaw. The police are trying to build the case that he killed Ryan."

She didn't say anything, just opened the door wider so I could step in. The drawn curtains darkened the room, but I could see that Gina wasn't exactly a neat freak. Clothes spilled from an open suitcase on the floor, a pair of shoes next to the closet slumped in toward each other, resting as they had fallen when they were kicked off. A melting bucket of ice sat on a small writing desk, along with a plastic glass and several empty Coke cans. The bed was made, but rumpled, a pillow pulled up against the headboard and a damp towel on the spread.

"You can sit over there," she said, pointing to a chair in front of the desk. She sat down on the edge of the bed, leaning slightly forward, resting her hands on her knees. She rocked almost imperceptibly back and forth. I pulled my chair closer, so that I was directly in front of her with a space of only about two feet between us. Unsure how long she'd tolerate my presence, I jumped right in.

"Gina, I know you saw James Saturday morning. He was in his front yard when you drove to your parents. You stopped and talked to him."

I knew no such thing, but given where the Coxes lived,

where James lived, and the shortest distance from the motel to
Gina's family home, it was a reasonable guess.

"Did he tell you that?"

"Gina, I think you know James didn't tell me that. But it's
true, isn't it?"

"Who says I saw him?" The words were defiant, but her
voice sounded nervous.

"It doesn't matter. I know you did. James is in trouble, Gina. I
think you can help him. You can start by telling me what you
said to him."

She got up and began pacing around the small room,
holding her left arm across her body as she rubbed compul-
sively up and down it with her right hand. Abruptly she sat back
down on the corner of the bed and began to talk.

"I didn't plan to go to any of the reunion stuff. I didn't even
know it was happening. I came home for my mother. She's been
sick, and I'm scared for her. She's not very strong. I know what
everybody is saying about me. But none of you know a damn
thing about my life. It hasn't been great. Nothing like I thought
it would be. Nothing like yours."

"Other people's lives always look better from the outside.
I—"

"No, let me finish. I know what the talk was after I came
back from North Carolina. 'What happened to Gina?' 'Gina's on
drugs.' 'Gina's a slut.' I wasn't on drugs. Though I was learning
all about drinking then. And I wasn't a slut, either. I was just ...
broken. I went with Mackie because he was broken, too. But we
were both too much of a mess to be with anyone. He ran out on
me in Milwaukee. Took all our money, left me with nothing and
no place to stay. I did a lot of things to survive, none of them
good."

"But Gina, surely your parents would've—"

She spread her arms, hands up as if begging me to understand.

"What, my parents would help me? My parents—my dad anyway—threw me out. And my mother, she was too weak. She's sorry now. I'm sorry, too, but that doesn't change all those years. And it doesn't change what Ryan did to me, and what my father did to me."

"I know Ryan hurt you, Gina. You made a lot of bad decisions because you were so heartbroken. I get that, but now you're hurting yourself. It was sixteen years ago. You can't let it define your life. You have to let go."

Briefly, she put her head in her hands and looked down. I must have really reached her. Sometimes, I thought, it just takes the right word at the right time. I mentally patted myself on the back for knowing how to get through to her. Until she lifted her head and gave me a mocking smile.

"I thought you were so smart, Leah. That's what Ryan always said, when he told me not to be jealous of you. 'Leah is saving my grades. I need her. You're beautiful, Gina. But she's smart.' Only you aren't very smart, are you, Leah? You can't even see what's in front of your face, not then, not now. I let go once, that's why everything bad in my life happened. I can never let go again."

"What do you mean?"

"My baby. I let go of my baby." Her eyes filled with tears.

"Your baby? What baby?" As I said the words, I knew Gina was right. I wasn't very smart. "You were pregnant with Ryan's baby, that's why you went to North Carolina. Not to take care of your grandmother. You gave your baby up for adoption, didn't you?"

She nodded.

"And that's why you—"

"Why I 'changed' so much? Why I stopped going to church? Why I didn't care about anything, or anybody? Yes, Leah. That's why. The last time I saw Ryan—I didn't know I was pregnant then —was the night before he left for Seattle. My parents would have killed me if they knew I was dating a boy outside our church. We always had to sneak around, but I didn't mind. I thought it was romantic. Like a movie. I'd tell them I was studying with a friend, or helping a teacher after school, or babysitting. On our last night together, I really was babysitting. Ryan told me to cancel, but I was the only person Marcy trusted with her baby, so I couldn't. He came over instead, after Marcy and Doug left.

"It was my last chance to see him. I cried, and he told me not to worry. As soon as summer came, he'd be back. And he'd get his mother to let him stay with his stepbrother Steven, so he could do his senior year back in Himmel. So, really, we'd only be separated for a few months. He told me to be patient and wait for him. I said of course I would. And I'd email him all the time, and I'd use my babysitting money to buy a throw away phone, so I could call him and he could call me, and my parents wouldn't know."

The scene she described was familiar. Ryan and I had much the same conversation, minus the throw away cell phone idea. Only we'd had it the afternoon of the day before he left. I hadn't realized then that it was because he was already booked for the evening.

"But he didn't call you."

"I never heard from him again. I emailed him over and over, but he never answered. The last time I tried, it came back with an error message. He'd changed his email. He changed his cell phone number, too. By then I knew I was pregnant. I was so scared. I found his mom and stepdad's home number. His mother answered when I called. She said Ryan was out with his girlfriend."

"That had to be devastating."

"I didn't know what to do. I couldn't make myself tell my parents. I started wearing baggier and baggier clothes. But in May my mom noticed. I was so ashamed for letting them down. My father was so angry. He didn't want anyone in the church to know about the baby. He said I had shamed him and my mother and our church. They kept asking me who the father was, but I wouldn't tell. Ryan had a new girlfriend. He didn't want me, and he wouldn't want our baby.

"They sent me to North Carolina, but not to my grandma's. To a home for girls like me. I had my baby, a little boy. In my heart I called him Caleb. It means brave. But I had to give him up. They wouldn't even let me hold him. They wouldn't tell me anything about who adopted him. I had to go home and pretend nothing had ever happened. My punishment for deceiving my parents, for shaming them, for turning my back on the church and on God, was to embrace my suffering. That's what my father said. But it hurt so bad, I tried to make it stop."

I remembered Gina back then. Laughing too loud, hanging out with the "loser kids," as we so compassionately called them, sneaking away at lunch time to smoke with the other kids on the margins, skipping class, riding on the back of Mackie's motorcycle ... going nowhere.

"Gina—" I leaned over to put a hand on her shoulder, but she waved me off.

"I did everything I could to stop thinking about my baby. But nothing worked. I tried talking to my mom once, but she just begged me to forget about it and come back to church. My father had never hit me, but he did when I said I hated the church and I hated them, and my mother cried. But I hated myself more. I knew if I could get Caleb back, everything would be better. Mackie said he'd help me find him. He didn't."

The despair and loneliness in those last two words was profound.

"What happened?"

"Lots of things. None of them good. Mackie left, took all our money. I was homeless for a while. I got a job waitressing in a bar. I thought I'd save money to go to North Carolina and look for Caleb. I didn't. I barely had enough to pay rent. I hooked up with one guy who had a place. He was an alcoholic. After a while, I was, too. When he left, I found another guy. And then another, and then another. And all the time, my baby slipped farther and farther away."

"You're sober now," I said. "What changed?"

"I woke up one morning next to a man I didn't know. I didn't even remember going to bed with him. I felt terrible, not like a hangover, but like my whole self was sick and disgusting. I just wanted it over. He had some pills. So, I thought, time's up. Let's finish this.

"Oh, here's a fun story, Leah. You'll like this. I can't swallow pills. I start choking when I try. So, there I was trying to kill myself, and I have to stop and crush the pills because I can't swallow. Hilarious, right? I couldn't even do dying right. I woke up in the hospital, and I couldn't stop crying. I was in detox for a while, and then they got me in a program. I've been working it ever since. It's why I came home. Step nine, 'make direct amends.' "

I didn't want to sound like a jerk, but she obviously had fallen off the wagon when she confronted Ryan. She read the expression on my face.

"Yeah, well, I thought I could do it. I mean, I knew I could talk to my mother, and I was prepared to try with my dad. But then I found out about the reunion weekend and that Ryan was in Himmel. I wasn't going to go. And then I thought, 'I've changed so much. Maybe he has. Maybe he'd want to know about our son.' I guess deep-down I still believe in fairy tales. I chose the reception, because there wouldn't be so many people there, and maybe Ryan and I could talk. I know I don't look so good anymore, but I bought a dress, and I tried really hard with my hair and my makeup. I wanted him to think I was still pretty. But I got more and more nervous."

I knew how the story ended, but she seemed to need to say it out loud. She stood up and began to pace again, clenching and unclenching her hands.

"I went to the liquor store next door. I just wanted a shot to steady myself. I could hear that voice inside say, 'No! Don't do it!' but I did. And, well, you saw the result. I was so far gone when I got to the reception that I thought maybe Ryan would even want to help me find our son."

She shook her head.

"So, when he acted like he did—as though he barely remembered me—well, I acted like I did. I don't know what would have happened if Marcy hadn't taken me back here. I was crying, and yelling, and probably not making any sense. She stayed right with me, got me in the shower, into pajamas, and into bed. It was the first time anybody had looked out for me in a long, long time. I don't even know when she left, but when I woke up with a splitting headache the next morning, the liquor bottle was gone. She cleaned everything, hung up my clothes, even put my shoes in the closet. She left me her phone number, but I needed more than Marcy could give me right then. I needed accountability. I got online and found an AA meeting at noon in Omico."

## 25

"What happened after you finished the meeting?"

"I felt a lot better. A lot stronger. I wanted to talk to my mom, before she heard about Friday night from someone else. I knew my dad was at a church retreat all day, so I went to see her."

"You saw James on the way to your mom's, didn't you?"

She looked at me but didn't say anything.

"Come on, Gina. James won't tell me the truth. I believe it's because he thinks he's protecting you."

"Protecting me? From what?"

"From becoming the number one suspect in Ryan's death."

She looked at me in bewilderment. "But *I* didn't kill Ryan. I didn't even see him after Friday. I told that to Sheriff Lamey already."

The way she said "I" made me ask the next question. "But you're worried James did?"

She looked away.

"Please, just tell me what happened between you and James on Saturday. If you think you're helping James, you're not. I have to know everything you know, or I can't help him either."

She sighed heavily, but then started to talk. "He was outside in his yard when I drove past. He waved at me. I'd been here for three days, and no one except Gail and Mary Ann had even acted like they knew me. It was the day after I humiliated myself. I was feeling pretty beaten down and pretty alone. So, I stopped."

"And?"

"And I guess James was feeling pretty much the same. He invited me in, we had some iced tea, and I made some joke like maybe after what had happened the night before, he wouldn't want to be seen talking to me. He looked at me funny. I thought it was because he knew and was embarrassed for me. But instead, he told me about being suspended from teaching, and no one wanting to talk to *him*, and he was surprised I'd stopped. I said I didn't know any of that, but then I told him about what I did at the reception. We both laughed then, not because it was funny, but because if we didn't laugh, what else were we going to do?"

"Is that all?"

"Mostly."

"Tell the rest, Gina."

"He said he'd always had a crush on me. But he was afraid to tell me because of his leg. And after Ryan told him what I said, he was glad he hadn't. I didn't know what he was talking about."

"Ryan never said anything to you about James, did he?"

"No."

"Did you tell James that?"

"I said that his leg didn't make any difference to me. That before Ryan came along, I liked him a lot. When we both worked at my dad's hardware store, I felt shy about talking to him. When I tried he hardly answered. I thought he didn't like *me*. He said he was so shy he didn't know how to talk to me. He asked me if it would have made a difference if I'd known that."

"And would it have?"

"I don't know. I told him it was too long ago, too many things had happened for me to look back and know what I would have thought or done. I was a different person. And then for some reason, I started to cry. He thought it was his fault and kept saying he was sorry. And then I found myself telling him everything—about Ryan, and the baby, and life after I left Himmel. He was so kind to me."

"What then?"

"He told me what Ryan had done to him."

"Done to him?"

"The boat. His leg. James doesn't believe it was an accident. He did at first, but later, after Ryan and I got together ... I don't think I should tell you this. It's for James to say."

"I don't think you need to tell me. Let me try this out on you. After James saw you and Ryan together, he was hurt and upset. And he started looking at Ryan in a different way. Ryan got almost everything he wanted. He was a good athlete, but not as good as James. That was the one place where James had him beat, and he didn't like it. Maybe it was spur of the moment. But Ryan gunned the motor, and James fell, and Ryan's attempt to 'rescue' him destroyed any chance James had to play football again. James couldn't prove it. He didn't even dare to say it, but it's what he's been feeling for a long time. Is that right? Is that what James told you?"

She nodded miserably. "Ever since I heard Ryan was dead, I've been worried. James was really upset at what Ryan did to me—to both of us. I know they had a bad fight at the reunion. If James decided later to go to Ryan's cottage ... Leah, do you think he did?"

"I'm not sure what I think just yet. Let's switch gears here. I want to hear more about your interview with Sheriff Lamey. What exactly did he say to you?"

"He said he already knew about what I did Friday night—

because of the story in *GO News,* and lots of people had told him about it. And he said he interviewed Marcy White, so I shouldn't bother to lie. He asked me where I was Saturday night, and I told him I was with my mother. Then, my dad came home, and we visited for a while, and then I came back here around eleven."

"And he didn't press you for more detail?" I knew the answer before she said it. Lamey was the worst excuse for a detective since Inspector Clouseau.

"No, he said he was going to talk to my parents, and he told me not to leave town. I'm not going to anyway. My mom has some tests next week. I want to be here for them."

"Just FYI, Lamey can't really stop you from leaving town unless he arrests you. That's only on TV, which is where Lamey got his investigative training, I'm sure. Maybe he doesn't need to hear more details about your Saturday night, but I do. I think you're leaving something out."

"I don't know what you mean."

"Gina, I'm not the enemy. Not yours and not James's. You already said you went to visit your mother, because you knew your dad wouldn't be there. But when he shows up, you just have a happy little family hour, and then go merrily on your way? I don't think so."

"Well, you're wrong then."

I went on as though I hadn't heard her. "It was the day after your drunk meltdown. You had just spent an emotional hour with James, learning some hurtful new things you didn't know, and reliving some old bad things you did. When you got to your mother's, you did what anyone—adult child or kid child— would do after the trauma you'd been through. You told her all about it. Including the fact that Ryan was the father of your child, didn't you?"

She looked at me as though I were a fortune teller whose

crystal ball had been hand-delivered by Nostradamus. Actually, it was just that some separate pieces of data were beginning to coalesce into information in my brain.

"Yes. She said she was so sorry that she hadn't stood up for me back then, but in our church—her church—wives are supposed to obey their husbands. My dad said I had sinned, and I had to take my punishment. When he said I couldn't come home, she felt like she couldn't go against him."

"Gina, did you really never come home in sixteen years?" My mother and I had had a very serious rift not all that long ago. For a little while, I'd wondered if we could ever repair it. But we hadn't been estranged for long before I had realized I couldn't live that way. I couldn't fathom not seeing her for years and years.

She nodded. "It was the way it had to be. We talked sometimes. But I was so messed up. It was better she didn't see me, didn't really know how bad things were for me. But it's going to be different now. Her heart attack was a good thing, she said. It made her stronger not weaker. She realized that she didn't want to die without having me in her life again."

As she said the last, her voice broke and I waited while she got a drink of water and then sat back down across from me.

"All right, so you had a good, meaningful, undisturbed talk with your mom while your dad was away all day at his church retreat. What time did he get home?"

"Around nine or so. I wanted to go before he got home, but Mom said I should wait. We should talk to Dad together."

"How did that go?"

"Like I expected, not like I hoped. Dad was angry that I was at the house. And he knew about me being drunk and making a scene. Someone at the retreat must have told him. He started on me about coming home after he'd forbidden me to be under his roof. I got just as angry at him, and I laid it all out. How it gutted me to give up my baby. How lost I felt. How alone. How awful it was when he threw me out. I gave him all of the nasty details about my life. When I told him that Ryan was the father of my baby, he really lost it. My mother had been standing behind me, with her arm on my shoulder to give me strength, I think. But I couldn't take any more. I started crying, and I ran out of the house.

"And what did your father do?"

"I don't know."

"You're lying to me again, Gina. You must have talked to your mother. It's been three days."

"Look, I don't know what my father did. I wasn't there. My mother asked me not to upset him anymore. She said that she'd do her best to bring him around. I don't agree, but she has to live with him. I didn't ask her anymore, because I really don't care."

"Gina, does your father have a gun?"

"Of course he has a gun. Just like about every other man I know in Wisconsin."

"I don't mean a hunting rifle. I mean a handgun, the kind you'd use for home defense."

"I don't know. But if you think that he's the one who shot Ryan, you're wrong. He's a hard man, but he wouldn't kill anybody. I don't want to talk anymore. I hope you can help James, but I don't know anything else."

———

Gina's account of the fight she'd had with her dad on Saturday night fit in pretty well with the theory I'd tossed out to Gabe a few days earlier. Warren would have been furious, and it would have been very natural for him to confront Ryan immediately. It seemed very unlikely to me that he'd gone to see Ryan for any

kind of civil discussion on Sunday morning, like he'd told the
police he'd done.

When I had pressed Gina, she clammed up, maybe because
she suspected the same thing I did. Even after everything,
Warren was still her father. It would be interesting to see what
Peggy had to say about things.

The Coxes live on a small farm that they run more for pleasure than profit. As I drove up, it looked like a picture from a
kid's book about country life. A rambling white farmhouse was
situated well back from the road, and behind and off to the side
was a big red barn. In the background were fields of something
—maybe oats or wheat? I'm a townie, not a country girl.

I pulled in the driveway and a collie with white and golden-
brown fur bounded up to me with a bark as I got out of the car.

"What's that, girl? Timmy's in the well?" I couldn't resist.

The front door opened as I patted the dog. A small woman I
recognized as Peggy Cox stepped onto the porch.

"Buddy, come here," she called. As he bounded toward her,
she stepped off the porch and said to me, "Hello, can I help
you?"

She was petite, like Gina, and pretty like her, too. The bright
sunlight glinted on the silver threads that ran through her chin-
length light brown hair, which was held back by a plastic head-
band. Her eyes weren't as large as Gina's, nor quite as dark, but
the shape of her mouth was the same. She wore a rosy pink
cotton blouse and a long denim skirt.

"Hi, Mrs. Cox. I'm Leah Nash. I don't know if you remember
me? I went to school with your daughter, Gina."

"Oh, yes?"

I wasn't sure if that meant, *Yes, I remember you*, or *Yes, why are
you here?* I decided to respond to both.

"I've just been talking to Gina. I'm investigating Ryan
Malloy's death."

"Investigating? You're not with the police, are you? Aren't you a book writer now?"

I really should consider getting business cards to hand out that say:

*Leah Nash*
*Non-Police Investigator*
*But Still Can Ask Questions*

"No, I'm not with the police. I'm working with an attorney who's representing James Shaw."

"Has James been arrested? I heard about his fight with Ryan. James was always such a nice boy. I can hardly believe it."

"He hasn't been arrested. I hope I can help keep that from happening. I wonder if you have a few minutes to talk to me?"

I saw her hesitate, and once again pulled out my trusty I-need-a-drink ploy.

"I'm sorry, but I'm feeling very warm all of the sudden. I guess this heat is catching up with me. Do you think I could have a glass of water?"

As I hoped it would, my request sent her into a flurry of apologetic hospitality.

"Oh, of course. I should have offered. Please, have a seat on the porch. The shade will help cool you down. I have some fresh-squeezed lemonade in the fridge, would that be all right?"

"That would be more than all right, thank you."

Instead of following her in through the screen door, Buddy opted to stay with me on the porch. I took a seat on a cushioned white wicker rocker and felt a little guilty. I was about to take Peggy Cox down a path she wouldn't want to travel and might find painful. Such is the lot of reporters, police, private investigators, and anyone else who has a job that sometimes requires poking the sore spots in people's psyches.

When she came back carrying a tray with two glasses of lemonade and a plate of molasses cookies, I felt a lot guilty. Nevertheless, I persisted.

"This looks wonderful, thank you. You didn't have to go to so much trouble."

"No trouble. I always have a pitcher of lemonade in the refrigerator during the summer. It's Warren's favorite. And I just took the cookies out of the freezer this morning. Too hot to bake today, that's for sure." She put the tray down on a small glass-topped table between us and sat down herself. I took a long sip from the glass I lifted off the tray, then put it down and picked up a napkin and a cookie. It would be rude not to eat one.

"Mrs. Cox—"

"Please, call me Peggy."

"Thank you, I will."

"I don't mean to be impolite, Leah. I'm just not sure why you're here? I mean, I haven't seen James—only in passing—for years. And Gina, she hasn't been home in a long while, so I don't know what she could tell you about him." Her voice was calm enough, but I noticed that she had picked up a napkin and was twisting it around one of her fingers.

"It's not really James I want to talk about. It's the night Ryan Malloy died."

She sat very still, but her eyes darted quickly away from me, to Buddy, to the floor, to the porch railing—as though searching for a safe place to hide. She settled on Buddy, calling him to her, and proceeding to take a deep interest in scratching behind his ears.

"Oh. Well, I'm afraid I don't have anything helpful to tell you. It was just a quiet evening here. Warren was at a retreat, and Gina and I visited. When he came home, we just talked some more, and then Gina went back to the motel. We spoke to Sheriff Lamey already." All the while she spoke, her fingers moved restlessly through Buddy's fur.

"I did say that I'd spoken with Gina, already, didn't I? Peggy, she told me what you 'visited' about. I know about Gina and Ryan and the baby. And I know Gina and Warren had words. Loud words."

Her hand stilled.

"Ryan wasn't a very nice person. I can see why someone might have wanted him dead," I said.

"Warren had nothing to do with Ryan Malloy's death."

"Peggy, I didn't mention Warren. Why did you?"

"Because you're coming here, saying things happened that never did."

"Gina isn't lying though, is she? She and Warren did fight, and Gina ran out of the house and left. What happened then?"

"Nothing happened. Warren and I talked a little more, and I went to bed, and after a while, so did he."

"How long was 'a while,' Peggy?"

"I don't know. Because I was sleeping. He went to church to pray."

"Does he do that often?"

"Sometimes."

"What time did he get home?"

"I don't know. Like I said, I was sleeping."

"What about Sunday morning? Why did Warren go to Ryan's cottage?"

"He went there because he wanted to invite him to church."

That was basically what Ross said Warren had told him. I still didn't believe it.

"I'm sorry, Peggy, but that doesn't make sense. You and Warren find out that Ryan was the father of Gina's baby, that he was the cause of a world of hurt for your family, and then

Warren just pops over the next morning to invite him to church? That's hard to believe."

She stood up then, and Buddy stood in solidarity by her side, softly growling at me, our recent friendship apparently forgotten.

"Maybe it wouldn't be, if you were a Christian. Warren prayed over it when he went to the church. In the morning he went to see Ryan, to offer him repentance. He wanted to invite him to come to the Church of the Covenant of Jesus and confess his sins so that God could forgive him, and Ryan could save his soul."

She said it with such conviction that I thought it was possible that Peggy really believed it. But I didn't.

"I'm sorry, Peggy, but I don't think that's true."

"I don't care if you don't. It's what we told the Sheriff, and he believes us, and that's what matters. I think we've talked enough now." Her hands were trembling, and her cheeks were as pink as the blouse she wore.

"I'm sorry I upset you. Thank you for the lemonade and cookies. And for the information."

I hurried down the steps as quickly as I could without outright running, lest she turn my former pal, Buddy, loose on me.

## 26

"*Chica*, did you know you have a box of babies in the back of your car?" Miguel asked, as he opened the passenger door of my car. He had phoned me from Parkhurst's garage as I sat waiting for him in the Elite. An emergency had sent his beloved yellow Mini Cooper convertible in for repairs.

"What?" I craned my head to look at the back seat and saw the box of dolls I'd promised to deliver for my mother. Uh-oh.

"Don't say anything to Mom. I was supposed to drop those off but I forgot, and now I've got too much going on. I'll have to do it later. Mom's church group is making clothes for all those dolls Vesta had at her house. They're going to give them away to kids at Christmas."

"Oh, that's nice ... I miss Vesta."

"Well, you had a different relationship with her than I did. She liked you. She hated me. But, tell me, what happened to your car?"

"I don't know. She was fine when I left the salon, but when I stopped at the light, she just quit. My poor little Mini. She's never done that before."

"How long did Frank say it would have to be in the garage?" A reporter without a car has a serious handicap.

"Two days, maybe. Can you drop me back at Making Waves? Aunt Lydia will let me borrow her car, I know."

"Don't you want to go to the Elite for lunch?"

"I would, but now I don't have time. I have to shoot pictures at the water ballet rehearsal at the high school. But I'll tell you quick while we drive what I found out about Lily at Making Waves. It's little but choice."

"Spill."

"Well, Brittany the colorist who does Lily's hair—I talked to her about yours, too, *chica*, and she told me she'd be happy to work on bringing out your copper highlights. We both think—"

"Miguel, focus. We can talk makeover later."

"Right. So, three weeks ago, she was in Madison for a Wedding Hair class and—"

"Wait a second. There's something called 'Wedding Hair'?"

His face registered dismay at my ignorance. "*Chica*, yes! Wedding hairstyles are art! The loose top knot with bangs, the French twist/bun combo, the chignon—"

"OK, sorry I asked. So Brittany was in Madison—"

"Yes, and when the class was over and she was leaving the meeting room at the hotel, guess who she saw holding hands, waiting for the up elevator? Don't guess, I'll tell you. Lily and Ryan!"

"Really! Did they see her?"

"No. She went back around the corner. She didn't want to embarrass a client. It's the code of the salon."

"But she told you?"

"Well, I was her shampoo boy during college vacations. And also, Brittany has been coloring Lily's hair for a year, and Lily still calls her Brenda. She feels free to abandon the code."

I pulled into the lot and parked behind the back door to the salon, but it was too hot to shut off the car and lose the air-conditioning.

"If you trust Brittany, I trust Brittany. And when we add in Wanda's story, I think we can be pretty sure Lily and Ryan were having an affair. You did great. So great that if you have time—and only if you have time, I have another something you can do."

"I always have time for you, *chica*."

I asked Miguel to track down Lily's friend, Mandy, if she existed. "I think she probably does. Lily's too smart to make her up out of nothing. What I'd like to know, though, is Mandy's version of how Lily's Mother Teresa day went with her, and exactly what time Lily left. Also, see if she knows anything about Lily's extracurricular love life."

"I can do that, no problem."

"Thanks, Miguel. I mean it. I can always count on you."

He grinned as he opened the car door, and this time I didn't reach over and mess up his hair.

My phone rang as I pulled back onto the street.

"Hi, Mom, what's up?"

"Are you still interested in talking to Jill Burke?"

"Yes, why?"

"She's at the theater now. I just got off the phone with her. You can catch her there. She's going to be a while. She's working on the treasurer's report."

"Thanks, Mom. I will."

———

The Himmel Community Players is housed in the renovated Regent movie theater in downtown Himmel. It's a cool building with a marquee out front that the Players still use to announce new shows. A glass-fronted display case beside the entrance always has a poster of a current or coming production. The popcorn and candy counter in the lobby looks the same as it did when we were very little and my mother took us to the movies to see the latest Disney flick. Inside the theater itself, the walls are still covered with murals painted in the 1930s—in a jungle motif, for reasons unknown. But, thankfully, the back-destroying old theater chairs with scratchy upholstery have been replaced with cushy, comfortable seats. The sound system and the lighting are new, too. It took a lot of fifty-fifty raffles, bake sales, generous community donations, fund raising shows, and a few grants to bring the Regent back to life, but it's amazing what a dedicated group of creative people can do when they put their minds to it.

The doors were unlocked and I went through the lobby, which still had the pleasant after-smell of popcorn lingering in the air, and took the stairs to the second floor, to the room that serves as office and board meeting space. A woman was sitting at the table, a laptop in front of her and spreadsheets beside her. I tapped on the door.

"Hi, are you Jill Burke?"

"I am, and you are?" She had blunt cut, shiny black hair, parted on the side, no bangs. Her eyes were light brown under soft black eyebrows. She had a pleasant warm voice, and a nice smile.

"I'm Leah Nash. You know my mother, Carol."

"Yes. I know you, too, at least by reputation. I've enjoyed your books. And I'm very happy that you and Miller are reviving the *Himmel Times*. I think a community newspaper is so important."

"Thanks. We're working to get more people to feel the same way," I said.

"What can I do for you? Is this about the Fall Fundraiser?"

"No, actually it's not about the theater at all. I'd like to talk to you because I'm investigating the murder of Ryan Malloy."

"I don't understand. I spoke with Joanna last night. She said that the police were close to arresting an old friend of Ryan's, James Shaw."

"He's been questioned, but so have a lot of people. I'm working with the attorney who's representing James. I'm doing some poking around, trying to get a handle on Ryan's backstory."

"Obviously, then, you don't think James did it?"

"I think there may be other people who wanted Ryan dead. Joanna is the one who originally asked me to look into it. But now that I'm doing some investigating for James's attorney, she's not very happy with me."

"No, she wouldn't be. She's always felt that James was the reason that Ryan didn't come home very often—almost never, actually."

"Because Ryan felt guilty about the accident?"

"More because some people in town blamed Ryan for James losing his leg. It made Ryan uncomfortable, she said." There was an ironic note in her voice that I followed up on.

"You didn't like Ryan?"

"I hardly knew him. The last time I saw him was when he graduated from college. Steven and I flew out for the ceremony. It meant a lot to Joanna, and she's always meant a lot to me."

"Did you run into him at Joanna's after he came back?"

"No. I make it a point to visit Joanna only when I'm fairly sure the rest of the family won't be around. It would be beyond awkward to run into Lily and Steven there, and Joanna doesn't need any of that nonsense in her condition. I'm just about past being so bloody angry at Steven that I could cheerfully smash a bottle of wine over his head. But I'm not at the post-divorce civility stage yet, even though it's been almost three years."

That was promising.

"I'm divorced, too. It's tough, isn't it? I don't think you can really understand how bad it feels, unless you've gone through it yourself. And at least I didn't have to live in the same town as my ex and his new wife, like you."

"That hasn't been much fun, but I'm damned if I'm going to be run out of town. Or out of the business either."

"You're still in partnership with Steven?"

"No, but Wisconsin is a community property state, and my attorney was very good. He made sure that I have an ongoing interest in the profits, in addition to an adjusted upfront division of assets. After all, I worked with Steven to build up and expand the dealerships. He fought me tooth and nail on the settlement —or maybe I should say Lily did. Steven is middle-aged crazy about her, and he'd do anything to make her happy. And me having an ongoing stream of revenue from the business definitely doesn't suit her. Too bad."

A woman scorned is a sad story, but a good source. I was getting lots from Jill without even asking much.

"So, things are going well for Steven, I understand. I know that he opened a third dealership not long ago. Emotionally, it might not feel so good, but financially you have to be pretty happy that the business is doing well."

"You wouldn't know to hear Steven tell it. Last year, he started making noises about unexpected expenses, slowdown in sales, increased overhead, blah, blah, blah, trying to prepare me for less money coming my way. I told him fine, I understood, but I'd like to have my accountant go over the books. Then, amazingly, things turned right around, no problems, no need for my accountant to bother. He could pay me just fine, right on time. I'm sure he was just poor mouthing to play on my sympathies, so he could build another addition for Lily, or take her on a trip to Paris. That's where they went for their honeymoon. Steven and I went to the Dells."

I smiled sympathetically and stood up to leave.

"Thanks, Jill. This was very helpful. I just have one more question. Do you know if Steven has a handgun—for home protection?"

"He did when we were married. I never liked it. I imagine he still does. It's not like he ever used it though—I'm not really sure he knows how." Then I could tell by the way her eyes widened that she knew why I had asked.

"You think Steven could have killed Ryan for the money, don't you?"

"No," I lied. "I'm not thinking yet. I'm just collecting information. Thanks for your time, I appreciate it. If you remember anything you think would help, please give me a call. Here's my card."

## 27

I'd made a pretty good dent on my to-do list: talked to Cole at Ride EZ, met with Gina, and had a bonus round each with Jill Burke and Gina's mother. My growling stomach made me think of Marcy White. I wanted her version of what happened Friday after she took Gina away from the reception. But when I called Himmel Tech, where Marcy taught in the culinary arts department, the secretary said she wasn't in on Tuesdays.

"You could probably find her at home. She likes to go fishing on Tuesdays."

I made a U-turn and headed out to Gray Lake. Marcy's cottage was actually a year-round home on the less attractive side of the lake across from the Burke cottage. The lots on that part of the water, and the cottages on them, are much smaller and much closer together. The beach is rocky instead of sandy. In place of luxury pontoons and large speedboats moored at the docks, most owners have small fishing boats, or kayaks and canoes.

When I pulled into Marcy's rutted gravel driveway, I didn't see her truck, but it could have been in her garage. I spotted her when I got out of my car. She was just tying her fishing boat up at the dock. I waved and walked toward her. She met me half-way, carrying a pole and a tackle box, but no freshly caught fish. Her long gray hair was in its usual braid. Her light blue eyes showed neither pleasure nor annoyance at my unexpected visit. She didn't smile, just nodded and waited for me to explain myself. I tried to do a little social chit-chatting to ease into things.

"Fish not biting today?"

"Not the right time of day. I should've gone out earlier." She kept on walking toward the cottage, so I walked along with her. She didn't ask me why I was there.

"You're kind of a pioneer woman, Marcy. Living off the land —or the water, I should say. Do you hunt, too?"

"My dad taught me. Don't do much. I like fishing."

We finished the short walk to her door in silence. She looked at me when we reached it, but didn't invite me in.

"Marcy, do you have a few minutes? I'm looking into Ryan's death for Gabe Hoffman. He's James Shaw's attorney."

"James was arrested?"

"No, it's more of a precaution at this stage."

"Why do you want to talk to me?"

"Because you were with Gina Cox Friday night. I just want to confirm some things with you."

She stopped in her tracks and stared at me. "You don't think Gina killed Ryan, do you?"

"No, I don't. But I'm trying to build a picture of Ryan and the people in his life."

"Gina wasn't in his life. He abandoned her sixteen years ago." We were at the screen door of the enclosed porch on the front of the cottage.

"True, but as you know better than most, she was definitely

in his face Friday night. I talked to Gina this morning. She said you were really kind to her, but she admitted her recollections are pretty hazy. I just want your take on things."

She waited a beat before answering, then said, "Well, you're here now, you might as well come in."

I'd never been inside the cottage before. The porch had a concrete floor, a couple of plastic patio chairs and a small table, on which sat a book, the memoirs of a well-known chef. A book-mark stuck out of the pages marking her place.

She put her fishing equipment in the corner and led me through another door into a living room with knotty pine panel-ing, a large stone fireplace, and vaguely nautical decorating touches. Other than its OCD-level neatness, it looked like all the other lower-end cottages on Gray Lake. They'd been built decades ago as weekend retreats for factory workers escaping tedious, but high-paying, union jobs. That was in the glory days of Wisconsin manufacturing. The jobs and the workers are mostly gone now, but the cottages serve as a reminder of a more prosperous era for the middle class.

It was Marcy's kitchen that set her place apart from others on the lake. Walking into it was a little like going through the wardrobe into Narnia, if Narnia was a stage set for the Food Network. The room was unexpectedly large and was an obvious add-on that had transformed the cottage into an L-shaped structure. The pristine space was tiled and filled with gleaming stainless-steel appliances, long work counters, a huge refrigera-tor, a freezer, and a six-burner, double-oven Viking stove. Pots and pans hung from a rack above a central kitchen island and floor to ceiling cupboards lined two walls.

"This is an amazing space, Marcy. You must have done a ton of work on the cottage after you bought it."

She nodded, and with typical Wisconsin understatement said, "I like it."

She led me to a small alcove just off the kitchen. It held a wooden table just big enough for two, and a short counter with a sink on which sat a coffee maker and a mug tree.

She gestured for me to sit, and as she washed her hands asked, "Do you want some iced tea?"

"Tea would be great," I said. Secretly, since it was after one o'clock and I hadn't eaten, I was hoping that she'd throw in some fantastic canapé that was just sitting around in her refrigerator or ask me to sample a new recipe she was testing. Alas, when she returned from the main part of the kitchen, it was with only two glasses of tea in her hands. Each was wrapped in a napkin to absorb the condensation. She took two coasters out of the cupboard and put one at each of our chairs before sitting down.

"Thanks," I said, then took a drink of tea before beginning. "Gina and I had a pretty up-front conversation today. She told me her real story and said that she had more or less sobbed it out to you on Friday night. Do you remember what she told you?"

"Of course I do. I wasn't the one who was drunk. She told me she was pregnant by Ryan, and her parents made her give up the baby. All of that. When she was all cried out, I got her in the shower. Then I helped her into bed. I sat with her. Made sure she was all right before I left."

"Have you talked to her since then?"

"I went over the next day. Gail at the front desk told me she'd gone out. So, I knew she must be all right. On Sunday, after I heard about Ryan, I called her. We met for coffee. She said she'd been at an AA meeting on Saturday when I stopped. She was upset about Ryan. Naturally. But she was coping all right."

"Did she say anything about the fight she'd had with her father on Saturday night?"

Marcy nodded. "Warren was angry about Gina being drunk

and making a scene Friday night. She got angry back. I don't blame her. Warren was too harsh with her. And Peggy—I don't see how a woman could put her husband ahead of her child. It's wrong."

"Gina must have been pretty upset after the scene with her father. I'm surprised she didn't come to talk to you afterwards."

"I was working at the reunion dinner. I didn't get home until after eleven, and I went straight to bed."

"Marcy, did you hear any loud, firecracker-like sounds the night Ryan died?"

"No. I already told the police that. Some college kids rented a cottage around the lake. They shot off fireworks all week. I didn't notice it after a while. Saturday I was dead tired. I have some *hors d'oeuvres* to make now."

She stood up, and it was clear she was ready for me to go. She was a humorless, no-nonsense woman, but her behavior toward Gina said that at heart she was a kind one.

"Marcy," I began, then hesitated, unsure if I should say what was on my mind.

"Yes?" Her voice was impatient. She'd given me enough time.

"I just wanted to say I know why you're helping Gina. And I know why you go to the cemetery. It's why I go, too. I understand."

"You may know the reason. But you don't understand. Only a woman who's lost her child can. Your mother can. Now, Joanna can. Gina lost her baby. She can understand, too. But not you. You don't understand. Goodbye. I have work to do."

———

If I had had any hopes that my words of compassion would touch Marcy's tender heart, forge a new bond between us, and perhaps even land me a plate of something delicious from her kitchen, she had briskly torpedoed them.

Back in my car when my cell phone rang, I saw on the dashboard screen that it was Ross. I wasn't quite ready to share any of my news, but I was eager to hear if he'd been able to break Steven and Lily's joint alibi.

"Ross, what's up?"

"I talked to your friend with the dog."

"Cil? Yeah, and?"

"She didn't want to come down hard on the time. Said she thought it was between twelve and one, but she'd only go as far as a guess."

"Yes, but the point is, Steven and Lily said they were home together at eleven thirty, so even if Cil is off a little, they still don't have an alibi."

"Oh, they got a story to cover that. Seems like when they went upstairs, after they had their cocktails, they took a shower. Together. Didn't mention it the first time we asked. Seein' as how it was their personal business. They were in their spa bathroom on the second floor, way up at the back of the house. The fan was on, they had music on, the water made noise, and they were, lemme see what Steven said, exactly."

I could hear him flipping pages. "Oh, yeah, here it is, they were 'absorbed in each other.' Couldn't hear anything at all. Sounds real—"

"Creepy? Yes. True? No. You don't believe them, do you?"

"Not sayin' I do. Not sayin' I don't. But at the moment they've still got an alibi that works."

"They're lying, wait and see."

"Got no time to wait and see. I got work to do. Later."

I could feel it in my bones. Steven and Lily were making things up, but proving it was going to be hard. My stomach began growling loudly again. I was sorely in need of something more substantive than the Doritos, Cheerios, and peanut butter I knew I had in my cupboard. I swung through McDonald's on the way home, picked up a quarter pounder, no cheese, some fries, and a large Diet Coke with plenty of ice. I like soda from a can, but I love it from McDonald's—or any place, actually, where it comes together in the moment with syrup and fizzy water. It's magical ... I'm easily enchanted.

Once home, I went into my building through the parking lot door, did not check-in on the newsroom, and scurried up the stairs to the air-conditioned bliss of my loft. When I got there, because I'm all about making meals special, I unwrapped my burger and put it on a plate, along with the fries. With the addition of a beverage, and my propensity for spills, I took the extra precaution of setting up a tray table next to my window seat to hold my meal. I retrieved my yellow legal pad, a pen, and then sat down and made myself comfortable.

Alternately sipping my Coke and eating my burger and fries, I stared blankly down at the street below and allowed myself to be almost hypnotized watching the cars pull up, stop, and go in the same repeated rhythm, regulated by the traffic light on the corner. Every time my mind wanted to start making lists or running through suspects, I forced my attention back on the cars coming and going below. When I finished my food, I wiped my hands on a paper towel and was ready to work. Something that had been niggling the back of my mind ever since I left the Ride EZ office had suddenly leaped into focus.

I flipped through my notes, checked a few things, and then grabbed my laptop and looked in the *GO News* back files online. I read the story James had told me about—the feature Andrea Novak had written about the boy recovering from a leg amputation. Next I looked for a story in the online archives of the

*Himmel Times*. After that, I Googled some names and checked what I found against a people search engine I subscribe to. In under an hour, I had the information I needed. Then I called James Shaw.

---

## 28

"James, the boy you mentored, the one who lost his leg, was his name Austin Mepham?" I was too excited by my idea to waste time on opening pleasantries.

"Yes, why?"

"Austin's parents, are they Tabitha and Monroe Mepham?"

"Yeah, that's right. Leah, what is this? Why are you asking me about Austin? Did something happen to him?"

"No, no, nothing like that. I'm just double-checking an idea I have. Now, James, I want you to think back, really focus, on what happened when your Good Samaritan picked you up by the side of the road the night Ryan was killed. I—"

"I already told Gabe, I told the cops, I told you, the whole thing is a blur."

"I know but try just one more time to remember. We'll take it slow, step-by-step. Humor me."

He sighed loudly enough for it to come clearly through my phone, but he followed it with a resigned, "OK."

"Good. Now, you fight with Ryan, your leg is hurting you pretty bad from the fall you took, and you're drunk. You don't want any help, and in your fuzzy state of mind, you think it's a good idea to walk home. You leave the fairgrounds, walk you don't know how far, but realize eventually that you're turned around and going the wrong way. Do I have that right?"

"Yes, but I—"

"Hold on now, it's almost your turn. When that realization hits, where are you? How do you know that you're heading the wrong way? What do you see that tells you that?"

"I don't know. I don't remember."

"Come on, you must have seen something that didn't look right, or how would you know you were going wrong? Close your eyes. Think about that night. It's still daylight, but it's getting dusky. Your leg is throbbing. It feels like you've been walking forever. You should be able to see your house pretty soon, but you don't."

"No. My leg hurt so much I had to stop. I had to sit down."

"Where, James? Where did you sit down?"

"On the bench. I thought if I could just stretch out ..."

"What bench?"

"It was off the road. Hard. Cool. Under a tree. I told you, I can't remember."

"Oh, but you can, James. You just did. There's only one place in Grantland County that has a stone bench under a tree by the side of the road. The Lauderman farm. You were on Marshall Road, going in the exact opposite direction from where your house is. That's where your guardian angel found you passed out, hours later. Now, let's try to remember more about him."

"It's no use. All I remember is getting helped into a car, and then waking up in my chair with a splitting headache in the morning, when the sun came through the blinds."

"James. You're starting to get on my nerves. I can't help you, if you don't help yourself. Now, think about that man. He's shaking you awake. He's getting you to sit up. You have to lean on him, because besides being drunk, your leg hurts like a mother. Concentrate. What comes to your mind?"

I stopped talking and let James have some space for recall. After a minute, he said, "I remember, I do remember something!"

"What, what is it?"

"Peppermint!"

That nailed it for me.

"Well done, James. I think you have just helped us save your butt."

"I don't understand."

"You will if I'm right. I have to go."

———

I wasn't sure he'd come. I'd been pretty vague on the phone. I looked up from my back-corner booth every time the bell over the front door jangled. Which wasn't that often, really, because I was sitting in the Eat More Restaurant, a diner where the coffee is great and everything else isn't. Finally, he walked in and, seeing me, swaggered back to my booth.

I nodded to the waitress behind the counter, and she brought over the two mugs of coffee I'd ordered but asked her to hold until my "friend" showed up.

"You took long enough to get here, Cole," I said.

He shot an appreciative glance at the pretty blonde who set his coffee down. He said thank you to her before he answered me.

"Now, that's not a very nice greetin', Leah, when I come all the way over here in the middle of my busy day. I'm not surprised though, that you couldn't wait more'n a few hours to see me again. Now, what's got you all fired up, besides you just can't keep away from me?"

"Nothing personal, believe me. You have a nephew named Austin Mepham. His mother is your sister Tabitha, and she's married to Monroe Mepham. Is that right?"

"That's right. But—"

"Austin lost his leg in a lawn mower accident two years ago. He's enrolled in a program that pairs kids who have had amputations with volunteer adults who also have had an amputation," I said.

"I don't see where you're goin'. Or why."

"I imagine it was a pretty terrible thing for your family when Austin lost his leg."

He dropped the smirk he habitually wore.

"It was. My sister about lost her mind, and Monroe, he didn't do much better. He was the one drivin' the mower. Didn't know Austin had snuck up behind him. Backed up right over him. He's doin' all right now, though, Austin is. Got him a special leg. We call him Cyborg. He likes that, like the comic book. Why are you askin' all this?"

I ignored the question, knowing Cole was curious enough to go along with me.

"James Shaw was Austin's mentor until a month ago, when the program asked him to step away, because of his troubles at school. Did Austin like him?"

"Yeah, good enough, I guess."

"How did he feel when the program dropped James?"

"He took it hard. They was close. He showed Austin he could still do things, be a regular kid. Helped him train for these special games, taught him little tricks how to manage his leg. He was good for Austin."

"James swears that he didn't kill Ryan Malloy. That he couldn't have, because he was passed-out drunk on the side of the road, for he doesn't know how long. He came to when a man shook him awake, got him into a car and drove him home. The trouble is, his memory is pretty hazy. He can't say for sure who picked him up, or exactly when."

"Now, I would call that a pretty weak alibi."

"Given your extensive history in making them up, I almost feel like I should defer to your expertise. But I think, in this case, you know that it's actually true."

"I have no idea what you're talkin' about."

"Yes, you do. You told me that after dropping Ryan off at the cottage, you took Marshall Road, and went straight home."

"Leah, much as I enjoy our time together, one cuppa joe don't buy you the rights to my whole day. What are you gettin' at?"

"You didn't mention that on your drive down Marshall Road, you saw James Shaw passed out on the stone bench by the Lauderman farm. And you didn't tell me that you picked him up, got him in your car, and took him to his house."

"Now, does that sound like the me you know and love, Leah? Why would I do any of that?"

"It surprises me, too. But I guess even you have some kind of feelings, Cole. James helped your nephew Austin. Helped your whole family, really. And one thing about you Grangers, you're a tight-knit bunch."

"You got it wrong. I didn't do anythin' like that. Don't try to get me involved in some murder investigation. I don't need that business in my life."

"Stop it, Cole. James remembered."

He looked nonplussed for a second, probably trying to figure out how the incoherent, practically insensible man that had been James on Saturday night could recall anything.

"It was your peppermints. You told me yourself, you always have some with you. And the one thing James can remember about his Good Samaritan is the smell of peppermint. Just like the smell from the one you popped in your mouth a minute ago."

"Is that all you got? 'Cause I have to tell you, it's not much. Nothin' the police are gonna take serious. I did not even see James Saturday night. I am not some bleedin' heart that goes around pickin' drunks outta gutters—or off benches, neither."

"You really won't admit that you were there, and you picked James up? You're just going to let him be charged with a murder he didn't commit?"

"I can't say what's not true. I wasn't there. I didn't pick up James."

"All right, if that's your story. But I'll find a way to make you admit the truth."

"You wound me, Leah. I'm a very truthful man. Just ask my mama."

I shook my head as I reached in my purse and said, "Call the waitress over, would you? I'll settle the bill, but I'm late making a call someone's waiting for."

He raised his hand to motion his pretty blonde over, as I looked at my screen and frowned.

"Oh, great. Just what I need."

"What?" he asked.

"My cell phone is dead. I promised to pick my mother up at three, and it's already three-fifteen. She's going to kill me. Can I borrow yours just for a minute?"

The cute waitress was back. I shook my head when she motioned the coffee pot to me, but Cole said, "Yes, I'll take a warm-up, darlin'. Although it warms my heart, just to see you standin' there."

She giggled. I said, "Cole, your phone, please? I really need to make this call."

Still focused on the waitress, who really should have known better, I watched as he tapped in his security code, 1,2,3,4. Seriously? But it wasn't my job to warn him of hacker dangers. He slid it over to me.

I punched in a number, and I pressed the phone to one ear. I covered the other with my hand as if to block out their flirty chatter. Then I gestured that I was stepping outside to make my call and slid out of the booth.

Once I cleared the back door, I acted fast. I tapped settings on his phone, then privacy, then location services, then system services, then significant locations. Up popped a lovely list of all the places he had gone recently, including the date and the time.

A rush of triumph went through me as I ran down the list of Saturday night stops: the fairgrounds for the post-reunion pick-up of Ryan; Ryan's cottage; Marshall Road. Then, ding-ding-ding! James's address. After that, and this one puzzled me, a location ten miles outside of town, Grantland Sand & Gravel, at one a.m. That was odd, but not relevant. Then home to Cole's address.

I had to get back inside before the waitress lost interest and Cole had time to become suspicious. I pulled out my own phone, which was actually fully charged, took a few pictures of Cole's travels, and emailed them to myself. The waitress was just leaving as I went back inside, holding Cole's phone out to him as I slid back into the booth.

"Thank you. I appreciate it more than you know."

"Anytime you want to show me just how much, give me a call." He pushed the bill the waitress had left over toward me and began to move out of the booth.

"Stay, just a minute, can you?"

"I thought your mama was waitin'."

"Did I say that? I meant Charlie Ross is waiting. For you."

"I don't follow," he said, a suspicious look creeping across his face.

"You lied to me, Cole, just like I said. I looked at location services on your phone. Here's a pro tip for you, you can block it from tracking you, but I'm glad you didn't. Otherwise, how would I know that you were on Marshall Road right by the bench where James passed out? And then you went to James's house, and then, here's an odd one, you went to Grantland Sand & Gravel, and then finally you went back home."

His expression had gone from puzzled to astonished to defiant.

"That's illegal, what you did."

"Sorry, no. You gave me your phone; you lost your expectations of privacy."

"All right, fine. But you don't have any proof of that. Like you said, I can delete location tracking and delete the history, and there we are. Your say-so against mine. And I told you, I'm not gettin' involved."

"Not even to save James from a false murder charge?"

"Not my circus, not my monkey."

"Then I'm glad I don't have to rely on your better nature. I don't need your phone. I took pictures. I took the precaution of emailing them to myself, and I'll be sharing them with Detective Ross shortly. So, I think you can expect a visit from him in the near future. And with those photos, I don't think he'll have any trouble getting your cell phone records, which will pinpoint even more accurately where you've been, and over a much longer time period. Have you been doing anything over the last few months that you wouldn't want the sheriff's department to know about?"

I watched as he calculated what that meant, no doubt running quickly through the various illegal activities he'd been involved with recently and how much trouble he—or others in his family—might be in if they came to light.

"All right, fine. After I dropped Ryan off, I was drivin' down

Marshall Road and I saw James, lyin' there on the bench at the Lauderman farm. He looked bad. I stopped to see was he even breathin', Then I got him up and took him home. I guess it's true like they say. No good deed goes unpunished."

"Thank you. Now we can prove that James's story is true, and that means he's out of the frame for Ryan's murder. But I'm curious. Why did you go to Grantland Sand & Gravel? It's miles out of your way."

"Nothin' to do with James, or anythin' else you need to know about. Not to be impolite, Leah, but you can take that curiosity and put it where the sun don't shine."

I'd pushed him as far as he was going to go, and I really was just curious, so I dropped it. I'd already gotten what I needed.

## 29

I could have flown instead of driven home, I was so elated. I flitted back and forth between going straight to Gabe's office to tell him James was in the clear, phoning him with the good news, or driving out to James's to put him out of his misery—for the murder part of his misery, anyway. I finally decided it would be the most fun of all to surprise Gabe with the news over dinner. And Gabe should have the pleasure of telling James he was in the clear. We could phone him together.

When I got home, I still had a couple of hours before I needed to get ready. Normally, I would go as is, but it was a celebration evening. I decided to take a shower, and yes, shave my legs, *and* wear my "nice" tank top and a summer skirt.

First though, I called Ross, gave him the quick take on my chat with Cole, then texted him the photos I'd taken. He agreed to call me back after he talked to Cole and checked things out and warned me not to "jump the gun."

It was hard to stick to my plan and let Gabe tell James. I knew it would be better that way, but I was anxious to share the good news with him. To distract myself, I decided to tick something off my list that was overdue, and now more important to nail down than ever. I called Miller Caldwell.

"Leah, hello. What can I do for you?"

"Hi, Miller. Just a quick question—or two. Do you represent Steven Burke?"

"No, he uses Kinney, McKittrick and Carlisle in Madison. A good firm his father used as well. Why?"

"So, you don't have any lawyer/client confidentiality reasons not to tell me if you've heard that Steven's business interests aren't doing so well, right?"

"I don't have any professional reasons, no, but I don't feel comfortable speculating about Steven's financial situation," he said a little stiffly, as though he was, perhaps, a little disappointed in me. Miller has very high ethical standards. It can be rather annoying at times.

"I'm not asking you to speculate. Well, that's not true, really, I would love it, if you'd speculate about Steven's fortunes or misfortunes, but not for idle gossip. I think the answer to whether or not Steven is in financial trouble could be important in Ryan Malloy's murder."

"I don't understand."

"I don't want you to, not yet. I'd just like to know if it's possible that Steven is underwater, financially speaking."

"I'll trust your discretion, Leah. And this is with the caveat that it is a rumor. I've heard that Steven took out a very large hard money loan."

"What's a hard money loan?"

"It's a short-term loan, usually for a year, offered by private investors instead of a bank, at a high interest rate. It's secured by real property the borrower puts up."

"Real property? You mean like a house?"

"No, it would be commercial property for the most part."

"You mean like the commercial real estate on which three different dealerships sit in three different cities?"

"Well, as a hypothetical example, yes."

"You said the loans have a high interest rate. How high?"

"Typically, twelve to fifteen percent, sometimes higher."

"Wow, that sounds like loan-shark territory to me. Why would anyone go for a hard money loan instead of one from a bank?"

"If you have the real property to back them up, the loans are easy to apply for, easy to get, and they come through quickly."

"But if your loan term is up, and you can't pay back what you borrowed, these private investors, the hard money lenders, they seize the assets you put up for the loan. So, whatever commercial property you used as security is gone, and you're out of business. Is that right?"

"If you can't pay the loan back when it comes due, yes, that would be the case."

"All right, thanks, Miller. That's all I need."

Steven's ex-wife, Jill, had said that a year ago he was having some financial troubles. Then, abruptly, he wasn't. Coop's dad had heard the rumor, and Miller had, too. Steven had been expanding his business. At the same time, he'd been spending a lot of money—on trips, and cars, and condos, and jewelry, and home makeovers, and now Lily wanted the Dunn house. A hard money loan might have looked pretty attractive to him as he waited for his business expansion to start generating the income he anticipated. But, if he'd kept building up expenses instead of income, he might need to get his hands on the whole estate when Joanna died, not just his half of it. And Ryan would have to die in order for that to happen.

Pleased with the addition to my theory about Steven, I moved to a different task on my list and forced myself to focus on keeping my promise to Clinton. I settled down to writing. I worked so hard that when I looked at the clock on my computer screen, I was surprised to see it was already six o'clock. Almost time to go to Gabe's. I had just finished a quick shower and wrapped a towel around my wet hair when my phone pinged with a text from Ross.

*You home?*
*I'm getting ready to go out to dinner*
*I'll be right up buzz me in.*

---

"I dunno, I think I'd go just a *little* more dressed if I was goin' out to dinner. But that's just me."

"You're hilarious, Ross." I had answered the door with my hair wrapped in a towel and my body wrapped in an old terry cloth bathrobe. "I was in the middle of getting ready when you called."

"Hey, I'm in the middle of a murder investigation, and you're the one who wanted me to tell you after I talked to Cole."

"I know. I do. Come in. He admitted it, didn't he? He had to. You had the photos. You saw where he went, right? Cole picked James up. You got him to admit it, right? James wasn't lying, you can see that, now, right?"

"OK, take it easy."

"But what did Cole say to you? What did you say to him? This gets James off the hook, doesn't it?"

"You got a Coke or somethin'? It's dang hot out there and I'm parched. Not the diet kind, the real stuff. Gimme one, and I'll tell you what's goin' on."

I produced a Coke, he waved off a glass, and dropped heavily on a bar stool. I sat on the one across from him and waited until he finished a long swallow of soda.

"So, what happened?"

"First tell me how you figured Cole for James's alibi."

"The peppermint, plus a few other things." I explained.

"Not bad, Nash. Not bad at all. Well, his story is a fit with James's. I'm still gonna need a warrant to get official cell phone records to back up those nice pictures you gave me. And Lamey's not gonna like losin' his favorite suspect. But, I'd say Shaw is sittin' pretty good on the murder charge."

"Can I quote you on that?"

"No way. You can tell Miguel to call the sheriff about noon tomorrow for an update on the case. Let Lamey do the talkin'. And don't bring me into it."

"It's got to be Steven who killed Ryan, don't you think?"

"Why him?"

"Because, follow the money, Ross. With Ryan dead, Steven gets the whole four million, that's why."

"You got anything concrete on Burke?"

"He's got the motive. He had the opportunity—that shower alibi is pathetic. He could have been waiting for Ryan at the cottage, killed him right after Cole dropped him off, and then he went home to fix up an alibi with Lily. Nobody stands to gain from Ryan's death like he does."

"I hate to burst your bubble there, Nancy Drew."

"What?"

"I got a badge that says I'm a detective and everything. I got a little more out of Granger than you did."

"Like what?"

"Like that last place he went, Grantland Sand & Gravel? I asked him to tell me all about that. Now, this is way off the record. I mean it. Cole said he was doin' some 'financial consulting' in confidence with a client who needed an out-of-the-way location."

"Right, because if you can't get an appointment with Capital One, Cole Granger is your second call. And your meet-up is a gravel pit. It sounds more like a drug deal than a financial consultation to me."

"Could be. But I don't figure Steven Burke for a drug dealer."

"Cole said he was meeting with Steven?" I couldn't keep the shock out of my voice.

"Yep. I think he's tellin' the truth, too. I used some extra persuasion on him. Told him I *might* see my way clear to over-looking any minor odds and ends that could turn up in his cell phone records, if he told me the truth. But for sure I'm gonna run down every last place his cell records say he was for the last six months, if I find out he lied to me. It'll be a little trickier to get a warrant for Steven's cell phone, seein' as he's such a fine, upstanding citizen. But I think if I bypass Lamey and go straight to the prosecutor, I can get it done."

"I thought you said you had to keep your head down with Lamey. He's not going to like it if you end run him."

"He'll be all right, if it pans out, and he can take the credit. If it doesn't, well, we'll see. There's layin' low, and there's layin' down. I'm not gonna lay down on the job, for any reason."

"Glad to hear it, Ross. But even if Cole's telling the truth, and Steven's phone records prove it, I still don't see why Steven would need a low-life like Cole to ... Ohhh, wait a minute—"

"Lightbulb go off there for ya, Nash?"

"Steven has a hard money loan. If it's due right now, he can't wait for Joanna to die. Those investors will want their money, not an I.O.U for what could be six days or six weeks, or six months from now before they could collect. Steven has to find a way to save his businesses right away. The only other place he can go is dirty money."

"I see where you're goin.' How's a nice, Chamber of Commerce guy like Steven gonna make that kind of connection? He's not," Ross said, answering his own question. "But Granger can maybe set it up for him."

It's not that Cole is some *Sopranos*-style mobster—though I'm sure he has his dreams. However, his family does exist on the lower rungs and outer margins of a number of sketchy-to-full-on-criminal operations. Some of them have their roots in Milwaukee or Chicago, where there's serious gangster-type crime—and gangster-type money from drugs, prostitution, insurance fraud, money-laundering, and loan sharking.

"But, Ross, even if Steven was meeting with Cole, it doesn't prove he couldn't have killed Ryan. He could've gone over to the cottage after that, couldn't he? It fits with the time of death window, right? Between midnight and four a.m.?"

"You been hammerin' me on twelve to one as the time of death, but now that it doesn't work for your favorite suspect, you decide you're all in on the M.E.'s time frame? Are you forgettin' the shots the neighbors heard? That was right when Steven was waitin' for Granger to show up."

"But maybe Betty and the other guy you talked to had the time wrong. Or maybe it was a car backfiring, or—"

"Come on." Ross was already shaking his head no, before I even finished. A response which, by the way, I hate.

"Not likely. When's the last time you heard a car backfire? Modern engines got fuel injection, they got computers that control fuel mixture, it doesn't happen. Give it up. Steven's got an alibi, and Granger's it. He was supposed to meet Steven at twelve-thirty, but he didn't get there until almost one o'clock, on account of helpin' James Shaw. So Steven and him didn't finish their little talk and leave until one-thirty. Ryan was already dead. And Steven couldn'ta got home until after two at the earliest. His phone records are gonna show he wasn't at the cottage. He's in the clear, Nash, face it."

I was silent as I said a sad goodbye to my favorite suspect. But Ross had just raised an important point.

"All right, Cole is Steven's alibi, Lily isn't. Then *Lily* is the one who doesn't have an alibi. She said she got home at eleven-thirty, but there's no proof of that. In fact, all she's got going for her now is the shower story, only this time, she's in it all alone. So, how about this, Ross? We already know she and Ryan were having an affair. So, Lily planned to use helping her sick friend not just as an excuse to get out of going to the reunion with Steven, but also as cover for a night of romance with Ryan. They arrange to meet at the cottage around midnight, only something goes wrong. They have a lover's quarrel, and Lily winds up shooting him. Then she goes home, and she's in luck, because Steven isn't back. When he does get home with whatever lame excuse he gives her, she's in no position to question him. Then in the morning, when he finds out Ryan is dead, Steven gets worried."

"You mean because he's gettin' all the money, and that makes him a suspect in his stepbrother's murder."

"Right. He knows he didn't do it, but his alibi is Cole Granger. He's not about to tell you guys that. Dealing with Cole doesn't fit his image. Besides, he doesn't want anyone to know how deep in trouble he is, financially. And if there's even a hint that he might have killed Ryan, Joanna could decide to change her will. And he desperately needs that inheritance."

"So, he tells the wife he needs her help, if they don't want to take a chance on losin' all that money, Ross said."

"Exactly! It works out great for Lily, because she's the one who has no alibi whatsoever. And she's the one who actually killed Ryan."

"I can see how that could work," he said.

"So you're going after Lily, right?"

"I'm goin' after the truth, Nash. That's what I'm gonna do. I'll be lookin' into Lily Burke's alibi. But there's two other people you left out who still need investigatin', Warren Cox and his daughter, Gina."

"You don't really think Gina did it, do you?"

"Why, 'cause you don't want it to be her? She's wide open on Saturday night. The only alibi she's got is her mother and dad, and her dad's not exactly on firm ground either. Hell, we don't even know for sure where Peggy Cox was that night. She says Warren went to the church to pray. Maybe he did, and maybe while he was there, she went and killed Ryan for screwin' up her family."

"That's crazy."

"Probably so. I'm just tryin' to show you, you can make anything fit inside the circle, if you draw it big enough. But my job is to draw it small, so only one suspect, the right one, fits inside in the end. And I ain't at the end yet. Now, you go your way, and I'll go mine. Just don't get underfoot, *capiche*? I don't need to trip over you with Lamey on my back."

"Fine. You'll come back asking for my help. Wait and see."

He snorted. "Don't stop believin', Nash."

## 30

I had just closed the door behind me and was walking toward my room when there was a knock. Ross, again. I didn't invite him in this time.

"Hey, I forgot. Did you get anything for me on what's buggin' Allie? Did you talk to her yet?"

"I did. I think you're right, her moodiness might be because of a boy. Well, a man, I guess. I think she has a crush on Troy."

"That little dweeb with the glasses? He's hittin' on Allie?"

"No, no, I didn't say that. I don't think he's hitting on her, but I think she likes him."

"He's too old for her. She's just a kid."

"Easy there, dad. I'm pretty sure Troy doesn't know that she's interested in him. Even if he does, he wouldn't do anything about it. First, because he's smart enough to know that he's too old for her, and second, because he's not exactly a player when it comes to women—or girls."

"Well, I'll be having a talk with her real soon about this Troy."

"Don't do that. Just let it run its course. She'll get over it, and she'll be fine. Just give her some space."

He looked at me doubtfully, but I thought I detected a touch of relief beneath the fatherly bluster. He probably wasn't any more eager to talk to Allie about romance than she was to converse with him on the subject.

"But there might be something else to keep an eye out for. When I saw Allie this morning, I got the impression she knows something about the whole James and his student email scandal."

"Like what?"

"Like it sounded as though she's friends with the girl who reported getting the email. Maybe everything isn't on the up and up there. But Allie backed away from it pretty quick when I tried to follow-up."

"Yeah? All right. Thanks for the heads up. I'll talk to her. Won't be tonight though, I gotta work late. I won't get home before she goes to bed."

"Try not to bring me into it, if you can avoid it. I don't want her to think that I go running to you with everything she tells me."

"Right. She might get the wrong idea. Like we're friends or something."

---

I shut my door for the final time, I hoped, and went to finish my big night preparations, feeling pretty good. Not only could Gabe and I cross James off the list of suspects, but it would be very satisfying if Lily turned out to be Ryan's killer. To make the day even better, my hair fell effortlessly into place as I blew it dry, and looked just how I wanted it to, a rarity in my experience. I hoped Gabe was ready, because I was seriously bringing it.

On the way over, I rehearsed several ways of sharing my good news. I could make him guess. I could play it casual and just toss it out over dinner. I could ask him about his day, which could in no way be as exciting as mine, and then wait for him to ask what I'd been doing. Oh, forget it. There was no way I wasn't going to burst out with it as soon as I walked through the door.

---

Gabe only locks his door when he's away, or he's ready for bed, though it had taken him several months to kick his big-city habit of barricading himself in whenever he was home. Just as it had taken me several months to acquire it, when I first moved to a city much larger than Himmel. I pulled up in front of his place, parked, ran up the sidewalk, tapped lightly on the front door, opened it, and burst into the living room shouting my good news.

"I've got proof James didn't kill Ryan, couldn't have! We've got a witness, and Ross is down with it! The best part is that James's imaginary good Samaritan isn't imaginary at all. You'll never guess who it was."

Gabe walked out of the kitchen, knife in hand.

"You'd better put that down, because you're gonna want to kiss me when you hear what I found out today. I just got James off the suspect list for Ryan's murder!"

He set the knife on an end table, gave me a hug and said, "Don't let anyone ever tell you that you don't know how to make an entrance. Sit down. Tell me everything."

I did. When I got to the part about Cole's phone, he stopped me with a kiss.

"If James doesn't take out a full-page ad in the *Himmel Times* thanking you, I will. Seriously, Leah, this is amazing. You're amazing."

"I am, aren't I?"

"No, don't joke. I mean it," he said.

"OK, well, thanks, that's nice to hear."

"That's it?"

"Uh, well, that's *very* nice to hear?"

"I'm trying to be serious here. I do think you're amazing."

Something in his voice made me feel a little uneasy.

"I was going to wait until after dinner, to say this, but I think—"

I tried to deflect what I was afraid was coming—the take-our-relationship-to-the-next-level talk.

"Why don't I help you get dinner on? We can talk while we're eating." I figured we had enough to catch up on that I'd be able to table the current conversation to another time—way, way in the future.

"No, I don't want to say this between mouthfuls of spaghetti. Listen to me, now, please."

There was no way out.

"OK, I'm listening."

"I've thought about this a lot. We've been seeing each other for a while now, but we're both so busy we don't see *enough* of each other. Between your job and mine, we're pulled in so many directions it's hard to find time for us. There's no one else in my life. I don't think there's anyone else in yours. I'm ready for something more. I hope you are, too. I'd like you to move in with me."

Although I had suspected what was coming, I wasn't prepared for the level of anxiety it set off in me. I felt cornered, trapped—panicked. I stared at him and watched his face gradually go from happily expectant to puzzled and concerned.

"Leah? Don't you have anything to say?"

I swallowed hard.

"I'm sorry, Gabe. I don't think that's a good idea. We're doing great the way things are. We have fun together. We respect each other. Why would we want to mess things up?"

"Why would moving in together mess things up?"

"Because it just would, that's all. I like my life. I like my work. I like my loft. I like the freedom to make my own decisions without checking in with someone else. I don't want that to change."

"It wouldn't have to."

"Yes, Gabe. It would. You know it would. We'd have to spend all that time getting used to sharing a living space. You'd get mad because I didn't pick up my towels. I'd get mad because you ate the last brownie. You'd have to remember to take the sheets out of the dryer. I'd have to apologize for reading with the light on. I don't want us to have to try to accommodate each other's ways. I want to keep my ways. Maybe I'm selfish, but that's how I feel."

"No, I don't think that's it. You're not a selfish person, Leah. And those are all trivial issues. Are you sure this doesn't have anything to do with Coop?"

I was so surprised that I was at a loss for words. But not for long.

"Please tell me that I heard you wrong. That you didn't just imply that the only possible reason I could have for not relinquishing my independence, my sense of self, even my home, for God's sake, is because I've got my eye on a different man?"

"Leah, I—"

"No. I'm not finished. Coop is my best friend, my oldest friend, the person who's been there for me at all the best and the worst times in my life, ever since I was ten years old. But we have NO romantic interest in each other. Zero. Zip. Nada. How can you just dismiss the reasons—the very real reasons—I gave you for not accepting your *fabulous* offer and decide that instead it's because—"

"That's not what I meant, and you know it!"

Gabe rarely gets angry, but he definitely was now. That was

all right. It matched the way I was feeling at the moment. His next words didn't do anything to de-escalate the situation.

"You're twisting my words to deflect the truth. Maybe you don't even know it yourself. But I know you—"

"No. Don't try to tell me that you know anything about me when you've just demonstrated so clearly that you don't. I don't want to move in with you, and it has nothing to do with Coop. If you can't hear what I said, then I can't help it. I feel like you're pushing me into a corner, and I'm asking you to stop, and you won't listen. I don't even know how we got to this point. But I'm leaving now, before either one of us says anything else."

"That's a good idea," he said stonily.

"I'll email you the details about James and about Ross's follow-up with Cole. I think it's better if we don't see each other for a while."

"There's something we can agree on."

Even though I was so mad I could hardly see straight, the coldness in his voice gave me pause. Did I really want it to end like this? As it turned out, after Gabe's next words, yes, I sure did.

"Say hello to Coop for me. I'm sure that's where you're going when you leave."

"And, we're done. Bye, Barnacle."

## 31

As I drove away, the tears of anger I had succeeded in holding back began to fall. I arrived in Coop's driveway before I even realized I was fulfilling Gabe's snide prediction. Coop heard my car pull in and came walking toward me from the backyard with a welcoming smile on his face, until he saw mine.

"What's wrong?"

"Oh, nothing," I said. "Tell me, are all men asshats? Asking for a friend."

He took in the smudged mascara under my eyes and said, "Come on out back. I was just having a beer. Want one? Or something stronger?"

"I'll take a Jameson, please. Straight."

When we were both seated on his patio, I used the washcloth he had handed me along with my drink to wipe away the mascara-tinged tracks of angry tears. Then I told him what had happened with Gabe.

"Can you believe he would say something so stupid? That I won't move in with him because of you? He didn't even listen when I tried to explain that moving in together just isn't something I want to do. I really liked him, but I guess I really didn't know him. I don't understand why *he* can't understand. He just dismissed what I said as though my independence, my work, my freedom to choose didn't make any difference. I'm mad at him and I'm mad at myself for not seeing that side of him before."

I took a bracing swallow of my whiskey before going on. "It was all going great. I had such good news for him, and we were going to have this nice dinner together, and then, no. He has to ruin it."

"You know, Leah, it doesn't sound like you gave Gabe a chance to say much. And I can't really blame him for being surprised that asking you to move in with him pissed you off. He probably thought you'd be happy."

"Hey, whose side are you on?"

The look he gave me guilted me into admitting, "All right, I know you're on my side. But, still, you think Gabe has a side?"

"Yeah, I do. Obviously, he wants more from your relationship, and you went off on him just because he asked. You're mad at him because he didn't seem to take your reasons seriously. But do you think maybe the real reasons are different than what you told him?"

"No, I don't. Could I have another drink, please?"

He went to refill my glass without comment. While he was gone, I thought about my conversation with Father Lindstrom. Was Coop getting at the same thing? I'd told Gabe it was about keeping my independence, my freedom, my home. Was it really more about keeping myself safe from getting too close to him, about my fear of—dreaded word—abandonment? Possibly, but only just. However, the not giving up my home part was definitely on point. It would take a pretty grand romance to pry me out of my loft, which Gabe and I were not.

Coop returned with my Jameson, this time on ice.

"OK, I don't want to talk about Gabe anymore. Want to hear how I solved Ryan Malloy's murder?"

"Wait a minute, I think you buried the lead. You know who killed Ryan?"

"Not exactly, but I know who didn't." I explained how Cole had taken James out of the running as Ryan's killer. And also, Steven.

"I'm glad to hear about James. But Steven was your favorite suspect. Now what's your plan?"

"I'm not sure I have a plan. I did what I said I'd do, help James. Now that I'm not working on the case with Gabe, maybe I'll just step back."

I downed half my drink in one swallow. "Yeah, no. I'm not doing that."

"Never thought it for a minute," he said.

"Can I have another drink, please?"

"How about something to eat instead?"

"I am kind of hungry. I didn't stick around for dinner with Gabe, delightful as that would have been."

"I haven't been to the grocery store this week, but I could fix you an omelet."

"Perfect."

I like to watch Coop working in the kitchen. He chopped onions and green peppers and mushrooms with a chef's knife, feeding the food quickly under the rapidly moving blade. While he sautéed them, I grated some cheese and beat the eggs with a little milk and some salt and pepper, then sat down to let him do the hard part.

"You're right. I do kind of hate to let go of Steven as Ryan's killer," I said sadly. "He's got the clearest motive, money. But, now that Cole provided a twofer alibi, one for James and one for Steven, it just won't work. But, there's still Lily."

"How's that?"

"She was having an affair with Ryan. That makes for a nice, spurned-lover motive. If Ryan had decided to dump her, that is. Which he no doubt would have at some point. That's his M.O."

Coop removed the vegetables from the pan, set them aside, and poured in the egg mixture before he said anything. "Have you talked to Charlie Ross about it?"

"Yes—about Steven and Lily, and Lily's affair that is."

"What are you holding back?"

"I'm not holding anything back. I'm pursuing a parallel investigation, that's all. Ross doesn't tell me everything he finds out, either."

"Ross is a cop conducting an official investigation. You're—"

"I'm what? A nosy reporter who gets in the way? You can say it. I've expended my anger quotient for the night. Besides, you're feeding me."

"I was going to say you're a gifted amateur who isn't responsible for making sure a full and fair investigation is conducted."

"I don't think I like the amateur part, but I'll accept gifted. I didn't tell Ross that Gina got pregnant in high school, and Ryan was the father. He has to do *some* work for himself, right? Besides, he probably already knows, and he thinks he's holding it back from me."

"Gina was pregnant? So, that's really why her parents sent her to North Carolina. That explains a lot."

"Doesn't it, though?" I watched as he added the sautéed vegetables and the cheese to the pan, folded the omelet over, slid it onto a plate, and handed it to me.

"It's looks great." I took a bite. "Tastes great, too."

While I ate, I asked Coop about work, but he changed the subject to a walleye fishing trip he was planning in the fall with a friend of his. I surmised he wasn't getting any happier at HPD, and that worried me a little.

"Want to watch a movie?" I asked.

"Maybe. What movie?" he asked cautiously.

Coop's all right with some of the classic films I like, but he's not that into *Laura* or *Leave Her to Heaven*, two movies I'll always stop and watch if they pop up when I'm checking out Turner Classic Movies. They're also on my list of go-tos when I need video comfort. But I have another one on there that we both agree on.

" 'Welcome, to *Jurassic Park*,' " I said, echoing a line from the movie that we had watched a million times on the VCR at his house when we were kids.

" 'Clever girl,' " he answered, also responding with a quote from the film.

I declined his offer of popcorn and claimed the couch, where I stretched out with a pillow behind my head. He pushed back in his leather recliner, and we streamed the movie that had nothing to do with our current lives, and everything to do with endless summer days and nights and less complicated times.

Despite the chasing, the screaming, the eating of people by dinosaurs, and the high level of tension throughout the film, I fell soundly asleep within the first hour. The drain of the anger I had felt at Gabe, followed by two stiff drinks, a full belly, and several days of too little sleep had done their work. Coop didn't wake me.

Sometime during the night, I dreamed that Gabe was putting a blanket over me. Then he leaned down and gently brushed my hair back from my forehead. I tried to wake up fully, but I couldn't. When I did, hours later, the dream seemed real for a minute. I couldn't help wishing it had been. A light blanket covered me, but I must have pulled it down from the back of the sofa in the night. I threw it off and stretched. I couldn't hear any noise coming from Coop's room. I wrote him a short note and left the house as quietly as I could.

---

## 32

It was only six a.m. when I got back to my place, so I figured I wouldn't have any trouble slipping in the back door of the building and up the stairs, unseen. I was wrong.

The rear doors for both the newspaper and my loft are in the same back entryway. Mine is on the right. The entrance to the *Times* is straight ahead as you come in. As I stepped inside, I saw Miguel walking toward me down the *Times* hallway. Any hope I had of going unnoticed was lost as he looked up, gave me a big smile, a wave, and hurried toward me.

"*Chica!*" he shouted as he pushed through the door.

"Miguel, why did you come to work so early?"

"No, no. I think the question is, why did you come home so late?" His grin was teasing, but I wasn't up for it.

"I had a not-so-great day yesterday. Well, let me amend that. Professionally it was good. Personally, not so much. I went over to Coop's to cry in my Jameson and fell asleep on the couch."

Immediately, he was all sympathy. "Do you want to tell *Ask Miguel* all about it?"

"Maybe later."

His eyes ran over my bedraggled appearance, complete with

couch-head hair, and he let it drop.

"Oh, but I have to tell you about Lily's friend Mandy. I found her on Instagram, and I DM'd her and she called me back."

"What did she say? Was Lily really with her Saturday night?"

"Yes. But Lily, she made up a little story for you. Mandy didn't ask Lily to come. Lily called and invited herself. Mandy was very surprised, because she and Lily, they don't text or talk at all anymore."

"That's interesting. Lily told me Mandy was clingy and wouldn't take the hint that Lily had moved on. What did she say about Lily leaving early, not spending the night?"

"Lily was never going to stay all night. Just until Mandy's husband got home at ten."

"This is getting better and better. If Lily left at ten, she could get to Ryan's from Ennisville by midnight, or even before, easy. It's less than a two-hour drive. Then, they could spend the whole night together. Steven didn't expect her home until the next day."

"But there's more. Mandy's husband was late. At ten fifteen, Lily said she had to leave."

At that point, Miguel engaged in a little dramatic retelling of Mandy's story.

"Mandy is tired, her mind is fuzzy from the medication, but she doesn't want Lily to go until Thomas gets home. She can't be alone. She can't even get up by herself, and her leg it hurts so bad! She begs Lily to stay. Lily won't. The next thing Mandy knows, her husband is shaking her, trying to wake her up. Lily is gone. It's two a.m. And ..." He paused until he got the desired response.

"And what?"

"And there is nothing left in the pill bottle! There were four pain pills when Thomas left. One to take at ten-thirty in the morning, one at four-thirty in the afternoon, and one again at ten-thirty at night. There should have been one left."

"You mean—"

"Yes! That's what Mandy thinks. Lily gave her double her pain meds, so Mandy would sleep and let her go and stop begging her to stay."

"Oh, man, that's cold. A little dangerous, too."

"Yes. Thomas, the husband, he was very mad."

"I would be, too. So Mandy knows for sure that Lily was there at ten-thirty though, right?"

"Yes, but she doesn't know when Lily left."

"Well, I'm gonna guess it was as soon as Mandy was deep in dreamland. It would have been tight, but if she pressed it—and there wouldn't have been much traffic at that hour—Lily could have been at the cottage by midnight or a little after. She had time to fight with Ryan, kill him, and zip back home to pretend to Steven that she'd been there since eleven-thirty. Then she got lucky, because Steven had his secret meet-up with Cole to lie about, so he didn't question her at all."

"What? Steven was with Cole Granger?"

"Yes, but it's not for publication yet. Also, James isn't a suspect anymore. I'll give you the details later."

"James isn't a suspect? What did he say when you told him?"

"Um, nothing. I didn't tell him. I imagine Gabe did, though. Which reminds me, I have to put a report together on the whole thing and email it to Gabe. I have to get busy."

I could see he didn't understand why I didn't have direct knowledge about whether or not Gabe had already talked to James. But he was sensitive enough not to dive for details at the moment. He just nodded and said, "OK. I'm in the office all morning. Come down later."

"Yeah, I will."

Once upstairs, I fulfilled my promise and wrote up a

detailed report for Gabe with everything that I knew, and also some things I couldn't prove but thought were true, with the caution that everything in it was confidential, except what he absolutely had to share with James.

I almost signed it "respectfully submitted" like Kinsey Milhone does in the Sue Grafton books, but I wasn't feeling that playful in relation to Gabe at the moment. After that I took a long shower and thought about how much I was going to miss having him in my life. But that wasn't my fault. It was his. Wasn't it? I didn't like the direction my thoughts were taking, but then I never do like raking over the ashes of one of my ill-considered temper flare-ups.

Father Lindstrom had told me not to let "the perfect be the enemy of the good." Gabe was a good man. I wanted him to be perfect. Which I, myself, was far from. Maybe I should call him. I hadn't behaved very well, and I could at least admit that and apologize. Would he even take my call? I probably wouldn't if the situation were reversed. I debated for a bit, then finally tried his office.

"Hi, Patty, this is Leah. Is Gabe busy?"

"Hello, Leah. He's getting ready for a meeting, but I'm sure he'll want to talk to you," she said. Patty Delwyn has been Miller Caldwell's secretary and protector for a long time. She had assumed the role with Gabe when he joined the firm, but she usually let my calls through. I waited as she connected me. But instead of Gabe, it was Patty who came back on the line.

"I'm sorry, Leah. Gabe is on another line. I didn't notice when we were talking. I can give him a message for you."

I doubted Gabe was on another phone call. When Patty told him it was me on the line, he must have said he didn't want to talk to me. She was probably surprised and a little curious, but Patty would never ask why.

"Um, no, that's OK, Patty, I'll try later. Thanks."

"And so, Miguel, that is the apex and the nadir of my last twenty-four hours. James is off the hook for the murder, and I'm on the hook for being an ass to Gabe."

We were sitting in the newsroom, Miguel at his desk and me on a chair beside it. He no longer had a private office, having relinquished that to Maggie when she stepped into the editor's job. But we were alone. Troy was doing an interview, Maggie was at a meeting, my mother was out somewhere, Courtnee was allegedly working on the monthly mileage logs out front, and Allie was handling the phones.

"Don't worry. Gabe likes you too much. He'll come around. Just be chill."

"I don't have much choice. Moving on from the soap opera that I have made of my life, how is *Ask Miguel* going?"

"Oh! You have to see this. How could I forget?" He swung his laptop around, and I saw that he'd been working on a reply to an *Ask Miguel* question. I read it out loud.

*Dear Miguel,*

*I sexted with my boyfriend, and now he's blackmailing me. He isn't even really my boyfriend. I just wanted him to be, that's why I sent him the photos. Only now I know that he did something really bad, criminal even. I told him if he didn't tell the police, I would. But he says if I do, he's going to put the pictures I sent him online. Everyone would see them, my dad, even! It will ruin my whole life. My dad will be so disappointed in me. But if I don't tell, someone could go to jail for something he didn't do. I don't know what to do.*

"Miguel, this kid is in real torment. And maybe in real trouble. We have to find out who sent it."

"I know. I think we could trace the IP address it was sent from, but what if she used a public computer, like at the library?"

"That's more complicated, but maybe we—"

"You don't have to look."

We both turned. Allie was standing in the doorway.

"It was me. And everything is ruined!"

Miguel and I glanced at each other in mutual shock.

"Oh, *niñita*! I'm so sorry."

She burst into tears. He walked toward her, his arms open. She fell into them, sobbing.

"Allie, sweetie, it'll be OK. Here, sit down," I said, vacating the chair I'd been sitting on, and leaning on the corner of Miguel's desk instead. She pulled away from Miguel, leaving a large wet patch of tears and mucous on his untucked, coral-colored shirt, which I knew he prized as his summer find. It was a testament to his kindness that as Allie apologized for crying all over it, he shrugged and said, "It's just a shirt. It will wash. But you, Allie, tell us. Everything."

Out poured a story that a number of adolescent girls could tell, even the really smart ones like Allie. She liked a popular boy at school. She thought he liked her, too. They texted, they Snap-chatted, they flirted, and he asked her for pictures. And he kept asking, and teasing, and flirting, and pressuring. Finally, because she wanted him to like her and was worried that he'd drop her if she didn't, she texted some photos.

"The pictures I sent him, they're so embarrassing, so humiliating. He promised he'd never show them to anybody. And now he's going to put them on the internet. How stupid, stupid, stupid I am!" She looked down at her hands, holding them tightly together in her lap.

"How bad are they, Allie?" I asked as gently as I could. "Are they just photos? Is there video, too? Or are—"

"No! Oh, no. It's not like video or anything!" Her head shot up. She swallowed hard before she elaborated.

"I'm in this, sort of, sexy underwear, you know." Her face and neck had flushed a red so bright it looked as though it would be hot to the touch. "And, um, I did some, you know, looking over my shoulder and tilting my head and stuff, you know, like models do. And in one ... I-I took off my bra. But you can't see my face," she quickly added. "I read you shouldn't do a picture like that and show your face."

I did my best to conceal my dismay as she covered that face with her hands.

"Allie, what is this boy's name? Why did you think you could trust him?" I asked.

"His name is Evan Luedtke. He said he had a secret about himself that he would tell me if I sent the pictures. But if I didn't, he'd know he was wrong about me—that he couldn't trust me if I didn't trust him. I know it sounds so ridiculous now. But I just liked him so much! So, I sent the pictures. And then Evan *did* tell me, but it wasn't just a secret about him, it was about something terrible he did ..." Her voice trailed off.

"What did Evan tell you?"

"It's Mr. Shaw. Evan and a friend of his set him up. He didn't tell me who the friend was. The pornography email to Emily, it's a fake. I know I should have told as soon as I found out, but I just couldn't. I tried to get Evan to tell the police what he did. But he wouldn't. I told him Mr. Shaw might go to jail, but he didn't care. I told him I'd go to the police. He said if I did, he'd post my photos online. And now my dad will know what I did, everyone, all the kids at school."

"Allie, hold on. Take it back a little. The email came from Mr. Shaw's computer, the police traced it. How did Evan do that?"

"He spearfished Mr. Shaw. You know, sent him a fake email that looked like it came from a real place, so Mr. Shaw would click the link in it. That's how he got Mr. Shaw's email password. Then, when Mr. Shaw was out of his classroom, he put this app on his computer, so he could get remote access. That night, he used it to get into Mr. Shaw's email. He wrote the email to Emily. Then he scheduled it to go out like at three in the morning, so it would look like nobody but Mr. Shaw could have had access to his computer. The next day after school, Evan had his friend stop Mr. Shaw and ask him a question at the vending machine. Everybody knows Mr. Shaw goes there for a Coke after sixth hour. While they were talking, Evan took the app off Mr. Shaw's computer."

I shuddered at the ease with which a life could be ruined by an adolescent with a few technical skills and an under-developed moral compass.

"Why did Evan want to hurt James that way?" Miguel asked.

"Because when Mr. Shaw failed him in biology, Evan wasn't eligible to play in the state baseball championship. He wanted to pay him back."

"Seems fair," I said, "payback for self-inflicted loss of eligibility for a baseball game equals total destruction of a man's career and reputation."

"I'm sorry, so, so, sorry," Allie said miserably. "I should have told. I—"

"Allie, stop. You did tell. Now, we start taking care of it."

"How? How can this be taken care of? My life is over. Evan's going to show those pictures, everyone will see them. I can never go back to school again!"

"Hey, let's take this one step at a time. The first thing you need to do is tell your dad."

"I don't think I can. He's going to be so mad at me. Even worse, he's going to be so ashamed of me. I'm so ashamed of me! And what about his job? He always says Sheriff Lamey is just looking for an excuse to fire him. Maybe I gave it to him. How can a cop have a daughter like me? Everyone's going to think I'm a-a-a slut! I've never even had sex! I hate myself!"

"Allie, don't say those things about yourself. Ever. You're a good person who made a bad mistake. A lot of girls—a lot of grown women—have done what you did. You have to tell your dad, you know that."

My heart hurt for the girl in front of me, her cheeks flushed and eyes red from crying, wearing jeans, a vintage Wonder Woman T-shirt, and a light blue pair of embroidered Converse high tops. She looked closer to twelve than fifteen, but she'd gotten herself into a very adult problem. I didn't have to work hard at all to know how much she dreaded telling her father what she had done.

"Will you talk to my dad with me, Leah? Please, I just can't do it by myself."

———

When I called Ross and asked him to come over, he was reluctant until I said it was about Allie.

"Is she all right? What's the matter?"

"Yes, she's fine. But she's ready to tell you what's been bothering her lately, and she asked me if I'd be there, too."

"Why does she want you there? What's goin' on? Are you sure—"

"Yes, I'm sure she's all right. We'll be upstairs at my place."

---

I'd set things up so Ross sat on one side of the island in my kitchen, with Allie and me across from him.

"Dad, I have to tell you something. It's not very good. In fact, it's pretty bad. And if you want to send me down to Texas to live with Mom and her boyfriend, I understand. I'm so sorry, Dad."

"Allie, what are you talkin' about? What is it? What are you sorry for?" Ross's eyes darted back and forth between me and Allie. She took a deep breath that turned into a shaky sigh. I squeezed the hand she held in her lap as she began her story. It was clearer and more organized than what had spilled out to me and Miguel, but it was punctuated by tears as well. Ross listened in silence, though his expression ran the gamut from shock, to anger, to sorrow, and back to anger.

When she finished, Allie looked at him with a mix of pleading and shame in her eyes. I held my breath. How he responded now could set the course of their relationship for years to come—maybe for a lifetime. He stood up, and so did I, moving from my place beside Allie. She turned to face him as he walked around the island, her body tense, like a deer ready to run at the slightest sound.

Neither one said a word. Ross stopped in front of her, shaking his head slowly and pressing his lips firmly together as though to keep his words from tumbling out. Then he stepped forward, and wrapped her in a big bear hug, rocking her back and forth. As she leaned into him, he patted her on the back and whispered over and over, "It's OK, Allie. I love you sweetheart. It's all right."

Which in the end, was probably the very best thing he could have said.

"I'll leave you guys to figure things out. I'll be down in the office if you need me. Just pull the door shut when you go."

## 34

I walked into the break room and saw my mother halfway inside the refrigerator, searching for something and muttering under her breath. She emerged triumphant, holding a covered blue plastic bowl aloft in one hand.

"You look like you just pulled Excalibur out of a stone," I said.

"I feel like I have. I had to practically excavate this tuna macaroni salad. There are so many Styrofoam containers of leftovers, mystery brown bags, and bottles full of fermenting things in there. No one throws anything out. They just push things around and jam another thing next to it and leave it there to turn into green mold."

"Doesn't sound like the refrigerator is sparking joy for you, Mom."

"That's why I'm emailing everyone with a warning: anything you value, take out of the fridge by five p.m. today. Anything left gets dumped."

"You sound kind of crabby."

"I am, a little, I guess. Want to join me for lunch in my office? I'll tell you all about it."

"Wow. A crabby lunch. Sounds great."

"Well, there is the tuna macaroni salad with my special dressing."

"OK. Sold."

My mother sat behind her desk and I was across from her in the guest chair. Placemats, silverware, and napkins, all pulled from the depths of the filing cabinet behind her, were in front of each of us, as were paper plates heaped high. My mother's tuna macaroni salad is epic. Besides your standard pasta and tuna, she adds peas, finely diced green and red peppers, onion, celery, and carrots and a dressing for which she is justly famous. She only makes the salad in the summer, and it is worth waiting all year for.

After I consumed my first forkful, I said, "All right. I'm ready. Crab away."

"Oh, it's not really crabby, I guess. More like frustrated and sad. I spent some time with Joanna this morning. I was with her when she heard the news that James isn't a person of interest anymore. She just collapsed—emotionally, I mean, not physically."

"Because she wanted James to be guilty?"

"No, it's not about James, really. She was just so invested in having an answer, and Steven encouraged her to think that James would be arrested soon. Now, who knows where Sheriff Lamey will look next? And she's getting weaker every day. I don't see how she'll have the physical, let alone the emotional, reserves to make it through the funeral on Friday."

I thought I knew what was coming next.

"Joanna realizes she wasn't fair to you."

"You mean when she accused me of exploiting Ryan's death, and of working against her instead of helping her, because I was helping Gabe?"

"Well, yes. She was so distraught. She made assumptions,

because she was too upset to think straight. You can understand that, can't you?"

"Yeah, sure, of course I can."

"Well, I thought maybe you could stop by and see her. Just let her know that you're still working on things—you are, aren't you?"

"Yes, I am. But there isn't much I can tell her. I've thought all along that Steven was the leading candidate, but it doesn't seem so now. I think Lily's a possibility, but I'm not going to tell Joanna that."

"Lily?"

"She was having an affair with Ryan. I'm not sure that qualifies as confidential since more than a few people either know or suspect. But—"

"I know the drill. Don't tell anyone. I won't, I won't."

"But anyway, yes, I'll stop by and see Joanna, if you think it would help."

"I do, hon, thanks."

I was just working up to telling her about Gabe and me, when she brought up the subject.

"How would you and Gabe like to go out to dinner with Paul and me on Sunday? We're going to Quivey's Grove in Madison. I think Gabe would enjoy it. You can take a little time out for that, can't you?"

"I can. I don't know about Gabe."

The tone of my voice alerted her that something was amiss.

"What's going on?"

I went through my story.

"I feel pretty bad for the way I acted. I just went off on him. I'm not exactly sure where it came from. When he started talking, at first I just sort of froze, and then I started to feel super anxious. I think I really hurt his feelings. I tried to reach him, but he doesn't want to talk to me.

"I'm sorry, Leah. But don't be so hard on yourself. Gabe may have been thinking about the idea of living together for a while, but he just sprung it on you. It's a big step. I don't think your reaction was so out of line. You've worked very hard the last couple of years to get where you are. It's natural for someone like you not to be eager to upend your life. He'll come around."

I appreciated the support, even if I wasn't sure what she meant by "someone like" me. I didn't care to explore it at the moment, so I changed the subject to something that I knew would capture her full attention.

"Allie's having a rough time, and it's going to get rougher. I think it would help if you know what's up, and she doesn't have to tell you herself." When I finished the story, the vagaries of my love life had receded completely, and her focus was on Allie's situation.

"Oh, my gosh. What that girl's been carrying around with her! I guess that's the kind of thing Coop's Citizen Task Force is supposed to prevent. And, by the way, you didn't have to explain sexting to me. Of course I know what it is."

" 'Of course?' I'm not sure I want to know what that means."

"Don't be foolish. I do read, and I do live in the twenty-first century, right along with you. I could just take that nasty boy Evan and turn him upside down and shake him!" Since my mother is about five feet two and a hundred and fifteen pounds soaking wet, that was unlikely. Still, it was probably best that she never be in the same room with Allie's blackmailer. "What's going to happen now?" she asked.

"I left Ross and Allie upstairs, but I imagine they've left by now. He'll get in touch with Erin Harper, I'm sure. She's in charge of James's email case, which happily is about to go out the window. It's pretty serious, what that Evan kid did, and Allie's going to be in some trouble, too. But she did come forward, plus she was the victim, not the perpetrator.

"And she's just fifteen, so whatever goes down, it'll go through juvenile court. If the boy—Evan—is under seventeen his case will, too, but the hammer's going to fall a lot harder on him. If he's lucky, he'll come in front of Judge Rathbun, and then he might get by with probation, counseling, and some serious community service time. As for the kid that helped Evan, he'll probably be in for pretty much the same thing. James might be able to sue the parents for fraud or damage to his reputation or both, but I doubt he will."

"I am so, so glad that you were out of high school before texting and Facebook and everything else took off."

"Why? You think I'd be sexting my boyfriend?"

"I'm sure you'd find something much worse to do," she said darkly.

Actually, I was glad social media hadn't been a thing when I was a teenager. I didn't need digital evidence of some of the stupid things I'd done when I was in high school—or after.

"You'd better not count on Allie this afternoon, maybe not tomorrow, either. She's got a lot to cope with."

"I like that girl so much. I wish she had more self-confidence —she's smart, she's pretty, but she doesn't have any belief in herself."

"Yeah, she's a great kid. And Ross is trying hard to be a great dad. He really stepped up today. It was nice to see."

"Yes, but she could use a mother figure in her life, especially right now. I don't suppose there's any chance of Charlie getting married in the near future?"

"Not that I've heard."

"I wonder ..." She left her thought hanging until I prodded her back into the conversation.

"Wonder what?"

"Oh, I was just thinking. St. Stephen's had a soup and salad luncheon the other day, and I took Allie with me at noon. Marcy White was there and—"

"You're seriously trying to matchmake Marcy and Ross?" I interrupted, incredulous at the thought.

"No, let me finish. I'm thinking about matchmaking Marcy and Allie. It could be good for both of them. The three of us chatted for a few minutes at the lunch, then Allie went to get something from the dessert table. Marcy paid her about the highest compliment she could. She told me that Allie looked just like her Robin would have, and Allie's about the same age as she'd be now. I've never heard her talk so easily about Robin before. Maybe Marcy could give Allie some of the attention her own mother never did."

"Maybe," I said, though I was pretty skeptical. "Marcy's not exactly the warm, nurturing type. She's more the brusque, don't-bother-me-kid type."

"Don't be so negative. You're the one who said Marcy was so good with Gina."

"Yeah, that's true, she was."

"Allie's looking for a sidebar for her vaccination story, isn't she?"

"Yes. I told her she needed to put a more human face on the story. She's supposed to find someone who can't be vaccinated because of age, or a compromised immune system, or allergic reaction, and who became seriously ill after exposure to the measles, or mumps, or flu, or whatever." I wondered where this was going.

"I think I'm going to tell Allie about Marcy's baby, Robin. If that doesn't put a face on the consequences of not getting vaccinated, I don't know what does. And it's a way for the two of them to talk, maybe each open up a little, start to forge a relationship."

"And I thought *I* was supposed to be the callous reporter

willing to do anything for a story. Do you think it's really fair to Marcy? Asking her to talk about Robin's death for the newspaper? I don't think she'll want to do it."

"Maybe not, but she might be ready. I think that sharing something like that with Allie might encourage Allie to share some of her own feelings. Allie's a sensitive enough girl to back off if Marcy doesn't want to do it. But, if they do connect, even a little, it could be the beginning of a beautiful friendship."

"All right, when you start with the *Casablanca* quotes, I know there's no deterring you. Maybe you should write an app. You could be the Tinder of potential parent-child match-ups."

"That's not a bad idea. Maybe I could find a more compatible daughter match."

"Your sarcasm doesn't fool me. Father Lindstrom told me that you said it was an amazing experience to have a daughter like me."

"I did. And I also told him it was an alarming, disturbing, overwhelming, and occasionally irritating experience, too. I see he left that part out."

"Back at you. Thanks for lunch. Let me know how the matchmaking goes. And yes, I'll stop by Joanna's this afternoon."

---

I expected to see Wanda when Joanna's front door opened, but it was a young woman wearing light blue hospital scrubs.

"Hello, I'm Leah Nash. I'm here to see Joanna," I said, extending my hand.

She gave it a brief shake and smiled. "I'm Felicity, Mrs. Burke's home care aide. I'm not usually here in the afternoon, but Wanda had an appointment out-of-town."

"Is Joanna feeling well enough to see me? I won't stay long."

"Oh, yes, I think so. She had a visitor just before lunch who seemed to really lift her spirits. I just gave her meds to her, though, so she may get a little dozy on you."

I followed Felicity down the hall. She tapped lightly on the door before opening it, then motioned for me to go in. From what my mother had said, I expected Joanna to be resting on the sofa, or perhaps even in a hospital bed. Instead, she was upright on her wingback chair, and when she saw me, she managed a smile.

"Leah, thank you for coming. Your mother said you might. Please, sit down."

As I did, she said, "I want to apologize to you, for what I said and the way I behaved the last time I saw you. I don't know what came over me."

"Grief, Joanna. It doesn't leave a lot of room for social niceties. You were hurting. I understand. You still are. No need to apologize, really."

What I didn't understand was the disparity between what my mother had described, and what I was seeing now. Joanna was obviously unwell, but her eyes had a light in them I hadn't expected. The coolness of her hand on mine told me that the pink in her cheeks was due not to fever, but to excitement. I was mystified but couldn't think of a tactful way to ask her why she no longer looked like a woman who might not last the week.

"It's true, Ryan's death is more painful than anything I've ever experienced. When the sheriff told me that James was no longer a suspect, and he didn't have anything to tell me about where his investigation was going, I just felt hopeless. Steven was wrong about James, and I don't trust the sheriff's reassurances. Please tell me that you'll keep looking. I still want Ryan's killer found with every fiber of my being."

"I meant it when I said Detective Ross is a good investigator.

He's a good man, too. I know he won't quit on you. I won't either."

"Thank you. It means the world to me."

"Joanna, my mother was very worried about your, um, emotional state, when she was here today, but you seem, almost, well ..."

"Almost happy? Is that what you're trying to say? You're right. I'm as close to happy as I'll ever be again without Ryan. I've had some wonderful news today. I have a grandson, Leah. Ryan's son. That means a part of my son is still alive."

I was stunned that she knew, and my face must have shown it. I was even more surprised when she revealed who had given her the news.

"Gina Cox came to see me just before lunch. I'm so glad Wanda wasn't here. Gina was so nervous that if Wanda had sent her away, I don't think she'd have come back. But Felicity let her in, and I am so grateful. She had such wonderful news. Did you know about Ryan's son?"

"Yes, Gina told me."

"I hope I can hang on long enough to see him found. Even if I can't, it feels so comforting to know that he's somewhere in this world. I told Gina I'd hire someone to find him. I'm changing my will, too, so that he inherits Ryan's share of the estate."

"I'm glad for you, Joanna. I had no idea Gina planned to tell you."

"I don't think she did, at first. She was very anxious. She was afraid I'd think that she was trying to get money out of me for herself. But I understand the need she feels to find her son. If you'd ever been a mother, you would, too, Leah. I'm so happy I can do this for my son's sake.

"Oh, I heard how he reacted when Gina approached him at the reception. But I'm sure he was just surprised, shocked even, to see her after so long. She admitted she didn't tell him anything—she was too out of control. I know if she'd been able to talk to him about the baby that Ryan would've wanted to find his son."

OK, so I'm an asshat. I couldn't help thinking that Ryan would not have been at all happy to have a sixteen-year-old son pop into his life. If Gina had told him, he would have brushed her off and not given his child another thought.

"Have you told Steven?"

"I will tonight. He and Lily are coming for dinner. I've already talked to my lawyer. He's making the changes, and he'll bring them for me to sign after Ryan's funeral on Friday." She paused, then went on.

"I can't believe I'm even saying the words 'Ryan's funeral.' I don't think I could get through it without Gina's news. I want Steven to know the change I'm making to the will. Although it really won't affect him, because the money will still be divided evenly, minus the fund I set up to find my grandson. I think Steven will be glad for me."

Again, I'm an asshat. Because I was pretty darn sure that Steven was not going to be happy that he wasn't going to get the whole four million. Even in death, Ryan could still stick it to him, by having a son who would keep Steven from getting the entire—and much needed—inheritance. Still, I opted for diplomacy.

"I think it's good that you'll be able to tell him the news yourself."

"I know I'm going on and on, but it was so wonderful to talk with Gina today. Like a miracle, really. Or a happy ending to a sad movie. I didn't know that Ryan was even seeing her when they were in high school. If only she'd told Ryan about the baby back then, things would have turned out so differently."

And that makes me once, twice, three times an asshat, because I didn't believe for a second that Ryan would have let knowledge of Gina's pregnancy affect his life in the least. Instead he would have taken active measures to ensure that he was free of any inconvenient entanglements.

Joanna had ended her last sentence on a stifled yawn, and I noticed that she was struggling to keep her eyes open.

"I'm going to let you get some rest, Joanna. I'll be in touch."

---

## 35

I made an unplanned detour on my way back home and drove to the Himmel Motel to see if Gina was there. When I knocked on the door, it opened right away to a smiling, Gina.

"Leah, hi! Come in." She opened the door wide. Instead of stepping into a gloomy space, as I had on my first visit, the room was flooded with sunlight that matched Gina's mood. It was still pretty messy, though. She moved a pile of clothes off a chair and shoved the covers over on the unmade bed to give herself a seat.

"I should pick up a little, I guess. But I'm too excited. I can't settle down."

Much like Joanna, Gina had undergone a radical change in her emotions, and she couldn't seem to stop smiling. It was nice to see.

"I think I know why. I just left Joanna's. I was really surprised when she said you'd been to see her, and that you told her about your son." I couldn't bring myself to say, "Ryan's son," despite the pleasure the phrase had given Joanna.

"I surprised myself. I didn't plan it at all. But I've been feeling a little shaky with everything going on, and I went to an

AA meeting this morning. We talked about the ninth step again —that's the one about making direct amends to people we've harmed. And it came to me—there was one major harm I'd done way before I started drinking, but it was the *cause* of my drinking."

"What's that?"

"Don't you see? It all started because I never told Ryan about the baby. I tried, but I should have tried harder. When I found his number and called his house in Seattle, and Joanna said he was out with his girlfriend, it crushed me. But for the baby's sake, I should have told Joanna right then. I know what you're going to say," she added, in response to the look on my face.

"Ryan wasn't the person his mother thinks he was, and he probably wouldn't have wanted anything to do with the baby. But I wondered if his mother might, especially now with Ryan gone. I was scared to see her, though. I didn't know how she'd react. I didn't know if she'd throw me out, or call me a liar, or maybe even think I was just trying to get money out of her. But I knew that I had to tell her.

"I turned myself over to my Higher Power. And it came out better than I could ever have expected. She believes me. She's going to help me find Caleb! I'll have to take DNA tests and Caleb will, when we find him, but I'm not worried about that. He's Ryan's son. He's the first boy I was ever with. There wasn't anybody else. I don't even care about the inheritance, but it will be wonderful for Caleb. He'll be able to live whatever kind of life he wants. I just hope he can forgive me for giving him up."

Having used up my asshat allotment for the day, I resolutely turned my mind away from the thought it kept pushing to the forefront. Namely, that Gina's son had probably already had a much better life than he would have had with a single parent, teenage mother, whose own parents threw her out, and a teenage father who was at best a disengaged narcissist. Joanna was thrilled now, because her grandson was a connection to the only thing truly important to her, Ryan. But it seemed likely to me that if Gina had come forward with a baby when Ryan was still in high school, that Joanna would have done whatever Ryan wanted her to do. And it wouldn't have been to bring his unplanned offspring into his carefree life.

"I can see why you're feeling so happy. Have you told your parents?"

"My mother. She asked me not to say anything yet to my dad. Not much chance of that. We weren't doing great before. Since I told him that Ryan was the father, it's as bad as it was between us when he threw me out. It's only because my mother said she'd leave him—which shocked me—that he's even letting her come to see me. I love my baby, well, my boy, I guess I should say—it's hard to think of him as almost grown.

"I love him so much that I can't understand how my father turned his back on me, his own daughter. I don't want anything to do with the kind of God that tells him to cut me out of his life. I would do anything to have my boy in mine. But I'm not going to waste any more time trying to change things. And I'm not going to let the way things are with my parents make me feel bad, either. I called Marcy and told her the news. We're going out to dinner tomorrow to celebrate. I haven't been this happy since before I met Ryan."

I had intended to ask Gina more about the night Ryan died, either to find a lead to something verifiable that would prove her innocence, or to find a hole in her story that indicated her guilt. And I wanted to press her more on what her mother might have told her about Warren Cox's movements that night. But I didn't have the heart for it. For maybe the first time in sixteen years, she felt really hopeful. Let her have her moment.

"Well, I should go. I just wanted to see how you're doing. Are you going to the service Friday?"

"I don't want to. All those people whispering and pointing. And the gossip will really be spreading by then. But Joanna wants me to, so I told her I would."

"OK, I'll see you then, I guess."

"Yeah, see you then."

---

The mix of good and bad news the day had brought so far had left me feeling like I was on a seesaw, tipping back and forth between elation and disappointment. I was really happy for James, getting out from under both life as an alleged pedophile/stalker and as a murder suspect, but I was worried about Allie. I felt glad for Gina—that she had a shot at finding her son, but worried about Steven's reaction. Lily could cause problems for her, too. But there wasn't anything I could do about any of it—for the moment, anyway. So, I sat down at my laptop and began working on something I *could* have a positive impact on, my manuscript.

I'd been working for a couple of hours when Ross called.

"Hey! How's Allie? How did things go?"

"She's good. It went good. We met with Kristin Norcross from the prosecutor's office and Coop."

"Coop? But Erin Harper is the investigator for James's case."

"She is, but she's at some kinda training today, so Coop sat in. I was real proud of Allie. She told her story straight, didn't make excuses. I think it's gonna be OK. Kristin told her it all goes through juvie, and the files are sealed, so no one will know what she did. Allie was so relieved she started cryin' again. Kristin, she gave Allie some tough talk, too. Told her sexting in

Wisconsin, even for teens, comes under pornography laws. I'm glad she hit hard on that. I didn't wanta have to be bad cop to my own kid."

"What about the boy, Evan? The one that actually framed James and blackmailed Allie?

"I guess he was a tough guy at first, but he finally admitted what he did, said he wasn't ever going to put the photos online, he was just tryin' to scare Allie into not tellin'. "

"Allie said a friend of Evan's helped him get to James's computer. Will anything happen to him?"

"Doubt it. Evan's sayin' he did it all himself, that Allie got the story wrong, nobody else was involved. I guess he doesn't want anybody to think he's a rat. I'm just glad my girl was brave enough to turn Evan in. His dad called me a little while ago. I thought he was gonna start runnin' down Allie, but he was real embarrassed. Wanted to apologize for his kid. Told me no matter what a judge decides, Evan's not gonna be playin' base-ball or anything else his senior year. And he's not gettin' his phone back for a good long time. Gonna have to use one of those grandma phones with no internet."

"That'll probably be the worst part of his punishment. It'll really cut into his social life."

"Yeah? Excuse me while I don't cry any tears for that little pissant. He should pay big time for what he did—to Allie and to Shaw. Allie called Shaw, by the way, just a little while ago. She was real nervous, but she wanted to do it. He coulda been a real jerk to her. I figure it's within his rights, after what he's been through. But Allie said he was pretty nice, considerin'. I'm proud of my girl."

"You should be, Ross. You should be proud of yourself, too. You did some outstanding dad work today. You said exactly what Allie needed to hear, at one of the worst and scariest moments of her life. Nicely done."

"Ah, I didn't say anything special. I just told her I loved her."

"That's my point, Ross. That's my point."

"Yeah? Well, all this nicey-nice stuff, it's gettin' on my nerves. I gotta go."

I couldn't help smiling after I hung up—and thinking that given the choice, I would have taken gruff, growly, stubborn, opinionated, but stand-by-you Ross in a heartbeat over my own charming, handsome, affectionate, but leave-you-in-the-lurch-all-alone father. Allie was a lucky girl.

Then I called Coop.

"Hey, you. Thanks for listening to me whine last night, and for the couch."

"You're welcome. Things any better?"

"They're OK. I've been thinking about what you said, and my mom said kind of the same thing. I really don't want to move in with Gabe, but I didn't have to take his head off just because he suggested it. I don't know what's going to happen. I tried to reach him today, but it's pretty obvious he doesn't want to hear from me. But, I didn't call for that. You already know that Allie dropped a bombshell today. Ross told me that you were in the interview with Kristin. Thanks for that. I'm sure it was a little easier because Allie knows you."

"Erin and the captain were at a training today. So, I sat in. That's all. I hope it helped Allie. Didn't go over so well with Erin, though."

"Why's that?"

"She thinks I was trying to take over."

"You weren't trying to do that. You were trying to help a kid who needed it."

"Yeah, well, Erin didn't see it that way, and technically, she's right. She should've been part of the team making the decision, not me. She's going to take it up with the captain."

"Uh-oh. I hope that doesn't mean more task forces, fewer actual cases, in your future."

"We'll see. Don't worry about it. I'm just glad things worked out all right for Allie and for Charlie."

"Yeah, how about that guy? Ross is really doing the dad-thing proud, isn't he? I never would have imagined it."

"He takes being a father seriously."

I remembered then that Coop had believed he was going to have a baby with his wife, Rebecca, and how much he had looked forward to it, and how badly it had ended. I changed the subject.

"My day was pretty full besides the Allie business." I told him about seeing Joanna and Gina, and my mother's scheme to bring Allie and Marcy together.

"Your mom could be on to something. Even if she isn't, you won't be able to stop her."

"Don't I know that."

"Runs in the family," he said.

Before I had a chance to protest, he asked, "Are you going to Ryan's funeral?"

"Yeah. Are you?"

"Planning on it. If I don't see you before, I'll see you there."

"OK, bye."

I was still holding my phone when a text came in. Gabe.

*I'm not angry, just not ready to talk. Thanks for the smart work you did for James.*

Fine. I'd made as many attempts at a *mea culpa* as I could. Now it was up to Gabe. I wasn't going to beg him to talk to me, or sit around like a broken-hearted high schooler waiting for the next text to come in. I had plenty of grown-up things to do, like make a plan for digging into Lily's alibi, look over the website stats and see if *Ask Miguel* was bringing more traffic to the *Himmel Times* online site, and, oh yeah, pound out some more chapters on my book, so I could keep this place and not have to move back in with my mother.

But right then, I felt the need for a little me time. I did a quick change into my jammies. Then I made a deep dive into a half-gallon of Breyer's Mint Chip ice cream, while watching *Gaslight* on Turner Classic Movies. Then I went to bed.

## 36

In the morning I wandered downstairs just before eight to see if Allie had come in, and to let Miguel know what had happened, in case he hadn't heard.

Curious to know if my mother's edict had been followed, I checked the break room refrigerator. It was pristine. As I closed the door, she came in carrying a container of what looked like Cranberry Hootie Creek cookies.

"A reward for good behavior?" I asked, as she placed her burden down on the counter and took the lid off. I grabbed a cookie.

"Positive reinforcement. We'll see if it works."

"I don't know, Mom. In my experience with break room refrigerators over more than a decade, I'd have to say, nature abhors an orderly fridge."

"Cookies!" Courtnee cried as she came into the room, followed by Troy and Allie. Right behind them were Maggie and Miguel.

Maggie boomed out in her cement mixer voice, "There better be strong brew in that pot, because I'm out of coffee at home, and that's not a good thing. And I don't mean that weak stuff you made yesterday, Troy. You could've fed that to a baby, and he would've slept the night through."

"Hey, Allie, how's it going?" I asked, while Maggie schooled Troy on the correct number of scoops per pot.

"Good!" She gave me a big smile and her blue eyes sparkled. She got a cookie for herself and was turning to go out front when Courtnee, who had been reading something on her phone, let out a small squeal.

"OMG! Listen to this on *Tea to GO!*"

She began reading breathlessly.

*We hear a certain county law officer's teenage daughter texted some very naughty pictures to her boyfriend. It's a crime in Wisconsin, so it's nice that her daddy has pull. GO News is a family friendly publication, so we won't be showing the photo we received from an anonymous source. But we hear the Himmel High website is seeing a LOT of traffic this morning. And visitors are seeing a lot of that certain girl.*

I looked at Allie. Her face had gone white. She stood as still as a French royal waiting for the guillotine to fall. And fall it did.

"How could anybody be that stupid? I mean, seriously, I—" Courtnee had apparently gone to the site as she talked, because her eyebrows lifted almost to her hairline. She looked up from her phone and stared at Allie with a shocked expression on her face. Allie turned and ran out of the room. Miguel followed her.

"What's going on?" Maggie asked.

"Allie was sexting and somebody posted her picture online," Courtnee said.

"What?"

"Sexting. She texted a picture of herself—"

"I know what sexting is, Courtnee. What I don't know is what it has to do with Allie."

"Well, you don't have to be all salty about it, Maggie. I was just—"

"Courtnee, I think the phone is ringing in reception. Come on, let's go," my mother said, taking Courtnee by the arm and almost physically pulling her out of the room.

I told Maggie and Troy the abbreviated version of Allie's story.

"Damn that Spencer Karr and *GO News*," Maggie said. "You expect that kind of gossip rag in a city, but here?"

"How did they even get the story if Allie's going through juvenile court?" Troy asked.

"Someone must have tipped them off," I said.

"The kid she sent the pictures to?" Maggie asked.

"I doubt it," I said. "From what I hear, his parents came down pretty hard on him. He'd have to be super stupid to do something like that before he faces a judge in court."

"It's Lieutenant Harper's case, right?" Troy asked.

"Yeah, and Erin will not be liking this kind of messing around with the investigation."

"Hey, Maggie, my sexting story is supposed to run this week, but do you think we should hold it for a little while? I mean, if we run a story about sexting in school, right after Allie's thing—that might just, you know, bring all eyes back on her, and—"

"You don't need to hold the story for me."

Allie had returned, and whatever Miguel had said to her, it must have been good. Her eyes were dry and her head was held high.

"In fact, you can interview me, Troy, if you want. I could tell kids some things about what not to do. It's too late for me. It's going to be pretty awful at school. But it still isn't as bad as it's been for Mr. Shaw. I let him take the blame for something he didn't do. I guess I can take the hit for something I actually did."

She turned to Maggie then. "I'm really ashamed, Maggie. I feel so, so bad. Not just for myself, but for my dad, and for the paper, too. I embarrassed everybody. I thought nobody was going to find out, but now everybody knows. I understand if you don't want me to work here anymore."

"Who said anything about you not working here anymore?" Maggie asked. "Experience is the best teacher, kiddo. Even when it knocks you on your ass. You're doing fine here. Now, don't you have a story due yourself? I want to see what's happening with your vaccination piece. And we'll talk later about whether Troy interviews you or not."

I heard the doorbell jingle out front, signaling that someone had entered the reception area. Seconds later Courtnee came back into the break room, no doubt having escaped while my mother answered a customer's question.

"Allie, I was thinking. I mean, it's not that bad. Well, it is *bad*, obvs, but it's not like you're one of the popular kids or anything, right? So it's just like, yeah, it's a surprise that someone basic like you does something sort of skanky, but nobody's gonna like, *care*."

"Thanks?" Allie said, the uptick in her voice conveying sarcasm that was lost on Courtnee. She looked at me over Courtnee's head. The half smile she gave made me think she just might be able to weather this. As they walked out together, Courtnee continued offering her brand of comfort.

"You should talk to Miguel. His cousin Sofia was like a prostitute or something, and it was in the paper and everything. Nobody said hardly anything about it, and she was a cheerleader!"

As is often the case, Courtnee's statement had barely a nodding acquaintance with the actual facts.

"Do you want to take that?" I asked Miguel, as the two of them moved out of earshot.

"No, it's all right. Courtnee, she's gonna be Courtnee. She's trying."

"I'll say she is, but not in the sense of the word that you

mean. What did you say to Allie to get her to come back in? It must have been pretty good."

"I just told her to do what I do, when I need to be strong."

"What's that?"

"I say to myself, WWLD."

"Is that another new texting shorthand I don't know? You keep forgetting. I'm on the thirty-plus side of the millennial cohort. What does WWLD mean?"

"It's simple. I told her think, *What Would Leah Do*? And then do it."

His phone rang then, and as he answered, he flashed me a smile and began moving toward his desk, leaving me staring after him in stunned surprise.

I started for the stairs to my place, but at the last minute I changed my mind. Instead, I waved to my mother, who was taking a classified ad from someone as I walked through the reception area. Then I went through the door and walked two blocks down to the offices of *GO News*.

## 37

*GO News* occupies a one-story, cinderblock building that had been an optometrist's office, then a Radio Shack, then nothing until Paul Karr gave his son Spencer the capital to buy and renovate the building. It would have been nice to see another downtown building rescued from deterioration and ultimate doom, if it hadn't been occupied by Spencer and his tawdry publication.

The front door of the *GO News* offices opened immediately into a small black and white tiled reception area. Two uncomfortable-looking black molded chairs sat along one wall. Framed posters of front pages from a variety of papers in the heyday of print journalism decorated the walls. It had to be a hipster/ironic thing, because Spencer Karr's publication couldn't even come close to the reporting standards they represented.

No one was at the sleek black desk sitting to the left of an open doorway leading down a long corridor. I passed several offices with closed doors as I marched down the hall, but my target was the last room on the right. I rapped sharply on the half door and walked in.

"You are, without doubt, the worst excuse not only for a journalist but for a human being that I've ever seen."

"Well, good morning to you, too, Leah." Spencer Karr looked up from the laptop on which he had been typing. "To what do I owe the pleasure? Please, have a seat."

"I won't be here that long. How could you print that despicable piece of garbage about a fifteen-year-old girl? And not only that, direct everyone who read it to the website and the actual photo that made her humiliation complete?"

"Freedom of the press, Leah. Ever heard of it? Give the people what they want. I've just been looking over our numbers, care to see?" He swiveled his laptop around so the screen faced me. "They're looking very, very good. Care to share yours?"

"We're doing fine, thanks, and without the smarmy innuendo and outright trash in your sickening *Tea to GO*. You might escape libel suits using blind items and anonymous sources— but one of these days you'll pick the wrong target. You're not a news site. *GO News* is a cesspool of misinformation, borderline plagiarism, mean-spirited gossip, and outright lies."

When I finished speaking—OK, yelling—he had an amused look on his face. He took off his blue-framed glasses and held them by one bow, as he leaned forward and began speaking in a condescending voice that grated on my last nerve. As he no doubt intended it to do.

"Leah, I understand. I truly do. You're feeling terrible. Your little dream about becoming the savior of community journalism is falling apart before your eyes. Your second book bombed, your publisher has dropped you, and you're realizing that you were just a one-hit wonder with your first book. But screaming at me like a crazed seagull is not going to help anything.

"You don't need to feel ashamed of your failure. You're just proof of the Peter Principle. Everyone rises to the level of their own incompetence—and then they fail, fall, or both. In the coming months, or possibly weeks, after you accept that the *Himmel Times,* the little paper that could, actually can't, come and see me. I might be able to find a spot for you."

I was so furious I was shaking. Angry tears stung the back of my eyes, but there was no way I'd ever let them fall in front of him. I mustered all the control I had, which wasn't much, before I answered him.

"Spencer, you've always been smart, you've always been rich, and you've always been a mean, nasty, little boy who makes himself feel bigger by making other people feel small. I could almost excuse that, because with Marilyn for a mother, it's got to be in the genes. But you have Paul for a father, too, so you had a choice. You went with asshat. Karma's a bitch, and I'll be right there cheering when you get yours."

"Is that a threat, Leah?"

"Consider it a warning. And consider this, too!" I held up my hand with a finger lifted in a gesture my mother would not have been proud of—but which I found immensely satisfying. As I stormed down the hall, Andrea Novak, my erstwhile employee and Spencer's chief minion, stepped out of one of the offices. I'd be lying if I said I didn't take a half-step to the left and deliberately bump her into the wall on my way out.

I hadn't really accomplished anything. Spencer wasn't going to change the way he operated. Allie wasn't going to be saved from ongoing public humiliation. The *Himmel Times* wasn't going to double its numbers overnight. Still, I felt much better. Go figure.

———

As long as I was out and about and in a fighting mood, I decided it was long past time to see Gina's father, Warren Cox.

Cox Hardware Store was one of several hardware stores in Himmel at one time. It's the only one that has survived the onslaught of the big box stores. It's still a profitable operation in downtown Himmel, as it has been since Warren's grandfather opened it in the 1940s. I walked in, and the sloping wooden floor creaked under my feet. Overhead the ceiling fans moved in leisurely circles, circulating cool air throughout the building.

The shelves were stocked with much the same merchandise the store has offered for the last fifty years. Hand and power tools, electrical and plumbing supplies, house paint, duct tape, small kitchen appliances, gardening supplies and lawn furniture in summer, snow shovels and Christmas decorations in winter. One section of the sales floor is devoted to gifts suitable for birthdays, weddings, showers—fancy candy dishes, anniversary clocks, pewter candlesticks. The store even has a gun shop in the basement, with all the fire power a Wisconsin hunter could want. Older people in town are fond of saying, "If you can't find it at Cox's Hardware Store, you don't need it."

You might think that the place would be run by a friendly elderly gentleman, ready to lean on the counter and have a nice chat about how much rain has fallen lately, or what kind of season the Himmel Tigers are going to have. You'd be wrong. I knew Gina's dad Warren fairly well from the years I spent working as a reporter at the *Times*. He's a tall, sharp-featured man in his mid-sixties, still strong and sinewy, with a fringe of grayish-brown hair circling his bald head. He competes every year in the Lumberjack Games during Paul Bunyan Days. Warren isn't out on the floor of his store much anymore—he leaves that to an assistant manager. Most of his time is spent in his office working on the books and, I presume, counting his profits. Warren isn't well liked, but he's well respected as a businessman who managed to keep his store afloat when most others like it went under.

I could see him through the glass window in the office at the back of the store. He was doing something at his desk when I knocked and poked my head in.

"Warren? Have you got just a minute?" He looked up, surprised at being disturbed in his den.

"Darrell is out on the floor, if you need some help, Leah."

"No, I'm not shopping today," I said, sidling in through the doorway, though I hadn't been invited. I took the lone extra chair in the room before he could shoo me away. "I'm doing some background work on Ryan Malloy's death and—"

"I don't want to be in a newspaper story. I've talked to the police already, and that's all I have to say."

"No, this isn't for a news story. Joanna Burke, Ryan's mother, asked me to check on some things."

"That's what the police are for, isn't it?"

"Yes, but I guess you could say I'm supplementing some of their work. I'm sure you've heard that James Shaw isn't a suspect in Ryan's death anymore. So, I'm just going back over the night of the murder. I talked to Gina and to Peggy already, and I want to confirm some things with you, just to make sure that I've got them right."

"I'm quite busy, and—"

"I understand. That's why I'll just take a minute. Now, you were at a men's retreat for your church on Saturday, and you got home a little after nine o'clock. Is that right?"

"Yes, yes," he said, perhaps realizing that I wasn't going to leave unless he threw me out bodily.

"But you and Gina had an argument, a very serious argument about Ryan Malloy. So serious that she left, and you did too, shortly after."

His face had turned a shade of red so dark that it almost looked purple.

"I will not discuss personal family business with you or anyone else."

"Well, you don't really have to discuss it with me, I already pretty much know it. You found out that Ryan Malloy was the father of Gina's baby. That made you pretty unhappy. You and Gina had a huge fight that left Gina crying and running out of the house, Peggy crying and staying at the house, and you not crying, but also leaving the house. You didn't get home until very late, maybe three or four in the morning, and you left again about nine."

I was flying blind here, as I had no idea when Warren had returned home, or when he left again. However I asserted it with great confidence in the hope that it would shake a little truth from Warren.

He stared at me in stony silence, but he didn't contradict me. So far, so good.

"Now, your wife said that you went to your church to pray after you argued with Gina. I assume that's because the argument was so upsetting to you."

"We didn't have an argument. A father does not argue with his child. If she is under his roof, she obeys his wishes. If she is grown and out of the home, she still must respect his authority as patriarch of the family."

"Uh-huh. But you did fight. Your wife told me, and Gina told me. I don't blame you for being angry, enraged, even. You had a nice life—pretty, compliant wife, lovely daughter, profitable business. You were a respected businessman, and an important man in your church. Then Gina messed everything up. She fell in love with a boy outside your church, she got pregnant, she shamed you. Your daughter was visible evidence that you weren't an effective parent—or patriarch—if you prefer.

"You're an elder in your church. You set the example, you uphold the standards, and then you find that your own family wasn't keeping them. Gina submitted to your will when she gave up her child. But when she came back, she rebelled. She refused to go to church. She ran with boys. She defied you. In your eyes, she defied God. So, you cut her out of your life."

"My daughter chose the path of sin. I had no choice. I must obey the teachings of the Church."

"But your wife couldn't keep turning her back on Gina, could she? After she had her heart attack and begged you to let Gina come back for a visit, you relented a little. But you wouldn't have her under your roof, not unless she returned to your God. Someone at the retreat on Saturday told you about Gina's getting drunk and making a scene at the reunion reception. You saw that nothing had changed. In fact, it looked like it was starting all over again. You were furious when you got home and found Gina there. Soon you were both hurling accusations at each other. And then she told you that Ryan Malloy was the father of her baby, and she left in tears. You left, too. You say to go to church to pray."

"I am not a hard man. I loved the daughter God gave me. But, I am a just man. There are laws of God that must be obeyed. Children obey their parents. Drinking is a sin. Promiscuity is a sin. My daughter is guilty of all of them, and more. I have prayed all these years that she would return to God. And that night, after she finally told me the truth, yes, I was angry at Ryan Malloy. And angry at Gina, too. But I went to church to pray that God would set aside my anger and set me on the path of justice. I heard His voice. It was my duty to bear witness of God's truth to Ryan Malloy. To urge him to atone for his sins by turning to God. To help him if he saw the light. That is why I went to the cottage. But when I arrived, it was too late. Ryan Malloy was dead."

"That's a very powerful story, Warren. It's one I know that your wife believes. Even your daughter would like to believe it, I think. But I'm more of a cynic. Hazard of my profession, I guess. It seems more likely to me, Warren, that you went to confront Ryan. You finally had a focus for all the pent-up rage you felt at the loss of the family God had given you to manage. You went to Ryan's to confront him, not to save him."

I was pushing him pretty hard, but I felt pretty safe, given that anyone in the store could look through the window and see us, should he leap across the desk and start choking me. Which, from the thunderous expression on his face, wasn't all that unlikely.

"I don't know exactly what happened Saturday night and Sunday morning, Warren. But I do have some ideas. And I'll be sharing them with the sheriff's department."

"It is not for you to judge me, or to spread lies about me. I walk in the path of God, and I answer to Him, not you. I did not kill Ryan Malloy. I was at my church praying for his soul and for Gina's. I will continue to pray that my daughter turns her face to God. I will pray for you, too, Leah. Because I believe you are in danger of Satan snatching your soul—if he hasn't already."

## 38

Although I'd argued with Ross for Lily as the suspect most likely, once Steven was out of the picture, my interview with Warren had moved him up a notch. I could easily see him taking some kind of Bible-based vengeance on Ryan. If she'd agree to talk to me, I'd like to take another run at Peggy. She knew more than she was saying, but her loyalty to her husband ran deep. When I got back home, I checked in on Allie.

"Everything going OK?"

"All right, I guess. Well, no, really it's kind of awful, but I'm OK. The school took my photo off the website, so that's a good thing. But I had to shut down my Instagram and Snapchat accounts, because I was getting so many gross messages from stupid boys, and some really mean ones from some of the girls. A couple of my friends texted me and said they can't hang with me anymore, and I'm disinvited from a trip to the Dells one of their moms is taking them on. I really liked her mom. But, I guess she didn't like me."

The plaintive note in her voice made me think of what my mother had said, about Allie needing a "mother figure" in her life. She had probably been getting that need met through her friend's mom. Now that avenue was closed. Maybe my mom's idea to connect her with Marcy would work out after all.

"I'm so sorry, Allie. But—though I can't believe these words are coming out of my mouth, and I'll deny them if you ever tell her—Courtnee was right about one thing. People will forget. You probably won't, but someday it won't matter nearly as much as it does now. And, I don't mean to scare you, but this isn't the last big mistake you're going to make in your life. If you're anything like me, you're going to keep making them. I was just lucky that *GO News* wasn't around for most of mine. All you can do is pick yourself up and go on."

"I'm trying not to whine. I know I did this to myself, but I don't know how to fix it."

"Well, some things you can't fix, Allie. But most things you can manage. You might not be able to get your friends back, but you'll find new ones, maybe better ones who'll stand by you. Meanwhile, you just keep going. You're strong. You'll get through this. It may not feel like it right now. But you keep your head up, and you're going to be just fine. OK?"

She nodded, but I thought it was more to make me feel better than because I'd been any real help to her.

I spent the afternoon writing, and off and on thinking about Allie, and wishing I could do something to get her through the next few days. Maybe Miguel and I could take her to the Dells. Tell her it was a reward for getting her vaccine story done. I drifted away from writing and started Googling things to do at the Dells. I had a pretty good list when I got a text from Ross. He had news and he was on his way over.

He refused the sandwich I offered, once he was seated in the kitchen.

"Nah. Already ate."

"I haven't. So keep talking while I make a sandwich. You want a Coke?"

"If it's not diet, yeah."

"You want a glass?"

He shook his head as he took a stool at the kitchen island. I slid the can over to him, then started making my PB&J sandwich.

"What's up?"

"Coupla things. They found the kid who put Allie's picture on the school website. Yesterday, Evan swore to Kristin and Coop that there weren't any pictures of Allie except the ones on his phone. Today, he said he 'forgot' that he texted one to his friend Josh. Just to show his buddy what a big man he is, that he could get Allie to do that. Then that jackass kid Josh thinks Evan's gettin' a raw deal, and it's Allie's fault because she went to the cops. Josh is some kinda hacker boy or somethin', he's the one who showed Evan how to set James Shaw up in the first place. Then Josh thought it was funny to hack the school website and post Allie's picture. Served her right, he said."

"He might be a computer genius, but that was a real dumb move."

"He thought he was so smart nobody would catch him. I'm tellin' you, it's a good thing I wasn't part of findin' that kid, because—"

"Don't say anything else. In case he turns up dead, I don't want to have to be a witness against you."

"Oh, I wouldn't kill the little bastard, I'd just like to make him wish he was dead."

"Seriously, stop it. But I'm impressed. Erin got to the bottom of this fast."

"Wasn't her. Turns out Josh's mother is on that sexting committee of Coop's. And Josh has a little sister he's not very nice to. She knew somethin' was goin' on from listenin' to her brother and Evan talk. She told Mom. Mom hauled Josh right over to Coop's house after supper last night. Coop scared the crap out of him, I guess. Hacker boy Josh is goin' through juvenile court, just like his buddy Evan. He's not gonna be playin' Fortnite or havin' any computer fun time for a good long time."

"Ross, you amaze me. How do you even know what Fortnite is?"

"I don't exactly, but one of the guys at work, he's always talkin' about it. I listen and I learn, Nash. I listen and I learn. And not to change the subject now, but just when were you gonna mention that Ryan Malloy was the father of Gina Cox's baby?"

"I thought you knew?" I put a disingenuous uptick in my voice to see how that worked. Not very well.

"No, that's not gonna play. You shoulda told me."

"You don't tell me everything."

"Maybe that's 'cause no one can tell you anything. That was a big thing for me to miss. I'd like to blame Lameass, because he was so bent on roundin' up Shaw, but I shoulda gone back and talked to Gina after he did. I know what a dumbass he is. I know you don't want to think Gina Cox had anything to do with Ryan's murder. But now that she's got her hooks into Ryan's inheritance, that gives her a motive besides revenge. She coulda been plannin' somethin' like this all along."

"Has 'her hooks in'? What do you mean?"

"I went over to Joanna Burke's last night about seven-thirty. Went to talk to her without Lamey over my shoulder. I just wanted to let her know I was still digging, and I wasn't gonna stop 'til I found her son's killer. That's when she told me about findin' out she has a grandson, and how she's gonna leave him Ryan's share of the inheritance. Steven and Lily were there too. They didn't seem near as happy about the news as Joanna. More like they just found out their winning lottery ticket got flushed down the toilet."

"I'll bet. But I don't see how that means Gina's 'got her hooks in' the money. It's going to her son, not her. All she wants to do is find him."

"Maybe, but a sixteen-year-old who comes into two million dollars? I don't know all the legal ins and outs, but don't tell me mama isn't gonna get somethin' outa that."

"So, you're willing to go all in on Gina, and not even look at Lily?"

"Did I say that?"

"Ross, I talked to Warren Cox this morning. He's so sure he knows what God wants him to do, it's kind of scary."

"Now you're after Warren? Ya mean I wasted all that time today shakin' up Steven and your favorite suspect Lily? Geez, Nash, I try to follow your lead, but when you keep changing your mind, it's pretty tough."

"Did you talk to Steven and Lily? Did you get Lily to admit where she was? Because I have more stuff I forgot to tell you that Miguel found out."

" 'Forgot?' I bet."

"No, seriously. I did. I only found out yesterday, and it was a pretty crazy day. And then this morning, I'm sure you'll recall, things got crazy all over again. I wasn't keeping this from you. Honestly. Here I am, telling you. Now. Lily's friend Mandy—the one in Ennisville—she didn't ask Lily to stay with her. Lily called and practically forced herself on Mandy. Why would she do that? And she wasn't supposed to spend the night either. She told Mandy she'd stay until her husband Thomas got home, which was supposed to be ten o'clock. When he wasn't there at ten-thirty, and Mandy couldn't reach him, Lily said she had to leave. Mandy was upset, so Lily fed her a double dose of pain killers to knock her out and she left. What would make Lily both lie to her husband and overdose a friend? A tryst with Ryan, that's what."

"I don't even know what a tryst is, Nash, but settle down. I got this."

"How?"

"I'm not sayin' anything more, so forget it."

"But you're going to bring Steven and Lily in for questioning, right?"

"Bye, Nash. I'll see ya later."

## 39

"Leah, are you sitting down?"

"I'm actually lying down at the moment, Clinton. It's only six-thirty in the morning."

"Well, it's eight-thirty in Nova Scotia."

"What are you doing in Nova Scotia? I thought if you left New York you turned into a pillar of salt."

"Funny girl. I'm looking for puffins."

"OK, stop. This is starting to feel like I'm Alice and you're the Cheshire Cat."

"I'm with my mother. Her birthday treat. My birthday nightmare. A boat trip to see puffins. But, you only turn fifty-nine ... now, what is it? That's right, this make six times."

"You're a good son, Clinton."

"I'm a good agent. No, make that a great agent. No, I amend it. The greatest agent in the history of literature! I sold your new book. And I got the rights back to your second one. We're changing the title, doing a different marketing push. Totally new. I like *Bury Your Past*. What do you think?"

"What?" I shot up from my reclining position and sat straight up in bed.

"The ears, girl, the ears! Take it down a notch. Yes. On the strength of your outline and synopsis, and my skill as an agent —because I don't have any more chapters from you, do I? That's a rhetorical question. I know—"

He broke off, and I heard a muffled, "Right, Mom, I'll be right there." Then he was back.

"I have to go, people are getting on line to board. Just wanted to tell you. In case I go down with the ship. Keep writing. Or start. Whichever." And he was gone, with his usual lack of formal farewell.

"Yes!" I shouted to no one, as I leaped out of bed and hurried to take a shower. A new publisher. A new chance for my second book. And a home for my third one. You bet I'd be writing. And contrary to Clinton's belief, I already had a fair number of chapters done. I could get a good four hours in before Ryan's funeral at one-thirty.

Ryan's funeral. That thought stopped me mid-scrub as I stood in the shower. Through all the questioning and the theorizing in my investigation, the subject on my mind had been Ryan's killer, not his death. That was for two reasons. One, his passing didn't exactly leave a hole in my life. Two, the world at large, it seemed to me, wasn't going to be much poorer because of his absence. But the funeral of someone I had gone from grade school through high school with, who was here one minute and gone the next, suddenly hit me.

Both of my sisters had died very young, but somehow I had managed not to consider that I wasn't immortal myself. It's hard to shake the idea that we have infinite time. Other lives might be cut short, but we bought the warranty, right? Yes, sure we'll die some time, but we convince ourselves that it's a long, long way off. For some of us, it is. For some of us, it isn't. But for all of us, it comes. Ryan's death loomed like a flashing billboard telling me my life was going by much faster than I wanted it to. It was a depressing, but at the same time motivating, thought. I ate some Honey Nut Cheerios for breakfast, made an extra-large cup of extra strong coffee and sat down to write.

---

St. Stephen's church, built of limestone from a nearby quarry in the early part of the last century, has beautiful stained glass windows that cast a rainbow glow on sunny days. A wide center aisle divides the rows of wooden pews that subtly shine from regular applications of beeswax and the comfortable behinds of generations of Himmelites. The building was filling fast. Ryan's funeral offered interest on three levels: he was a native son who was a little bit famous, which thrilled some. His mother Joanna was a woman with a terminal illness, now burdened by the loss of her son, which stirred deep sympathy in others. And Ryan had been murdered, which evoked horrified fascination in all.

Joanna had asked my mother to sing "Amazing Grace" during the Mass, so she was seated in the choir loft with the organist. I saw Coop up ahead, but his pew was full, so I slid into a seat in one of the last rows. I didn't expect to see Gabe. Still, I looked around for him. He wasn't there.

The organist began to play more loudly—a tune I recognized only as a sad funeral song. Joanna, leaning heavily on Steven's arm, made her way to the front of the church. I saw her eyes flick from side to side, and I thought she must be searching for Gina. It looked like she was a no-show. She'd already given her all once to Himmel's gossip mill. Who could fault her for not wanting to make another contribution? But when I felt a poke on my shoulder from behind, just before the Mass started, I turned half-expecting it to be her. Instead, Ross whispered a greeting in my ear and I nodded, then turned forward as the service began. It had been a long time since I'd attended a Mass, but I discovered I still remembered the moves.

It was hard, as all funerals are, even those of people I don't have a deep connection to. It guts me when the soloist sings, whether it's "Amazing Grace," or "The Old Rugged Cross," or "You Can't Always Get What You Want," which was played at the funeral of an old professor of mine. Secular or sacred, I cry. It's not a delicate sniff either. It's a sob from the very depths of the saddest, loneliest parts of my soul. It's a mourning lament for every person I ever loved who has died.

I don't really get this celebration of life stuff, the whole don't be sad they're gone, be happy they were in your life. No. The person is dead. You'll never see them in this life again. And who knows if there's another one after this? Not me. It's just a damn heartbreaking, gut-wrenching occasion. So don't try to make it into mourning lite. Funerals are all about the darkness for me.

As people returned from taking Communion, a minor commotion a few rows ahead caused me to look. Coop was standing, excusing his way down the pew as he pulled his phone out of his pocket. He held it to his ear as he exited his row and walked quickly to the door. At least he'd had the fore-sight to turn off his ringer. At a funeral I attended a few years ago, a weeping grandson was choking out the words of the eulogy he'd written for his grandpa, when a cell phone went off and the sounds of James Brown singing "I Feel Good" pealed through the chapel. In the midst of life we are in death, and sometimes in the midst of death, we are in life.

Outside after the service, Joanna sat in a folding chair with Steven and Lily on either side of her as people approached with hugs and handshakes and condolences. There would be no graveside service, because Ryan's body had been cremated, and Joanna was taking his ashes home. But the Burkes were hosting a funeral meal at the parish hall.

I stood waiting for my mother among the crowd gathered on the steps, spilled out in the yard, and lined up on the sidewalk that ran in front of the church. The murmur of conversation rose as people greeted friends and relatives they hadn't seen since the last funeral they'd attended. Occasionally, there was a burst of laughter. It wasn't disrespectful to the dead, it was just the necessary acknowledgement of the living to each other that they were still alive.

I saw my mother coming out of the church and lifted my hand in a wave. As she waved back and moved toward me, I noticed that the buzz of conversation was growing louder. People were looking at their phones, reading, and then turning to each other. I hoped it wasn't a *GO News* scoop that the *Himmel Times* had missed. As I reached for my own phone to check it out, Ross came up to us.

"I just heard. Gina Cox is dead."

"Gina is dead," I repeated, my lips saying the words, but my mind unwilling to accept them.

"Yeah. Gina Cox, they found her body about an hour ago."

"Where? How?"

"At the motel. Don't have the details. Just that it looks like she drowned in the bathtub."

"No. That doesn't make sense. She's not a toddler. How could she drown in a bathtub?"

"She could if she wanted to."

"What do you—are you saying she committed suicide? She wouldn't do that. She was happy. She was going to find her son. She wouldn't kill herself. Are you the investigator on this?"

"Nah. It's an HPD case. The motel's in the city limits."

Coop's abrupt departure from the church now made sense.

"What's going on?" my mother asked as she joined us. "It sounds like the Tower of Babel out here."

Ross told her.

"No. That's too much. Gina, dead? Charlie, I don't understand. How could she drown in a bathtub? Is that really what the police think?"

"You sound like your daughter. I dunno anything except she's dead, and they found her in the tub."

"Has anyone told Joanna yet?" she asked.

Our eyes involuntarily turned toward where Joanna was sitting. Steven had bent down and was whispering in her ear. Her hand went first to her forehead as though shielding her eyes, then she shook her head slowly, and began to stand up. She was halfway upright when her hand clutched at her chest. Steven reached out to steady her, but she slumped from his grasp and fell to the ground.

Fresh murmuring spread through the crowd as everyone became aware of what was happening. Ross rushed toward Joanna, his ear to his phone as he called for an ambulance. Some people surged forward for a closer look when they realized something dramatic had occurred, but they parted and fell back like the Red Sea at Ross's commands to step aside, make room, get out of the way. Soon, we heard the scream of a siren growing louder as it came closer, drowning out the sound of the crowd's excited chatter. Within minutes, EMTs had arrived and worked with practiced skill to check Joanna's vitals, start CPR, get her onto a gurney, and then into the ambulance. They moved so swiftly and surely that it was like watching actors unerringly hit their marks on a stage. But this was real life, not a play, and we all knew Joanna might not make it to the second act.

"I don't care if it's only three o'clock. Crack open the Jameson, I need a drink," my mother said.

We'd come back to my place after Joanna had been whisked to the hospital. Most people had gone on to the parish hall to take part in the planned funeral refreshments, but neither of us had any appetite for the food or the ghoulish speculation that was certain to be part of the gathering.

"You don't have to ask twice," I said. After I poured us each a shot over ice, I lifted my glass.

"To Gina."

"To Gina," she echoed. She took a sip, then said, "Leah, you don't think Gina could have killed herself, do you?"

"Mom, no! Why would you say that? She was just about bursting with happiness when I saw her two days ago."

"I was just thinking—worrying really. She was so young. You just think of old people, don't you, when someone dies in a bathtub? It just crossed my mind, that's all. She had such a hard life, that girl."

"Yes, she did. But she felt like things were finally turning around for her. She wasn't depressed, a little anxious, maybe, about going to the funeral and facing people. But nothing serious enough to make her think about killing herself. I'm a hundred percent on that."

"Well, I'm glad for that, at least. The son of an old college friend of mine committed suicide years ago. It wasn't the grief that destroyed Bethany, it was the burden of guilt she felt for not being able to stop him. I'd hate for Peggy to have to contend with that."

"I notice you didn't include Warren. He's so self-righteous, it's hard for me to believe that he'll suffer much, no matter how Gina died."

"Leah, that's not true. Warren is Gina's father. He may not love her the way you or I think he should, but I'm sure that her death is causing him a great deal of suffering. I feel very sad for Warren and Peggy—and for Joanna, too. All three of them have just lost a child, and Joanna lost another link to Ryan. But what's really tearing me up is that after all the disappointments and hardships she made it through, Gina died just when the one thing she really wanted was within her reach. And now, when her son is found, both his birth parents will be dead."

"I agree. It's pretty much the worst O. Henry twist ever. Although, if Joanna doesn't pull through, I doubt anyone will be looking for Gina's son."

"But, it's in her will. Joanna set aside a fund to search for her grandson, and for Ryan's half of the estate to go to his son."

"I know she did. But she also told me that her attorney was coming to her house today after the funeral for her to sign the papers. If she dies without doing that, I'm pretty sure Steven won't be carrying out her intentions. He'll be thrilled to get the whole estate all to himself."

"But, he'd have to. He knows what she wants."

"He should honor Joanna's wishes from a moral standpoint, yes. But you were a paralegal for a lot of years, you know he doesn't have to. Until a new one is signed, the current will is valid. I think when money is involved with morality, Steven operates on a sliding scale of justice."

"I wish we knew what was happening. Why don't you call Coop and find out?"

"Mom. Much as I'd like him to be, Coop isn't my personal hotline into HPD. He's got to be up to his neck in things right now. Even when I do hear from him, he might not tell me much."

When my phone rang, we both looked at it expectantly. It wasn't Coop, though.

"Ross, what's going on?"

"Joanna Burke had a second heart attack at the hospital. She's dead."

"Oh." I felt an odd hollowness in my own chest at his words.

"All right. OK, thanks for telling me. Bye."

I turned to my mother, but she'd already guessed the news from my expression.

"Joanna died, didn't she?"

I nodded.

"Damn."

I nodded again.

## 40

---

After my mother left, I poured myself another Jameson. Then I sat in the window seat, thinking about Gina and the son she'd never see, and Joanna and the grandson she'd wanted so badly to provide for. Fate, or God, or whoever's hands are supposed to be on the wheel has a really lousy sense of direction sometimes.

The sound of a phone on vibrate pulled me from my reverie. I felt around for my mobile for a few seconds before realizing the buzz wasn't my phone. It came from the intercom in the back entry to my apartment.

"Yes?"

"It's Peggy Cox, Leah. Can I come up?" Now that was unexpected.

"Uh, sure, of course."

The woman who stepped into my apartment looked very different from the shy, lemonade-dispensing Peggy I'd seen just days earlier. Her soft brown eyes, which had been wary and uncertain then, now looked at me with flinty determination. Her voice didn't tremble with nervous anxiety. Instead, her lips formed a firm straight line of resolve. Though her face showed the obvious signs of grief—eyelids puffy from crying, nose reddened from constant swipes with a tissue—she was composed.

"Warren knows I'm here, but he didn't want me to come. I had to. I'm sure you already know about Gina."

"Yes. I'm so sorry for your loss, Peggy."

She gave me a brief nod in acknowledgement, but then said, "I don't need sympathy right now. I need help. Can I tell you some things?"

"Yes, sure, Peggy," I said, curious about where this was going. When we were both seated, she began her story without any preamble.

"I saw Gina. I found her in the bathtub."

I was shocked. I'd assumed that a maid had discovered Gina. Again, I tried to offer sympathy, but Peggy waved it away and continued speaking.

"After Warren went to work this morning, I called Gina. I usually call her in the morning after he's gone. She didn't answer, so I left a message. And then I texted, and then I called her again, and then I got worried. I drove to the motel. Her car was there, so I went to her room. There was a Do Not Disturb sign on her door, but when I knocked she didn't answer. I went to the front desk, and Gail came with me and used her passkey to let me in."

I shuddered inwardly as I imagined the scene. The room quiet and dark with the curtains still drawn. Gail flicking on the light. Peggy looking around, seeing the bed empty, settling on the door to the bathroom, calling Gina's name. Only an eerie stillness in response. Peggy's stomach plummeting as she opened the bathroom door. Then, her worst fears confirmed. Her daughter, motionless, cold, not breathing.

"Gina was dead. I could see that right away. Gail called the police, and I called Warren. When the police came, they said we should go home to wait, and they'd come to see us. They did come, but what they told us was wrong. It didn't happen like they said. I know that's not how Gina died. It's wrong," she repeated.

"What did they say? What was wrong about it, Peggy?"

"The police found a bottle of pills in Gina's room. Illegal ones. I can't remember the name. The bottle was open, and some were spilled on the desk. They said they'd have to wait for the toxicology report. They think Gina took some, and then took a bath and fell asleep. The pills are the first wrong thing. Gina didn't take pills. She couldn't swallow them."

My mother's question about suicide had flickered in my mind as Peggy spoke. I remembered what Gina had told me about the time she tried to kill herself—that she'd ground up pills in order to do it.

"Peggy—"

"I know what you're going to say. That Gina could have crushed the pills. That's what the police said."

"It's true, isn't it?"

"It's true she *could* have. But she had no reason to. She was happy, Leah."

"I saw her Wednesday night, and you're right. She was happy and excited. But she was nervous, too. Joanna wanted her to go to Ryan's funeral. Gina really didn't want to—all those people, all the whispering, everyone talking about her being drunk at the reception. Maybe she wanted something to calm her down?"

She shook her head in frustration. "Not pills. No. She wouldn't risk buying illegal drugs and getting in trouble with the police. Not when she was so close to getting her son. That was everything to her. And they didn't find any alcohol in the room, no empty bottles, nothing. Because she didn't take anything, not pills, not alcohol."

"OK, I agree it seems unlikely."

"Not unlikely. Wrong. The second wrong thing is that she was in the bathtub. Gina never took baths. Always a shower. She used to say, 'Why would anyone sit in dirty water to be clean?' "

As a showers forever girl myself, that made sense to me. I take a shower almost every day, but I haven't taken a bath since I was old enough to shower alone.

"Did the police know about her son? That Joanna was going to help Gina find him?"

"Not until I told them. But it didn't seem to matter. They already made up their minds. They said Gina was unstable—they know she was drunk at the party. They say she took pills, fell asleep, and drowned in the bathtub. They think it's her own fault. Nothing I said made any difference, not the pills, not the bathtub instead of a shower, not the clothes either. They were nice about it. But they think I'm just a mother who can't accept that her daughter's death is her own fault because she used drugs."

"You said the clothes didn't make any difference. What clothes? What about them?"

She leaned forward and held her hands spread apart for emphasis, as though making one last effort to make me understand. "Everything Gina had been wearing was folded. All her clothes. Her jeans, her blouse, her underwear, her bra. They were in a little neat stack on the toilet seat. The bathroom was perfectly clean, too. That wasn't like Gina, ever. She would never have folded her clothes like that. She'd leave them in a pile on the floor."

Thinking back on my two visits to Gina's room, I had to agree it seemed out of character. Casual chaos was the most generous description of Gina's living space.

"What about the main room, the bedroom?"

"It was normal. Messy, bed half-made. Like that. It was only the bathroom that was so clean. No streaks on the mirror, no toothpaste with the top off, no makeup bag with things spilling out on the shelf. Every single thing was put away. That wasn't Gina."

"Peggy, you said Warren didn't want you to come to see me. Does that mean he agrees with the police? Or does he feel like you do?"

"You have to understand about Warren. I know some people think he was too hard on Gina. But that's only because he loved her. When Gina was little, she followed him all over the farm, and he was so good with her. She was a real daddy's girl back then. He was always so proud when the ladies at church said what a pretty little girl she was, and what good manners she had. He has always loved her. People don't know that side of Warren."

Her eyes begged me to see him the way she did, as a parent whose unforgiving sternness sprang from love. I didn't, even with Peggy's testimonial. But I must have managed to keep my expression neutral, because she continued.

"When she got older, and all the troubles started, Warren was only angry at her because he was afraid for her. Afraid that she wouldn't come back to God. She can't be forgiven if she didn't come back to God. I'm afraid, too. I'm afraid Gina died without God's forgiveness." For the first time her voice quivered and her composure broke.

Muted sobs heaved up with a force that shook her body and strangled her breathing. She made no attempt to stop the tears coursing down her cheeks, or to cover her face. Instead, she balled her hands into fists using them to hit her thighs so rhythmically and mercilessly that I sprang from my chair and grabbed them tightly in my own.

"Peggy! Stop, please, stop. Maybe Warren couldn't forgive Gina, but I'm sure God did. Gina came home to you. And she came home clean and sober. If you have faith in God, and in Gina, you should have faith that God forgave her."

I'm not exactly an atheist, more of a doubter who still has a little hope. I wished that a true believer was here to allay Peggy's savage fears for her daughter's soul. Still, she began to quiet down, perhaps translating my fumbling words of comfort into something that fit with her own deeply held faith. Her sobs gradually subsided. When she seemed to have recovered, except for the occasional shuddery breath, I got her a glass of water. She drank the entire thing without stopping before she spoke again.

"I pray that you're right. I hope Warren will pray with me, too. But you can see why I have to know what really happened, can't you? All the things that make sense to the police don't make sense to me. Everything is wrong: the pills, the bathtub, the clean bathroom, the clothes. It's not my daughter."

"But people do unaccountable things sometimes. They act out of character. They do the kind of thing that makes their friends say, 'What got into her?' Or, 'That's not like him at all.'"

"I understand that. But I'm not talking about 'people.' I'm talking about my daughter. Leah, I need your help. I want to know if someone killed my daughter."

As she said the words, I realized that they had been lying in wait in my own subconscious ever since I'd heard the news about Gina's death.

"Who do you think would do that and why?"

"What about Joanna's stepson, Steven Burke? He must have been angry that half of his inheritance was going to go to Gina's son. People do terrible things because of money," she said.

Reluctant as I was to give Steven absolution for anything, casting him as Gina's murderer didn't really make sense.

"Killing Gina wouldn't stop the money from going to her son, once Joanna changed her will. And there's no way Steven could have known that Joanna would die before she signed the new will."

"Maybe he thought he could change her mind about the will if Gina wasn't around."

"Even if that was true, how would Steven get Gina to take the drugs?"

"He could put them in food or soda or something. Maybe they were Joanna's pills. He could get those easy enough."

"Possibly. But it's not as though Steven could drop off a hot dish loaded with drugs for Gina to eat. They weren't friends, or even friendly."

"No, but he could have called her and said he had something important to tell her. He could've brought coffee or something with the pills already in it. He could have given it to her while he told her that he'd make sure her son was found even after Joanna died. Then when she got sleepy, he put her in the bathtub and drowned her."

Peggy's overriding of my every objection gave me a glimpse into how Ross must feel when I'm trying to make a case for my own theories. It was like being hit by an ocean wave of certainty, over and over again. I dove back in.

"Even if things had happened that way, I can't see Steven neatly folding Gina's clothes and tidying her bathroom. Can you, really? Why would he?"

"I don't know. But why would Gina either?"

I didn't say anything for a minute, because I was turning over in my mind just how unlikely it was that Gina, in the throes of a drug-induced haze, would have left behind a neat pile of clothes and a pristine bathroom. But if someone knew about surface DNA, or had fingerprints to hide, or hair, or spilled water on the floor from a dying woman thrashing in the water, he might have taken extra pains to make sure nothing looked out of place or was left behind when he was through.

Something floated near the surface of my mind just then but sank before I could grab it.

"Peggy, I know that you need to make sense of Gina's death. And I don't know the answers to the questions you're asking. Maybe there aren't any." However, even as I spoke an idea crept into my mind. I didn't want to say anything about it to Peggy yet. It was pretty out there.

Her face fell. She obviously thought my words meant that I, like the police, believed she was an overwrought mother, unable to accept reality. But what I was actually thinking at the moment would have disturbed her a lot more.

"I didn't read your book, the one about your sister," Peggy said. "But Gina told me about it. That's why I thought you'd understand. That you'd care. But you don't," she said. Her voice now flat and defeated.

"I do care, Peggy. I know the cop who's the lead investigator. David Cooper was in the same class as Gina and me. Even if you think he wasn't listening to you, I'm pretty sure he was. I'll talk to him. I'll let you know tomorrow what I find out."

Relief flooded her face, and she grabbed both of my hands in hers.

"Thank you, Leah. But David Cooper isn't the one in charge of the investigation. The woman in charge is named Erin Harper."

## 41

I had been stunned when Peggy told me that Erin was in charge of the case, and as soon as she left, I tried to reach Coop.

The investigation into Gina's death should have gone to him. Coop had done some seriously good work in the last year—work that got him well-deserved recognition. I'd suspected that relegating him to the minor leagues, as his captain Rob Porter had done by assigning him to the task force he hated, might be motivated by professional jealousy. But this latest move cemented my belief that Rob was afraid Coop was smarter than him, better than him, and should have his job. Coop was unwilling to attribute ulterior motives to his one-time friend. But in my estimation, Rob wasn't one to let friendship stand in the way of career advancement.

When Coop didn't answer my text or my call to his cell phone, I tried the direct number to his HPD office. It rang four or five times before someone picked up—and it wasn't Coop.

"Himmel Police Department, Darmody." Dale Darmody is a patrol officer who's been on the job long enough to retire but is showing no signs of leaving. He isn't the brightest guy, but nobody loves the job more than he does.

"Hey, Darmody. It's Leah. Is Coop around?"

"No. Didn't you hear?"

"Hear what?"

"Coop doesn't work here anymore. He quit today!"

"What?"

"He quit today."

"I know that's what you said, Darmody. I meant why, what happened?"

"He had a big blow-up with Lieutenant—I mean Captain—Porter. Coop thought he was gonna be lead investigator on Gina Cox, but the captain gave it to Lieutenant Harper."

"Why did he do that?"

"Dunno. But she's pretty mad about James Shaw. Word is, she told the captain that Coop was disrespectin' her, and that he interfered in her case. She said she was gonna file a complaint. So, the captain put her in charge of the Gina Cox case. Squeaky wheel, I guess. When Coop found out, all hell broke loose."

"That doesn't sound like Coop. He's not an all-hell-breaking-loose kind of guy."

"I know. But he sure was mad today. Walked right out. Told the captain what to do with his task force. And the job."

"Wow. This is. Wow. I'm shocked. Thanks, Darmody. Talk to you later."

———————

I knocked once on the door, then walked into Coop's kitchen without waiting for an answer. My first clue to his state of mind was the fairly large collection of empty Leinenkugel bottles lined up in front of him. My second was his effusive greeting.

"Hi, Leah! C'mon in. Good to see you!" His grin was a little off-center, and he bumped his knee on the table as he stood up to greet me. He gave me the kind of hug you might give to a friend who's just returned from six months in a war zone.

"Good to see you, too, Coop," I said, disentangling myself and leading him back to the table. "I just heard the news. Looks like you're drinking your troubles away."

"Troubles? No troubles here. No worries, no troubles, no job, no nothing. Want a beer?"

"No, thanks. Let's just sit down and talk a little."

Coop enjoys a beer or two, occasionally a shot of whiskey, rarely a glass of wine. I'd never seen him drunk, and I'm not saying he was at the moment. But he was definitely on the better-not-drive side of sober.

"What happened today?"

His story was a little more fleshed out, but basically Darmody had it right. Rob Porter passed Coop over and gave Erin the assignment he should have had.

"I can see why you were mad. But quitting? Right on the spot?"

"Wasn't on the spot. Been comin' for a while. You trust your guys or you don't. If Rob doesn't trust me to do my job, then I can't do it."

"Maybe it's not about trust, and it's more like he's worried that you're showing him up, and that Erin knows how to play the game better than you do."

"Doesn't matter. It's time. Like my dad says, you got to know when to hold 'em and when to fold 'em."

"Actually, I think Kenny Rogers says that. Not to take anything away from your dad's excellent Karaoke version of 'The Gambler.' "

"Don't mess with me, Leah. I'm a little buzzed, OK? You know what I mean. It's Rob's department. I been back for a while. Nothing lasts forever. It's time for me to move on. That's fair to Rob, and fair to me."

"Maybe you won't feel that way in the morning. I mean, did you burn all your bridges at work? Is there a way you could talk to Rob, or maybe to the chief? Get things straightened out with Erin?"

He shook his head. "Nope. Don't want to. I'm not a good fit anymore. Gonna have to find a place where I am. Friend I worked with in Madison, he moved to Florida last year. Might try there."

My heart sank, but I could see as he cracked open another beer that this was not the night for rational discussion. It was also not the night for talking through the out-there idea about Gina's death that had sprung into my mind during Peggy's visit.

"I should go. You should maybe eat something and call it a night?"

"No, not hungry. Don't go. Let's watch a movie."

I think it's not a bad thing for people to cry in their beer by themselves, sometimes. And I really wanted to think through the reasons Gina might have been killed, and who might have done it. But it's rare that Coop is the one who wants company, and he'd come through for me already in the past week.

So, I settled down on the couch with him to watch his choice, *Gone, Baby, Gone*, a good, but dark movie, which seemed to suit his mood. Halfway through he fell asleep, and his head began tilting toward my shoulder. I didn't have the heart to wake him. So I sat as still as I could, and he dozed quietly, except for an occasional soft snore. When the film ended, I shook him gently.

"Hey, wake up. Movie's over. Go to bed."

He stared at me, bleary-eyed for a minute, then stood up a little unsteadily. It looked like his nap had resulted in him feeling more drunk, not less.

"Are you OK?"

"Yeah. Fine. Yeah. Go, go," he said, stumbling a little in a way that showed he was not quite as fine as he claimed.

"I'm just going to walk with you to your room. Just to confirm how very fine you are."

I put my hand under his arm, but he didn't really need it. When we got to his bedroom door, I said, "Thanks for the movie. I hope you don't have a headache tomorrow."

"No, it's all good." He took a step inside, then turned back.

"If I go to Florida, I have to move." He spoke in that very slow, careful way people do when they've had too much to drink but are trying to prove with their careful diction that they haven't.

"Well, that's pretty much the way it works."

"I'll miss you," he said, putting a heavy hand on my shoulder.

"I'll miss you, too."

"You could come with me."

"Yeah? I have a newspaper to run into the ground right here. Plus, I think one of my old editors from the *Miami Star Register* still has a hit out on me. It'd be a lot more convenient for me if you just stay. Why don't you think about doing that?" I said.

"I love you, Leah."

"I love you, too, Coop. Call me when you feel up to it tomorrow."

---

Although it was almost ten when I got back from Coop's, Miguel's car was still in the parking lot. I stopped by the newsroom and found him typing away at his laptop.

"Miguel, did you hear that Coop quit?"

"No! When? Why?"

I explained.

"Tomorrow, first thing, get official confirmation from the department. Then put up a brief online so *GO News* doesn't get there before us. Then you can check with Coop. I don't think he'll say much. See if Rob Porter or the chief have a comment. Include the usual background—"

"*Chica*, I know how to write a story. I used to even be the managing editor, remember? Why are you so wired?"

"Sorry. I know you do, Miguel. I guess it feels good to do something that comes easy, like giving out news assignments, instead of something that's really hard, like trying to figure out if a crazy idea I have about Gina's death could really be true."

"Lucky for you, my specialty is your crazy ideas. Tell me."

"Come on upstairs and get comfortable, this could take a while."

When we got to my place, Miguel took a Coke from the refrigerator and sat down on the sofa. I preferred to pace. I gave him the police theory of Gina's death and the reasons Peggy didn't accept it.

"I think she's right. I don't think Gina's death was accidental, and I'm sure it wasn't suicide," I said.

"But who would kill her?"

"Well, who had a motive for Ryan's murder?"

"You mean Gina's."

"No, I mean Ryan's, because I think they're connected."

"You mean by the money? Because Steven wanted Ryan's share of the inheritance? And then he would lose it anyway to Ryan's son?"

"No, though that did occur to me. But Steven's out of Ryan's murder, because even though he had a motive and the means, he didn't have the opportunity. His alibi is solid. I've been very fond of Lily as my runner-up suspect. Her alibi doesn't hold up, and she was having an affair with Ryan. However, though it pains me to admit it, there's no proof that

Ryan dumped her. And if he didn't, she didn't have any reason
to kill him.

"I think her cell phone records will show that she actually
*was* at the cottage that night, because she had a prearranged
meeting with Ryan. But when she got there Ryan was dead. She
didn't want to have anything to do with murder—or with Steven
finding out about her affair. So, she zipped home and lied to
Steven about what time she got there."

"She just left her lover lying there? She's got no heart, that
one."

"Agreed."

"Then who is left for Ryan's murder? Gina?"

"Not Gina. Her father. Warren Cox. The man who 'found'
Ryan's body. Warren has no alibi. His wife and daughter both
admitted that he was in a fury that night. He's an eye-for-an-eye
kind of guy, and he wanted revenge. I guess it's more Biblical to
say vengeance, isn't it? Ryan destroyed Warren's family and
turned his daughter away from God. Think about it. Warren has
a gun shop, right in the basement of the hardware store. He
could take a gun, use it, clean it, and put it right back. It could
be there now, hiding in plain sight. Warren is the trifecta: motive,
means, opportunity."

"But you said Ryan's death is linked to Gina's. How?"

"Well, I don't have it all worked out, but even before Peggy
came to talk to me, Gina's death made me uneasy. I didn't think
it was suicide—she was too happy and hopeful when I saw her
Wednesday. But accident didn't feel right either. Still, I had a
hard time letting myself think murder, because there didn't
seem to be any motive. Until I realized there was."

"*Chica,* come on. Don't leave me hanging."

"All right. Gina had no money. She wasn't involved with a
jealous boyfriend. She'd had a hard luck life, no reason for
anyone to envy her enough to want to kill her. She had no

power. She wasn't standing in anyone's way. True, her son was in Steven and Lily's way, but killing Gina wouldn't prevent Joanna from changing her will."

"But those are all the reasons why there wasn't any motive to kill Gina," he said.

"Ah, but see, I was wrong about one of them. It sort of flitted into my head when I was talking to Warren, but it came on full force while I listened to Peggy. Gina *did* have power. She had the power to drive a wedge between her parents, the power to humiliate Warren, the power to lessen his standing in his church, the power to destroy his world all over again. It was clear to him the night they fought, the night he learned about Ryan, that Gina would never bend to his will. She would never accept Warren's church, or his God, or his right to control her life. Warren had to kill her, if he wanted his life back."

I could see from his expression that Miguel wasn't with me on the theory.

"OK, what don't you like about it?"

"For Warren to kill Ryan, *chica*, that's one thing. He was furious, it was impulsive, a crime of passion! But Gina, it's so different. The way you say it, she was drugged. She was drowned. Her bathroom is all clean. Her clothes are all folded. That's not like Ryan's murder at all. And why would her father wait to kill her? Why didn't he kill her the same night?"

"Maybe because when he killed Ryan, he still thought he might be able to "save" Gina. He might bring her back to the church she was raised in. But when he found out that Joanna was going to help her find her son, he knew that things wouldn't change. In fact, they'd get worse, because Peggy wanted Gina back in their lives. She would want her grandson, too. Warren was losing control."

"Maybe that could be a reason. And maybe Warren did kill Ryan. But the way Gina died, I don't think Warren could do it, so cold like that. And where would he get drugs? I don't think that can be it."

I wanted to tell him he was wrong. I wanted to be right. But as I listened to his words, I knew they made sense.

"Damn it, Miguel." I sighed. "Why do you have to be so smart? And so honest? I really thought I was on to something."

I sank down on the couch beside him. He put his arm around my shoulder.

"I'm sorry. Don't look so sad. You already saved James. And Allie. You are pushing too hard. Ryan's murder, now Gina, the *GO News* pressure, your new book pressure. It's too much. Maybe you should let Detective Ross solve Ryan's murder by himself. And I don't think Erin Harper will mind if you don't help her with Gina."

"I'm sure you're right on both counts. But I hate to leave Peggy with no answers."

"Better no answers than the answer is her husband killed their daughter."

"That's definitely true. You know, I wish every time I fell on my face, you were the only witness. You do an excellent job of catching."

"I'm always happy to make your landing soft."

I yawned then, involuntarily and hugely.

He laughed. "I know when it's time for me go. *Buenas noches.*"

"Good night, Miguel. And thanks."

## 42

It had been a long, emotionally draining day. Before I took Miguel's advice and crawled into bed, I opened all the windows wide. A welcome cold front had moved in, and I knew I'd sleep better with a cool breeze drifting in. I only got through one paragraph in the book I was reading before my eyes closed, and it slipped from my hands and hit me on the nose. I turned off the light, but it was a restless night.

·I dreamed that Joanna Burke was in my office, and she was giving Gabe's dog Barnacle a shot, but then she said, "You need one, too, Leah. It's truth serum. So you'll know the answers." The scene shifted quickly, as it can in dreams. Joanna was gone. Allie rode in on her bike with Barnacle in the basket and handed me a stack of papers.

"It's my story. You'll love it. Here's a brownie from Marcy," she said. But as I reached out to take both, Allie became Vesta, and instead of papers and a brownie, she was handing me a crying baby. The transformation from Allie into Vesta jolted me awake. I got up for a glass of water. When I went back to bed, it took me quite a long time, punctuated by much tossing, turning over of my pillow, and switching from back to side, before I finally drifted into a troubled sleep filled with unsettling dreams.

My last one was of Annie. We were walking together, talking and laughing. As is the way with dreams, I didn't question that we were both adults, though she had been only eight when she died.

"I'm so happy you're alive, Annie. All this time, why did I think you were dead?"

"I am dead, silly. Everybody here is," she said, as she opened her arms wide. As I followed their sweeping arc, I realized we were in the cemetery.

"But I'm not."

She looked at me with a sad smile, and then began to fade away.

"Don't go, Annie! Stay, please, stay!"

I woke, sitting straight up in bed, my arms stretched out, my face wet with tears, and my heart racing.

---

After that, there was no going back to sleep. Besides, it was close to seven. I got sluggishly out of bed and stood in the shower until the water ran cold and released me from my stupor. It was a bit brisk in my apartment, the temperature having dipped to an unseasonable low of fifty-eight degrees during the night. However, the forecast predicted a return to ninety-plus and high humidity later in the day, so I left the windows open to take advantage of the fall-like temperature before the heat wave resumed. Maybe a cool breeze would blow the fog out of my brain. That, and an extra strong hit of caffeine.

I'd intended to spend the morning regrouping from my

failed attempt to find a link between Gina's death and Ryan's. I'd promised Peggy that I'd talk to the investigating officer, but now that I knew it wasn't Coop, I wasn't that enthused about the conversation. As I inhaled my coffee and felt a surge of energy, I decided to use it on something totally different, but more personally important. I was nearly at the halfway mark in my book. I knew exactly where I was going, and I had the research done and organized. With some focus and a block of uninterrupted time, I should be able to push past the midpoint and start the long descent to landing. I put my phone on airplane mode, and that is what I did.

It's funny, but when I'm having trouble writing, the time drags on and on. Five minutes can feel like an hour. But when the words flow easy, as they were doing, it's just the reverse. An hour goes by like five minutes. My stomach rumbled around one o'clock, and I made a peanut butter sandwich and carried it and a glass of iced tea back to my laptop. I know, it's a bad idea for liquids to be near computers, but I like living on the edge.

Finally, at four-thirty, I pushed back from my desk, lifted my arms overhead, looked up and stretched as hard as I could. It felt great, and I felt pretty good about myself. At least I could still write about crime, even if I'd lost my touch solving it. I switched my phone back on and saw several texts. The first one was from Allie, at ten.

*Almost done with my vax story. Talking to last source today. Can you look at it tomorrow?*

I texted back an affirmative, then read the next message from Coop.

*Meet at McClain's at seven?*

*Yes.*

The third one I took a little longer to answer. It was from Gabe.

*Can we talk? Seven at my place?*

*Can't do seven. Will nine work?*

His reply came back immediately.

*Yes. See you then.*

I'd been waiting for days to talk to him, but now that it was set, I didn't know if it would be the end of our beginning, or the beginning of our end.

The last message was from Erin Harper.

*Call me. Re: Gina Cox*

I started to, but then rethought it. She probably wanted to ask me about how Gina had seemed on Wednesday when I saw her. I could truthfully share that she had seemed very upbeat and happy, with no evidence of either drinking or drugging. But as I thought about my last conversation with Gina, I remembered something. Gina had said she was going to have dinner with Marcy the next night, because Marcy was basically the only friend she had in town to celebrate with. Which meant, of course, that Marcy was probably the last person to see Gina, except for her killer—if there had been one, that is.

I knew I should let Erin know. And I would. Just not right that minute. I wanted first crack at what Marcy remembered about the evening before Gina died. Gina's mood, any mention of expecting someone later, anything that might point toward someone who could have had reason to want her dead.

In my defense, my motive wasn't just to get one over on Erin if I could. Though that would be sweet, given what she had done to Coop. I had another reason to talk to Marcy as well. I wanted to tell her how sorry I was about Gina. As her teenage babysitter, Gina had been the last link to Marcy's baby daughter. She was the only other person around who had held Robin, fed her, changed her, and rocked her. Now, Gina's death and her connection with Robin might be causing Marcy to feel the loss of her daughter with renewed intensity.

Grief is that way. At the start, it rips you apart, tearing through your heart. Then, slowly, its ferocity begins to diminish until it sits in quiet retreat and lulls you into thinking you've tamed it. Then a trigger—like Gina's death might be for Marcy —makes your "tamed" grief spring to life, and once again it savages your heart like the wild beast that it is.

When I walked out the back door on my way to Marcy's, I was surprised by how much warmer it was—and wet feeling. By the time I turned into her driveway, the sky had clouded over and there was a very light mist in the air. I parked and hurried up the path to knock on her door. When I did, it opened slightly, as though the latch hadn't caught the last time it had been shut. I stepped partway inside and called out.

"Marcy? Marcy, it's Leah Nash."

There was no answer, so I walked in further. Maybe she was in the far reaches of her enormous kitchen and hadn't heard me.

"Marcy, it's Leah. Are you home?" By then I had reached the kitchen. It was perfectly tidy as I'd expect from Marcy, with all surfaces and appliances gleaming. On the way out, I poked my head in the little alcove where I'd had coffee with her. She wasn't there. I hadn't expected her to be. But I was surprised by what I did see.

One chair was pushed away from the table almost to the counter. Two cups sat on the table, one half-full of coffee. I picked it up to see if it was still hot. It wasn't. The other held the sludgy caramel-colored remains of a brew liberally dosed with cream and sugar. The scene was very unlike the neat freak orderliness of Marcy.

As I turned to go, I bumped into the out-of-place chair and stumbled a bit. I grabbed the counter to hold onto my balance and knocked a small bottle that had been next to the sink onto the floor. Thankfully, it was empty. The label revealed it had contained a prescription for Xanax. Maybe that's why Marcy seemed a little less tightly wound to my mother. I pushed the chair back in and left, pulling the door hard to make sure it latched.

Once outside I looked toward the lake, but Marcy's boat was tied up at the dock. It had been a well-intended but wasted trip. I put my car in reverse and was backing out when a flash of blue metal caught my eye. Leaning up against a tree, mostly hidden from sight, was a bike that looked like Allie's. When I saw the retro-style orange helmet hanging from the handlebars, I was sure it was hers.

That explained the two cups of coffee. Marcy was the "one last source" Allie had mentioned in her text. Allie, like most kids her age, drank coffee, but also like most kids, she had a hard time with the bitter taste and always added creamer to hers. Obviously, she had ridden her bike out to talk to Marcy about Robin. She'd been the drinker with the bit of caramel-colored sludge left in her cup, and Marcy must have been the half-empty black coffee. But where were they now? I peeked through Marcy's garage window and saw that her truck was gone.

Uh-oh. What if Marcy had opened up about Robin, and then invited Allie to go see the family mausoleum? That was such a part of Marcy's regular routine, she probably wouldn't even think about how uncomfortable, not to mention creepy, a kid Allie's age might find it. And Allie would've been too polite —or maybe too anxious to get the story—to say no.

I tried Allie's cell phone, but it went right to voice mail. That confirmed my suspicion. Appropriately enough, the cemetery is a known dead zone. You can't get a signal except on the higher elevations. It was still misting and tendrils of fog had begun to weave their way through the trees. I decided to rescue Allie. If the fog thickened, she wouldn't be able to ride her bike home anyway. I was due to meet Coop in twenty minutes, but I sent him a quick text.

*Picking Allie up at cemetery. Be a few minutes late.*

I grabbed Allie's bike and opened my trunk, ready to move things around to make room for it. I didn't have to, because everything that belonged there was still on the back seat of my car. Along with the box of dolls I had yet to deliver. Oops. I got the bike in, secured the trunk with a bungee cord, and took off.

The cemetery isn't far from Marcy's. I saw her truck as I pulled in the gates and parked next to it. When I got out of my car, I looked in the direction of her family's mausoleum. The gauzy fog was becoming heavier, but I was able to see Marcy walking up the hill with Allie next to her.

"Marcy! Marcy!" I called, cupping my hands together and shouting, before I stopped to think that bellowing across the graves probably wasn't the best cemetery etiquette. Still, I wanted to catch them before she made Allie go inside. I'd only been in a walk-in mausoleum once, as part of a "Death and Dying" class in college. The cold granite, the stained glass, the small bench, the empty crypts waiting for deaths yet to come ... I had made some excuse and rushed out. Maybe Allie was made of sterner stuff, but she'd been through enough emotional stress recently. I hurried up the path toward them and shouted again, "Marcy!"

She turned and looked right at me, then turned away. Allie stumbled. I realized then that she hadn't just been walking with Marcy, she'd been leaning on her. Marcy wrapped an arm tighter around her. She bent down a little so that her cheek rested on the top of Allie's head. Just like she had when she led Gina away the night of the reception. Things suddenly began to feel very weird.

I ran flat out, the fog thickening around me. "Allie! Allie, are you OK?"

A breeze shifted the fog, and for a second I could see them at the door, Allie propped up by Marcy.

"Marcy, wait! It's me, Leah!"

I sprinted forward, then stumbled and fell, sliding down the hill on the loose gravel of the path, scraping my knees and the front of my hands where I tried to break my fall. I scrambled back to my feet. Marcy turned once more, one arm still around Allie, the other holding the key to the bronze door of the mausoleum.

"Go away! Robin and I don't want you here."

The fog shifted again and they disappeared. I heard a heavy thud as she pulled the door closed behind them. And I knew without doubt who had killed Ryan Malloy. And why.

## 44

"Marcy! Allie! Marcy! Let me in!" I shouted. My thoughts raced as rapidly as my fists beating against the unyielding door.

"Marcy!" I pressed my face against the stained glass inset in the door, but I couldn't see anything. I pounded on the door again, then on the glass. But even if I succeeded in breaking it, that wouldn't help. It was far too small to give me access. Again I shouted, though I knew it was futile.

"Marcy, what's wrong with Allie? Let me in, please! Marcy, please!"

"No. Go away. Robin is asleep."

A chill ran through me as I remembered the empty bottle of Xanax. How much had Marcy given Allie? She had lost touch with reality. Somehow in her mind, Allie had become Robin. I tried to get through to her again, this time in a more conciliatory way.

"I don't want to disturb Robin, Marcy. But I need to talk to you, just for a minute. Won't you open the door, please?"

"You can't take Robin. She needs me. She's *mine*. Now go away!" The determined fury in her voice was clear, even with the muffling effect of the door.

I didn't have time to parse everything out. I just knew I had to get Allie out of there. I needed help. I turned and ran down the hill toward my car. The wind had risen and was blowing the fog away. But it had brought with it dark storm clouds. A sudden clap of thunder sounded, but it was no louder than the pounding of my heart.

Out of breath, I yanked open the car door. I grabbed my phone. I hit speed dial for Coop, but the call wouldn't go out. No service. Of course there wasn't, I knew that. Allie wasn't safe. How many pills had Marcy given her? I had to get her out now. I couldn't stand her dithering. Shit, shit, shit!

My eyes fell on the box of dolls sitting on the floor of my car. Then on the blanket on the back seat. All at once, I had a plan. Not a great plan. Maybe not even a good plan, but I had to try it. I shoved the phone in my pocket, grabbed a doll, wrapped her in the blanket, and ran as fast as I could, rain pelting down on me and lightning crackling overhead.

---

A faint glow shone through the stained glass in the door as I powered up the hill. When I got to the top, I pulled out my phone. Two bars. I punched in 911. I blurted the situation out nonstop, not even giving the operator room to interrupt with a clarifying question. There was no time.

"This is Leah Nash. I'm at Maple Hill Cemetery. A woman having a psychotic episode has drugged a teenage girl and locked them both in the mausoleum at the top of the hill. I need police and an ambulance, fast." I hung up, turned off the ringer, and tossed my phone aside. I didn't need a call back panicking Marcy in the middle of my Hail Mary play.

I paused to adjust the doll on my shoulder, wrapping it up

so that a tuft of its fine black hair showed above the blanket. I pressed it close and shouted through the door.

"Marcy, please, let me in. I need to talk to Allie."

"Robin and I don't want you here."

"But Marcy, that's not Robin. It's Allie Ross, the girl from the paper, remember? I have your baby. Robin's out here with me. She's starting to fuss. I don't know what to do."

I turned and walked a few steps away, patting the doll on the back. I made whimpering noises that I hoped, given the thickness of the door and Marcy's state of mind, would pass for a small baby's cries.

"Please, Marcy. Robin's really starting to cry. She wants you, not me."

I walked around in a small circle then, jiggling my arm so that the doll bobbed gently up and down, as you would do to try and soothe an infant. No response came from Marcy. I made the cries louder.

"She won't stop. I don't know what to do."

I walked a little farther away, so that Marcy would have to step outside to reach me. Half-turning so I'd be able to see her coming, I continued to sway and bounce, whispering *there, there*, as I leaned my cheek down on the little plastic head.

The door handle clicked. I upped the crying. Then I made my voice harsh as I shook the doll. "Robin. Stop crying! Now!"

Marcy rushed forward. I turned as though to keep "Robin" away from her.

"Give her to me! Robin, Robbie, it's mama."

I whirled quickly around and thrust the doll at Marcy with a lunge that threw her off-balance. I ran into the mausoleum. In the light from a flashlight Marcy had leaned against the wall, I saw Allie lying on the bench. Her head was tilted to the side and her breathing was shallow.

I knelt beside her and tapped her cheeks, "Allie, wake up! It's me. Allie?" Her eyelids fluttered. I slipped my arm beneath her to help her sit up.

*Whack!* Something hard hit my shoulder and made me drop her back down on the bench. I swung around from my kneeling position and looked up. Marcy stood over me, her face contorted with rage. The pretend Robin was dangling from one hand. A real gun was held firmly in the other.

"This isn't Robin. You tricked me!" She flung the doll aside and it hit the wall.

"Marcy, you're right. Of course you are. That isn't Robin. But neither is this."

I gestured toward Allie. I tried to speak in a normal tone, as though Marcy had simply made an everyday error, like mistaking a moth for a butterfly.

"This is Allie Ross. She looks like Robin though, doesn't she? She came to talk to you about your baby, right? You gave her coffee. Why did you bring her here?"

"I brought Robin."

"No. This is Allie. Robin is already here. You come to visit her every week, like I come to visit my sister Annie. Robin is just a baby. Allie is almost grown."

Uncertainty flickered in her eyes, and she shook her head in confusion. The hand holding the gun dropped to her side.

"Marcy, did you kill Ryan?" Again, I tried to keep my tone nonthreatening. Conversational, even.

"He killed my baby."

"I know. He was carrying the flu virus. He got sick with it the day his family left for Seattle. Joanna told you that. Then later, while you helped Gina the night she was drunk, she told you about Ryan. That he had come to your house while she was babysitting the night before he left. You knew then that he was the one. He gave the virus to Robin, and she died. That's why you killed him, isn't it?"

"Yes. I rowed across the lake. I waited for him. He had to pay and his mother had to pay, for Robin. I told him why. Then I shot him. Then Joanna found out what it's like to lose your child. It was her turn to suffer." She spoke as though she were reciting a dream she'd had a long time ago.

"And Gina? You killed her too, didn't you? Why?"

Unexpectedly, Marcy's eyes filled with tears. "Life for life. Eye for eye. No pity. It's in the Bible. I had to. She told me her baby was coming back. My Robin was still gone. That wasn't right."

"You put something in Gina's drink, like you did with Allie, didn't you? And then when she was sleepy, you got her undressed and into the tub."

She nodded.

"Gina sank down, but she started to wake up. I put my hands on top of her head. I pushed her down. Then she was quiet. Like a baby. I had to do it. For Robin."

"I understand, Marcy. Everyone will understand. But this is Allie, not Robin. I need to take Allie now. I'm just going to stand up. Then I'll help Allie up. OK?"

She didn't answer me. She was staring now at the small crypt in the wall behind me. The one engraved with Robin's name. She still held the gun limply at her side.

I moved slowly to a standing position, watching Marcy all the while. She had retreated inward, her eyes were staring but not seeing.

I shook Allie's shoulder. She moaned softly. I slipped my arm under her and pushed her up to a sitting position again.

"Allie," I said urgently into her ear, "Come on. Stand up."

Allie began to rise.

"No! Leave Robin alone!"

Marcy rushed forward to push me away from Allie. I pushed back with equal force and a lot more fear. She stumbled and we both fell. The gun went off. The sound in the small space was so loud that for a minute, I couldn't hear anything but the ringing in my ears. I rolled away from Marcy. She was holding her hand against her side. Blood was seeping out between her fingers. Her expression was confused, as though the shot had wakened her from a dream and she didn't recognize her surroundings. The gun had skittered under the bench, but she wasn't in any shape to go after it.

Allie had sunk back down to a sitting position, but her head was lolling. I had to get her out of there. I half-pulled, half-pushed her to her feet, keeping my eyes on Marcy, who showed no sign of moving.

"Come on, Allie." She leaned heavily on me as we shuffled the few feet to the door. As I got Allie through it, Marcy started a keening wail that pierced my soul.

"Noooo, noooo, don't take Robin. I want my baby."

The rain was coming down hard as I stumbled outside with Allie. It hit my head and ran down my neck, sending shivers through my body. Though maybe that was the adrenalin surge powering down. I kept looking over my shoulder as I walked Allie unsteadily to a concrete planter and positioned her behind it. Marcy was still crying for Robin with heart-rending sobs. I could hear the police and ambulance sirens approaching.

I knelt down and took Allie's face in my hands, lifting up her head so I could see her eyes.

"Allie? You all right? I need to go back and check on Marcy. You'll be OK? The ambulance is almost here. Can you hear the siren?"

She blinked her eyes a couple of times and nodded her head groggily. But as I stood, behind me I heard the thump of a heavy door closing. Then the loud, reverberating crack of a gunshot.

## 45

"What were you thinking, Leah? Running after Marcy when she had a gun?"

We—me, my mother, Miguel, and Coop—were with Ross in a family waiting room at the hospital while the ER staff checked Allie over. I'd given them all a quick overview of what had happened at the cemetery already. My mother hadn't been happy with my decision-making.

"I told you, Mom. I didn't know she had a gun. I didn't know much of anything until she locked herself and Allie into the family mausoleum."

"*Chica*, you were very brave."

"Don't encourage her, Miguel," my mother said.

"How did you get her to open the door?" Coop asked.

I explained about the doll.

"Good thinking," Coop said.

"Desperate thinking. It's probably the most scared I've ever been."

Ross, who was sitting next to me, surprised me by grabbing my hand. "My girl means more to me than anything, Leah. You saved Allie's life. I'm never gonna forget that."

He let go of my hand and pinched the bridge of his nose, then quickly brushed his hand over his eyes as though relieving an itch.

Tears welled up in my own eyes.

"Ross, I—"

He cut me off before I could finish. I guessed that he'd had enough sincere emotion for one evening.

"Why didn't you tell me you suspected Marcy? You were all over Steven and Lily, and even Gina's dad, but all the time you were thinkin' Marcy?"

"No. I wasn't. I didn't suspect her until I was at her cottage today. Even then it was just a weird feeling, because her kitchen alcove looked so untidy, and Marcy is freakishly neat."

"Why did you go there, anyway?" Coop asked.

"Because I remembered Gina had said she was having a celebration dinner with Marcy on Thursday. I wanted to ask Marcy about how Gina had seemed, what she'd said."

"And you wanted to get one over on Erin Harper, and talk to her first," Coop said.

"Well, yes, that, too. I wasn't feeling very motivated to help Erin. And she hadn't listened very well to Gina's mother, either. I thought she could wait just a little—or find it out on her own."

"How did you know to go to the cemetery?" Miguel asked.

"I knew Allie was going to be talking to Marcy about Robin. When they weren't at her house, I thought she might have taken Allie to the cemetery, to show her the family mausoleum where Robin was. I wanted to spare her that if I could."

"The text you sent me was one of your stranger ones. '*Picking Allie up at cemetery.*' Maybe I should have followed up," Coop said.

"I wish you had. Once things fell into place, I didn't have a way to send an SOS, because of the bad cell phone coverage out there. I called 911 as soon as I got to the top of the hill, but things started happening pretty fast."

"When did you know Allie was in danger?" my mother asked.

"When I saw Marcy walking her up to the mausoleum. She leaned down and put her cheek on Allie's head. She did the same thing with Gina. I'd had the clues I needed all along. I just hadn't recognized them. Until it was almost too late."

"But you were still right, *chica*, even if you didn't know it," Miguel said loyally. "You said that Ryan and Gina's deaths were linked."

"But I had it figured out wrong."

"You got to the right answer before I did," Ross said. "You can hold that over my head for a while if you want. My thank-you gift to you."

"Charlie, I'm glad Leah was able to save Allie. But I have to say I'm not that crazy about the risk she took. You'd already called 911, Leah," she said, turning to me. "The police were on their way. You could've waited for them."

"No, I couldn't. Marcy was unstable to say the least. I didn't know how many pills she'd given Allie. I didn't know what she was going to do to her. I couldn't just stand around and wait. Besides, I don't think Marcy wanted to shoot me. She shoved me away from Allie, because she didn't want me to take 'Robin' away, and we fell and the gun just went off."

My mother shuddered. "Marcy's intentions aren't much comfort."

"No, they're not," Coop said. "The bullet probably ricocheted off those granite walls. It could have hit you, or Allie, instead of Marcy."

"Well, it didn't, so let's just be glad about that and talk about something else. What's happening with my two favorite former suspects, Ross? Did you get anything more out of Lily about where she really was the night Ryan died? I doubt either one of them will be saying anything more, now that we know Marcy killed Ryan."

"Funny you should ask, Nash. I had a real nice talk with the Burkes this morning. Apologized for botherin' them. Said I was real sorry about Joanna, but I was on the trail of a suspect in Ryan's murder that I thought was really gonna pay off. Lily was standin' there, but I made it like Steven and I needed to talk private. Said I just needed to run a coupla things by him.

"He was fine with that, but she had her antennae up, I could see. But Steven thought we were gonna have a man-to-man talk, so he sent her off. His stepmother dyin' before she could change her will seemed to put him in a real good mood."

"What did you say to him?" I asked.

"I told him I was a hundred percent sure he didn't kill his stepbrother. He liked that. Got a lot less friendly though, when I laid it out that I knew his real alibi was Cole Granger, and I knew about his money troubles. He huffed and puffed some, but I told him I had the phone records that showed his movements, and Granger to confirm it. He backed down then, said he made the alibi up because he didn't wanta upset his wife, and he didn't want his financial situation comin' out."

"What about Lily? Did you bring her in, smash her alibi?"

"No, I talked to her separate. She's pretty sharp. I just cut to the chase with her. Said I knew about her affair, had witnesses, and I also had phone records that showed where she was the night Ryan was killed. And I knew she was at the cottage."

"You got Lily's records already?"

"Nah. I was just—"

"Lying?" my mother asked.

"Now, why do you have to go and call it like that, Carol? I was bluffin'. It's legal. Saves a lot of time, sometimes. I can lie, and the witness can believe me, or not. We all got choices. Turns out, Lily believed me. My grandma always said I had an honest face.

"She was supposed to meet Ryan that night. But when she got there, he was already dead. She freaked out, got home just before Steven rolled in around two. He told her he went to the office to do some work after the party, 'cause he didn't think she'd be home. She told him she got there a little after eleven, 'cause her friend felt better. Next morning, when Steven got the call that Ryan was dead, he panicked. He knew he'd be a suspect. Lily agreed to say he was home at eleven-thirty, because that's her alibi, too. They didn't count on the neighbor tellin' Leah about them not bein' home when they said they were. They made up the shower story to take care of that."

"I knew it! I knew they were lying. What happened when Steven found out about Lily and Ryan? And when Lily found out about the money?"

"Nothin', 'cause I didn't tell 'em. When I finished with Steven, I told him it wasn't my call, but I didn't see any need to put his personal finance troubles out there. He seemed real happy with that. Told me to be sure to go to Burke's Auto next time I was in the market for a car. When Lily and I finished, I thanked her for being so honest."

"What? They both lied to the police. They obstructed justice. Steven was consorting with gangsters—or he would be if Cole had managed to set him up. How can you just let them both off?" I asked indignantly.

"It's Lamey's call in the end, you know that. And we both know which way it would go. Some things you gotta fight for, Nash. And some things, you let karma do the work. It's a crime to lie to the police, but it's not a crime to be so stupid in love with your cheatin' wife that you run your business into the ground. Or to be so cold you can walk away from the dead guy you're supposed to be in love with and act like nothin' happened. Figure they kinda deserve each other. But I'll admit, I didn't have Marcy in my sights as the next suspect. I was actually gonna have another talk with Warren."

"Detective Ross?" We all turned as a nurse came into the room. "You can see your daughter now. Is there a Leah Nash here?"

I raised my hand.

"She'd like to see you, too."

As soon as we walked into the room where Allie was sitting up on the edge of a hospital bed, she held out her arms like a little kid wanting to be picked up.

"Dad!"

Ross did the next best thing and swooped in with a big hug.

"Alley-cat, you scared the heck outta me!" He pulled back and held her at arm's length, as if surveying for damage. "You OK? You sure?"

"Yeah, I'm sure. I'm kind of fuzzy on some things, though."

"What do you remember?" I asked.

"I remember mostly what happened at Marcy's. I just needed one more interview for my story. She was really nice. I told her that I wanted to show that when someone doesn't get vaccinated, it can affect more than just that person. That's all I needed to say, because she started talking all about Robin, and how she died because somebody didn't believe in vaccinations.

"She showed me pictures of Robin, and she said it was OK if I used one with the story. Then I thanked her and started to go, but she asked me to stay. She'd been so nice to me, I said sure. While we were drinking coffee, she told me how she didn't think she'd ever have a baby, and then finally she got pregnant with Robin, and she said how happy she and her husband were. I asked her about her husband. She told me they got divorced, and he had a new baby with someone else.

"Then she touched my hair and told me Robin would be

about my age, and that she had curly dark hair and blue eyes, too. Then she called me Robin. I said, you mean Allie. But she looked at me funny. By then I was feeling kind of funny myself. I told her again that I should go, and she said she'd give me a ride. I stood up, but I felt sort of dizzy, and really, really tired. I remember getting into her truck, but then it was like I was dreaming and I knew it, but I couldn't wake up."

"I'm pretty sure she put Xanax in your coffee."

"Why would she do that?"

"She was delusional. By then she had already killed Ryan and Gina."

I let Ross explain the details before I chimed in again.

"I think killing Gina, even though she had justified it, really preyed on her mind. She genuinely cared about Gina, and after she killed her, she started losing it. She'd been obsessed with Robin's death for so long. When she looked at you, she saw Robin. And what she wanted most of all was to be with Robin.

"In her mixed-up mind, that meant taking you, her grown-up Robin, to where baby Robin was—the family mausoleum. She had a gun. I wouldn't be surprised if the rest of her Xanax prescription was with her, too. She would probably have given it all to you at the cemetery. Then, when you stopped breathing, she would have killed herself, so she and her 'Robin' would be together at last."

Allie didn't say anything. She'd been through a lot the past few hours. I hoped I hadn't traumatized her more with my theory. But when she spoke, I found my worry was unfounded.

"OMG! You mean I was going to be killed? That is so amazing! This will make my story the greatest thing ever. I have to get out of here. I need to get it ready for you to read. I—"

"You, kid, are goin' home with me. You're gonna eat somethin' and then you're goin' to bed. Got it?" Ross's voice was no-

nonsense and his expression was stern, but he didn't fool Allie any more than he did me.

She hopped down from the table, gave him a hug and said, "OK, Dad, you're the boss."

And then she smiled at me.

## 46

As I walked to my car in the hospital parking lot, my phone vibrated with a text. Gabe.

*Are we still on?*

I looked at my watch. Ten o'clock. I was supposed to be there at nine.

*Yes. Be right there.*

I stood very still and took a deep breath before I knocked on the door. When Gabe answered it, he was wearing a T-shirt and cargo shorts. His feet were bare, his hair slightly damp as though he'd taken a shower not long ago. I wished I had.

"Leah, come in, please." He stepped aside, and I followed him to the living room, babbling as I went.

"Thanks, yes. I didn't really forget. I just got caught up in a few things. The Ryan Malloy murder is solved, and Gina Cox, too. And Marcy White is dead, but Allie's all right. I should've gone home to shower and change. I must look pretty bad, but I went right to the hospital from the cemetery and I—"

He stopped and turned to face me and put a finger lightly on my lips.

"It sounds like I've missed a lot in the last few days. I want to hear it all. But first I want to apologize. You were right. I was pushing you. But it's because I've been worried that if I didn't get more of a commitment from you, I might lose out."

I admit to a teeny, tiny, thought about taking the easy way out. I had been the one who acted like a jerk, but if Gabe wanted to apologize, hey, who was I to stop him? But that only lasted for a second.

"Stop. You're reading *my* lines. You had a right to be angry. You still have one. I didn't mean to hurt you with the way I reacted when you brought up moving in together. I don't want to move in with you, that's true. But it's not because I don't care about you. I do. But when things start to get a little serious, I get a little nervous."

I stopped for a minute, thinking about what Father Lindstrom had said, and decided I owed it to Gabe to go full-on honest. "I'm not very good at relationships. I choose the wrong people, or they choose me, but either way it ends badly and it hurts. I don't like to be hurt. So, it's easier not to get in too deep."

"You don't worry about that with Coop, though, do you?"

"That's different, and you know it. Or you should. Coop will never not be in my life—at least I hope so. But he's not in love with me, and I'm not in love with him. Just ask him. I trust him because he's earned it. And I think he trusts me for the same reason. But you and me—that's a different kind of relationship."

"Leah, I just have to say this. I'm not sure that you're right about how Coop feels. But as long as your feelings for him aren't what's making you back away from me, I can live with that."

"Gabe, you're making me kind of mad all over again. I'm not backing away from you. I'm here, aren't I? Is it so hard to think that men and women can be friends? I have lots of men friends: Miller Caldwell, Miguel, Charlie Ross, Father Lindstrom, Darmody, Marty Angstrom the insurance guy—"

"I'm sorry. I don't want you to be mad at me. I'm trying to

make amends here, OK? I can accept that you love Coop as your oldest, best friend. And for the record, of course I believe that men and women can be friends. But also for the record, I'd like to point out that fifty percent of your list includes two gay guys, and a Catholic priest. It's not the strongest evidence for your argument."

"Seriously, if you don't—"

"No. I do, I do. If you're willing to see where things go—no pushing involved—I'd be very happy with that. You're right. One or both of us could get hurt, but we could also wind up with something pretty nice. What do you say?"

"I say OK. I'm not giving up my loft."

---

I woke up early the next morning, confused at first at not being in my own space. Then Barnacle's soft snoring at the foot of the bed reoriented me. I looked at Gabe and thought that it might be nice to regularly wake up next to him, instead of occasionally. But not yet.

I grabbed my phone and checked to make sure the *Himmel Times* had more on the Marcy White story than *GO News* had. We did. Maggie had come back in and rousted Troy and a stringer to help Miguel, so the coverage was good. Whoever Spencer Karr had put on the story hadn't contacted me. And Ross, I knew, wouldn't have talked to *GO News* after what they did to Allie, unless he was ordered to. So all they had was Acting Sheriff Lamey.

Victory was sweet. However, we couldn't afford to savor it for long. If we didn't build some bridges with Erin Harper, who had to be pretty upset, the *Times* would get frozen out of any police news except for standard press releases. Miguel would be a good one to take the lead on that mission.

As I got out of bed, Gabe said sleepily, "Hey, where you going? It's early."

"Sorry, didn't mean to wake you. I've got book pages to write, and staff to congratulate, and a perfectly worded, gloating, email to send to Spencer Karr. Plus, it's our bi-weekly Sunday breakfast at my house for me and Coop. Want to join us?"

I mentioned that especially, to see how he'd react, after what he'd said about Coop the night before.

"What's on the menu?"

"Cheerios."

"I think I'll sleep a while longer."

"I've got Pop Tarts, too. You know you love the way I toast them."

"Tempting as that is, I'm going back to sleep. I'll call you later."

He passed the test.

## 47

"OK, I've fed you whole grain cereal. Provided two flavors of Pop Tarts. And made coffee the way you like it, just this side of sludge. So, can we please have a serious discussion?"

Coop and I were in my kitchen, cleaning up after the delicious breakfast I'd made, which was pretty quick work, because I used very few dishes.

"About what? You and Gabe? Did you get things sorted out?"

"Yeah, I think so. I mean, we had a good talk. We both apologized, and we're going to see how things go. I know I should be more open, and I want to make trust my default position with Gabe. I'm really going to try not to let bad past relationships ruin current ones. But ..."

"But what?"

"But I always do, don't I? I mean, I've been the way I am for a really long time. And I always *say* I'm going to be a nicer, better person. But I never really am, am I? Come on, you can be honest. You know it's true."

I expected him to say something funny, or maybe sarcastic, or maybe both. Instead, he didn't say anything.

"Hey, come on. You could at least say you believe I'm going to try, even if you don't think I can get there."

"What I believe, Leah, is that you're already one of the best people I know. If you have to change for Gabe to think so, maybe he's not the one."

"I thought you liked Gabe."

"I do. But I like you better, and I don't like to see you being so hard on yourself."

"Now that's a twist I didn't see coming. You're always telling me I should this or I shouldn't that, or to be more patient, or don't be so bossy."

"That's just to help you keep on course, not to change you."

"I see. Well, it's going to be hard to do that from Florida. Though I suppose there's always Skype. And planes. I hear planes go back and forth between Wisconsin and Florida quite regularly these days."

"Florida? I'm not moving to Florida."

"But you told me you had a friend who was going to get you a job there."

He shook his head. "That was just the Leinenkugel talking. I'm not going anywhere."

"Then what are you going to do? I know, let's open a private detective agency. Nash and Cooper Investigations."

"Now, there's a quick way to end a friendship. No, I don't have any interest in being a PI."

"What then? Try to get back in at the Madison police department? Try for something in Omico or Hailwell? Wait, isn't Kristin from Hailwell? Can she help you out? You know, if you weren't so stubborn, you could go to Chief Riley. I'm sure he'd like to have you back."

He shook his head. "Nope. I won't go over Rob Porter's head. He deserves his chance to run the department the way he sees fit. Thanks for the suggestions, but I already know what I'm going to do."

"So, tell me, already."

"If things go right, there might be a new sheriff in town this fall."

"Lamey isn't exactly new. You're not saying you want to work for him, are you?"

"I was thinking more along the lines of him working for me."

"Shut up! You're running for sheriff?"

"You don't think it's a good idea?"

"I think it's a great idea! You'll be your own boss. You can work some cases if you want to, because you'll have an undersheriff to handle the admin stuff. And Jennifer is capable of way more than the secretary things Lamey has her do. You're a great team leader. Ross would love working with you. And best of all, Art Lamey won't be the sheriff."

"If I win, that is. So, can I count on an endorsement from the *Himmel Times Weekly*?"

"Endorsement? Absolutely. I could run your campaign, too. I can—"

"Let's not get carried away. I'll settle for the endorsement. I'm thinking about asking my dad to come and stay with me for a few months and run my campaign."

"That's perfect."

"Yeah. I kind of think it might be."

"I'm glad you're not going."

"Me, too."

**DANGEROUS PURSUITS: Leah Nash #7**

A club dancer found dead in a field.
A hotly contested local election.
A wet-behind-the-ears reporter, eager to prove his chops.

And crime reporter Leah Nash is in the middle of it all, tenaciously hunting down the truth—whatever the cost may be.

*Dangerous Pursuits* is the seventh standalone book in the Leah Nash series of complex, fast-paced murder mysteries. If you like quick-witted dialogue, daring female characters, and plots with lots of twists and turns, then you'll love Susan Hunter's riveting novels.

**Get your copy today at
severnriverbooks.com/series/leah-nash-mysteries**

# ACKNOWLEDGMENTS

Thanks are due to friends who helped me think through the plot at the very beginning, and to the beta readers who caught mistakes and inconsistencies and gave me helpful feedback. Special appreciation to Anonymous (she knows who she is) whose insights always make my stories better.

A shout-out to Matt Ogle of Ogle Computers, who helped me figure out a clue that required more technical knowledge than I have. Also, another thank you to my daughter Brenna, whose on-point remark sent the story in a new, and better, direction.

As always, I'm grateful for my husband Gary Rayburn, who provided the usual steady supply of encouragement, an endless stream of chai lattes, and a listening ear as I worked out key plot points.

Finally, to all the readers who take the time to email me with comments, questions, and reading suggestions. I appreciate every one of them.

# ABOUT THE AUTHOR

Susan Hunter is a charter member of Introverts International (which meets the 12th of Never at an undisclosed location). She has worked as a reporter and managing editor, during which time she received a first place UPI award for investigative reporting and a Michigan Press Association first place award for enterprise/feature reporting.

Susan has also taught composition at the college level, written advertising copy, newsletters, press releases, speeches, web copy, academic papers and memos. Lots and lots of memos. She lives in rural Michigan with her husband Gary, who is a man of action, not words.

During certain times of the day, she can also be found wandering the mean streets of small-town Himmel, Wisconsin, looking for clues, stopping for a meal at the Elite Cafe, dropping off a story lead at the *Himmel Times Weekly*, or meeting friends for a drink at McClain's Bar and Grill.

**Sign up for Susan Hunter's reader list at**
**severnriverbooks.com/authors/susan-hunter**

## DISCUSSION QUESTIONS

- What do you think the title *Dangerous Ground* refers to?
- How did the book make you feel? Were you amused, upset, bored, angry, intrigued?
- How do you feel about *how* the story was told? Did it start too slow or end unresolved?
- Which characters did you relate to the most/least?
- Did any parts of the book stand out to you? Are there any quotes, or scenes you found particularly compelling?
- What themes did you detect in the story?
- Did you learn something you didn't know before?
- Were you satisfied or disappointed with how the story ended?
- How do you picture the characters' lives after the end of the story?
- How does this book compare to other books you've read in the same genre?

Made in United States
Orlando, FL
17 March 2023

31138192R00232